Of Chaos and Eternal Night

RD Pires

Ether Books

Other works by RD Pires

The Tides That Reign Saga
Design of Darkness

A Vast, Untethered Ocean

Novellas and Anthologies
In Death Do Flowers Grow
A Sky Littered With Stories

For Alexander
for whom I would happily cheat death

Contents

1

The Gateway

Ten Years Ago

From the tower came five tolls.

Theo Sahiron heard them and watched his parents exchange solemn glances.

His mother, Medina, was round-faced with perpetually flushed cheeks. Dark hair sat in a tight bun at the nape of her neck. She wore a neat, ironed dress with a silvery scarf arranged just so about her shoulders. But though her presentation was exact, the sharpness of her appearance was purely cosmetic. Where others might have lines on their faces from persistent worry, she had smooth, youthful skin. Her hands were more used to turning the pages of books than they were to scolding.

She lifted the hem of her blackberry dress and knelt on the floorboards. At this level, Theo was almost as tall as she.

Her words began to dance.

"Theo, my child, dressed handsome and bright
In manner but mild, we'll walk through the night
Keep close to me and then never you'll fear
The shadows, together we'll make disappear."

Theo giggled in delight, not giving much weight to any of her words—and why should he? He had never feared the dark as other children might. In Ipsitfel, darkness was more common than light. What was darkness to him but another place for hiding?

"Aren't you handsome?" His mother's voice was silvery. She ran a hand over the shoulders of his tunic—white, for youth. "Look at me, Theo."

He squirmed, remembering why he wore the starched clothing. "I don't want to go. Do I have to?"

She smoothed his hair. "Yes, my love."

"But I don't want to." Even at his young age, he knew pleading wouldn't change her mind. It never did.

"You're going anyway, Theo. Don't argue with me." His mother's voice retained its kindness even through the firm edge.

"But why? I never had to go before."

She made him face her, holding his chin with her thumb and forefinger. She had that look on her face; the one she always got before she said something to change his mind. This time, he resolved that it wouldn't work. "My boy. Tell me, do you one day want to be a grown-up like me and Daddy?"

He looked back at her, as wary as his youth would allow. "Yes," he said and glanced up at his father.

"Only babes and the incapable stay home from Descensions. If you don't start attending the ceremony now, you will never grow older. You will stay a babe forever, and then what will happen?"

He shrugged, but she urged him with a raised brow.

"What?" Theo asked. He tried to seem casual, but her words worried him.

"You will have to keep changing your friends, because they'll all grow up. Your father and sister and I won't know what to do with you because you won't have any birthdays or join in any holiday festivals..."

Theo moaned, the last bit having crumbled his defenses. "Well, alright."

"Besides, you are old enough now that people will begin to wonder why you aren't coming." Damon Sahiron's face was all angles, his jawline prominent from just below his earlobes to his chin. Bushy brows shaded slate gray eyes. But though he was stern, his wide lips were prone to smiling and his sharp features could become softer than any cloud. "We don't want them to think we don't care about the importance of Descensions—for all our sakes. Would we? You'll understand."

Theo nodded—certain in the way children often are that he would *never* understand and this was all unnecessary. He knew, however, that he was far outnumbered.

Laila came down the narrow stairs, one hand gingerly tracing the banister and the other tucked into a pleat of her white skirt. Whereas Theo had inherited their mother's darker skin, Laila's terra-cotta complexion matched their father's. She didn't say anything when she reached her family gathered on the first floor. Instead, she perched on the seat in the corner by the window. Mister Sahiron grinned at the sight of her. "Well, don't you look beautiful."

"Thank you, Daddy," she replied. Her voice was just as silvery as her mother's.

"Did you braid your hair yourself?"

"I did. Gwendolyn at school showed me how. She said braids during the ceremony will make your family stronger."

"Wasn't that nice of her to tell you," Medina said. Theo watched as she considered his sister. The braids were impeccable, one from either side of her head, meeting in the back and perfectly centered. "You're already much better at them than I."

"By Kouros, we need to depart," Damon said, urgently. He pulled a tin pocket watch from his vest and opened it with his thumb. "We can't be late."

Theo's mother surveyed both him and his sister. Laila remained poised while Theo fidgeted uncomfortably. Tonight would be their first Descension as a family. The thought made Theo nervous, though also excited. He knew Descensions were a serious event, but he couldn't help his imagination filling in the blanks of what he didn't understand. His father's presence was calm, but his mother was visibly anxious. She always got this way before the ceremony.

"Everybody ready?" his mother said.

Theo tugged on his sleeve, intrigued by the purity of his tunic. Nothing else he owned was as clean and stiff. His dress clothes were thinning and faded from overuse, while the ghosts of mud-wrestling matches and climbing races stained his play clothes. By contrast, this tunic was new. He had never seen it before today.

"Come," his father said, opening the front door and ushering them out.

The sun was well on its way to setting and the evening air was crisp, pinching the cheeks and nose. They filed out of the house—Theo's father closing the door behind them—and set off along the cobblestoned street. At first, they were met by few other people, but the roads would become more crowded the closer they got to Cirillo Square.

Theo skipped along, happy to be outside. He barely noticed the cold that made his mother draw her jacket tight around her. He made a game of jumping from stone to stone, but only ones that were the same shade of rain-washed blue. Laila skipped along with him for a bit, laughing once even, but then she fell into step beside her mother.

Theo kept jumping until Damon caught him in midair and lifted him with incredible strength. His weight was nothing to the man. Theo sometimes wondered how long it would be until he had strength like his father's. Damon held his son against his side, carrying Theo in a way he had come to do less and less as the years passed. From this position, they could see eye to eye.

"Do you know where we're going?" Damon asked.

Theo could picture the place in his mind. He tried to remember the name his teachers used, but the word eluded him. "The hole in town square."

"The Gateway," his father corrected. "Do you know why?"

"Because someone has died."

"That's right." They rounded a corner and were met with more of their neighbors, all filing into the street from their homes or their work. Some carried lanterns, dotting the crowd with squares of light. Others were content to walk by the light of the streetlamps. A general hum took shape in the crowd. "Theo, it may seem strange at first, but I want you to understand that Descensions are necessary and good for everyone in Ipsitfel. The tradition began in a time before anyone can recall. But though the origins are hazy, the results have stayed engrained in the people's minds. This is our pact with Death, the reason our village has survived when so many others have not. As long as we do this, our crops continue to grow, our wells do not run dry, and we escape disease. It's how we remain alive and hea lthy."

Theo nodded. He hoped his father would continue holding him. Being carried provided a much better vantage point than his short stature allowed. No sooner had this thought crossed his mind, however, than he found himself on the cobblestones again. The crowd of villagers pressed tighter.

As they crossed Ashmore Bridge, Theo leaned over the railing to peak at the black Stick River flowing under them. Somewhere down on the banks was the miniature house he and Laila had built last week using river rocks and loose twigs. It was too dark now for him to make it out.

In the corner of his vision, Theo saw a shadow sweep along the bank, away from the flow of villagers, but when he looked, no one was there. What a strange trick of the light. He lingered for another moment before realizing he was losing his family.

On the other side of the bridge, the crowd slowed.

Descensions happened in the town square. That's where they always were and undoubtedly always would be. If one could stand over The Gateway in the center of the square and face North, they'd see the old clock tower. Like the town itself, the clock tower—often referred to as Viseyne Tower, for it was built as a gift from Aon Viseyne, the first historically recorded mayor of Ipsitfel, to his grand-daughter Imelda Viseyne—was a strange amalgam of architectural styles and crude quick fixes. It had been partially destroyed in a battle during one of the Great Regional Wars many years ago, then rebuilt, then partially knocked over again due to poor rebuilding. The village had often seen trying financial times and so the resulting recon-structions had been completed with whatever the villagers had lying around. Since then, there had been various talks about restoring the pride of Ipsitfel, but the clock ticked and the face shone eternally in an amber-glow that fought the fog with unwavering resolve, and so the tower was left well enough alone. Better not to mess with things that worked fine.

The Sahirons shuffled into Cirillo Square and took their place at the back of the slowly building mass. There were some villagers who arrived early to reserve spots beside the grieving family, closest to the Gateway—those with veils drawn and small medallions hanging from their necks—but otherwise villagers found somewhere to stand and didn't care much about where that was.

As soon as they stopped, Theo realized he would be buried by the throngs. A forest of bodies stood oblivious over him. This was only exacerbated as the crowd thickened and they were pushed closer together. Even if he asked, his family couldn't move now. He was stuck.

The clock in Viseyne Tower struck half past five and silence overcame the villagers.

Theo danced on his tiptoes, trying to catch a glimpse of anything at all. Before tonight, he used to stay with Missus Munter—who was much too crippled now in her old age to come to the ceremony—and he knew that a Descension could take up to an hour. If he had to stand here that entire time, he needed to see something at least. Nobody seemed to want to help him, though, and as he cast himself this way and that, his mother turned to him and put a finger to her lips. The boy complied, but only for so long as young children are able. Someone was speaking.

"My fellow villagers, may the light of Caelum guide you all. I welcome you tonight to this; our eldest tradition here in Ipsitfel." That must've been the governor. He repeated much of the information about why the town held the ceremony, then went on to eulogize the deceased and what they did for a living.

A subtle shift opened a hole in the spectators' legs, wide enough for Theo to fit through. He knew that if he wanted to see more, now was the time. He looked up at his parents, who were paying rapt attention to the governor's words. Even his sister listened, staring blankly at the back of the man in front of her. Would they notice him leave if he came back quickly? He just wanted a peek.

Theo looked again at the opening and back at his family. They were all so serious and concerned, but he couldn't see why. How could they expect him to stand there quietly, knowing nothing?

Crouching low, Theo darted through the gap, trying not to bump anyone in the process. He'd find a place to climb. If he got up on a lamppost, he'd be over everyone's heads. Yes. That was it! A lamppost.

Priding himself in his clever plan, Theo searched the forest of spectators for one of the iron posts anchored into the ground on thick stones. He'd climbed them before when nobody was looking; he'd have no problems now.

Up ahead, he could see a clearing in the crowd. Theo turned toward it, hoping he'd find what he sought there.

The governor droned on, his words unintelligible even though they were the only sound in the square. Theo was steps from the clearing, pushing gently on people's legs to clear the way now. A youthful mind throws caution to the wind early and often. Almost there. Almost able to see. Hopefully, he hadn't missed any of the interesting bits, whatever they might be. The things adults whispered about, the things about which schoolchildren spread rumors—

He burst into the clearing, hands to the cobblestones, and only had time to realize he'd stumbled out onto a path running from beneath the clock tower to the center of Cirillo Square before someone grabbed him by the collar and yanked him back.

It was only just in time. A procession began to pass through where he'd lain a moment before.

Theo didn't look up at who was holding him, entranced as a group of villagers marched past at a mournfully slow pace. A man with long auburn hair that curled around his face led the way. Dark stubble sprouted on his jaw like grass, much darker than the hair on his head. Behind him walked an elderly couple holding hands, their midnight blue clothing starched and unaffected by the breeze.

But what was most intriguing were the six figures bringing up the rear of the procession. They all wore trailing blue capes. Bright, ornate medallions hung from their necks—the same as the faithful gathered closest to the Gateway. Theo didn't have time to see what was embossed on the medallions before they'd passed him. Each figure wore a pair of white gloves, and they held a long wooden board between them. Lying on that board was a person. Theo watched—still and attentive now—while they passed him by and brought the body to the Gateway.

Villagers were not allowed to approach the center of Cirillo Square. It was cordoned off by a brick fence topped by an ornate iron railing, a precautionary measure as the Gateway was a very large hole in the ground. The fence was opened for one occasion only, and that was the Descension ceremony.

Theo screwed up his face, trying to remember the scraps of stories he'd retained. The hole had existed for as long as anyone could guess—perhaps predating the settlement and even humanity itself. Over the years, the village grew around it. The stonework in Cirillo Square was neat and patterned, except for near the hole, which was bordered by a circle of rounded river rocks. If anyone had ever attempted to cover the Gateway, nobody living could recall. As the songs were sung, the hole could not be hidden. It would always find a way to resurface.

The Gateway measured roughly a dozen paces across and opened unto an impenetrable blackness. Some said people had dropped lit torches down the hole, but the fire vanished into the darkness before hitting the ground. Some said the bottom could not be seen simply because there was no end to the Gateway. It continued on forever.

Theo watched the trail of people cross through the open fence into the enclosure. The elderly couple and the man at the head of the procession were visibly stricken by sorrow, but the bearers showed no emotion. When all were inside, the gate was shut. The governor concluded his speech.

"...will be greatly missed, but she joins the dead in keeping our community alive."

Beyond the fence was a wooden pulley that hung over the lip of the Gateway.

One of the bearers hooked the rope threaded through the pulley with a long rod. At the end of the rope was a harness. With the same deliberate pace at which they had walked, the carrier moved back to the deceased woman and deftly wrapped her in the restraints. They tied it off with another, thinner rope and proceeded to hand the end of this to the distraught, long-haired man.

Theo wanted to get closer, but the hand holding him back was firm and he was forced to relent. Then, all around him, the villagers began to sing. Quite suddenly, as if by some cue, their voices rose in a mournful melody that precipitated out of the fog like water.

"Gently you go, breathing the night
The moon and the stars come, guiding by light.
Pity the mountain that howls and grieves
But tend to the bowed willow mourning its leaves."

The blue-cloaked bearers lined up one behind the other, and very gently they used the pulley to lift the body from the wooden board. As they did so, the dead woman swung out until she hung suspended above the Gateway. Her hair fell free from her face, longing for the darkness beneath her. In the light of the now-risen moon, her dress waved at Theo, the breeze causing it to illuminate in oscillating patterns. Her arms extended back as far as her shoulders would allow, splayed helplessly. Her back bent in a graceful arch, curling toward a hungry earth.

And then they began to lower her.

Inch by inch she sank while the blue-cloaked voices chanted unintelligibly in unison and the villagers continued their elegy.

"Only with death do the living remain
Pardoned of famine, of thirst, and of pain
A fate we may fear, a fate we may know
Maybe again we will meet down below."

Theo understood.

Realization struck him and he gasped. He was suddenly afraid and in awe, and did not understand why but he couldn't stop watching. His eyes widened in incredulity. *This* was the ceremony of Descension. This was the solemn ritual he had thus far been missing.

"Theo, there you are," his mother hissed. Somehow, her voice managed to be even softer than normal. She took his hand, but she couldn't tear away his gaze. "Thank you so much, Mister Rhodes. I'm sorry if he was a bother."

Theo didn't hear the mumbled response. He was enraptured by the proceedings. The woman was now almost completely submerged beneath the lip of the hole. The man who had led the group, who held the thinner rope, was overcome. His shoulders shook with grief, and he swayed on the spot. Nobody came to his rescue, though; nobody approached the fence. Not even the elderly couple in the enclosure moved to console him. Their hands remained clasped, their eyes downcast. Looking away, as if that might make it all easier to swallow.

"Come on, Theo. Follow Mommy."

But he didn't move, and she didn't force him to.

When the woman in the harness had been lowered out of sight, when the farthest carrier had reached the end of the rope, the governor nodded solemnly.

"Theo, don't look," his mother said, but it was too late.

The man with the tear-stricken face let out a gruff gasp of anguish and pulled the rope he'd been handed. For a brief moment, it snagged. Then it came loose, no longer fastening the harness. In the complete silence, Theo waited for the sound of the body hitting ground. It never came.

The harness was reeled in. Empty.

2

Seer Stone and Scolding

Present Day

Quiet engulfed the dreary street.

Theo watched as a gust of wind blew tufts of fog across the road, obscuring the buildings at the other end. Barren branches of short trees hung over the cobblestones, their plots evenly spaced and giving the impression that the trees were marching in two single-file lines down the sides of the lane.

"You're going to see Mary Alba?" Ismena asked as she caught up to him, but Theo didn't respond. Instead, he took off down the street, combing his fingers through the fog. He knew he was being unusually *un*forthcoming about his intentions, but he couldn't help it.

"You don't like her?" he said, acting as if he didn't already know.

"It's not that I don't like her," Ismena said. "I just find her rather... vague."

Theo shrugged.

The grungy building materialized under a crooked, wood-tiled roof. Moss grown by the constant fog overfilled the gutters and the shutters hung half closed as if frozen, impervious to the breeze.

The building stood back from the street, farther than the build-ings around it, as if hoping to hide in the shadows, though the bright lantern hanging by the front door prevented it from doing so entirely. A worn, wrought-iron gate stood ajar, unsure whether to welcome anyone in.

The two slid through the opening without touching anything, then traipsed up to the door past the twisting, barren bushes and masses of vines.

"I hear she's got an animal graveyard around the back," Ismena mumbled.

"I've never seen it," Theo said.

"Do you come here often?"

DING.

The ring was as deep as the bell in Viseyne Tower. For a moment, there came no response, and then the door cracked open. Sapphire eyes and close-cropped chestnut hair peeked out. They scanned the porch before the door swung the rest of the way, revealing a tall boy with a wide smile. His clothes were oddly mismatched—a sleek purple vest over a maroon shirt with the sleeves rolled to up his elbows, and brown trousers that didn't seem to be made of any well-known material. Leather wraps and bracelets of various metals traveled up from his wrists—and yet every piece of the outfit made perfect sense on him.

"Theo," he said.

"Roman!" Theo said.

Roman's mouth tipped to the side in an attractive smirk. "And Ismena!"

"Roman Alba," she said, less enthused.

The boy stepped back and gestured into an oval room with a sweeping hand. Oil lamps burned on teal walls. To their left were great racks of lush fabric: silks that seemed barely there but held bold colors, and thick, heavy cloths with intricate patterns Theo couldn't have dreamed in a hundred dreams. On the other side of the room hung long dresses with beads and lace. Scarves that looked fit to adorn queens. Blouses, skirts, the whole lot. In an instant, Roman's wardrobe seemed demure by comparison.

Opposite the entrance, a white door sat open, allowing a view of the hallway beyond. Theo knew it led to the part of the house where Roman and his mother lived, but the door was usually closed. Curious, he tilted his head to peer through the opening. At the far end of the hall, he could make out what looked like two figures sitting pristinely on a bench—statues, maybe? Veils hung over their heads, blocking their faces.

Just then, Roman slid behind a till atop a long counter and nudged the door closed with a foot.

"What are those?" Theo asked, curious as to why the Alba's would keep statues covered and in such an odd place.

"Nothing. Nothing at all.," Roman said, taking a seat on a stool. He was a year or two older than Theo and Ismena, with an accent owed to his non-Ipsitfelian origins. "The timing of your visit can't have been better. I only just got back yesterday."

Theo laughed. "Did you?" He and Ismena locked eyes for a brief moment. She looked bemused. His face turned hot.

"We had *no* idea," Ismena said.

"Yeah, got in real early, see. Before most folks are up, I expect. Slept like the dead after that." Roman smiled.

"Where'd you go?"

"You've got taller" Roman said to Theo, ignoring her question.

"You haven't been gone *that* long," Theo said.

"Feels that way, it does."

"Where were you?" Ismena tried again.

Roman straightened up. "How've you two been?"

Ismena glared.

"Alright," Theo said.

"Staying out of trouble, I should hope? No more running around on the village wall?" This made Theo's face flush harder, and he tried to hide it by showing interest in some of the items beneath the glass tabletop.

Roman laughed. The sound was light and reassuring.

"I'm only joking," he said with a wicked grin. "Latrice Petunia is a swamp of pollywogs if ever I've seen one, and I encourage you to be late to more shifts at the bakery." He leaned forward on the stool, his adornments jangling as he gripped the edge of the counter. "Last summer, the old twat found Beatrice Pitcher and me tossing stones into the woods. Wasn't doing nothin' else, nothin' naughty. She went fucking mental on us, saying we was bad. Saying we didn't know what we was doin'—which don't make a lick of sense. Then the old hag went and told me mum we was trying to bring devils into the town. Fuck that. I haven't got a death wish."

"Were you punished?" Theo asked.

"Nah. Mum knows that's not how you bring dark omens in. But it's the principle, isn't it? Petunia still went and ratted on us for something she didn't know squat about." He leaned back against the wall behind the counter, and Theo nearly followed.

"Why were you throwing stones?" Ismena asked.

"I'd got my right boot stuck in a tree. Had to get it down, didn't I?" He grinned with the side of his mouth, a silver sheen in place of his canine. A wink followed, sapphire eyes glinting like gemstones right at Theo. "I only got the one pair."

"That wouldn't do to lose them," Theo agreed.

"But what was your boot doing in the tree?" Ismena asked.

Roman slapped the counter jovially. "Wouldn't you like to know, miss?"

It was Ismena's turn to hide her pinkening cheeks.

Roman leaned forward again, resting his forearms on the glass. "Anyhow, what is it that brings you two to my mother's wayward emporium? An' don't say it's the fabrics, I'll know you're lying."

He eyed their plain, pattern-less clothing with a raised eyebrow.

"I was...wondering if you'd heard about Eldra's party," Theo said, not wanting to admit that he'd just been excited for the boy's return to Ipsitfel. He was painfully unaware that, like most adolescents, his acting left much to be desired. Shields built of emotions make for poor hiding places. "It's in three days."

"Look at you wanting to make sure I'm on the up and up," Roman said. Theo could feel Ismena's eyes on him. Of course, Roman had known. Everyone knew about the party. "We had the invitation slipped under our door when we arrived. I must say I'm somewhat surprised. Most folk 'round here find us a bit dodgy."

Theo laughed awkwardly. "Yeah, but Eldra's never cared about public opinion. Do you think you'll go?"

"Would be rude of me if I didn't."

"Well, glad to have answered that question," Ismena said. She grabbed Theo by the arm.

"Wait!" Roman said. For the briefest of moments, his casual demeanor disappeared. "I'm glad you came by. It's damned boring minding the shop on my lonesome. There's not a soul what comes in here during the day, hardly. You can see." He gestured around the empty showroom.

"We don't mind staying with you," Theo said.

"Do more people come at night?" Ismena asked.

"Wassat?"

"You said that hardly a soul comes here during the day. Then they must come at night. Why is that?"

The mischievous shade in his grin deepened. "I'm glad you asked that, miss."

Theo and Ismena drew up against their side of the counter. Roman stood and turned, bending over to rummage through a chest of drawers against the wall. Theo took the moment to admire the other boy's buttocks, which was always a pleasant sight.

When Roman stood again, he was holding a brass pyramidal stand with a scarlet stone perched on top. The stone was jagged, amorphous in shape, though all its many sides were smooth. It could almost have been glass and filled with liquid, the color was so crisp. If Theo wasn't mistaken, every light in the room dimmed. His eye couldn't help but be drawn away from the older boy and instead to the stone. The urges to touch it and back away from it occurred simultaneously. The pull was magnetic, the resistance instinctual. Roman set it down on the countertop—the clink heavy when the metal stand met the glass—and slowly took his hands off the brass base. He wiggled his fingers mysteriously, not touching the scarlet surface.

"A bit of shine makes for a good show, eh?" he said.

"What is it?" Ismena seemed to be struck by the same urge as Theo. Her fingers twitched.

"It's me mum's Seer Stone. She's an oggie, you know." Roman put his tongue between his teeth.

Theo decided he *did* want to touch the scarlet jewel, the building urge too much to keep at bay. He lifted a hand that had gone trembly all of a sudden and made to place it against a wonky angle that looked like it would fit perfectly in the curve of his palm—

A woman in a teal dress burst into the room from a door half hidden by curtains and beads. She had iridescent chestnut hair—the same color as Roman's but with a more noticeable shine—pulled into a half ponytail. On her face were thin glasses with stony rims white enough to be talc. Two large purple gems sat on the index and little fingers of her left hand.

"Is there someone here, Roman?" she said brightly. Her accent, though educated, was over-pronounced. Almost affected. When she spotted Theo and Ismena by the register, her step faltered only the smallest amount, which might've gone unnoticed if Theo's attention hadn't been so fully wrenched by her sudden entrance. "Who's... Ah, you're Damon's son, correct? Theo. And I recognize you—*Don't tell me.* It's Lena?"

"Ismena, actually."

"Of course," Mary Alba said with a bow of her head. She glided behind them as if drawn along a current in the air, the great sleeves of her dress masking her hands from sight. The normal laws of movement didn't seem to apply to the fabrics.

"Are you looking for anything in particular, dears?" she asked airily. As she drifted, she paused to stare at an iron hook hanging above a painting of a rhododendron. Theo exchanged a glance with Ismena, wary of the typical, diaphanous antics attributed to Mary Alba. He didn't want to feel the *I told you so* lecture emanating from her eyes though, and looked away. Roman's mother continued, "Perhaps a vest for young Theo Sahiron? I have fabrics unlike anything you've ever felt before—you like the one my Roman wears? It's from Rimi."

Theo had never heard of a place called Rimi, but unwilling to show his ignorance in front of Roman, he nodded as though impressed.

Mary Alba twisted, brushing a skirt forth as she descended upon Ismena, who stood closest to her. "Or perhaps a dress for you, Miss Ismena?"

Ismena averted her gaze, but Theo noticed it catch on the garment Mary Alba held. The skirt was as deep a blue as the sky on a rare clear night.

"You're hardly a girl anymore," Mary Alba continued. "Beautiful. A woman almost. You ought to shine like the heavens. I talked to the clouds, had them bring me stars so I could stitch them into the fabric. I traded them knowledge in exchange. Can't you see the stars sewn in? How they glisten?"

"Mum, they're not here to play dress-up."

"You lot're old enough to know what you like, Roman. I'm only makin' suggestions." The polished accent dropped when she addressed her son. "Don't listen to him. You can look at whatever you like, dear." And instantly back again.

Theo smiled at Roman, who rolled his eyes with dramatic flair. If Theo wasn't mistaken, the Albas had subtle powers of persuasion. Mary Alba was hypnotic, approaching with a gentle lilt aided by her deep, soothing voice. Tension diffused while she floated beside you and cooed into your ear. Theo didn't know yet how to describe Roman's power. Only that it suffered few similarities.

He turned his gaze back to the Seer Stone. Roman stood sentinel over it, an arm planted on the counter to either side. He'd wanted to show it to Theo—had wanted him to see something in the stone, perhaps. Roman probably knew how it worked. Or perhaps the only necessary action was a touch. The rich scarlet blazoned in Theo's pupils, saturating the hazel in his irises with a hue undeniable.

Mary Alba said, "I wouldn't—"

Theo's palm rested on the cool surface, which was even smoother than he would have guessed, like touching water. Roman jumped in surprise, perhaps not realizing Theo had been leaning over the stone. Theo hadn't remembered walking over to it either. Touching it, he felt unchanged, but Mary Alba's face was transfigured, and she gazed beyond him with deep concern in her round black eyes. Her hand with the rings went to her chest, covering her heart as if to calm it. She gasped.

"Why is Age watching you?"

Theo frowned and withdrew his hand from the stone, turning his palm upward to check for any marks. It looked as unchanged as he'd felt.

Mary Alba surged forward, her teal dress swirling around her. "Crushed by the sea. Endless forest. The Zealots' Flower. And... and..." She blinked, her eyes flickering desperately around as if trying to catch the fading images. "And..."

Nothing.

"What are you talking about?" Theo asked.

"I—I don't remember." Mary Alba lifted the hand from her chest to her head. The great rings had come askew. Her breath mellowed. "I was not prepared to See for you, boy. I usually do not read until after dark."

"Sorry," Theo said. "I didn't know."

"Ignorance is the excuse of the young. No one else."

"It just caught my eye."

"Yes, well, the future has caught the eye of many a man." She was almost cross. Almost. Her shoulders sagged briefly, the folds of the dress billowing. "Don't touch things that aren't yours. You ought to be more careful where the worlds meet."

"What was all that you said?" Ismena asked, her voice layered with concern. "Age is watching? Crushing? What sort of—"

"I don't know, dear," Mary Alba sighed. "I was not ready to catch the flickers as they came to me. Now they're gone, and that's that. They've diluted."

She turned back to Theo. "I'm sorry if I frightened you, boy, but please do not touch any of my instruments unless you are looking for a reading."

The last phrase came out like a suggestion.

Theo eyed the stone again. Its glint seemed a little brighter now—mischievous—but that could've been his imagination. *Crushed by the sea? Age watching me?* The idea would be alarming if he put faith in it, but he'd heard his parents talk about Mary Alba's *other* profession. The one where she solicited dangerous knowledge from a wanton storytelling deity in the underworld. Still, the idea was tempting, and they'd never said she was wrong, necessarily. Just that it was a path no sane person took. Perhaps he could return another time. After dark. "No, thanks. I was just... having a look."

Mary Alba stared blankly for a moment, as if still bringing bits of herself back into the room. Her eyes were a lugubrious blue. Darker than her son's. She smiled. In that instant, Theo couldn't help but agree with Ismena: Mary Alba *was* vague.

"I see," she said, floating through a display of sheer scarves. "Well, we've had our look, haven't we? And now there are other things that need attending. Say goodbye to your friends, Roman."

She drifted back through the half-hidden doorway, the hem of her dress and the rolling sleeves spilling outward in her wake. In the next instant, she disappeared, nothing left of her presence except the soft rattle of the beads falling into place.

Roman smiled with less vigor than before. His disappointment was obvious. "I guess I'll see you at the party then, eh?" He'd mastered the art of summoning enthusiasm, and quickly busied himself with putting away the Seer Stone.

"We'll see you around, Roman," Ismena said. She grabbed Theo's arm and led him away.

"Bye," Theo said.

Roman nodded, resting his arms on the glass top again. The shine of his eyes was the last thing to fade once the pair slid out the front door and onto the porch. The gray-toned gloom of Ipsitfel greeted them again.

"What was that nonsense about?" Ismena hissed as they trod the path to the gate. "Where's she getting off, saying shit like that? *Age is watching you?* What a load of stupidity."

"She couldn't really help it," Theo said. "I think it just came out of her."

"Yeah, it just came out of her, and I'm the Angel of Ascension." Ismena crossed her arms.

Theo looked back at the house retreating behind the iron gate. If the Albas cleaned up the exterior, they might attract more visitors, even with Mary Alba's reputation. They—

A figure retreated from a window on the upper floor, the curtain falling back into place. He couldn't see what they looked like; the glimpse had been too quick.

Theo blinked, turned away, and laughed. "I didn't realize you felt so strongly about her."

"I told you, I thought she was *vague.*"

"Vague doesn't mean you dislike someone. Is this because she calls you Lena?"

"Haha. Very funny. You're a regular jester, you know?" She shook her head. "That family is unsettling."

"I agree—Mary Alba is a bit much to handle," Theo said, "but I think Roman's alright."

"Yeah, I noticed." Ismena hadn't slowed her pace, even now that they were back on the street headed for Cirillo Square. "I think you should know, if you don't already, he's not the type of friend we want."

"What do you mean by that?"

"He's just not, Theo. His cohort includes Marcus Hawthorne and Goran Becker."

"So—"

"So, that means he's like them—shifty, scheming, manipulative. I mean, did you see the way he smiled at us? Like we were meat, and he was a hungry wolf." She was unstoppable now. "And he just brought out that Seer Stone as if he didn't know we could get in trouble using it."

Theo tried to recall if he'd noticed anything manipulative about Roman's smile. Nothing came to mind. In fact, he rather liked the comparison of Roman to a wolf.

She finally stopped walking and pivoted to confront him. "All I'm saying is if you're going to make friends—or more—with Roman Alba, just... be careful, alright." She put a hand on Theo's shoulder.

Theo opened his mouth to argue but thought better of it. He knew Ismena's mind was made up. Words would not persuade her.

Besides, her opinion of the Albas was not what troubled him most. More than anything, what resounded in his mind were the words Mary Alba had said to him when he'd touched the Seer Stone. What did she mean, "age" was watching him? *Crushing sea. Endless forest.* And the Zealots' Flower? He'd never heard of that before. Even without knowing what she meant, Mary Alba's outburst was less than comforting.

3
A Numberless Birthday

Miss Eldra Vromía lived in a sprawling estate on the bank of the Stick River west of Cirillo Square. While the majority of the houses lining the streets of Ipsitfel were modest and similar, Eldra's was bold and gothic and sat on expansive grounds with moping trees and unruly hedges her many gardeners could never quite keep up with. If one did not understand how mist materialized, they might think it emanated from her house, for the fog around her property was so thick, the lights from her mansion could scarcely be seen from the road.

Many a time, the subject of Miss Vromía and her house arose during regular conversation in Ipsitfel. Mainly, the villagers wondered why it was so different architecturally from the rest of the town in both style and size.

"It was the first building here," schoolteacher Maud Leocota had said once, "built even before Viseyne Tower or the courthouse."

And this could have very well been true. But who was to know?

The townsfolk gossiped about hearing that Eldra paid no taxes on her estate, which would have been a brash affront to the tax-paying citizens.

"She is incredibly old," Claude Archaios explained, clutching his cane with trembling fingers in order to remain upright. "She comes from a time before taxes were invented."

This was probably not true.

In any case, while the villagers could agree on most things said about the ancient Eldra Vromía, they could not decide just how old she was. Some said she was close to ninety, and that they knew because they'd sworn they'd heard this person or that person discussing their grammar school days together. But no two people who'd talked this way about her had been the same age.

A select few would tell anyone with an open ear that Eldra had to be at least 160. You could tell by the innumerable wrinkles on every inch of her skin, which were as good as tree rings. But Theo had never paid these people much mind. After all, how could anyone be so old? The truth was, in her many years of life—and most especially in recent times—she'd frequently fallen quite ill to the point where someone always proclaimed that her death had arrived.

She always pulled through.

As such, much hubbub arose when invitations were slid under front doors for Miss Eldra Vromía's birthday celebration. To incite further fervor, it was to be held at her mansion. Very few people had been inside—even some of the gardeners claimed they'd never stepped foot indoors—and this very fact made the invitation all the more enticing.

"There's no mention of *which* birthday this will be for her," Medina Sahiron noted with disappointment. Theo watched as she combed both sides of the single sheet of thick paper again. His father shook his head.

On the night of the party, Theo stood in the hallway before the floor-length mirror. He tied and untied the blue velvet bow around his neck with exasperated gasps. So uncomfortable was the ghastly thing that he couldn't imagine why anyone bothered—and who had decided this was formal wear in the first place? In Ipsitfel, *boys* wore bowties. The men wore ascots under vests. At least, the ones his father worked with did. Why couldn't he have one of those? Ascots didn't threaten to choke the wearer, and he thought they looked rather charming.

Damon ascended to the landing behind his son. "What are you doing?" he asked with a smile. *He* was wearing an ascot and vest—one with a rather nice dark red hue. Theo wondered if he'd gotten it from Mary Alba's.

"I can't get this thing damned tied correctly," Theo whined, staring down at the current iteration, which had three leaves.

"Let's watch our language." Damon walked up behind him. Theo had grown significantly in the past year, but still had about a foot to go if he were to eclipse his father's towering figure. "Give it here," Damon said, and began his work. "By Kouros, we're going to need to get you new trousers soon—I can almost see your ankles. That's the trouble with buying nice clothes for growing boys. They never last long. Either they become too short or they are ripped to pieces by horseplay."

He squeezed Theo's shoulder affectionately. Then, in a swift movement, Damon pulled and the bowtie slid perfectly into place at the base of Theo's neck. It didn't even choke.

Theo was grateful for his father's help, but also ashamed that he still needed it for something so small. He didn't meet Damon's gaze in the mirror, his eyes falling somewhere below his father's chin. A tin pocket watch rested in the breast pocket of the red vest. The top of it, where the chain hooked on, peeked out over the fabric.

Following his gaze, Damon pulled it out. "My father gave it to me when I was a young man—when I first started at the bank. Our family lived on the farms in the village outskirts back then, didn't have much, and we made our way into town only to come to market. When your grandfather passed it on to me, he said I would 'make something yet of the Sahirons,' more than he ever had. He told me 'a man who makes something of himself is always conscious of time.'"

"Was he right?" Theo asked. One of his father's hands still rested on his shoulder, and he was careful not to move lest he withdraw it. His father's gentle but strong grip had always enlivened confidence and determination within him.

"I don't agree so much with me making more of our family than he did, but rarely have I failed to keep the watch with me." Damon slid the timepiece back into the pocket. Then he stood tall and clasped his hands behind his back, all business again. He surveyed his son's reflection. "We will get you new trousers soon. Perhaps for your birthday."

"And what about the other thing?" Theo asked.

"What?"

"The other thing your father said. About time. Was he right about that?"

Damon smiled again, his neatly combed mustache bristling. "He was right about everything else. You mustn't let time rule you, but you should never forget it's there, always walking alongside you, lest you become complacent."

He turned and Theo followed, descending the narrow stairs. Medina and Laila were waiting at the bottom. Laila had tied her curls back in a half ponytail, but still they fell over her shoulders. With age, Theo's sister had only ever grown more beautiful. Boys had even approached Theo for advice about how to impress her.

Like their father, Laila was tall; and like their mother, she was outwardly warm toward others. Few peers excelled as aptly in academia as she, her thirst for knowledge driving her into the field of law. Perhaps the way she wore her acquired learning was what made her most beautiful—shoulders back, gray eyes always observant. She had turned every one of her suitors away. A boy who wanted her for more than her beauty, she said, would befriend her first and know her

.

Their mother, Medina, was wearing her usual bun, pulled tight at the back of her head. "Are we ready?" she asked.

In answer, Damon opened the door and beckoned them out.

An immediate din of excited voices greeted the Sahirons. Most citizens walked along the streets, though the wealthier townsfolk took horse-drawn carriages. Not everyone had agreed to attend the soiree—those who didn't trust Eldra for her rumored age opted to refrain—and they watched from their windows as the throngs filed past, hastily pulling the curtains when they were spotted lurking.

Theo followed the stream of people past Viseyne Tower and into Cirillo Square. The line split around the Gateway, and he eyed the pulley, the governor's platform, and the locked storage chest, wondering as always, what it would be like to stand beyond the fence.

They left Cirillo Square and entered the west side of Ipsitfel. Suddenly, Theo found himself enshrouded in the fog surrounding the Vromía estate. He was used to the town's misty atmosphere, but here the lampposts had been reduced to glowing, floating orbs. His mind buzzed with curiosity. Any number of things could be skulking about unseen. Crossing into the estate unlocked a world he'd never been privy to. He itched to stray from the cobblestones and tried to placate this urge by listening in on the conversations around him.

"... easily three hundred years, Marge. Look at the stones! We haven't had roads like these..."

"By the light of Caelum, Foster, she didn't *build* the place herself. She inherited it. Her great-great-grandfather—"

"I'd heard it was her great-great-*great*-grandfather."

"Well, Matilda, we'll just have to see what's written on the cake."

"There will be cake, won't there?"

"... I'd've brought a raincoat if I knew it was going to be like this. My shawl is positively sopping..."

"... festooned over a bear rug. I said, 'Harold, nobody wants to see your bunions on display... '"

"... what do you think they've done with all the secret passages in the house?"

Secret passages. Now there was a thought he hadn't yet considered. Could it be true? Theo had always liked to imagine secret passages in his home. In reality, it was far too small to contain a secret anything—not even a secret cupboard. But in a place as massive as Vromía Manor... well, doubtless there were more passages than he could dream up.

Light grew stronger up ahead, a solid block of yellow, glowing mass that could only be the mansion itself. Maybe the unusual architecture everyone spoke of wasn't comprised of stone but pure light. That would be strange indeed.

The mansion's features broke through the mist, and at once Theo could see a great building with large-paned windows—the better to see the fog with—surrounded by arches and balconies and turrets as he'd never gazed upon before. The stone foundation rose from the ground as if grown, giving way to curling, gilded filigree and pitched roofs. Lanterns sprouted from symmetrical points, while the massive double doors at the front beckoned entry to gods.

It was filled with all manner of Ipsitfel's folk.

People could be seen through the windows, chatting in the foyer and the study. Some had found their way to the dining room to pick at the hors d'oeuvres, while others remained standing out in the fog on the portico or the front lawn.

It was easily the largest gathering Theo had seen outside a Descension—more crowded than any of the busiest days in the Cirillo Square market when Theo had shopped with his mother or sold bread for Miss Petunia—and the strangest part was that everyone seemed to be enjoying one another's company. They weren't mourning or morose. They were laughing and smiling and dancing together.

When they entered the foyer, Medina placed a hand on her son's shoulder and said, "Why don't you find some of your friends, Theo? We'll come find you when it's time to leave."

Theo nodded, wondering how he could find anyone in this place. The manor was so large he would've lost himself even if it wasn't full of people. Each of the rooms opened to another that he hadn't seen before. And though the carved wooden ceilings lost none of their grandeur, he found them melding together in an indistinguishable medley of opulence. This was a far cry from the Sahirons' narrow hallways and modest rooms. Any doubts about whether Eldra's home held hidden treasures vanished.

The only remaining question was where to start looking.

Theo tried the handle of a glass door at the back of one of the rooms and found himself on a dimly lit back porch along the water's edge. Stick River flowed past at a leisurely rate, reflecting whatever soft moonlight made it to the surface through the fog. An uneven, wooden dock jutted out over the water. Though the opposite bank disappeared into the night, shrouded in shadow, he could just make out the black tips of narrow treetops reaching toward the sky on the other side.

Contrary to the rest of the estate, this porch was quaint: small and made of simple unpainted wooden planks. A rough wooden railing slid beneath his fingertips, worn and warped by weather. The awning sagged in the center under a tumult of seasons, and a single lamp centered along the wall was all that illuminated the space. If light weren't streaming out through the glass door, the barely-there glow could've been quite pleasant.

"It's all a bit much, isn't it?" said a familiar voice in the darkness.

"It is," Theo agreed.

"She's got two parties inside—them what wants to live out their fantasies of wealth, and the other half who're only here for the gossip. What about you?" Two chairs sat in the far corner of the porch. Roman leaned forward in one of them.

"I got dragged along. Didn't have a choice," Theo said, which wasn't entirely true. He'd wanted to come ever since Roman had pledged his attendance.

"No, I meant what're you doing out here?" Roman's voice said he was smirking, but Theo couldn't quite see it in the dark.

"I was looking for Ismena. Has she come around?"

"Haven't seen her."

Theo crossed his arms, feeling a little cold now that he was outside and uncrowded.

"Then again," Roman continued, "there're enough folk here that finding her could prove impossible. Maybe she's hiding from you."

"That could be the case."

"Don't know why she'd want to." Roman leaned back in the chair again, his torso disappearing into shadow. He crossed one leg over the other. "She's probably gettin' her fill of the duck skewers. They get the best of us—I've had six myself. D'you want to sit?" He gestured to the empty chair.

Theo looked back into the room, drawn by the glow of the hanging lanterns. Then he drifted to the wooden chair, leaving the beam of light coming from the door. Once the glare had gone, Roman was easier to see.

"Your mum's keen on scarves, isn't she?" Roman asked.

"What makes you say that?"

"I saw you lot earlier as I was walking through the square. She'd got that royal blue one. I realized I haven't seen her without a scarf before. She must have hundreds." He moved his hands around his neck as if stroking a scarf himself.

Theo laughed. "She's got about a dozen, yeah. She's always going on about the patterns and the colors and whatnot."

"She could come to the shop sometime. We've got loads of fabrics that would make pretty scarves. I'm surprised she hasn't."

Theo gulped, not wanting to relay the things his mother had said about Mary Alba.

"Is your mother here?" Theo asked, thinking the intrigue of Eldra Vromía's mythic life span and the mysteries of her manor would appeal to Mary Alba.

Roman shook his head. "No, she's got other things that need doing. Things that need watching over."

Thinking of how many people were at the party, Theo said, "You couldn't possibly have any customers tonight. I think the whole town is here."

"I don't mean the shop." Roman laughed. Theo thought he might explain, but the other boy just sat quiet for a few moments before nodding toward the other bank of the river. "D'you ever think about having a look out there?"

"What? The woods? They say—"

"I *know* what they say. *Death lives in the woods.* I'm asking what you think."

Theo let his gaze wash over the black mass of forest across the waterway. For a moment, he thought he spotted a figure gliding through the trees, dark and shadowed. His heart leapt, but the vision faded as soon as he tried to stare directly at it.

"I don't know. I suppose they could be right. Somewhere far inside there are probably deadly things. But people go out there—I mean, didn't you? And you came back fine. One simply must take precautions."

"I've seen you going out to the edge of the woods on occasion. Beyond the wall. You don't seem afraid," Roman said. "I admire that."

Theo beamed. Then quickly cleared his throat and wiped the expression away. "I've never run into anything bad. Definitely not enough to justify the scary stories."

"People get their jollies telling others not to do what's fun."

"I've received many a lecture because of it."

"That's because you refuse to be a good boy and follow the rules."

They sat back in their chairs and watched as shadows crossed in front of the light through the glass door. The muffled sounds from inside grew, threatening to overtake the calming song of the crickets.

"It's your turn to answer my questions," Theo said.

Roman chuckled; the sound was melodious. "Alright, fire away."

"Where were you?"

"What d'you mean?" Roman asked. "I got here when all this lot did."

"No, I mean you were gone for a month and you only came back three days ago. Where've you been?" Theo said.

The older boy shifted in his chair. Theo took this to mean he'd made Roman uncomfortable, though the light tone of his voice didn't change. "Ain't you a nosy little mouse," he said. Theo bristled at the "little" distinction. "I've got my own travels and things."

"Yeah, I know that," Theo said, feeling sheepish. "I just thought—I wouldn't tell anyone. It's only because I knew you went out there—"

"Why'd that bother you?" Roman asked, chiding. "Were you scared for me?"

Theo's color deepened. "Well, yeah. Death lives—"

"*Death lives in the woods.* I know, I know. Gods, everyone in this town loves that phrase. Don't forget, me 'n' my folks came from out there. Wasn't here I was born like everyone else."

Theo did remember. It was why the Albas talked differently, why villagers were so quick to distrust them at the slightest opportunity. And why Theo had been so interested to meet Roman in the first place.

"I just... I care about what happens to my friends," he said.

Roman didn't respond for a full few minutes, staring out into the water with implacable focus. Theo assumed that he was done with the conversation—Roman sometimes did that when he didn't like the topic of conversation—but then he spoke again. None of the mischievous charm remained in his voice, nothing but sincerity. "I was out getting my father."

"Your father? Didn't he leave—"

"A year ago? Yeah."

"People said he'd done wrong to your mom."

Roman shook his head. "People spout about three loads of shite a day. He didn't do nothing to me mum. *Nothing* that she didn't tell him he couldn't do. And *nothing* that was bad by her."

"I'm sorry," Theo whispered. "I didn't know."

"S'alright."

"So, did you find him?"

"What?"

"Your dad. Did you find him?"

"Wasn't no matter of finding him. I knew where he was." Roman lifted his hands and placed them behind his head, looking much more relaxed than Theo felt, even if the topic of conversation remained somber. "But no, he didn't come back with me."

They sat in silence again, listening to the insects hum just below the din inside. Theo searched for things to say but didn't know how he could revert to easier discussions without coming off as dismissive.

"I just might go," Roman said, then sighed. "Not home, though. I don't want—I suppose I'll take a walk."

"Did you want me to come with you?" Theo offered.

Roman stood, shoulders tensed. He stared out at the river for a few more seconds, letting the night sounds fill the space between them. In another instant, he was back to his charming, enthusiastic self. Spinning on the spot, he flashed a grin and said, "Nah, you'll be wanting to stay once this lot's in full tilt. Maybe find your friend."

"I came to see you." Theo didn't mean for the confession to come out, but he had panicked at the idea of Roman leaving. Immediately, he clamped a hand over his mouth, feeling his face flush with heat. He was glad for the shadows.

To his relief, Roman grinned. It was that self-satisfied, smug, and yet completely charming grin that made Theo's heart thrum. "Is that so?" the boy asked. He leaned forward so that their faces were inches apart. "You've paid with honesty. I suppose it's only fair, then, that I give you your dues."

He pulled Theo's hand away from his mouth and kissed him gently on the lips. It was less a kiss than a peck, but Theo still felt his heart soar. It was as if a thousand fireworks went off inside him at once. A confusing, calamitous cacophony that rattled him to the core. He didn't want it to end.

"I'll see you around," Roman said.

And with that, he left through the door. Theo followed a few seconds later, but by the time he reentered the amber glow of the festivities, Roman had already vanished.

4
Eldra Evinced

Theo's shoulders slumped in disappointment, having found himself without company once again. Around the room, people mingled, their conversations unintelligible even as he attempted to single out voices. Against the opposite wall, Theo spotted his mother with her royal blue scarf. She was in a deep dialogue with a gray-haired woman Theo knew only as one of the court judges.

Turning on his heel, he decided to go find Eldra's famous conservatory his mother had gushed about, but that task turned out to be easier said than done. The manor was labyrinthine, folding around itself in indiscernible ways. After sliding through several doorways, he came upon a long, narrow room where only a few clusters of attendees lingered. One group huddled at a low table upon which lay a white sheet cake.

"... not even a number in sight..."

"'Happy Birthday, Eldra.' You think they'd have the decency to put *which* birthday..."

Thinking he'd rather not get near the trio of disappointed partygoers, Theo drifted away through another door, but as he made to close it behind him, wisps of another conversation arose, this time tense and paranoid.

"... fields drying up, even though Adonia Sykes says they got plenty of rain this season," said one voice.

"How can she even tell how much there'll be?" croaked another. "I'll bet once they've harvested—"

"Her family's only been at it for generations, Bert," said a third. "She's been harvesting since she was a tot. You don't think she knows when the crops take ill?"

"All I'm saying," Bert replied, "is that every year my father would lament the imminent crop shortage. And every year was the same—we were *fine*."

"That was grain, Bert," said the first voice. "Dolothyia knows we've always got a surplus of grain. Adonia's got potatoes and carrots. You know, vegetables."

"The drop-off is sudden enough that the zealots are whispering. They think the agreement is broken. They think these are bad omens."

"Do they really? That's never a good sign."

"They whisper about *everything*," Bert said, exasperated. "Look, it's not as though we've got rotting corpses lying about. We'd *know* if something were wrong with the ceremony—"

"Having fun, dear?"

Theo's heart leapt in his chest and he spun on the spot, slamming the door closed much harder than he meant to. Behind him stood a stout woman with startlingly white hair that conspicuously contrasted her brown complexion. The lines on her skin were so deeply etched, so pronounced, that he wondered if they sank right through her flesh to the bone. He realized in an instant that this must be their hostess. She wore an olive-green dress hemmed in a muted gold trim—shockingly plain when compared to the opulent decor of her residence.

"Sorry," Theo mumbled. "I just caught a bit of what they were talking about and—"

Between her sagging cheeks, Eldra smiled at him, and Theo's worries that she'd be cross to find him eavesdropping on her other guests seeped away. "Not a problem," she said with a voice like wind through an old forest. "The most interesting tidbits are never said directly to our faces."

Theo nodded, feeling his face flush a shade.

"Are you Miss Eldra Vromía?" he asked to confirm his suspicions.

"I am," she said, and wrapped his hand in hers. There was a tremble to her touch. "And who might you be?"

"Theo," he said. "Theo Sahiron."

They shook hands.

"Did you want to go out to see your guests?" Theo asked, stepping aside to let her pass.

Eldra shook her head. "Good heavens, no," she chuckled. "When I agreed to have a party, I never guessed this many people would come. Who knew I had so many friends, when I normally get so few visitors?" She winked. "But now that they're here, I'm having trouble getting up the courage to greet them all. Would you walk with me, my boy?"

Theo nodded again, and she took his arm. In slow strides, they made their way down an empty narrow hallway. Instead of ornate wallpapers or brightly colored panels, the walls were simple, darkly-stained wood. The sudden disappearance of filigree and fabulosity gave Theo the impression that this was a private corridor. Flames flickered in sconce lanterns, making a company of four out of the two and their shadows.

At the end of the hall was a pale green door separated into eight glass windows, beyond which the conservatory unfolded: a glass room under a domed glass ceiling. Outside, the world was dark, and only the silvery light of what moon could be seen through the fog lit the room. It was simultaneously eerie and extraordinary. Standing amid a wealth of unique greenery, Theo could make out the silhouettes of flowers he had never seen before, vines with leaves as large as his face, and trees whose shapes defied gravity.

They walked to the center of the room, which consisted of a circle of the most vibrant roses Theo had ever seen. Even in the dark, their colors shone clear: bloody scarlet, shimmering ivory, and blushing pink. Eldra tilted her head skyward. The clouds parted just enough that the moon swathed her aged features in its glow.

"I've spent a lifetime decorating a hundred rooms, but my favorite has always been this one," she said. "It's the only room that decorates itself, wouldn't you guess. I merely help it along."

Theo couldn't think of anything to say, minding his poise with his feet flat on the slate floor and his hands clasped behind him.

Eldra lifted a hand to caress a white blossom vying for attention. Compared to her wrinkled skin, the petals were pristine. "I used to come to this room almost every night in my youth—to enter the world of stars and darkness. It was my escape. My parents never knew at the time, of course. And I never told them. Some secrets we keep for the sake of having secrets."

"You've told me now, though," Theo said. "So, it's not a secret anymore."

"I have others." Eldra smiled. "Some in this very room."

Excitement rushed through Theo's veins. Was she hinting at what he thought she was? Suddenly, the conservatory called to Theo in a different way, but he knew it was rude to leave mid-conversation.

"Are you as old as they say you are?" he blurted. Remembering his manners, he added, "If you don't mind me asking."

Eldra chuckled again, the sound of tree limbs creaking in a breeze, and let the flower spring away from her grasp.

"I'm as old as say some, not so old as say others, and I suppose that means I'm older than most," she said. "Old folk lose count after a certain number of years."

The knowing look she gave him made Theo believe she was not like most old folk. As his eyes began to readjust to the darkness, he took a few steps away, trying to search his surroundings without being obvious. Blades of grass peeked between the stones in the path. On his right, lilies yawned. If Ismena were with him, they could find the secret passage faster.

"But how can you be so old?" he said, mind elsewhere. "No one else comes even close."

"Now how would you know that, young Theo?" she said. "I haven't told you my exact age."

"I guess you haven't," Theo said. He looked back at Eldra, who shrugged.

"I suppose death has yet to come for me. I couldn't say for certain. Perhaps they are afraid."

"Death is afraid of you?"

"Stranger things have happened."

Theo scratched his head, trying to think of circumstances stranger than that. When an answer eluded him, he pressed forth with the next thought that came to mind.

"Do you get lonely in this house? It's so large. I think I'd want someone to share it with."

This time, Eldra laughed outright. "Now you sound like the gossipers, always wanting to know why I never married." She clasped her hands together and bowed low to a crop of honeyworts, inhaling their scent. "I'm alone because I choose to be, and I have never married because I have never wanted to marry."

"Haven't you ever been in love?"

"What do you know of love, boy?" The blue honeyworts shook like bells in her hands, their dark flowers hanging as if to smell her palms. "I was in love once, but it was the only thing in this life I couldn't have, and so I lost it."

She wasn't looking at the blossoms anymore, but somewhere past them. The traces of her smile had gone. She looked, perhaps, older than she had before. Seasons marked her face. When she stood upright again, the wispy moonlight touched her skin and she appeared rejuvenated, her momentary lapse of senescence at an end.

"You speak in riddles," Theo said, resuming his visual search. The pond looked promising, but would he know the entrance when he saw it? "Like the rhymes my mother used to sing me. Older people do that."

Eldra barked into the domed ceiling. "And you are blunt. Your youth makes you far too eager to get your message out. But enough chatter. I suppose at some point I must appear before my guests. They'll be disappointed otherwise." She beckoned for Theo's arm again, shuffling up beside him. Laughter still filtered from her mouth and she muttered to herself in unintelligible disbelief.

As they crossed the threshold of the conservatory, Eldra gave his arm a squeeze. "Oh, and if you're interested," she said, "you might take a good look at the mosses."

5
Secrets and Scarves

The moment he and Eldra parted ways, Theo dashed through the rooms in search of Ismena. The party was now in full swing, and somehow the number of guests had multiplied since Theo arrived. Ipsitfel folk spilled from every doorway and crowded every corridor. Yet Theo found his friend with little trouble through sheer determination—driven by urgency. He had as much direction as he was likely to get tonight, and he had no intention of wasting it.

"There you are," Theo said, taking an empty seat beside her. His friend turned away from her conversation with an older girl he recognized but couldn't name.

"Theo!" Ismena said. "I meant to come find you, but time got away from me. Tom thought you might've—"

"How is he?" Theo asked, not wanting to be rude though he didn't truly care about her older brother's well-being. Tom maintained the wells all over town.

"Oh, the same, you know. Always complaining about fishing for loose buckets and endlessly braiding rope." Ismena shrugged. "Anyway, I looked everywhere, but I couldn't find you. Oddly enough, I ended up chatting with Miss Petunia for a while."

Theo made a face without thinking.

"Oh, she's not *that* bad if you're nice to her. To be honest, I found her rather funny. I didn't realize she had four cats!"

"Yes, Whiskers, Curtains, Bonbon, and Mortimer. They're always trying to sneak into the shop. They get fur in the frosting and then *I* get into trouble!"

Ismena laughed, as if this behavior were endearing and not obnoxious. "And where were you?"

"I sat on a porch out back with Roman for a while, and then I met Eldra. Listen—"

"Oh! You met her? I think someone said she's about to give her speech. Did she tell you how old she's turning?"

"Yes—I mean, no, she didn't say. But listen, she *did* tell me where there's a secret passage."

"A secret..." Ismena pursed her lips as if to dam a sudden flow of words. Theo watched her struggle to pretend the idea didn't intrigue her as much as it did. Her legs, which were crossed at the ankles, swayed back and forth.

"Do you know something?" he asked.

His friend relented. "I overheard Robin Deckle from the library saying that *supposedly* there'd been a tunnel built between the manor and the woods. A long, long time ago. But—"

"I know where the entrance is!"

Ismena sat up straight. "Theo."

It was too late. He'd stood and was racing for the door.

"Come on!"

"Theo, wait!" Ismena chased after him, regret straining her words. "Eldra's speech!"

"Don't worry she practically pointed it out to me." Through the first door. Wrong way. This was the ballroom where he'd found the back porch. Theo doubled back.

"Please, people are gathering."

"Then they won't know we're gone. It's the perfect time."

"I really don't think that's true!"

The two rushed through a chain of rooms, weaving in between groups of adults whose thirst for wine and whiskey had not yet been quenched. Several called out in alarm as the pair darted past and one woman almost lost her slice of cake. Ismena shouted apologies as she went, but Theo could not be stopped.

At last they entered the narrow room where the cake had sat before cutting. Theo slowed to a walk, nervous that Eldra might be hiding near where she'd found him before. When he opened the door at the other end of the room, however, the long, dark hallway was empty.

"It's this way." Theo gestured forward.

"No, Theo."

"I just want to see if it's real."

"We can't."

He was walking down the corridor already, his shadow moving from before to behind him each time he passed a light fixture. "This was where I met Eldra. As we were leaving, she told me to check the mosses."

"She might just be proud of them. They can be deceptively tricky."

"No." Theo shook his head. "She was definitely giving me a hint."

Even though Theo had been inside minutes before, entering the conservatory without Eldra felt transgressive. The hairs on his arms and neck stood on end, his sense of hearing heightened. He loved every minute of it. Before, the plants had held an ethereal beauty; now they made grotesque shapes in the dark, reaching out for the ankles or the unsuspecting head. The glass room was a labyrinth of unbidden space, particularly near the roses, which made every effort to scratch his arms.

Where would the mosses be?

With Ismena's reluctant help, Theo combed the room, peering over every bush and under every rock. Several times, his clothes caught on thorns he hadn't seen, the stems clinging to him while their flowers bowed in his face. The mosses weren't behind the stack of orchids on their steel shelves, nor beneath the topiary. Theo was just about to check around the roots of an aspen when he heard Ismena whisper his name.

Theo froze. "What is it?"

"I think I've found them."

Getting off his hands and knees, Theo joined his friend behind a stone wall which was covered top to bottom with mosses in every shade of green. On the ground before her, half covered with grass, dirt, and rocks, was a square wooden platform. When he knelt closer, Theo could see a rusted handle just large enough for two fingers.

"Alright, you found it. Let's go back," Ismena said, looking around.

"Well, let's be sure first." Theo gripped the handle and yanked on it as hard as he could.

At first, he thought it might not move, but the more he tugged—and with Ismena's eventual help—the platform began to tilt. Roots from the grass growing around and over it ripped, adding a crunch to the air. Dirt fell away. Rusted hinges buried for years beneath the surface howled in resistance.

And then it was open. With the hatch door leaning against the wall of mosses, a deep, dark pit extended below. It reeked of stale air and wet muck.

"How far down do you think it goes?" Theo asked.

Ismena grabbed a rock and dropped it in. It landed with a thud in less than two seconds.

"Not far," Theo remarked, then rolled onto his bottom to drop his legs in.

"What are you doing?" Ismena asked.

"I'm going to take a look."

"You said you just wanted to see if it was real."

"And I'm still not convinced," Theo replied with a smirk.

"You're unbelievable," she whispered. "It's pitch dark down there. How are you going to see anything? How are you going to *decide* that you've gone far enough? Or is your plan to get lost and killed?"

"Don't you mean 'or'?"

"I mean 'and.'"

"I'm just going to go down, feel around a bit, and then I'll be satisfied." Theo held up his open palm. "I swear."

"Well, I swear that I'm not going with you."

"That's fine."

"So you're going alone."

"Yes."

"Alright."

"Alright." And with that he lowered himself in.

The drop was shallow enough that if he stood straight with his hands up, the edge of the hole was just out of reach. If he jumped, he could still grab the lip and Ismena could pull him up. She looked down at him reproachfully, his head hovering above the shadows.

"I'll be quick," he said.

Then a loud crack pierced the quiet. Theo felt something hard and cold hit his neck, and the next second he was plunged into darkness as the hatch swung closed.

"Ismena!" Theo shouted, touching his neck where the small projectile had hit him. Though the area stung, he couldn't feel any blood.

"Theo!" Muffled sounds from above. "I think the bolt on one of the hinges sheared!"

A flurry of movement and grunting preceded momentary silence. Then Ismena cried out, and the door lurched upward but immediately fell back into place.

"I can't get it open on my own!"

Theo jumped, but his hands only briefly brushed the underside of the door, not enough to help. Fear rose in his chest and he cried out, jumping again and again while the moist ground smeared beneath him. "I can't reach!"

As he came down, his knee caught the wall of the pit. Losing his balance, Theo tipped over and fell with a squelch. Mud caked his trousers and jacket, making them stiff and cold. "Ismena!" he yelled.

"I'm going to get help," came her muffled reply.

Theo rolled over onto his elbows, tilting his head up to where he knew the hatch must be. There was nothing but an empty darkness. The air was moist and fetid. Already he was starting to shiver, the chill aided by his damp clothing. He must be filthy.

All became still.

"Ismena?"

She'd gone. In her place was a pregnant silence. How long would it take her to find someone? Would she go looking for his parents, or the first adult she came across? He didn't care much what some random adult would think when they saw him, but he did worry what his parents would say. One thing was for certain: they wouldn't be happy.

Assuming, of course, they could get the hatch open.

Theo rose to his knees, and a faint sound of dripping came to him. He turned and looked out at an openness that could only be felt. Black, empty space stretched beyond the senses in one direction. This must be the secret passage.

As if coerced, he stood and began to tiptoe into the opening. His hands went to the walls on either side of him. Damp earth and protruding roots. Step by step he followed the path. It sloped downward at a shallow angle, just enough to pull him further into the dark. An errant thought came to mind. *You could find where it leads.*

Someone would come back with Ismena; he should wait for them beneath the door.

Or he could come out of the passage on the other side.

In the woods.

Drip. Drip. Drip.

Theo paused, heart hammering. *Death lives in the woods.* That's what his parents had always said. That's what any of the elders always said. And nobody went into the woods unless they absolutely had to.

But Roman did, and he survived.

Drip. Drip. Drip.

The way back was sealed. If the other side was open, he would have no choice but to enter the woods. It was the only way out. That wasn't his fault. He hadn't known the hatch would break. Was there a hatch on the other side, or was it open to the woods? If there was no second door... The possibility of a hundred hungry beasts wandering through the passage with him scurried up his spine. He clenched his teeth.

CRACK.

Theo jumped and ran, uncertain from which direction the sound had come and in which direction he was going. Blindly he fled, the soles of his shoes almost incapable of finding grip in the slick mud. He ran with his arms outstretched, searching the darkness.

And then he slammed into something as hard as rock.

Stars exploded in front of his eyes, the first thing he'd been able to see in the last quarter hour. He fell to the floor again, and with a wet thud, the stone he'd collided with came down beside him. Water splashed over his face, instantly soaking through his clothes. It puddled on the ground beneath him. His hair became matted to his face. Out of habit he brushed it aside, though it did nothing to help his vision. Water was jetting out of the ceiling above, coming down in a powerful stream. Louder and louder. Roaring in his ears.

He was below the river! He had to be.

Which meant the passage was collapsing.

With water pouring down from above, Theo felt in the darkness, trying to determine which way the ground was sloping. He needed to find his way back to Eldra's conservatory. If he didn't, he would drown as the passage filled. In his panic, though, he couldn't feel any slant to the ground. It was all wet, and the water kept coming. Liters upon liters cascading from above.

The puddles!

Placing his hands flat on the ground, Theo concentrated. Water splashed all about, but most of it was running in a steady flow to his left. That must be the way further down. Quickly, he crawled to the right, clutching at the mud and roots all around him.

The crashing water grew to a onslaught as the hole in the ceiling widened. Water already covered his ankles. He had to move faster. He had to run.

Pulling himself off his knees, Theo shook the throbbing in his head away and began to amble up the passageway. His balance wavered; his footing unsteady. The rushing consumed his ears. He was shouting, but he couldn't hear himself above the din. All around him, the darkness was impenetrable.

With an almighty crash, a powerful fist of water collided with his back and he was thrown forward, his head snapping, feet lifted from the ground. Water splashed into his open mouth as he slid to the floor beneath the wave. He was completely submerged. All was black. He tried swimming. No sense of direction, no strength left, no air.

He was going to drown in this passage. He was going to drown in the darkness.

Then hands wrapped under his arms. Theo was only half aware that he was being held tightly, dragged through the water like a rag doll. He could not react, the strength in his limbs gone.

He broke the surface, lobbed through the mouth of the pit and pulled the rest of the way onto dry land. Behind him, someone else emerged and was helped up as well. Air returned to Theo's lungs, and he opened his eyes to light. Dim moonlight, but light nonetheless.

His father—every inch as wet as he—appeared over him. Terror and concern gripped his face. Damon had him by the shoulders and was jostling him. "Theo!" he called, and Theo heard his voice louder with each repetition. "Theo! Are you alright? Theo! Theo..."

—◦—

The streets were nearly empty—something Theo had never seen before. He was used to throngs of people—the vibrant commotion of Cirillo Square—but save for a few pairs of travelers here and there, not a shadow crossed the cobblestones. Then again, he had never been out at this time of night. The quiet was eerie.

His mother hurried him along. For a good five minutes, she said absolutely nothing. Laila trod a few steps behind, her head bowed and her hands behind her.

Theo's father had stayed at the manor to help figure out what could be done about the collapsed passageway. Though the conservatory itself hadn't suffered much damage, there were concerns that the foundation below might continue to deteriorate due to the flooding.

But Damon Sahiron would see that a solution was found, given that his son had caused the trouble. He was good at finding solutions.

At the very least, Eldra hadn't seemed angry. If Theo wasn't mistaken, she almost sounded pleased that he'd interrupted her birthday speech.

"I cannot stop you from being curious," Theo's mother said suddenly, "but I hope you understand how badly you just frightened me and your father."

Theo found he didn't have a response.

"You're lucky Missus Vromía was not upset."

"Miss."

"What?"

"Miss Vromía. She's never been married."

They stopped abruptly, and Medina shot him a look that said this was clearly not the time for him to correct her.

"You shouldn't have gone down there. Who knows how old that passage is. You could've died." She held a hand to her chest and was quiet for a moment as they continued walking. Long enough that her heels on the stones took on a rhythmic quality.

Then she sighed. "Are you grasping any of this?"

Theo *was* sorry. Every time his parents admonished him, he became wracked with guilt. Yet time and again, he found himself in trouble—and always for the same things. For being too rash, too reckless, too forgetful of the rules. He didn't have their patience though. Not yet. Perhaps not ever.

"I'll try not to do anything like that again," he said.

She put a gentle hand on his back.

"Oh, you're freezing," she said, unwrapping the great many rolls of scarf from around her neck. The royal blue fabric caught the light of the lampposts and shimmered in the darkness like waves of water. Medina quickly wrapped it around her son's shoulders and made him hold it closed in the front.

"We're not so far," Theo protested. "I'm fine. You'll be cold."

"Nonsense," she said. "With your clothes wet, you're likely to catch ill. Wear it, Theo. And keep it. You never know when you'll want for warmth."

"You can have my shawl, Mother," said Laila.

Medina turned back and brought her daughter under her arm. "No, thank you, my dear. You are a generous child. You are both my beautiful children. I wish nothing bad would ever happen to you. Even if I recognize I can't make that so."

This, perhaps, made Theo feel the worst. He knew his mother had done an exceptional job protecting him and his sister. When bad things *did* happen, they were usually of his own doing. As the trio stepped up to their front door, Theo wrapped his mother's scarf—now his—more tightly around him. He cherished its warmth; both as an added layer and a sign of her love.

It smelled faintly of jasmine.

6
Atonement

The night had yet to end.

Theo could feel his eyelids growing heavy. As the evening's excitement waned, he found he had to blink more than usual to keep his head up. The moment they entered the house, his mother led him into the bathroom where he washed reluctantly in scalding water. Then he dressed in his night clothes, and his mother instructed him to wait in the living room. Though she'd offered that he sit down, Theo didn't trust himself to do so without falling asleep. Instead, he stood motionless beside the hearth, staring at the ash-coated bricks inside the chimney.

Laila went straight to bed after muttering a soft goodnight. He envied her, but sleep was a reward of the wise.

When he was beginning to wonder whether his mother had forgotten about him and maybe his punishment was to stand there all night without sleep, hurried footfalls came up the front steps and the door to the house swung wide. Damon stood in the orange glow of the foyer lamp looking unmistakably exhausted and haggard. His dark hair clung to his forehead in the front, though it stuck out at odd angles elsewhere. His clothes hung stiffly from his frame, having dried with a ground-in layer of mud. He did not look pleased—not in the slightest—and when he spotted Theo standing stock-still in the living room, his very square jaw tightened.

Damon closed the door behind him with a soft click. He clasped his hands behind his back and walked the *one, two, three, four, five* steps to the living room, eyes never leaving his son.

Theo found he could not hold his father's gaze.

When Damon stopped, the ticking clock became the only source of noise for a long stretch of painstakingly slow seconds.

"Well," Damon began, "what have you to say?"

"I'm sorry—"

"Do you have any idea how distraught you made me and your mother?"

"No, I—"

"Do you have any idea how stupid that was of you to do?"

"It's just that—"

"And do you have any idea how much damage you've done to Miss Vromía's house, most especially her beloved conservatory?"

Afraid his father wasn't finished yet, Theo held his tongue.

"Well?" Damon asked.

"I'm sorry," Theo said. Then added, "It was such a long party and I couldn't find Ismena and Roman left so I had nobody to talk to. And someone had mentioned secret passages, so I was curious and *I just wanted to know*. I just wanted a look—I didn't know it was on the verge of collapse."

Damon shook his head. "So you just waltzed around someone else's home, without their consent, and when you found a hidden passage, you decided you had a right to use it?"

Theo trained his eyes on the floor.

"The world doesn't work that way, Theo."

"I just wanted to see where it led."

Damon held up a hand and Theo fell silent.

"You could have died. What if Ismena hadn't been able to get to anyone in time? What if I hadn't been able to pull you out of the tunnel before you'd passed out in the dark? It was black as pitch down there—you're damn lucky I found you as quickly as I did." Damon's hands came to rest on the back of the couch, the only thing between them. He sighed. "You're very lucky Miss Vromía isn't asking for recompense."

Theo found this to be too much. He swallowed hard, fighting the stinging in his eyes. Unable to help himself, he looked up at his father and found that most of the anger had fallen from his face. He looked worried and fatigued. Dirt powdered his jaw and forehead. His collar stuck out at an angle on the left side. Without a word, Theo walked around the couch, stood before his father, and embraced him. For a brief moment, Damon did not reciprocate—stiff and upright—and then he relaxed and his arms engulfed his son.

"I admire your curiosity, Theo—it's one of your best traits. But you must couple it with critical thinking or it will get you in far worse trouble than it's worth." Damon held Theo by the shoulders and looked him in the eye. "I don't want to see you harmed."

"I know," Theo said, though it came out as more of a whisper. "And I'm sorry I wrecked our dress clothes."

Damon's eyes widened as if the thought had not yet occurred to him. Then he squeezed them shut in resignation. "Dammit," he breathed. He clicked his teeth together, something he often did when he was searching for a solution. "We'll have to try to get them clean—see if they're salvageable. I hope they are."

He looked down at what Theo was wearing now. "Speaking of which, is this your mother's scarf?"

"Yes, she gave it to me so I wouldn't be cold on the way back. All my clothes were still wet. Said I could keep it."

"It looks like it needs to be washed as well."

"Some of the dirt... might've come off on it, yeah."

"You shouldn't be wearing it over clean clothes."

Theo clasped it tighter around himself. "I didn't want to take it off."

"She gave it to you?" Damon mused. "This particular scarf was her favorite. We'll have to do something about that."

Theo nodded.

"Alright, well if you've washed up, I think there's been enough excitement for one night. Go to bed. We'll talk more in the morning." Damon ran a hand through his hair then looked at it, as if trying to discern whether it came away any filthier than before.

With a pat on the back using his other hand, he dismissed Theo, who felt as though maybe he'd missed the part about punishment. Had he misheard? Perhaps his father was too tired to do any sentencing tonight; that would come later. For now, Theo mounted the stairs, thankful that he was still alive and vowing that he would never again let his curiosity take control of him.

———◦———

Theo was certain he had just shut his eyes and pulled his blankets up under his chin when the door of his room opened. His father strode in, a self-satisfied smile on his face.

"Good morning, Theo."

Theo grunted. "What ghastly hour is it?"

"It's the start of the day."

Theo felt the end of the bed sink beneath his father's weight. Reluctantly, he sat up. "I haven't got anywhere to be today."

"I know," his father said, "but I have something I want you to do this morning. A small atonement for the blemished night. Unless you'd rather be punished?"

Guilt scrambled up Theo's intestines, and he nodded. "Alright."

His father lifted his hand and revealed a pair of golden coins.

"Take these," he said. "Go to Cirillo Square this morning and get your mother a new scarf. Not just the first you see—Believe me, I *will* know. Get her one to replace the scarf she gave you. One that she will like. Do you understand?"

Theo looked back at his father. He didn't know much about choosing clothes. Sure, he could tell which ones looked nice and interesting, but he'd never picked any out himself. It was always whatever his family could afford. Whatever they already had for him. How was he supposed to choose something for his mother?

"Yes?" his father asked.

Theo took the coins and held them in his fist. He nodded. "Yes."

"Good." Damon ruffled his son's hair. "If you leave now, you can be back in time for us all to enjoy a nice Sunday together."

And with that, he stood and left the room.

Theo sat dazed for a few moments, his body aching from lack of sleep. He was beginning to gather the first wisps of coherent thought when he noticed something gray and round sitting on the end of his bed—his father's tin pocket watch. It lay face down, the chain piled loosely beside it, fallen unnoticed from his father's trousers. Theo leaned forward and grabbed it, turning the device over in his hand. It was still warm.

Opening his mouth, Theo made to call after his father but thought better of it. Lying open in his palm, the watch was no heavier than an apple. What a useful thing to carry around—it conjured images of the men who strolled Cirillo Square. If his father hadn't noticed it fall out of his pocket, he certainly wouldn't notice if Theo kept it for an hour or two. If he ran into Roman, he could even find a way to show it to him. And once Theo had returned from his errand, he could lay it on the dining table and pretend he'd never had it. Yes, he liked the way it felt in his hand.

Awake now, Theo rolled off his bed. Given how late they'd come home last night, his mother and sister were probably still asleep, oblivious to the errand his father had risen early to give him. Suppressing mumbles about the unfairness of it all and reminding himself over and over how much trouble he *could* be in, Theo dressed and combed his hair, shoving the coins and the watch deep into his trouser pocket. Of all the ways he'd ever been asked to atone, this was by far the easiest. And for addressing the worst trouble he'd ever caused, the deal was even greater. He bounded down the stairs—remembering only at the bottom that he probably should have tried to make less noise—and slipped out into the brisk, foggy a ir.

The spirit of emancipation inflated his lungs, and he was immediately cognizant of why early mornings in Ipsitfel were his favorite times—especially early mornings after a town-wide gathering, when the streets were still sleepy. The cold was biting but for a moment, until he wrapped the royal blue scarf about his neck. Then he traipsed over cobblestones, his weathered soles clomping carefree on the hard surface. The usual fog obscured the faces of the buildings around him, creating the illusion that he jogged in a gray-green cloud.

Without thought, Theo dipped into a narrow alley off Slade Street. He skipped through a puddle and bounded over a pile of discarded crates. The brick buildings drew in on either side of him, their aging walls vaulting upward into the drifting mire beyond sight. At the end of the alley, he took a large step, prepared himself, and leapt high through the air. Deftly, he grasped the top of the back wall—the city's wall—and scrambled upward, pulling himself on to p.

There was no need to rush into the town, so why not take the scenic route?

Hands outstretched to either side, Theo walked along the top of the wall. On one side, the town slid past: wooden fences, rear gardens, windows glowing yellow in the morning. On the other side, an empty stretch of grass and dirt, the portion of the Stick River which wound around this side of the town, and then a solid, impenetrable mass of woods. Trees with gnarled branches and knotted trunks reached for him across the wide barrier of no-man's land. He did his best not to look straight at the forest, a fear learned from every townsperson he'd ever met. But every so often, he allowed himself a peek, curiosity taking brief control.

He was approaching the arched eastern gateway—he always climbed around the outside of it, shimmying along the edge of the stone sill with his back to the great inscription of 'Ipsitfel'—when it happened. Where the woods came closest to the wall, a shadow moved, burying itself in a thicket of brambles. Theo strained his eyes, fighting the poor visibility to see what had caused the disturbance. Though the fog continued to drift through the line of trees, the forest returned to a standstill.

Theo moved a step farther along the wall without taking his eyes off the spot. He was *certain* he'd seen something. Something dark. Something tall. His heart raced. What could it be? Was it the same figure he'd spotted darting out of sight at the party yesterday evening? Whatever it was was shy. He imagined a large, lumbering creature curious to see what happened within the walls but not wanting to be caught looking. Maybe a beast with big, round eyes and a shining black coat.

The sentry at the gate hadn't seemed to take notice—though they never paid much attention, which was why Theo had rarely been caught. He took one quick look around and hopped to the ground outside the wall.

Never had his heart beat so fast. The thrill of this forbidden venture filled him with a rush of elation. He felt invigorated, terrified, and invincible all at once. What was in the woods?

Theo emitted a soft coo, hoping to lure the creature back out of the trees. He leaned this way and that as he approached the undergrowth, trying to get a better glimpse into the darkness. Nothing came to him. The woods were as still as he'd ever seen them. How could something so still be dangerous? People were afraid of the woods but only because, above all else, people feared what they didn't know.

"Theo! Where are you going?" The voice was shrill and harsh.

Theo stood upright, his excitement giving way to regret. He spun and saw Laila marching up behind him, her hands balled into angry fists, eyes flaring. Usually cool and collected, he was surprised to see her this emotionally charged.

"L-Laila," he stuttered, dumbstruck.

"What are you doing here?" She stopped her march a hands width from his face, nostrils flared, posture overbearing. He couldn't help observing for the first time that she looked quite like their mother, although he couldn't remember their mother ever being this angry. "Death lives in the woods."

"I saw something." He pointed behind him at the trees.

"Do you think that gives you any excuse to wander outside the town?" She crossed her arms. "After what you did last night, Father made one request of you this morning—only one—and you couldn't fulfill even that. I followed you because I was hoping you'd learned something. I thought maybe you'd understood—but here you are being stupid *again*."

"I was still going to get the scarf, I just came here first."

"Of *course* you were still going to do it. Of *course* you just came here first."

"Well, sorry I'm not perfect like you."

"Don't you dare make this about me." Laila lifted a finger, and Theo saw how much it trembled with fury. "I have made my mistakes, but at a certain point I looked at myself and realized what I had to do to stop making them. I realized I was not the only person my choices affected. Take some personal responsibility, Theo. Don't try to make this my fault."

"You came outside the wall too."

"Because someone must always put themselves in danger to save you. You are *selfish*, Theo. You are impulsive!" Laila stepped back, breathing hard, and let her words sink in.

Theo made to reply, but nothing came to him. He looked behind him at the woods and then at the ground, feeling shame creep over the collar of his sweater. He couldn't look at his sister, thinking only of the task his father had given him and the time his father had meant for the family to spend together when it was done.

But he'd only wanted to peek into the woods—to see the creature he'd glimpsed. He wasn't going to stay for long; it was just a look. They'd have never known. He *knew* he would've been back before the time was missed.

Before any tension between the siblings could dissipate, another figure came running at them out of the fog, this one frantic with waving arms and fearful shouts. She was nothing but a dark shape bobbing up and down for a long while before her features came into focus, but soon enough Ismena had reached them. Panic-stricken. Eyes wide and worried.

"Laila!" she screamed. "Theo!"

Laila turned to meet her. "Ismena? What is it?"

Ismena had trouble catching her breath. Her hands fell to her knees and she wheezed as though she'd run a very great distance. "I can't... You have to... help..."

Laila's gaze met Theo's for a brief moment, all the anger gone. "Ismena, what's happened?"

"You have to come quick," Ismena heaved. "Your house... your house is on fire."

The words dropped like a stone in Theo's stomach.

"By Kouros!" Laila swore. In the next instant the siblings were sprinting side by side across the grass, back toward the wall. Theo had more practice, and he scaled it deftly, coming down on the other side on heavy soles. He didn't wait for his sister; he took off running through the alleys. The cobblestones were slick from the mist and more than once he almost lost his balance. Behind him, he could hear his sister's pounding footfalls in pursuit. He couldn't spare a thought for where Ismena had gone.

Up ahead, over the rooftops, tendrils of dark smoke rose into the sky.

Ipsitfel's alleys had never seemed so antagonistic, but now they bent this way and that—an endless labyrinth of passageways barring him from his destination. Spilling out onto the main road, Theo bounded across the bridge over the Stick River. He no longer registered his heavy breathing, or his pounding pulse, or the wind whipping in his ears. Everything was static except for the glimpses of smoke drawing slowly nearer and nearer. He could smell it. The choking stench of fire filled his lungs.

When he could finally see the flames, he came to a halt.

Aggressive yellow and orange tongues flailed through the windows, leaving black streaks crawling up the outside of the house. Smoke billowed through the air, the fog thickened with ash. Burning wood crackled in his ears. He could see nothing inside. Nothing through the flames. The home he had left only an hour before had transformed into a bright, monstrous creature, swallowing the life he and his sister had shared.

Laila! She was beside him. Struck just as motionless.

"Everything was fine," she said monotonously. "When I followed you, everything was fine..."

Sparks rained into the sky.

Their stupor broke and both siblings darted forth at once.

"Mother!" Theo screamed. He could barely hear himself above the roaring flames. A few faces had gathered around them, townsfolk bringing buckets of water to stop the fire's spread, but none were his parents. "Father!"

Someone grabbed him. His shirt pulled taut in their clutches. He tore at their grip without turning to see who it was, not taking his eyes from the disaster before him. Someone had his sister too. She screamed throat-tearing wails.

"Father!" Theo was crying, and he wrenched himself away, taking Laila by the hand and pulling her with him.

"Don't!" a voice shouted.

Toward the flames they sprinted.

"Stop!"

Theo called out for his mother and father again and again until he found himself on the ground, crushed by the weight of another. Ash sullied the moisture on his face. He looked up at the burning house, watching the fire curl into the endless sky.

7

Lamenting the Sahirons

The black vest had been easy enough to put on, but he struggled with the bow tie. After several infuriating attempts, he decided to do away with it all together. What did it matter if he was missing one, unimportant part of his suit? Beneath, Theo wore the only pair of trousers and boots he had left. He couldn't bring himself to take the blue scarf from around his neck, even though—according to tradition—vibrant colors were avoided during the Descension ceremony. But who would make more than a half attempt to get him to reconsider?

Numb was the only word he could use to describe his emotional status.

Theo stood in the courtyard of the Temple of Preparation, staring at a fountain that no longer worked. He'd stood there for the better part of the last hour, watching as insects landed on the overgrown vines and birds came to bathe in the stagnant water. Only once had he seen his sister today. She busied herself with coordinating the proceedings, preventing her own emotional outpouring through task-oriented distraction. She'd cried only once since that morning, and remained elusive otherwise.

Theo had spent the last two nights sleeping on the sofa in Ismena's living room. The worn upholstery had been uncomfortable:

soft where it needed to be firm and unforgiving where it needed to be pliant. He'd tossed and turned through the evening hours until the first signs of light found their way through the curtains. But the truth was, even the most comfortable mattress would've done him no good. How anyone could expect him to sleep was unfathomable. He had lost both his parents. He might not sleep for a long time. And maybe never peacefully.

The condolences were almost worse than the deaths themselves. Every time he'd managed to stem the flow of tears, another apology at his devastation ripped off the fragile scab. The well-wishers seemed to time themselves perfectly, waiting for just the moment when he'd recovered to come along. "You poor dear," they said. "I'm sorry for your loss."

And perhaps that was why he could no longer feel. He had nothing at all to give. He had condensed all his sorrow into tears and every last drop had been wrung. There was nothing left.

He'd never known that was possible.

The doors at the top of the stairs swung wide. Laila emerged, her long dark hair lying loose over her shoulders. Her black dress moved only to allow her quick steps, and otherwise stood still and vertical like a heavy velvet curtain.

Behind her came the figures in blue capes, a dozen split between the two wooden stretchers. Their eyes were all but hidden in shadow, and they looked at neither of the siblings. Theo didn't want to be near them. He didn't want to accidentally catch a glimpse of the offerings they carried. He loathed the caped figures. How dare they carry what didn't belong to them?.He swallowed the instinct to shout in their faces.

Laila, however, came to the stretchers and tied a small drawstring bag around the wrist of each prone body. Afterward, she looked at

Theo for the first time since descending the stairs, as if shocked by his presence.

"Come on," she said. "It's almost time."

As if on cue, Viseyne Tower began to toll. Everyone in the courtyard stood in disassociated silence while the notes rang out over Ipsitfel. Each clang was a club to Theo's heart. How could he be expected to follow through with the ceremony?

When the last of the resounding tolls had died, the Temple keeper came forth from a room off the side of the courtyard and solemnly opened the gate. A pensive expression haunted her features, as if she no longer trusted herself to acknowledge the mourning. She'd seen enough of it in her life. The sorrow never changed. She would see another come the next few days or weeks.

Cobblestoned streets opened before them. The procession began. Waiting outside the courtyard was a small group of assorted friends of Damon and Medina Sahiron. People who'd been close in life and had grown up with them. None of Theo's relatives lived in the town anymore. His grandparents had died when he was young, and his aunt and uncles had moved long ago to larger cities far away. He therefore found little comfort from the gathered mourners.

By this time, the streets had emptied and the procession moved like a caravan of ghosts searching a deserted land. Lanterns held by various mourners created a circle of light that followed them beneath the gaze of vacant, dark windows. Theo pulled at the hem of his white tunic, anxiety compounding with each step. How much farther was Cirillo Square? He found he didn't know anymore, though he'd trod these streets more times than he could count.

And then, all too suddenly, he could hear echoes of the governor's voice, extolling the communal benefits of the ceremony and lamenting the profound loss of Medina and Damon Sahiron. The tone was appropriately mournful, and to anyone else it might have been understood as genuine, but anger built up in Theo. The governor's words were empty. He didn't know Theo's parents beyond mere acquaintanceship. He didn't know what their deaths meant. The governor may have seen death before, but he couldn't empathize with the surviving children of this "beloved couple." The governor didn't feel the unfairness of Medina and Damon being snatched from life without a moment's notice. He didn't feel the gut-wrenching pain of realizing they were in that burning building—a building they called home—trapped and turning to ash when they had so much life left in them. Governor Sutton knew *nothing*.

Yet everyone standing around looked to him, nodding along as if he so perfectly summarized the tragedy.

"Theo." Laila's hand to his chest stopped him walking any farther. He might've fallen into the Gateway had she not intervened. The procession had stopped without his realizing.

Someone took his arm. Ismena was beside him wearing a disconsolate expression. When had she gotten here? Her eyebrows were drawn together in concern.

The ones in the blue cloaks were harnessing Theo's mother first. Ismena's grip tightened on him, but the restraint wasn't necessary. He watched in paralyzed horror as the pulley took hold of his mother's fragile form. Medina Sahiron, once a picture of kind intelligence, bared her soul to the sky. Her limbs fell back, her head draped in a moon-silver scarf to disguise the loss of hair and the long burns on her face. She was as in control of her body as a rag doll.

The villagers began the Cimmerian Elegy.

"Gently you go, breathing the night
The moon and the stars come, guiding by light
Pity the mountain that howls and grieves
But tend to the bowed willow, mourning its leaves."

Then they began to lower her, the rim of stones rising as the Gateway swallowed her whole. A cavernous void opened inside Theo, as large as the one before him. He gasped without meaning to, unable to get the oxygen his lungs needed.

"Only with death do the living remain
Pardoned of famine, of thirst, and of pain
A fate we may fear, a fate we may know
Maybe again we will meet down below."

Laila was given the rope for release, and the leading member of the blue-cloaked figures nodded. They couldn't possibly expect her to—

His sister squeezed her eyes shut and pulled. Though not very hard, the effort was enough. The rope in her hands tensed for a brief moment before slackening, and she raised her face skyward, unable to watch. The ropes dangling into the Gateway recoiled as their load broke free. Medina Sahiron was gone from them in both body and spirit.

It was Theo's turn to grip Ismena's arm. This wasn't right. He couldn't let them dispose of his parents' bodies like this.

Then the figures in blue harnessed his father.

No part of Damon's skin was left exposed, so badly had he been disfigured by the flames. Theo had glimpsed him when the villagers removed his father from the ruins. His charred and mutilated face was completely unrecognizable. What proof did Theo have that this was his father, save the sinking feeling in his chest? He would never see his father's face again; he hadn't thought to study it, cherish it, memorize every minute detail.

The body was lifted over the hole, limp as his wife's had been.

"Gently you go..."

Theo dipped a hand into his pocket and felt the tin watch that was still there. Perhaps if he hadn't decided to keep it, maybe if he had run after his father to give it back, things would have played out differently. There was no logical reason why having his pocket watch would have changed Damon's fate, but who knew how the future might have differed.

Who knew?

It wasn't fair. It wasn't right. That indignant anger flared again inside him. Losing both his parents in one morning wasn't bad luck; it was conspiracy against him. From whom? The whole of Ipsitfel? The universe, perhaps? He didn't need an answer for it to be true. He didn't deserve this. They were meant to have long, happy lives together. They were meant to be a family. He still needed them. He still very much needed them.

He would not stand for their premature demise.

Theo didn't watch as his sister pulled the rope a second time. His mind was elsewhere, following a sequence of events that had yet to play out. This would not be the end, he decided. This would not be the final goodbye.

8

A Very Bad Idea

Lavender—the flower of Ipsitfel—coated the floor of the entryway. They had been sent by various mourners offering their condolences. In the three days since his parent's Descension, they'd begun to wither.

"Things will be better soon," his sister said, lingering beside him. Her voice was so utterly lifeless that he had a hard time believing her.

Instead of responding, Theo nodded.

"I know I've asked before, but the offer still stands. We can find another bed for you if you'd like, love." Alayna Bareen, Ismena's mother, entered the room. "We haven't got another sofa, but I'm sure if we piled up enough blankets, we could make something comfortable to lie in."

Laila tried to smile, but the attempt was weak. "Thank you, Missus Bareen, but I'm staying with Gwendolyn Shears. Her family's just around the corner, so it's no bother."

"Are you sure?"

Laila nodded. "Yes, thanks. You've been wonderful to Theo."

"Oh, he's no hassle." She turned to him, "You're a good lad. The both of you are wonderful."

They expected no response from Theo, and he did not disappoint.

"I don't know what we would've done without friends to take us in."

Missus Bareen *tsked*. "You poor dears. You've been through so much. *Too* much for people so young, if you ask me."

She put a hand to her mouth as her eyes filled with tears. She had done this several times since Theo's arrival. If he had run out of tears, then Alayna was making up for the dearth. Laila hugged Missus Bareen.

"I'd better go," she said. "It's getting late."

"You have a good night," Alayna said.

Laila and Theo locked eyes. Neither felt a need to pretend for the other sibling; they both knew exactly how the other was feeling. Buried by sorrow, there wasn't room for niceties like *good night*. The chances of having one were too slim.

Laila left, disappearing into the cold night.

"My dear, you must be exhausted." Alayna rested a hand on the banister beside him. "Did you want me to fix you a cup of tea before I turned in?"

"No," Theo said. He stared at the closed front door through which his sister had vanished.

"Well, let me know if you need anything," Alayna said, and mounted the stairs. "Don't hesitate to wake me up. I'm more than happy. Anything you need, love."

Theo waited until he heard the door to her bedroom close. He counted under his breath one full minute. Then he darted into the living room, feeling underneath the sofa for the item he'd hidden only hours ago while the Bareens were distracted by dinner. Once retrieved, his stockinged feet made no noise as he crept up the staircase.

At the landing, Theo darted off to the right, tiptoeing until he reached the door at the end of the hall. Ismena had gone off to bed about an hour before, but she was a light sleeper, and it wouldn't take much to wake her up. He knocked quietly three times and listened for rustling inside. One quick movement was followed by an extended silence, as though maybe she were contemplating whether to respond. Theo was just beginning to think he needed to knock again when the door cracked open.

Ismena's eye appeared. "Theo?" she whispered. "What're you doing up here?"

"Ismena, I need you to help me with something."

"What time is it?" she asked. Then yawned. "Is everything alright?"

"Yes," he said. "I mean, no. I need your help."

The brow above her visible eye dipped. "What's happening?"

"I need you to come with me," Theo said, gesturing behind him toward the landing.

Ismena hesitated, as if, now that she could tell Theo was not in any imminent physical or emotional duress, she was suspicious. Every other light in the house had been extinguished save for the sconce along the stairs. The rest of her family had obviously gone to bed, but here was Theo requesting that she follow him downstairs.

Then she noticed what he was carrying.

"Theo, why do you have that rope? Where did you—Have you been in Tom's things? Did you steal that?"

"Ismena," he pleaded. "I really need your help."

"What is going on, Theo?" she demanded.

Theo raised his palms, willing her to keep her voice down.

"I'll tell you if you come with me."

"I think you can tell me now. And why are you wearing that?" she asked, her eyes going to his white ceremonial tunic and his mother's scarf. "Theo, for the last time, what is going on?"

"I can't tell you yet," Theo said. "I'm not sure of it myself."

They stood in silence. Theo felt Ismena's eyes searching his own. She had to come along with him—she always came along with him.

If she didn't... well, he'd have to find another way, which was less than ideal.

"It's alright," he said, defeated. "I can ask Roman—"

"I swear, if this is something stupid," Ismena mumbled, feeling through the darkness for a coat and closing the door to her room as she left. Theo whispered his thanks multiple times as the pair trod lightly across the landing and down the stairs, scuttling between the pots of lavender to the front door. The smell of the flowers followed them out onto the first step, but was soon cut off by the outside world. Disparate light from the streetlamps replaced the warm glow in the house.

Ismena drew her coat more tightly around herself, and Theo did the same of the blue scarf, shivering.

"Now where?" she asked.

"Cirillo Square," Theo said. And he set off through the town. Behind him, he could hear Ismena sputter in surprise, but she followed. Under normal circumstances, he might've run to the perimeter wall and trod along the top around the outskirts of town, but not tonight. The Bareen residence was not as close to the wall as his home had been, and his mind buzzed with determination. He didn't have time for the scenic route.

They skittered through the streets of Ipsitfel. For most of the way, they met only the odd lit window glowing yellow behind a sheer curtain. Without a lantern, the pair were nearly invisible. If anyone glanced outside, all they would see were obscurations in the fog.

Then Ismena threw out a hand to stop Theo from rounding a corner. He came to a halt just in time to hear voices, though they were too low to discern what was said.

Theo peeked around the side of the building. He spotted three cloaked figures walking down the lane, a raised lantern held by the one in the middle. By the gold glow, he could see the medallions hanging from their necks.

"Zealots," Theo breathed.

"Don't call them that," Ismena hissed. "My father says it's disrespectful."

"Adults call them that all the time."

"We should go back."

"No," Theo snapped, a bit too loud. He clenched his teeth shut, but none of the three cloaked figures appeared to hear him. "They're leaving."

Indeed, the trio turned down another alley in the next instant and were gone. Theo waited a breath and then waved his friend forward. They said nothing to each other the rest of the way, and, perhaps, Theo kept himself a few steps ahead of Ismena so that she never had the chance to strike up conversation. He knew what she would say, what anyone might say had they a clue what he intended. Her protests would be appreciated—given that he assumed she had his "best interests" at heart—but unwanted all the same. His was a very bad idea, but maybe the only one that would bring him peace.

At last they reached Cirillo Square. The clock on Viseyne Tower shone over them, ticking its tongue in disapproval. The bank, the courthouse, the bakery—all the doors were shut and the shutters pulled. The lights were doused except the streetlamps. The Gateway sat in darkness.

"You can't pull them out again."

"What?" Theo said. He turned around.

"You can't pull them out again. That won't do anything. You'll only recover their bodies, nothing more."

"Ismena, I know—"

"Their spirits... their souls will still be gone." She put her hands on the fence that surrounded the Gateway, peering over the rim into the black abyss a few feet beyond. "Besides, there's no way you'll be able to hook them. I've heard people swear there's no bottom."

"Ismena," Theo said. She pierced him with a harsh stare. "I know I can't fish them out."

She huffed, looking around the plaza, checking for spying eyes. "Then I don't know why you led me out here."

"I'm going in after them."

Ismena gripped the fence and stared at him, mouth agape, as if she couldn't have possibly heard him correctly. Theo understood. If anyone else had said those same words to him, he would have thought them mad. But he had all his faculties about him. He'd thought the plan through. He meant what he said.

"Theo... don't be an idiot. You don't know what you're saying."

"I *do* know what I'm saying. I've thought it over."

"You can't go down there. You're not dead! Living people aren't allowed—"

"There's no other way, Ismena. Don't you see?"

"No, I don't see."

"You remember the teachings. I know you do. Death claims a person, right. The soul is expelled from the flesh and, in the *terrible* lands beyond the woods, wanders unseen until they are guided to the underworld."

Ismena nodded. "Yes, but souls don't wander in Ipsitfel. We have The Gateway. When we cast the bodies below, their souls follow and find their final resting place."

"Exactly."

"Then I don't understand."

Theo rolled his eyes and concluded his plan with fervor, "that means if I go down there too, I can find the bodies and souls of my parents and bring them back. It makes sense."

Ismena remained stern for a moment longer, and then her features softened. She stifled what looked like a sudden urge to cry. Theo searched her gaze, waiting.

"I know it hurts," she whispered. "None of this should have happened to you or Laila. You don't deserve it. But you need to listen to yourself. You don't know what you're saying. It *doesn't* make any sense at all."

Theo shook his head. "I do know what I'm saying. I need to do this."

"Theo—"

"They weren't supposed to die—"

"Listen—"

"My parents were healthy and strong and loving."

"Sometimes bad things happen to good people."

"Not this." Theo's gaze wandered over the edge of the hole. "Not this. Not to them."

Ismena didn't respond; maybe she couldn't bring herself to. Not when the fire burning in his eyes was so strong. Instead, she stared out at the Gateway, a string of possibilities playing out behind her eyes. Judging by her expression, none of them matched the hopeful outcome Theo envisioned. For the living, nothing lay beyond the Gateway.

"I know I'm asking too much," Theo said, "but I need you to understand that I need to do this. I know I can change what happened."

"You'll die." Ismena's voice was hoarse. "If you go down there, that's what'll happen."

"You don't know that."

"I'm more certain of that than anything else."

He sighed, closing his eyes and bowing his head. On some level, he regretted asking her to come along. But she was his closest friend, and he'd hoped she would eventually see things his way. Perhaps that wasn't a possibility. She might sympathize with him, but she didn't understand the turmoil he endured. He needed his parents back. He didn't want to spend the rest of his life dreaming of their faces. Maybe it wouldn't be every night, but it would come just often enough to remind him that they were missing. Remind him that there would never be mornings when they'd wake up in the same house and walk to the bakery to purchase a fresh pastry or two just so they could talk about how good Miss Petunia's apple turnovers w ere.

"You don't have to help me," Theo said. "I'm not going to make you do anything you don't want to do."

"Good," Ismena said. "Then let's get back to the house. I think I'm starting to freeze."

Theo hopped the fence in one agile leap, landing softly on the other side.

Crossing the threshold quickened his pulse.

"What are you doing?" Ismena hissed. "I thought you said—"

"Go home," Theo said. "You don't have to help me."

"Theo! Don't be stupid."

"I'm not being stupid."

He pulled the rope off his shoulder, letting the coils fall to the stones while he grasped the end.

"Don't do this, Theo." She looked around, growing desperate.

"It's alright. Go home, Ismena."

"I'll... I'll start shouting. Someone will hear and come find us. I'll tell them what you're trying to do."

"What?" Theo's heart raced. He looked through the iron bars at his friend.

"I mean it," she said. "They'll stop you and put you under close watch so you don't try this ever again."

He didn't know how to respond, frozen simultaneously in shock and anger. Ismena seemed to be just as paralyzed by her own threat, her eyes wide and fearful. She had never threatened him so harshly before and meant it.

"You would do that?" he asked.

She didn't respond. She didn't move at all.

"My parents were taken from me, Ismena." The words almost seized in Theo's throat, but he forced them out. "I need to get them back. I *need* to. This is the only way I have a chance at doing that. Don't you see? I don't have any other options. If you stop me... I don't think I could forgive you."

He turned away, unable to look her in the eye while she decided what would happen to him tonight. Perhaps he should've gone straight to Roman. The other boy would have helped him, no question. Theo was sure of it. He might have even joined Theo. But Theo trusted Ismena more—they had been through more together. He never guessed she'd betray him. Maybe he'd been wrong.

No matter—he couldn't make this decision for her.

Regardless of whether she was going to help, he was here now and he couldn't go back. He might lose his nerve if he held off another night. Theo turned the pulley so that it hung off the side of the Gateway.

"Dammit, Theo." With great difficulty, Ismena hoisted herself over the fence.

"You don't need to help me," Theo said again.

"If you're going to do it anyway, I might as well make sure you do it right."

Theo smiled in gratitude, his first genuine smile in several days. He breathed a sigh of relief. "Thanks."

"Don't make me regret it."

They threaded the rope over the pulley. This close to the edge, it sounded almost as if the cavern below had a wind of its own, circling to and fro beneath them and whispering incoherent words to the surface above. Theo was suddenly afraid the draft might kick into a vortex and suck them in with a strong gust. It was enough to make him shiver, but he pressed on, tying a loop near the end of the rope for him to stand in.

"Now, all I need you to do is lower me in. The rope's pretty long, so I imagine even if you don't get me to the bottom, you'll get me pretty close."

"But what if there is no bottom."

Theo sighed. "Then I'll holler and you can reel me back in. But there will be a bottom. There has to be."

Ismena raised an eyebrow. No, they didn't have any idea how far down the ground was, but Theo didn't want to dwell on this detail of his plan. He pressed on.

"I'll hop off then and go find my parents. They can't be too far yet, I imagine. So... just give me a couple days, and I'll call up for you every night until you come back."

There were so many holes in the plan, Ismena didn't seem to know where to begin. She opened her mouth as if to protest, but Theo, not wanting to leave her the chance to pick it over, handed her the rope on the other side of the pulley.

"Are you ready?" he asked.

She nodded apprehensively.

Theo gripped the rope with both arms, lifted his foot into the loop, and swung out over the empty air. His heart thudded in his chest as the void opened beneath him. The potential endlessness of it seized him by the bottom of his shoes and threatened to drag him down into the depths. Theo gasped, finding it hard to breathe. He locked eyes briefly with Ismena, who looked just as frightened as he felt.

"Okay," he said.

For a moment, he thought maybe she wouldn't move. Then, slowly, mechanically, Ismena began to let the rope out. Theo held his breath, teeth clenched, as the rim came up to meet him. First his feet, then his calves, his thighs, waist, and torso. Last, but not least, his head. He descended by the stray strands of moonlight, silver fog descending alongside him. Down he went, feeling the gargantuan, empty space widening in all directions. Nothing but open air all around. Above him, the Gateway shrank until it was just the size of the tip of his thumb, hovering overhead. The rope creaked, and each time another length was let out, he swayed slowly back and forth, in and out of the fading light.

"That's all I can do," Ismena called. "If I let you go any more, I don't think I'll be able to keep a proper hold."

Creak. Sway.

"That's alright," Theo said.

Hands in a death grip, he took one foot off the loop and allowed it to dangle. Nothing but air.

Creak. Sway.

"Can you see anything?"

Theo looked around. "No."

"Can you feel anything?"

"No to that too."

"Should I pull you back up?"

Creak. Sway.

Maybe it really was a bottomless void. Maybe it had been a stupid idea after all. But he *couldn't* let his parents go. This was just a setback. An unfortunate, time-consuming setback. How quickly would his parents' souls depart? He sighed, feeling tendrils of defeat creep into his mind. Perhaps if he and Ismena found a longer rope? It would have to be fast.

"Okay, pull me up," he said. He lifted himself to get his foot back in the loop.

Creak. Sway.

Having been pushed too close to the end, the knot gave way.

Theo wasn't prepared for his arms to carry his weight. He cried out as he slid, the rope burning his palms before leaving him. Then he fell, tumbling through open air. His shout was lost to the wind in his ears and the raucous drumming of his heart.

That was it, he told himself. *You've lost it all.*

And then he wondered if maybe that was alright.

The fall did not last long.

With a great *oof*, Theo landed on something soft enough to cushion his fall but not soft enough to deprive him of pain. He bounced and rolled down the side of what appeared to be a steep slope of similar objects. Tumbling over and over, Theo struggled to slow his descent and orient himself. Collision after collision with the firm but pliant surface jostled his body. Light from the hole above flipped past in rapid succession. A particularly rough tumble sent him bounding, and he reached out his arms for a handhold. When he crashed against the slope again, he grabbed the first thing he could and—after almost wrenching his arm out of his socket—came to a halt.

His surroundings took a few more minutes to resettle. Debris skipped past him down the slope. The world reeled behind his shut eyes. Pain dotted his back and shins in several places. Theo moaned. He had to right himself; he had to look around to be certain the way he thought was up *was* up. And to figure out what was he holding on to.

Theo opened his eyes. His hand was tightly fastened around someone's arm.

A few moments passed before he realized the body the arm belonged to was buried beneath countless other arms... and legs, and heads, and hands. Lifeless bodies, gray and bloody and in varying stages of decay, contorted around each other in a mound that stretched out of the darkness toward the dot of light above. Sightless faces stared up at the world above with skulls half caved in from impact. Twisted arms stuck out at grotesque angles, sharp bones jutting through ripped flesh. It was a miracle he hadn't been impaled.

Theo's stomach knotted and he screamed, his grip on the corpse releasing.

Down again he tumbled, but this time the fall was much shorter. He hit the ground—the *real* ground—and though the wind was once again knocked out of him, he backed away from the macabre mountain as fast as he could. His hand landed on something soft. Theo looked down upon sunken cheeks and blind eyes. He fell to the left and barely avoided landing on a torso that was swollen as if waterlogged. They were all around him. Bodies of the deceased littered the floor of the cavern as far as the eye could see until they disappeared into complete darkness. He had found the bottom of the Gateway.

9

The Ferrywoman

Theo couldn't stop gaping. It wasn't exactly horror that he felt, more a mixture of fear—at the innumerable corpses in disarray across the cavern floor waiting patiently to become animated—and intrigue. Here was an abbreviated history of Ipsitfel's past: generations of its deceased piled beneath the city streets. Who knew at what sluggish pace the bodies down here decayed—for it was certainly slower than the animals he'd seen who died in the harsh winters and were left to decompose amid the elements.

When his stunned trance broke, Theo realized a faraway voice was shouting his name. The pair of syllables bounded over a great distance. But where... Could it be Ismena? His eyes traveled upward over the towering mountain of corpses at the circle of light high above him. He could just make out what looked like a head eclipsing the light. She called again.

"Theo!"

"I'm alright," he said, but when she didn't react, he realized she must not be able to hear him. He looked around at the company of the dead; surely they wouldn't mind if he shouted. Still, it felt wrong, as if disrupting their crowding quiet would be irreverent. "Ismena... Ismena! I'm alright."

"What happened?" came the response.

"I think my knot untied."

"Are you hurt?"

Theo felt his arms and legs. Besides what would be a few bruises, nothing seemed too damaged. Not until he touched his ribcage on his right side did he cry out in pain.

"Theo!"

"It's alright," he called. "I'm alright."

"I'm going to throw down the rope again. Can you get back up to it?"

"No. It won't reach. Besides, I'm down here. That's what I wanted."

"What are you going to do?"

"I'm about to find out." Theo brushed himself off. His white tunic was now streaked with dirt and gore. *What am I going to do?*

"If you're hurt, you should come back up."

"I'm alright—really. I won't be able to reach you. I'll have to find another way back."

"I'll return every evening. Maybe I can find something longer."

"Thanks," Theo called.

A pause. "Come back alive."

Theo smiled though he knew she couldn't see him. He turned away from the Gateway, facing the night that surrounded him at the bottom of the cavern. Come to think of it, how could he see anything at all? From above, the Gateway led into a black, impenetrable pit. Yet from down here, his vision was little worse than the trip from Ismena's home to Cirillo Square.

Theo froze, convinced something had moved in the darkness. Or perhaps his eyes were playing tricks on him. Every corpse that was half lit by the moon seemed to look away when he laid his eyes upon them. Theo's stomach churned. They were all just too fresh, too full of flesh and bodily fluids. If this was every corpse that had been tossed down the Gateway since Ipsitfel had been founded, then the ones at the bottom of the mountain should be no more than bones.

Instead, they glistened with blood, their ligaments laid bare, crushed by the weight of a million corpses above them.

He had to get away from the sight. He was becoming entranced by the nightmarish vision.

Turning around, Theo reached out his hands. He felt his way through the dark. Whenever he kicked the side of something stiff and heavy, he cringed and tried to step over the body, though more often than not his foot simply landed atop another. He couldn't avoid them all, piled here and there, two side by side or one lying across the other. Once, he even tripped and fell completely forward. He didn't bother to contemplate what wet, spongy part of the corpse's anatomy broke his fall. Scrambling to his feet, Theo shuffled away before the thought made him gag.

Finally, his fingers met a rough rock face. It extended straight up from where he stood, high into a blackness his eyes could not penetrate. Theo breathed a sigh of relief. The cavern wasn't infinite. Now, to find a way out.

Cautiously, he felt his way along the wall, his eyes straining with an almost painful effort. Jagged to the touch, the surface felt dry and very solid. He ran both hands along it, searching for even the slightest opening. Now that Ismena was gone and he wasn't falling, the only sounds he heard were his breathing and the occasional rock disturbed by his blind steps.

As the wall continued unbroken, seeds of doubt took root in his head. Was this the extent of what the Gateway guarded? Could it really be nothing but a large cavern where the corpses piled year after year? A faint floral aroma came to him in brief wafts. He was surprised there was no stench; otherwise the rotting odor might have risen through the Gateway and the villagers would've realized what little was down here. Mounting disappointment frustrated him, but then another thought occurred: this meant the bodies of his parents were in this room, and perhaps not so difficult to find. If they had not stuck at the top of the mountain, then they might be somewhere near the foot. He couldn't determine how he'd feel coming across their disfigured faces.

Suddenly, he stumbled forward and found himself at the mouth of a wide passage. A slight breeze passed through, and Theo's heart leapt. Blind still, he started through the tunnel, his pulse quickening.

The passage was straight, level, and narrow, carved neatly into the rock wall as if by the hands of a deity. Once he'd entered, Theo wondered whether his eyes were somehow adapting, or if some other power was at work. He could *see* the passage clearly, though there was no source of light.

Rock became gravelly sand beneath his feet. The walls fell away to either side. And in the darkness, Theo could barely believe what he saw.

He was standing on a rocky shore.

Before him, the land sloped down into black water, the surface of which was perfectly glassy and smooth. The shore curved in either direction around the rock face from which he'd emerged, disappearing out of sight and into the dark. Rock outcroppings dotted the beach, like crouching monochromatic figures. And out on the water: nothing. It faded beyond sight where it became indistinguishable from the black horizon, an ocean disappearing into the starless night sky.

What was this place? How could such a large cavern exist? An ocean housed beneath the surface of the earth. It wasn't possible.

And where could he go now?

To his right, there was nothing but shoreline curving around the rockface, but to his left...

A tall column rose out of the ground about forty paces away. There wasn't enough light to make out any colors, though he would have guessed it was white or something close to it. The base had to be at least twenty paces wide. At the top, almost swallowed by the dark, stood a pointed roof over a row of windows. Theo had seen drawings of lighthouses in the storybooks about the world beyond Ipsitfel, but he hadn't imagined they'd be so tall.

He walked to it, sinking slightly into the ground with each footfall. Theo had never encountered real sand before. The texture was strange; similar to that of mud, but dry. The sand didn't so much suck at his feet but made room for them, making it hard to move quickly.

The base of the lighthouse was made of stone, but most of the structure was a clay of some sort. There was no doorway, though 'Ipstifel' was inscribed just above where a door should've been. How very strange.

Theo sighed, quickly giving up on the idea that he could use the tower to make light. He plodded away from the obelisk, and was in the midst of wondering whether he should follow the shoreline to the right or the left, when the faintest of glows appeared. Desperate for illumination, he snapped his head around to look out across the water.

A lamp drifted toward him, and behind it he could just make out the outline of a small boat. As the watercraft drew near, he could see the boat was wide enough for a small company, with planks for sitting at the front, center, and back. He could see no sail nor paddles, but the solitary passenger sat at the stern with their hands on a tiller, holding the boat true.

She had red hair that fell in waves to her shoulders. Her pale face caught most of the light from the lamp, but the rest of her body was cloaked in heavy, brown robes. She looked at him as she approached, her gaze attentive but emotionless. The boat came right up to the shore until Theo was certain she was going to ground it, but then the woman took her hands from the tiller and immediately the boat stopped moving.

"Who are you?" was the first thing she said, in a paper-thin voice that held more kindness than Theo had expected from her hard stare.

"I... I'm Theo Sahiron," he said. "From Ipsitfel."

Then he considered if it was prudent to have told her the truth.

"What's wrong with you?"

"I'm sorry?"

"You're different," she said, eyeing him with suspicion. She stood, but didn't leave the boat. "You haven't died."

Theo stood stock-still, wondering how she could have known—or how someone who was dead might've looked to her. The thought crossed his mind that maybe she didn't know for certain, and maybe he could deny it and convince her otherwise. All he could guess from her accusatory tone was that she'd have preferred him to be dead.

In the end, he decided he knew too little to be convincing.

"No, I'm not," he said.

"How did you get here?"

"I came through the Gateway."

Her eyes swept their surroundings as if expecting an ambush or looking for someone eavesdropping behind a rock. "Nobody would go through the Gateway. Are you lying to me? Be careful—I'll know if you are."

Theo didn't ask how, but he believed her. "I'm not lying. I used a rope to lower myself down."

He didn't know if it would matter, but he didn't want to incriminate Ismena.

She studied him, statuesque for the better part of an uncomfortable minute. He felt her dissecting him, felt as though he were naked and she could see every freckle and scar on his skin. Between them, the light danced, making the shadows play across her face.

"Why?" she asked.

Theo swallowed. "My parents were not supposed to die—they were both healthy and happy—but there was a fire in our house and they didn't make it out. I came to bring them back."

She didn't respond with words, but a short sigh escaped her lips. Theo looked past her at the dark water beyond her boat.

"They're out there, aren't they? I need to find them."

She continued to study him, hesitant to answer.

"I *need* to find them," Theo pleaded.

The ferrywoman closed her eyes. "Children should not be without their parents," she said in a soft, small voice. Theo wanted to argue that he was not a child—he was closer to a man than a boy. But if being a child would get her to help him, he would let it go unchallenged. "If they've died, then they're down here," she said. "I don't know how can I take you if you haven't been sent here through the ritual though. You need payment to cross the sea."

Theo's heart leapt with hope. She would help him; he only needed to find payment. What was her price? He thought of what he knew about the ritual, piecing together fragments of information he'd preserved from half-listening in class and in lectures from his parents. Why hadn't he paid more attention? If he hadn't treated it all like superstitious ramblings—but he couldn't have known the stories were real. Theo focused his thoughts. He was spiraling. The bodies were carried out by the people in blue. They were secured to the harness. Oh, but before that, the small drawstring bags were tied to their wrists. What was in those bags? Wasn't it just money? Did he have any—

Theo buried a hand in the pocket of his trousers. The coins his father had given him to buy his mother a scarf were still there. He brought them out.

"I've got payment," he said. "Is this enough?"

She looked almost disappointed to see the money. Nodding, she stuck out an upturned palm. Theo dropped the coins into her hand.

"Come aboard then," she said.

Having never been on a boat before, Theo faltered. He put his hand to the bow and surveyed the wooden craft. Age had stained the boat a mixture of dark hues. The plank across the front where he assumed he was to sit sagged from the weight of countless passengers. He had thrown many twigs into the Stick River and watched them float along the current, but they had been small and bore no load. He was skeptical this boat could do the same.

"I have carried many souls across the Corporis Sea. You are not the first and you will not be the last," she said. Maybe she was used to passengers hesitating. "This boat will not sink. Come aboard, then."

So Theo did as he was told. One at a time, he raised his legs over the side and entered the boat, leaving the dark, sandy shore behind him. Up the shoreline, he could just make out the mouth of the tunnel he'd come through. How small it looked compared to everything around it. The sheer cliff disappeared into the darkness above, which the lantern could not penetrate. The world had to be up there somewhere, a ways away, where the eyes could not see. He would return to this shore, would come back to Ipsitfel again with his parents beside him. He knew this in his heart.

His still-beating heart.

The boat moved away from the beach, returning fully to the water. Theo didn't divert his gaze even as he and the ferrywoman turned and headed out to sea. Rocks huddled in batches in the sand, the obelisk rising into the air.

"Your lighthouse doesn't work," Theo said. He assumed that this was the shoreline only she returned to. It made sense, therefore, to call everything on it hers.

"It is a beacon for those returning home," she replied. "Very few get the chance to see it."

And then the shoreline was swallowed completely by shadow, and the two sat alone on a black and endless sea.

10

Across Black Waters

The ferrywoman had to possess some sense that Theo didn't, for she sailed them into the darkness without checking any maps or nautical instruments. For maybe fifteen minutes, Theo sat at the bow of the boat, head swiveling, trying to make out anything around them. But it was only black water stretching off beyond the circle of illumination granted by the lantern. Eventually, he gave up watching and reached back into the pocket of his trousers where he kept the tin watch. He'd felt it when he found the coins and retrieved it now with trembling hands.

The fall hadn't damaged it—another, small miracle. The watch retained its dull shine and its hands ticked ever onward around the pale face. The lid maybe swung in a crooked arch, but as far as he could tell it had always done that. A calm came over him as he watched the hands travel from number to number.

The calm could not quell the flurry of questions building inside, however.

"Who are you?" he asked finally, looking up from the watch face.

The woman had been staring past him into the darkness, but now they locked eyes.

"I'm a ferrywoman," she said simply.

"Yes, but *who* are you? What's your name?"

The ferrywoman had to think for a moment. Either she had difficulty remembering, or she was uncertain whether she should tell him. Theo had never met anybody unwilling to give their name, so his immediate assumption was the former, but something told him that names in this world were more important than in the land above. Names held power. She might be wary of giving him hers because she didn't trust him.

"When I was alive," she said, "I was called Demeres."

"Was alive?"

"Well, I'm not anymore, am I."

Theo surveyed her very solid, very real form. Perhaps *alive* meant something different down here too, for when he thought of the opposite, he imagined the corpses lying in the cavern beneath the Gateway. If this woman wasn't alive, well, she couldn't be dead, could she? She was a state he couldn't yet grasp.

"I *am* dead," she said, as if hearing his thoughts.

Theo's eyes widened, although a small part of him had already suspected and now began interjecting a thousand new questions.

"But if you're dead, how can you be moving? How can you be steering us right now?" He gripped the side of the boat as the thoughts rattled off his tongue.

"Many beings live here, the likes of which you've never seen before. As for humans, we were alive when we lived above, but we passed on. Our state of being in this world is not what it once was, and yet not the same as the beings who were born here either."

For Theo, this explained nothing, but he sat at the head of the boat mulling her words over for quite some time. If this woman was as dead as she said she was, that meant his parents would be alive down here as well—or the same type of *alive* as Demeres, at any rate. His head spun. This was evolving into more than he'd bargained for. He hadn't expected things on the other side of the Gateway to be so...complicated.

"So then, Demeres, are my parents on a boat like this?"

Demeres shook her head. "No. I am a ferrywoman tasked with bringing souls from the shores of the living to their final resting places. If your parents died, then they will not be charged with the same fate as I."

"The final resting places?" Theo asked. Everything this woman said brought more questions.

Demeres sighed, as if answering his inquiries was taxing. "The Isles of Death." She nodded out at the impenetrable black beyond the bow of the boat. "Upon the Corporis Sea, any of the eleven Isles of Death can be reached by boat. When a human dies, they are ferried across the waters to whichever island reflects the life they lived before their passing."

Theo thought of all the bodies below the Gateway, the gory mountain that rose to a peak high above the cavern floor. He thought of all the other corpses that had rolled down the sides of that mountain and lay in the dark, decaying at an unnaturally slow rate. There were thousands—maybe millions—of them lying hidden in shadow like discarded waste.

"Then why were there so many bodies back there?" he asked. "Back the way I came."

"Those were their living bodies," Demeres explained. "They were spent in life above. Only the soul enters this realm; it is form enough."

And solid enough, for Theo watched her steer the craft, holding to the tiller with hands that moved and gripped just like his own. He wondered again how she made the boat sail. It was clear from the impeccably placid surface that there was no current or tide. The ripples the boat made as it cut through the water died quickly. Was the water truly black? Or was the color only the result of the total lack of light in this underground realm? If he dipped his hand beneath the surface and brought it back out again, would it emerge dripping with black liquid? How quickly would his hand disappear beneath the mirrored surface? The sea might suck it under into a realm his vision could not penetrate. His mind conjured images of sightless creatures navigating the inky blackness, waiting just below the boat for a curious boy to dip his fingers in. There could be any number of them keeping pace with the tiny craft, surrounding the human travelers. A shiver ran through him at the eerie thought. He would never know—or hopefully never know—if these wonderings were fact or fantasy.

Regardless, he kept all extremities on board.

Equally troublesome was the endless void above; he couldn't be certain how high it stretched. The more he thought about it, the smaller Theo felt, and he continued to shrink as they sailed away from the Gateway.

Absentmindedly, he clicked the pocket watch open and closed in his palm.

"What... What do you call this place?" he asked. "Where we are, what is it called?"

Demeres turned the tiller toward her, and Theo felt them adjust course. Why she'd done so he couldn't guess, as the nothingness around them remained unchanged. "It doesn't truly have a name."

"Really? How can that be?"

"Humans are so obsessed with naming all things. Gods know every concept must have a title, otherwise we cannot cope."

"Well, names are kind of necessary, aren't they?" Theo said. "It'd get a bit confusing if my friends were constantly referring to me as 'you there.' Then everybody'd be turning around whenever they called."

"I suppose, then, it doesn't have a *proper* name," Demeres said. "I've heard it referred to in many ways by many different beings who call it home."

"Can you tell me which is your favorite name, then?"

"No," Demeres said after a pause. "The name is far too long and beautiful. It encompasses many stories and individuals and places more complex than I could convey. If I started telling you now, I would not finish until your task was accomplished—or failed—and even then, I know I would blunder through it."

Theo laughed, thinking that was an odd answer to give. No name could be that long. "How about your second favorite?"

"I once heard a deity call it Nochlan."

Theo repeated the name. On his tongue, it left a taste of longing, though he couldn't place why. *Nochlan.* Demeres said it better than he did. The way her mouth curled around the word left it ringing in his ears.

"Are there many of you?" Theo asked. "Ferry people, I mean."

Demeres thought for a moment, looking down at the floor of the boat. "I suppose there must be," she said. "I've met only a few, but mostly I interact with the souls I ferry."

"Does it get lonely?"

"It's not a fate I would choose again."

"How did you become a ferrywoman?"

At this, Demeres' mouth became very thin. Theo might have imagined it, but he felt the boat hasten. Apparently, this was not a subject she was willing to discuss.

"You ask a lot of questions, Theo," she said.

"I just want to know... There's so much to ask about."

"My passengers don't usually ask me many things."

"Then what do you talk about?"

"They generally tell me stories of their lives before: who they were, what they did, what they left behind. I've been at this assignment long enough that I don't have much left to say. I mostly listen."

"But how can they not have questions?"

"Their souls are still clinging to the life that just ended." Demeres looked up at him again. "They regret actions—or a lack thereof. They reminisce. They miss their loved ones."

"Do you miss any loved ones?"

Again, he had touched upon a subject Demeres wasn't prepared to discuss. Reluctantly, Theo let the conversation die as the lingering question dripped down into the Corporis Sea. It wouldn't matter soon, he told himself. She was taking him to his parents, and then he would leave this world—Nochlan—behind for a very long time.

Theo rubbed his eyes; he was getting tired. He couldn't tell how long he'd been awake, but it had to have been a full day at least. After all, he and Ismena had snuck to the Gateway in the dead of night. The darkness was getting to him, making his eyelids heavy.

The ferrywoman noticed. "Your mortal faculties have not yet worn off."

"What d'you mean by that?" Theo asked, unsure if he should feel offended.

"While you're down here you'll lose your desire to eat, sleep, make waste—"

"I'm not going to *what*?"

"Of course. You're drifting away from the mortal world."

A faint something was taking shape far in the distance, much farther than he'd thought possible given how closely the darkness pressed in on them. Theo grappled with everything his guide had told him before realizing with some thrill that what he saw was light. There was an end to the sea of night! They were miles off still, but the light was unmistakable. His heart leapt, the sleepiness staved off for another time. Was this perhaps one of the Isles of Death? If so, that must mean his parents were on that island.

Before he could get too excited, Demeres interrupted his internal celebration.

"I'm taking you to Dolothyia, the Guardian on Eirini," she said. "Dolothyia keeps record of where every soul in the underworld has been sent. She'll be able to tell you where your parents are."

"She will help me?"

"Unless you mean to search each of the eleven isles, she is one of the few who *can* help." Demeres paused. "She and I have met several times before, and she can be amicable, but I must warn you not to cross her, Theo. She is a powerful being."

Theo hung on the word *being*. Excitement still flooded him at the prospect of someone who could facilitate his reunion, but a tremulous mixture of anxiety and uncertainty churned in his heart as well.

"Why do you call her a Guardian?" he asked.

"The Guardians are bound to their islands. Each is responsible for what happens there and for the souls that come ashore," she said. "When we meet Dolothyia, you must let me do the talking."

"Why is that?"

"Because what you're trying to accomplish is not encouraged," Demeres said. "If she knows what we're attempting, she'll try to stop you. Or worse."

Theo didn't think he wanted to know what *worse* entailed.

Ahead of them, the light grew closer, and with it, Theo began to ascertain the shape of the island. He couldn't yet gauge how large it was, nor could he distinguish much but an amorphous mass of something other than the dark nothing, but the sight held his eyes captive all the same.

How far he felt from home.

II

The Island of Eirini

An hour passed before Theo could discern what was on the stretch of land. The flat peak of a mountain rose into the sky from some central location—the only major change in elevation he could see on the island. All light came from a smattering of fires burning brightly from the shoreline. Squat huts crowded the water's edge, over which thick trees stood sentinel, their wide trunks splitting suddenly, almost comically, into thin branches at the very tops. Most of them, Theo noticed, were bare.

Demeres and Theo sailed into a harbor with a shallow gravel shore, small enough that Theo thought the whole thing could've fit comfortably inside Cirillo Square. All along the shore, torches stuck out of the ground with flames dancing on their tips. Theo couldn't decide whether they were a welcome or a warning, but he found he still preferred the fires to the void of being at sea either way.

The boat stopped a foot or two from running aground. Demeres took her hand from the tiller.

"Are you sure we've come to the right place? It looks empty," Theo said.

Demeres shook her head. "They're deciding what our intentions are."

They. Theo scanned the shore again, straining his eyes against the shadows. The tree line stood back from the water about a dozen paces. Peering into the maze of trunks, he could see boulders and bushes and wild undergrowth, but little else. No people, that was for sure, though he was reminded of the darting shadow he'd seen in the woods back home.

Then, small faces appeared one by one, blinking at him from the dark. Creatures emerged from the forest, waddling onto the shore like young children. Once visible, Theo understood how they had hidden so easily. Their entire bodies were covered in thick pale fur that flawlessly resembled the bark on the trees. Each had a perfectly spherical head, which was nearly twice the size of their plump bodies. They walked on two stubby legs, but their gangly arms were so long that their hands nearly dragged on the ground. Every inch of them was covered from head to toe with the fur, save for their eyes, which were nothing more than sunken black holes right in the middle of their round heads.

The creatures made no sounds as they crept out of the woodwork. They slid down from branches, crawled from under tree roots, or simply stepped away from whatever trunk they leaned against and stumbled onto the shore. None of them stepped into the water, but they stood as close as possible to the still, dark line and soundlessly watched their anchored visitors, heads tilted in curiosity.

Demeres cleared her throat.

"Liberi," she said in a mellow but pure tone, "we hope you're here to welcome us."

There came no response. None of the furry creatures gave any indication that they'd heard her at all. By now, a large gathering of at least a hundred had assembled on the gravel beach, the trickle of converging creatures coming to an end. If Theo had to give them an emotion, he would have characterized them as permanently surprised judging by their round, hollow eyes. Neither welcoming, nor threatening.

"We're here to see Dolothyia," Demeres said.

Again, the liberi did not react, but something else did.

"I am here." A woman descended onto the shore from the shadows. She was adorned in an opalescent dress of emerald and white that draped her long frame and trailed behind her. In form, she appeared human. Her black hair sat braided around her head and down her back, and her skin was a deep umber color. Yet, when she observed the boat, Theo felt she wasn't just seeing them, but learning about them with abilities he didn't possess. In one sweeping gaze she might've viewed his every childhood memory. In one sigh, she might've listened to each of his secrets. And somehow, despite these mystical characteristics, the word he would have used to describe her presence was *motherly*. She had a welcoming aura, nurturing, and knowledgeable.

At once, the liberi erupted into a low din, sounding like mumbling elderly folk with croaking, quavering voices. They waddled to the woman, surrounding her while murmuring ecstatically the entire time.

"Dolothyia," Demeres said.

The woman's gaze lingered on the ferrywoman for a brief moment before she broke into a haunting smile of recognition. "I remember you," she said. Her voice was deep. "Your name was... Demeres. Correct?"

"Yes."

Dolothyia spread her arms. "Welcome back to Eirini."

"Thank you. It's been some time."

"But a blink in the grand scheme of existence."

"May we come to shore then?" Demeres asked.

"Of course. Of course, my dear."

With a sudden lurch, as though Demeres were trying to waste no more of the Guardian's time than she had to, the boat moved up onto the shore, pulling itself half out of the water. Gravel ground against wood until they came to a stop with the diminutive figures of the liberi huddling around them.

Dolothyia laughed. "Let them through. Give them space!"

She reached forward and gently pushed aside a handful of the creatures, who continued to mumble incoherently while staring at the newcomers. This carved a path that Demeres and Theo used to leave the boat. One of the liberi brushed Theo's exposed forearms, and he was pleased to note that the ashen fir was incredibly soft. Softer than any fabric he'd ever felt back home, in fact.

"But I must ask you, Demeres," Dolothyia said, as if continuing an earlier thought, "who your passenger is."

Theo froze, unsure whether he should be the one to answer. He looked from the Guardian to Demeres, who gave an almost imperceptible nod that he should tell her the truth. Despite never having had qualms before about speaking to strangers, Theo felt his insides knot. She was not just another adult, but a deity of some sort. Should he be wary about giving her his name?

"I'm Theo Sahiron."

"Theo Sahiron." Just as he'd feared, the way Dolothyia said his name left him feeling vulnerable—exposed—as if his simple statement had revealed everything about him. Dolothyia turned to the ferrywoman, who now stood outside the crowd of liberi. "Why have you brought him here?" she asked, not unkindly. "Shouldn't you be taking him to his island?"

"I..." Demeres hung her head in shame. Theo wondered if she was going to give up their plan without any persuasion. He understood why she would: Dolothyia exuded authority. He didn't feel comfortable lying to her. But Demeres held her ground. "I have failed at interpreting him. His arrow lies precisely between two islands, and I cannot tell which pull is stronger."

Dolothyia nodded. "Perhaps your senses are ebbing," she mused. "Surely you've collected enough payment—"

"I haven't," Demeres said firmly.

At the interruption, Dolothyia paused, a bemused smile plastered on her face. She didn't look angry, but suddenly, Theo felt he understood why it wouldn't be wise to cross the Guardian. Her eyes twinkled dangerously, though no part of her body moved. She wasn't used to being interrupted. After a tense minute in which Theo couldn't remember breathing, she looked down at the liberi gathered around them and clapped her hands.

"Everyone, up the hillside. It's time for your lesson," she said, and her aura of motherliness strengthened.

The liberi scampered away, mumbling enthusiastically as they did so. They rushed back into the forest of barren trees, waddling as fast as their squat legs could carry them. Theo wanted to laugh, but felt the act might be inappropriate. He swallowed the urge. In a matter of moments, they were all gone, and the trio was left alone on the shoreline.

"I will help you discern his path, but first the liberi need their rest. I sent them to watch because I saw your light on the water, but now they have gone too long without relief. I don't think we will have any more visitors for a while," Dolothyia said.

"Do they sleep?" Theo asked. "Like people above."

Dolothyia smiled at him and gestured for the pair to follow her as she too made her way toward the trees. "They do indeed. But night and day do not exist here as they did in your world. If I'm not careful to give them rest periodically, they will fall into a trance. It is very hard to wake them from it."

Theo nodded. He wanted to ask more questions, but Demeres had placed a firm hand on his back in warning. Her message was clear. The less he spoke, the less chance he had of giving himself away. Instead, Demeres engaged Dolothyia in conversation about the island and its welfare. It was clear she'd been here a few times before, the first being when she became a ferrywoman.

Theo fell into step behind the women, matching their pace but keeping to himself. The ground sloped gently up toward the center of the island. There was little underbrush, but gnarled, twisting tree roots protruding from the soil made the trail impossible to traverse without concentration. At times, the loops of thick root came so high he found it easier to duck beneath them than to climb over.

Then he saw something that startled him, unprepared as he was to come across the figure. For a moment, he thought some animal was standing in wait, ready to attack, but when it didn't move, he realized it was one of the liberi.

The child-sized being stood still, moving only enough to breathe at a measured pace—though the rise and fall of its chest was so slight Theo could've believed he imagined it. Wide, empty sockets stared off, unseeing. Arms hung limp at its sides. It didn't react when he approached, nor when he waved a hand in front of its face. The liberi could have passed as a statue had Theo not suspected otherwise.

"I found him in this state," came Dolothyia's deep intonation. "He slipped away as the others slept. Curious creatures, liberi. They love to roam the forest, climbing and hiding as they will. But they cannot survive without being told what to do."

"He is in a trance?" Theo asked.

"Yes," Dolothyia said, "and he will not awake of his own accord."

"Can you wake him?"

She sighed. "Sometimes I can, and sometimes I cannot. It depends on the liberi—how old they are, how long they've been this way before I find them, how strong their fortitude."

"And what happens if you can't?"

Dolothyia placed a hand on the liberi's head, smoothing the pale fur with affection. She seemed genuinely melancholy for the small being trapped by its own naïve curiosity. Theo wondered how often this happened, how many liberi found themselves in this state and beyond her help. Then she withdrew her touch, and her gaze drifted up to the black sky as if she couldn't bear to look anymore. "Eirini is known for its forest of trees," she said. "You do not have anything like these where you came from. They grow tall in height and wide in girth; their roots stretch out but never tangle with any of those around them. They also thrive without ever bearing leaves or flowers. They are called metaliberus trees."

She strode off into the forest once more, her pace deliberate.

12
Fallible Guardians

For the rest of their journey, Theo made sure not to trample any of the thinner roots running over the ground. Dolothyia's implication had lent a curious, watchful feeling over the forest, though it was not unwelcome, as it reduced the sense of threat he'd learned to associate with the woods.

Their destination lay at the top of a hill. They found the liberi waiting in a wide amphitheater made by the sunken ground. At the other end, looming over them all, was the largest tree stump Theo had ever seen.

The trunk had to have been at least thirty meters across, the bark striated with deep furrows all along its length. Thick roots larger in width than he was tall fanned out over the far end of the amphitheater, creating a covered space almost like a stage. The top of the stump hadn't been cut; it looked like the rest of the tree had simply fallen down. Jagged spires rose into the air like fingers pointing into the black sky.

All around, torches cast an orange glow over the scene.

When they arrived, the liberi turned to look at them expectantly.

"The liberi have lessons before they rest," Dolothyia explained, "so they will dream of what they've learned and remember it."

"Should we wait for you somewhere until you're finished?" Demeres asked.

"You can, or you may stay if you choose."

As Dolothyia walked away, Theo expected Demeres to ask him his preference, but she didn't. No doubt she already knew his curiosity had rooted him to the spot.

The Guardian of Eirini descended through the liberi on an aisle they had left down the center. They didn't make any of their mumblings, but sat patiently, watching her go. The train of Dolothyia's dress swept behind her like the trail of a comet: white and green and shimmering. The diminutive forms of the creatures threw into contrast her already impressive stature.

She arrived at the bottom of the amphitheater and turned to face her audience. With a sweep of her hand, the torches dimmed and the shadows lessened. The fires crackled, sending sparks like red rain falling to the sky.

"Tonight," she said, "we learn of Sacer, the human mother."

Though she didn't speak loudly, the silence of the gathering meant she was easily heard. Theo knelt on the outer rim of the amphitheater, above the creatures. He was eager to soak in Dolothyia's words. Demeres remained standing, though her face showed rapt attention.

"During the earth's twentieth cycle," Dolothyia began, "Sacer gave birth to Urithi. A mild-mannered child, Urithi grew up to be beautiful and intelligent. And because she was more beautiful and intelligent than Sacer had ever been, Sacer let her do what she wished and run their household.

"When beasts threatened, Urithi encircled them in a wall of stones for protection, and when it rained, she covered their heads with thatch and branches to keep away the water. Sacer wove them blankets, but Urithi wove them clothes to keep warm during the cold season.

"'You know so much more than I do,' Sacer would say to her daughter, 'but what you've furthered, you've learned first from me. Therefore, I am still useful to you.'

"Urithi would smile at her mother and say, 'Mother, of course you will always be useful. I will always care about you.' And this kept Sacer happy.

"One day, Urithi discovered a fantastical food that could keep them alive forever if she put it in the ground outside their home. The food loved the rain and loved the sun, and when Sacer and Urithi ate it, they tasted its sweet nutrition and grew healthier than ever before. Sacer marveled at her daughter's knowledge. Each cycle, Sacer ate the crop from one half of their land, and Urithi ate the other."

Suddenly, Dolothyia spread her arms wide, and the torches dimmed even further. Theo found himself leaning forward on his knuckles.

"Then one day, a woman dressed all in black came to their door. She held more grace than Sacer and Urithi had ever seen, and they feared her but let her into their home, not wanting to be disrespectful.

"'I see you have discovered a food that makes you live forever, Urithi,' the woman said, and the mother and daughter did not ask how she knew Urithi's name.

"'I have,' Urithi said, proud but also wary.

"'Very good, very good,' the visitor said. 'And now you are with child.'

"Sacer turned to her daughter. 'Urithi, is this true?' she asked.

"Urithi beamed. 'It is true, Mother. I am with child.' The two embraced and were happy.

"Sacer said, 'Be ready, my daughter. As you were to me, your child will have more knowledge and more beauty than you could possibly possess.'

"'This I am hoping for,' Urithi said. But the visitor had not come to speak of this good news, and she was not finished. She sat on one of the chairs Urithi had made, drawing her black garments around her.

"'Each year, Sacer eats half of your land and you the other,' she said. 'What will the child eat?'

"'I will sow more land,' Urithi said.

"'But you have planted the whole clearing,' observed the woman. 'Outside that, the trees are thick and the underbrush is thicker. Do you mean to move the trees?'

"'This is true,' said Sacer.

"'This hut is sturdy,' the visitor continued, 'but there are two sides of the mat and two chairs. You use one half of the hut, Sacer, and you the other, Urithi. Where will the child live?'

"'I will make the hut larger,' Urithi replied.

"'You could, but then you would lose some of the land to plant the food you eat. You will not have enough for the year, and you cannot build onto the other side of the house, for the trees are thick and the underbrush is thicker. Do you mean to move the trees?'

"'This is true,' Sacer said.

"At this, Urithi became very distressed, wondering where her child would live and what they would eat. It was not long, though, before Sacer, who had been sitting on the sleeping mat, stood.

"She said, 'When the baby is born and needs more food than her mother's milk and more bed than her mother's arms, will you come back, visitor? For you are Death, and I will go with you into these woods.'

"And the visitor nodded. Urithi may have been smarter and more beautiful, but one thing she did not have more of than her mother was wisdom. 'I will come back for you then, Sacer,' said the woman dressed in black. 'You will come with me, and thus leave enough for your daughter and her child to thrive.' At these words, Sacer was happy."

Dolothyia spread her arms wide. "This is why humans gladly greet death: that when they leave the world another may take their place and have what they need to live and thrive."

Finished with her tale, Dolothyia was greeted by silence. With another wave of her hand, the flames surged atop the torches again. Dolothyia remained in the pit of the amphitheater while the liberi rose as one and began to trudge away, their gait betraying their sleepiness. None of their mumbling could be heard, only the soft patter of their footsteps.

Theo knelt aghast, mouth open, as the liberi waddled past him. He trembled slightly, a quiver in his hands, but didn't move until each and every one of the small figures had disappeared. Demeres appeared at his side and placed a hand on his shoulder.

"Are you alright?" she asked.

"Why did she—"

But Demeres' grip tightened, and he looked around in time to see Dolothyia drawing close. The Guardian almost floated. Anyone else might've caught the hem of the dress beneath their feet, but she didn't. Perhaps the fabric moved itself to prevent being trodden on. She stopped when she had reached them. Theo gazed up at her. Throat dry, he found he couldn't say anything. Instead, Demeres helped him to his feet.

"They will rest now," Dolothyia said, nodding in the direction the liberi had gone. "They love hearing the old stories and always ask for more. If I told more than one a day, though, I'd run out too quickly. As it is, I must repeat them every so often. But come, that is not why you are here."

The Guardian motioned, and they followed her around the outside of the amphitheater. Distracted still, Theo stumbled as he wandered too close to the rim, and nearly fell down the incline. He managed to right himself and glanced up at Dolothyia. She didn't seem to have noticed. Demeres, however, reached out a hand and pulled him away from the edge with a concerned look.

The gargantuan stump loomed above them, reaching into the darkness. Standing next to it, Theo realized just how massive the tree must have been, and how old, given the dry, sharp chunks of bark that clung to it. Around the back of the trunk, they came across a simple wooden door hidden from view of the amphitheater.

Dolothyia placed her hand flat against the wood. The door opened with little effort. Theo and Demeres followed her inside.

He'd expected the Guardian to live opulently in a large, intimidating home draped in fine fabrics. The dwelling inside the old tree proved him wrong. It was all one room, with a washbasin against one wall, a cot against another, and an assortment of bookshelves and trinkets organized elsewhere between. On a table near the center of the room was a large star chart, which confused Theo who'd yet to see any stars in Nochlan. The most decorated item was a tall armoire tucked neatly into a far corner. Intricate carvings of vines and leaves covered the corners, while the iron handles resembled twig wreaths. He supposed that was where she kept her lavish gowns. Other than that, the place was simple, pragmatic, and almost dull.

Dolothyia headed straight for the central table and moved the star chart aside. Then she pulled out one of the four chairs and sat. Her dress folded around her to fit between the arms.

"What did you think of the lesson?" she asked. "Please, sit down."

Stiffly, Demeres did as she was told. Theo considered for a moment whether he would oblige. He was still recovering from the fable. The Guardian didn't seem to be in a rush to make progress, and this too disturbed him. However, he ultimately decided that if they were not imminently leaving, he might as well accept her hospitality.

"I think I've heard that story before," Demeres said. "Although not that exact version."

"I'm sure it's been told enough times that the root story has been distorted—"

"Why do you lie to them?" Theo asked, finding his voice.

Demeres' mouth fell open, and she looked at Theo in disbelief.

Dolothyia only smirked. "Lie to them?"

"That story you told. Urithi and Sacer. It's not true." Theo knew he was supposed to act courteously toward the Guardian, but the words tumbled forth uncontrolled. "You said humans 'gladly greet death,' but that's a lie."

Dolothyia could've interrupted him, but she sat in her chair with the small smile frozen on her lips, letting him finish.

"Humans don't like death," he said. "They run away from death because it means losing their loved ones. They spend their whole lives pretending death doesn't exist just so that they don't go mad trying to avoid it. How could you tell the liberi that? How could you lie? They look to you for guidance and knowledge. You're—you're a mother to them."

Theo realized he was breathing heavily, and perhaps closer to shouting than was necessary. After all, nobody was arguing with him. Demeres had closed her mouth, staring fixedly down at her folded hands.

When it was apparent that he'd finished his jeremiad, Dolothyia replied in a calm, warm voice. "You are correct. I am not being wholly truthful. But I am speaking honestly about life and death. About how people learn what those before them learned and more; and about how they, like everyone before them, also die. That is not untruthful."

"But why lie to them about how humans feel concerning death?"

"The liberi will never experience life like you, like someone who has lived above. Nor will they ever experience death in the same way—no, not even when a member of their own vanishes into a trance. They love each other as a body, as one, but they do not know where that body of the past ends and the body of the now begins. Some will disappear to become the trees, and they'll be none the wiser.

"While they live, though, they remember the emotions in the lessons I teach them. The stories too, but mostly the plain, obvious emotions. It's enough to learn about human death without learning about human loss. So I teach what they can comprehend, even if it's not always the whole truth."

"That seems an unfair trick," Theo said.

"But necessary, sometimes," Demeres said, sitting up.

"And how can you know that?" Theo asked.

"Part of caring for others is making judgments they cannot make for themselves," said Dolothyia.

"How can you be sure you've made the right one, though?" Theo asked.

"I don't," Dolothyia replied. "Obviously, my lessons do not always find their mark. As you can see, our forest is filled with trees."

"What if lying to them about this gives them false ideas about death?" Theo asked.

Dolothyia was silent for a moment. "I'm not beyond fault."

"You're a Guardian, aren't you?"

"Nothing in this world, not even the universe itself, is infallible, Theo Sahiron."

He found he had no answer. It would seem both women were in agreement on this topic, though Theo continued to struggle to accept the response. His parents surely hadn't lied to him. Had they?

He tried to recall conversations they'd had, the lessons and stories they'd told him at night before he went to sleep. Joyous laughter filled his head, times of sorrow too. He could remember standing in the kitchen with his mother and sister while Medina taught them how to cut vegetables. Something so mundane and yet somehow poignant. They'd made stew, an iron potful of roiling vegetable stew. Everything Medina said at that point in his life was law, never questioned. Surely, he hadn't been wrong about that.

"That's not why we're here though, is it," Dolothyia continued. She hadn't posed it as a question.

"We need to know—" Demeres began, but the Guardian waved away her words with a hand.

"I know why you're here, and it hasn't anything to do with where *he's* supposed to go." Dolothyia tilted her head in Theo's direction. "I would've thought you knew the rules and would resist, Demeres. But I suppose we all have our soft spots."

"You knew?" Theo asked.

"Oh, yes. I can tell with these sorts of things."

"You can read minds?"

Dolothyia shook her head. "No, my boy. I'm not gifted in that sense. Do not look at me with such surprise; it's not difficult to tell. You can't be more than fifteen years of age. You look as though you've been dropped down a muddy shaft. And here's the most important part—you don't appear to be dead."

"Is it that obvious?" Theo once again felt incredibly vulnerable in the presence of the Guardian.

"Maybe not to everyone down here," Dolothyia said, "but it is my business to know the dead."

Demeres nodded in defeat. "I should've known you couldn't be fooled."

"What was your plan, then?" the Guardian asked. She sat back in her chair. "Assuming I had your name already listed, were you going to hope it was on the same island as your parents?"

Hearing Dolothyia state their true intent with such bluntness made Theo recoil.

Demeres' voice came out soft and apologetic. "I knew you kept records of every soul assignment. I just didn't know how the records were kept or where."

From the sound of things, Dolothyia was unlikely to help them. Theo's hopes sank to the floor. If she turned them down, they'd have to find another method to locate his parents. Demeres seemed to think Dolothyia was the only one with the answers, but perhaps there was another way. Theo was willing to search each of the eleven isles if the circumstances required. Of course, this was all assuming Dolothyia didn't send him back up to the surface or decide that he had to remain in Nochlan forever.

The Guardian stood, pushing her chair back with an elongated screech. She went to one of the bookshelves. Her gaze slid up and down until she found what she was looking for: a brass, globe-shaped instrument with hundreds of symbols carved into it, none of which Theo had ever seen before. Next, she went to the armoire and dipped her head inside for a brief moment. She emerged with a green silken sash and draped it over an arm.

"I ask that you move quickly," she said to the pair, who had watched in silence as she traipsed about. "If I'm going to help you cheat Death, we'd better do it before I change my mind."

13

The Book of Mortal Names

They left Dolothyia's home, the Guardian hugging the sash and ball to her chest. Though the light cast by the torches was low and the ashen trunks of the trees stood empty, Theo crept as Dolothyia did, wary that someone might be watching. His gaze darted back and forth, combing the dark landscape for prying eyes. But the liberi had all gone, and not another soul seemed to live on the island.

He expected them to head back toward the cove, but instead Dolothyia led them into the underbrush. Theo and Demeres followed, trying to make as little noise as possible, but this proved a futile task. With every step, some sort of dry bush or twig appeared. Dolothyia however, didn't have the same issue. She wove through the forest as easily and soundlessly as a needle through fabric. It didn't help that the pace she kept was rather fast for anyone trying to be stealthy in an unknown landscape.

After an extended period of stumbling, Theo discovered it was best to hop from tree root to tree root, which seemed to be the sturdiest and quietest option. Unfortunately, Demeres couldn't do the same as her dress and cloak kept catching on stray branches. She had to bundle the excess fabric in front of her to keep it out of reach of the undergrowth, restricting the extent to which she could stretch out her legs.

Deeper and deeper they plunged into the forest of metaliberus trees. The light from the liberi encampment was good and gone now, and only a pale glow from an invisible moon gave them any sense of their surroundings. Curiosity at this phantom illumination intrigued Theo. It reminded him of the dim visibility in the passage beneath the Gateway, but he found he couldn't keep peering up through the branches without sacrificing his footing. He then took to memorizing their path, but they twisted this way and that so often that he gave up on this task as well. He began to suspect that Dolothyia wasn't even following a path. Her abrupt, randomized movements suggested she was heading wherever her mood told her to go. Worry and doubt crept into his mind.

Just when Theo was plucking up the courage to say something, Dolothyia came to a halt. Her traveling companions halted as well, drawing level with her now that she wasn't speeding through the underbrush.

"Where are we going?" Theo asked, trying not to sound out of breath.

Dolothyia spun on the spot, drinking in their surroundings as if trying to decide whether or not this was the opportune location. He wondered if she'd heard him.

"The names and assignments for all souls have been recorded in books. I hide those books so that prying eyes may not use them to wreak havoc." She glanced pointedly at Theo, who bristled at the implication. He had no intention to wreak havoc. "The location cannot be stumbled upon. In order to find it, you must be looking for it." Dolothyia bent down and laid the sash out on the ground. Then she placed the brass ball in the center of it and pulled the four corners together, forming a sack.

"A finder's spell," Demeres said.

"What's that?" Theo asked. "What did you put in there?"

Dolothyia nodded. "That was a dreamscape," she explained. "You lock a dream inside so that you can remember or revisit it again, should you wish. But in a finder's spell, it doesn't matter much what the object is—only that it carries significance. You must leave, in the sash, something you care about losing, to gain that which you care about finding."

Despite standing in the underworld among dead souls and mystical beings, Theo was shocked to learn that spells were real—and not at all what he'd envisioned.

"And has no one stolen a look at the book before?" Demeres asked. "Forgive me, but a finder's spell seems such a simple protection."

"Well," said Dolothyia, "in order for it to work, you'd have to know that the book was kept in a room, and that the room was in this forest. As of yet, I've not had any issues with marauders."

Dolothyia reached up and tied the ends of the sash to a low-hanging tree branch. It hung there, swaying slightly, with the weight of the dreamscape pulling the silken fabric taut. Theo expected more to happen, but after another moment, the two women turned away and headed off into the trees. Theo followed, but kept looking back to see if the finder's spell was still there.

"You must allow yourself to lose it," Dolothyia said, and Theo understood from the tone of her voice that she was indeed sad to see the dreamscape go. He wondered what sort of dreams Guardians had. It seemed such a human experience. Not the fodder of immortal beings who could whatever they wished at will. In losing the dream, did that mean Dolothyia could never have it again? Or could the dream occur by happenchance some night in the future? Theo willed himself not to look back anymore, instead imagining little creatures like the liberi coming forth to claim their offering.

After another few minutes, Theo saw the glow of a lamp ahead and knew the spell had worked. The orange light was a stark change from the blue darkness—he'd begun to grow accustomed to the night.

As they wound their way through the maze of thick trunks, Theo realized they were coming to a cliff face. They must be below the volcanic-looking mountain he'd seen at the center of the island. A doorway made of smooth white stone was embedded in the rock. It rose up the face at least twice his height and four times his width. Lanterns hung on posts to either side of the door, their flames obscured by frosted glass. Theo wondered if a place like this could really only be found by spell. It seemed so conspicuous.

"The Room of Fates," Dolothyia said. Theo could make out these words inscribed over the door in neat, serif letters.

Dolothyia approached the door and gripped its gold knob with steady hands. Turning it, she pulled, and the door opened slow and heavy. "Come," she said when it was just wide enough for them to fit through. Demeres slipped in first, then Theo, and the Guardian followed last, pulling the door closed behind them.

They had entered a library.

One circular room awaited inside, lit by those same, hanging lanterns. Except for the door, the entirety of the curved wall was taken up by bookshelves, most of which were nearly, if not completely full. Thick volumes with dark spines of deep red, green, and blue sat in uniform rows, bound with golden accents. In the center of the room stood a wooden podium, carved with reliefs of various creatures holding up the platform. Theo spotted a human among the unknown species, a man with a deep, furrowed brow and a curling beard.

Upon the podium lay a single open book.

Theo guessed that this must be the most recent of all the tomes. He rushed forward, eager to find his parents' names, but Dolothyia called out harshly.

"Do not touch it! If you touch the book, you will sign your name and die."

Theo stumbled to a halt.

Dolothyia swept past him to the podium. Theo, keeping a safe distance, moved around behind her to get a better look.

The page the book was open to was half filled. Two columns of writing lined the paper, the one on the left a list of names and the one on the right, Theo guessed, a list of the islands to which each name belonged. As he watched, a name scrawled itself in red ink below the last entry. *Tomas Magrin*, it said. Then, beside it, *Aaru* appeared.

There were far more names than folk in Ipsitfel. These must be folk from cities beyond the woods.

Demeres drifted over to Theo and placed her hands on his shoulders, maybe to hold him back but also to console him. Theo realized then that he hadn't prepared himself for what was to come next. He hadn't considered the impact of seeing his parents' names inscribed in their handwriting in blood-red ink. Apprehension knotted his stomach.

Dolothyia ran a long finger down the left column of the page, then the one opposite, but she didn't find the names listed on either. She flipped back several pages. Theo read from behind her, starting from the top left.

Vihaan Arapur.

Shomei Kotashi.

Cyprian Alba.

Julia Amare.

But Dolothyia had gone back too far. The Guardian flipped forward again. She found them before Theo, listed on the right-hand page near the bottom. They were together.

Medina Sahiron.

Damon Sahiron.

His mother had died first, then his father right after.

Theo felt a jolt of pain in his chest. He told himself to breathe, unable to turn away from the scrawled names that were both comforting to see and painful to look at. Across from each name, the same word had been written in the second column, and that eased his constricted chest. At least they had gone to the same place. Until that moment, the idea that they might not have hadn't occurred to him. If he'd know it was a possibility, he would've been all the more frantic.

"Caelum," Dolothyia read. "The mountain of clouds."

"Island of beauty," Demeres said. She squeezed his shoulders comfortingly. "I consider that a rare place to be assigned. I have yet to ferry any souls to Caelum."

"That's a good thing, then. Isn't it?" Theo said. "If it's the island of beauty and few are sent there, that must mean they were good."

Demeres shrugged. "The islands are not necessarily divided among good and bad the way people above think. In this place, you are divided more by your characteristics in life, less by punishment or reward."

As Theo struggled to formulate an opinion as to whether he thought this was fair, Dolothyia spoke up. "You cannot approach the Isle of Caelum in the normal manner." She released the book, and it returned to writing itself. Dolothyia stared pensively. "Not every Guardian is as welcoming as I, and surely not in a place where human souls reside. If they see you are not there to take residence, they will be suspicious of you both."

"Is there another way?" Demeres asked.

"Yes, on the opposite side of the island from the harbor. Beneath the cliffs."

"You sound reluctant to suggest this," Demeres said.

Dolothyia nodded. "I am."

"And why is that?"

Dolothyia placed her fingertips together and rested them beneath her narrow chin.

"You're running out of time, Theo," she said. "The longer your parents stay here, the more reluctant they will be to go with you."

"What?" Theo asked, taken aback. He turned to Demeres. "You didn't tell me there was a time limit."

"I--I didn't know," she replied. "I only every ferry the souls. I do not know what happens to them afterward."

"Between here and Caelum is the island of Kouros," Dolothyia cut in. "To make as hasty a journey to Caelum as is necessary, you will have to pass closely to Kouros."

At these words, Demeres inhaled sharply, her hands flying to her mouth. Lost, Theo looked between the ferrywoman and the Guardian. He'd heard the term Kouros before—many of the townsfolk used it as a curse—but he'd never thought of it as anything other than a word. Demeres' reaction gave him a sinking feeling. Kouros could not be good news.

"Of course, the quickest way would be the canal through the center of Kouros, but I would never recommend such a heading," Dolothyia said, her mouth a solemn line. "Stay beyond the reach of the beings that reside there."

"How much longer do I have?" Theo asked.

"I cannot say," Dolothyia replied.

"How long does it usually take?"

"There is no one time span, just as there is no one length of life for every mortal body. It depends on how strong their ties are to their living memories." Dolothyia gestured for the pair to follow her back to the door. "I only suggest that you be as quick as possible." She hesitated. "There is another reason."

"What's that?" Theo asked, dreading the answer.

"Your own connection to the mortal world is thinning," the Guardian explained. "It will last longer than theirs for it is stronger, but it will not hold forever."

Theo didn't need to ask what would happened should it break.

"We have to get back to the boat," Theo said. Fresh worries addled him now—worries he hadn't foreseen when he'd set out to retrieve his parents. Though he reluctantly stayed back with Dolothyia and Demeres, their insufficient pace felt like wasting time when he could be sprinting to the boat. Caelum sounded far, but he reasoned it had to be close enough for him to reach in time. Otherwise, Dolothyia would have told him the quest was impossible.

"Why are you helping me?" Theo asked as they trudged through the metaliberus once again. The phantom silver sheen had returned to bathe the landscape in a barely visible light. He felt his eyes adjusting from the bright Room of Fates. "I know it goes against your purpose, that it goes against death. So why are you helping me?"

Dolothyia kept a steady pace, fingertips lingering on each tree that they passed. "I don't like what you're trying to do, and normally I would not aid *any* traveler who was attempting the same. But every human child has a journey to face. I feel this is yours. I cannot explain why, but I want to help you."

It was an odd response, one that Theo wasn't sure how to take.

He thought they might stumble across Dolothyia's spell along the way back, and hoped she'd have the chance to reclaim the dream she'd lost, but he didn't see it again. Instead, after a much shorter trek through the woods than before, the flickering lights of the liberi village appeared through the night. The vacant amphitheater had become imbued with the eerie aura of the abandoned. Fires danced unappreciated. The gargantuan tree—the back of Dolothyia's home—stood sentinel over emptiness.

Theo thought about asking if he could see the liberi once again. He'd spent but a brief period among them, and yet he felt melancholy leaving them behind without one more glimpse. The hurry to cast off dissuaded him, though, and he followed the two women into the trees on the other side of the camp. He realized they spoke in hushed tones, not exactly attempting to keep their conversation from him, but to keep private nonetheless.

"You forgo much by helping him," Dolothyia was saying. "Don't you want to go back for another soul? If your debt—"

"He paid for normal passage," Demeres said.

"Normal passage. This is not normal passage, Demeres."

"It's not," the ferrywoman agreed. "I want to help, though, same as you do."

"Of course you do." The look Dolothyia gave Demeres convinced Theo that she knew something about the ferrywoman he didn't. "When you're done with this, if, as it seems, you are in no rush to move on, why don't you visit sometime? I like to have good company when I can get it, and you have been good company to me. Most are in such a hurry to get to their own islands."

"Maybe I will," Demeres said.

Before Theo knew it, they had reached the cove. Their boat sat where they'd left it on the shore. Beyond lay the glassy black surface of the Corporis Sea. He found himself less than excited to sail the black waters, but the urgency of his journey superseded his reluctance. Dolothyia took his hand, and he turned to face her.

"I wish you luck, Theo Sahiron. I hope that whatever comes about, you are satisfied." Without waiting for him to respond, the Guardian threw her arms around him and drew him into a close embrace. The satin folds of her dress enclosed him, and for all the regality she embodied, and through his lingering hesitance over the stretched truth she had told the liberi, he felt remarkably comforted by her hold. A protector's hold. It was an embrace he hoped to get from his parents at the end of all of this.

"Go now, and hurry," Dolothyia said. She let go, and Theo and Demeres climbed into the boat.

As soon as Demeres placed a hand on the tiller, they slid back into the sea with a light scrape. Dolothyia walked beside them as they left the shore, her dress billowing out in the black water. She followed until the surface was at her waist, then stood still, watching them sail away. They left Eirini's cove on the waveless sea, gliding out across the black water until the Guardian was but a dot in a diminishing landscape.

14
Questions

Theo was the first to break the silence.

"I want to go through the canals of Kouros."

Demeres looked at him and shook her head. "You don't know what you're saying."

"I do," Theo insisted. "Dolothyia said that was the shortest way."

"Dolothyia should not have mentioned it," Demeres said irritably. "That she did is unfortunate, but a subtle reminder that she is not, nor never has been, human. Deities are indifferent to mortality. Regardless, we can't go through Kouros."

"*We* can't, or *you* won't?" Theo asked.

"They are one and the same. To do so would be to end your journey before even getting close."

"How do you know?"

"Because Kouros is not a place you ever want to visit."

"I thought there were no islands of punishment."

"It's not an island of punishment. Not for those who reside there, at least." Demeres sighed, staring ahead into the darkness beyond him. "Kouros is the island where many... *less* than friendly souls end up. Those who gave in to their darker impulses in life, people who prized their own desires and wealth above that of their fellow humans."

"We don't have anything for them to take," Theo said, gesturing around at their empty boat. "We have nothing,"

"It doesn't have to be a physical item."

"What else is there?"

Demeres was silent, her patience holding strong. "Clothes and money are not the only things that can be taken down here," she said, which was not any less vague. "They will accost us without reason, without knowing whether or not we have anything worth their trouble."

"We don't need to stop. If we just sail through the canal—"

"The Kourosites will not let us pass unbothered. They will see us coming. They will wait by the banks of the canals. They will trap us."

"Then you've already given up on my parents," Theo said. His voice had risen so that it sounded strained in his ears.

"We might still make it if we go around."

"*Might*. Dolothyia seemed doubtful." Theo struggled to control his exasperation. He didn't want to shout at Demeres, but she didn't understand the urgency. Somehow, she didn't grasp how dire the circumstances were. If they didn't go after his parents with all haste, then what was the point in him descending through the Gateway? "How much longer is it?"

"It adds only what amounts to a few days in your world," Demeres said. She wouldn't meet his gaze.

Theo seized handfuls of his hair, and for a few moments sat at the bow in frustration, trying to keep tears from spilling over by staring hard at the bottom of the boat. He noticed his soiled vest: now a brownish-yellow, the color of old paper. Those stains would never be removed.

Delaying the journey by sailing around the entirety of Kouros could not be the reason he lost his parents, and he wasn't about to head back home for the sake of his own connection to the mortal realm. If Theo found their souls after it was too late, he wanted it to be despite doing everything in his power to get to them in time. Demeres was his only obstacle. He needed to change her mind; he needed to *show* her that there was no other way.

His tone softened. "Is going through the canal at Kouros the straightest path to the cliffs of Caelum?"

"More often than not, the quickest path is not the best to take."

"But is it the quickest?"

She sat back, unhappy. "Yes. I suppose it is."

"Please, Demeres, you said you would help me, and I need your help now. Dolothyia told me my parents are running out of time. The longer it takes to get to them, the less chance I have at bringing them back."

"*If* you can bring them back."

Theo nodded. "If I can bring them back. If I can get to them in time, it will have to be because we went through Kouros."

Demeres shook her head, quieting. Her eyes closed, a token of her insoluble patience. Though it wore thin, it never broke. If she'd ever had children, she must have been an excellent mother. Theo could feel her weighing his pleas against what caution told her to do. He dug his hand into the pocket of his trousers and found the watch. Warm metal touched his fingertips. He drew it out and turned the watch over and over in his palm. He had a feeling that if she refused now, there would be no changing her mind.

"Before he died, my father told me 'A man who makes something of himself is always conscious of time,'" he said, sliding his thumb over the dull exterior. "I thought he chided me for my carelessness, but that wasn't quite right. He meant that I should realize time is not infinite. It's not even guaranteed. I need to be more efficient with my time. To go after things I believe are true and right." Theo looked up at Demeres, feeling the warmth of tears on his face. "I wish I'd understood that before it was too late."

The ferrywoman closed her eyes and sighed.

"You are an impulsive child, Theo. You would put yourself at unnecessary risk to charge blindly forth." Her words made Theo cringe. He broke her gaze and looked out again at the black sea. "But I have also sworn to ferry souls who have paid their due across the water. I have agreed to help you, and so against my better judgment I will do as you ask. Understand this, though: I am a ferrywoman; they cannot force me to leave the water. I cannot step foot on any island designated for human souls. Not until my debt is paid. You, on the other hand, are extraordinarily vulnerable. Whatever happens once we enter the canal is beyond my control. If they somehow manage to grab you..."

Theo ignored her concern, focused instead on the second mention of her debt. He would ask her about it when he wasn't so dependent on her good graces. Theo nodded in gratitude, not yet trusting himself to speak.

With that, Demeres gripped the tiller more tightly and the boat adjusted its heading. Relieved, Theo shoved the watch back in his pocket and clasped his hands in his lap instead. He could make it through the canal. If she kept up this speed and they kept their heads down, who knew? They might not even be bothered. After all, he wore a dirty tunic and a scarf that looked more distressed than its fabric should have been able to take. He was reasonably inconspicuous. As for the risks, what mattered most was getting to his parents. From the moment Dolothyia had told him their time was limited, every second felt more precarious than the last. He had to get to them before their window closed, before they began to forget. He didn't want to consider the alternative.

Theo looked up, watching Demeres lead them across the sea. She focused her gaze somewhere beyond him, her hair pulled back from her face, though there was no wind. The ferrywoman had to be older than Laila, though he would guess she was younger than his parents. This must be the age at which she'd died, now her eternal appearance so long as she remained in Nochlan.

"Demeres," he said, struck by an idea he couldn't hold back, "have you ever had to ferry someone you knew?"

Her lips unpursed themselves, her hard stare releasing. Theo knew immediately he had touched on a delicate topic—there seemed to be many of those where the ferrywoman was concerned—but unlike before, she grew morose instead of stern.

"I have," she said. Her voice was soft, the sharp edge from her reprimands gone. "I've ferried a number of souls whom I recognized."

"Is it difficult?"

She struggled again for words. "Not always. Sometimes it can be quite pleasant, actually. A sort of reacquaintance. I am not required to return to the shore where I collected you," she continued. "In fact, I've traveled to a few others. I choose the direction of the boat, but my heading draws me. I have found several shores from the land of the living since I became a ferrywoman. I prefer our own. I like to see that our people make it safely across."

"How many ferries are there?" Theo asked.

"I couldn't tell you," Demeres said. "Maybe thousands, perhaps hundreds of thousands. I don't know."

"Do you take everyone from our shore?"

"No. Remember, I did not ferry your parents. Depending on how frequently people die, someone may come while I'm ferrying another, but I take as many as I can."

"Have you ever taken anyone who was close to you? A family member?"

Demeres didn't respond to the question. Instead, irritation flecked her tone again. "You ask too many questions, Theo."

"Sorry," Theo muttered, though he wasn't truly. How could she expect him not to have so many questions? Maybe the passengers she carried didn't ask much, but death could've brought them a semblance of peace, of acceptance. He was alive. He warred with the very notion of contentment.

Theo pulled out the pocket watch again. It was becoming a habit. Turning it over under the light of the lantern, he pressed the clasp and it opened. The inside was as unremarkable as the outside: dull and unadorned. The hand had even stopped moving. When did it break? He squeezed it shut between his palms again. He would find his father before it was too late. He would give it back to him, and hopefully Damon wouldn't be angry that his son had taken it.

"Was that your father's?" Demeres asked.

"Yes." Theo held it up between his thumb and index finger for her to see. He expected Demeres to reach for it, but she didn't. "He always carried it with him when he was alive. On the last day I saw him, he accidentally left it on my bed, so I kept hold of it. I meant to give it back."

"It's nice," Demeres said.

"It's plain," Theo said.

"That doesn't mean it isn't nice. I'm sure he would've wanted you to have it."

Theo nodded. That may have been true, but that inheritance was meant to happen years in their future. "I didn't mean to bring it with me, but I forgot it was in my pocket. Everything happened so quickly. It's stopped working now. The fall must have damaged it after all."

"Will you keep it?"

"No. I'm going to give it back to him. I'm just holding it until we get to Caelum."

Demeres said nothing more.

The boat continued across the eerily calm black waters. There was no sky, there was no sea. The horizon simply disappeared into a void, a sight that would have been oppressive were Theo alone. He couldn't imagine the solitude Demeres endured each time she delivered a passenger to one of the islands. If all went well, this time she would travel back to his shore with more company than she'd left with.

"How did you become a ferrywoman?" he asked after what had to have been at least half an hour of silence.

But while she had, until then, begrudgingly given him some sort of response to every question he asked, this time she looked him in the eye and said absolutely nothing. He didn't feel the need to repeat his question. She wouldn't answer.

15

A Land of Fire Keepers

Someone was calling his name.

The sound rose slowly, as if from a distance. Then it was all around, yanking him out of his dream. In the world of sleep, he was flailing, but on the floor of the boat he lay still and simply opened his eyes. A vacuous void blanketed the view above him.

He blinked.

"Theo," Demeres said again.

He lifted his head to look past his prone body at the ferrywoman. She sat by the tiller with her red hair dyed a fiery orange by the lantern. Though she'd said his name calmly, he could see anxiety on her face. That could only mean one thing.

Theo scrambled onto his knees, peering over the bow.

Approaching them rapidly was a wide, low island emerging out of the darkness. In every way, it was the opposite of Eirini. Where Dolothyia's home had been a forest of trees, this island was uniformly covered in stone and clay buildings. Instead of a mountain at the center, there was only the gentle roll of the land, like the shallow mounds formed when tilling fields for sowing. Most of all, while Eirini had been cloaked in night, with only the few torches at the shore and the liberi settlement, this island was covered in light. Everywhere Theo looked, fires burned—in lanterns hung from buildings, on torches lining the roads, and in great plinths scattered across the landscape. There was no doubt in Theo's mind: this city was many times larger than the Ipsitfel he'd left behind.

"Kouros," Demeres said.

"Kouros," Theo breathed. He couldn't deny that the island, which seemed itself to be ablaze, had a pyrocentric beauty to it—mesmerizing in the same way that light seems to draw all things. He didn't want to tear his gaze away, but the longer he stared, the louder Demeres and Dolothyia's warnings echoed in his head. This was a place to be feared, and its troubling reputation caused his pulse to quicken.

"Where is the canal?" Theo asked.

"The canals run through several parts of the island, but the one we want is there, below the large tower."

Theo followed the trajectory of her pointing finger to a cylindrical column at least twice the height of any of the buildings around it. Atop the tower, the walls curved together to form an oblong dome. Light shone from windows in the roof and along the spiral staircase that must be inside. At the foot of the tower, Theo could just make out the arches of a bridge supporting a road. The closer they sailed, the clearer the canal became.

When they could be no further than a kilometer away, Theo felt himself tilt forward as the boat slowed. In another second, the lantern at the bow had dimmed until it was almost out. Light from the island led them instead, coaxing their small craft into its reach. Theo could see hundreds of people milling about the streets, and without reason this filled him with trepidation, even though none of them had noticed their boat.

"Shouldn't we keep going fast?" he asked under his breath. How well did their voices carry across the sea?

"I don't want to draw any attention to us," Demeres said, though her hand fidgeted on the tiller.

"What if they notice us anyway?"

"Then this boat will sail faster than I've ever sailed it before."

He had the impression that her words were not mere hyperbole; so said her tense posture, at least. Oddly enough, they seemed to have no issue remaining inconspicuous. At any moment, Theo was certain someone on land would point them out and initiate a chase through the infamous canals, but the moment never came. They sailed closer and closer to the island, the only occupied boat on the water, and not a soul turned their way. Despite the relief it might have brought him, Theo instead felt an eerie unease. He felt *ignored*, and that too was worrisome.

Now, less than half a kilometer from the mouth of the canal, the meandering residents came into sharp focus. Theo noticed—with some embarrassment that caused him to flush and lower his gaze—that the inhabitants of Kouros didn't wear much clothing. Instead of the long-sleeved tunics and trousers, or the dresses people wore in Ipsitfel, they walked around with exposed legs and arms—torsos even. The reason for this became readily apparent moments later, as a wave of heat washed over Theo, followed by the acrid odor of flames.

He should've expected as much given the multitude of fires burning everywhere.

Within a few minutes, the mouth of the canal greeted them, and the city closed in on both sides. People crossed the bridge overhead, but none so much as glanced over the railing.

The heat became stifling. Surely, they didn't need so many fires to keep the island illuminated. If they extinguished even half of the plinths, visibility on the streets would remain unencumbered. Sweat beaded on Theo's forehead. He considered removing the scarf from around his neck, but ultimately decided he'd rather deal with the discomfort of heat rather than the discomfort of its absence.

Demeres muttered to herself, her eyes darting constantly as she steered the boat. Even in the light, the water remained perfectly black, creating mirror images of the buildings bordering the canal. The reflections hung from the water's edge like clothes hung from a line to dry.

Past the second bridge, Theo wondered if maybe the inhabitants couldn't see them at all. Had Dolothyia perhaps helped them out with an invisibility spell and not told them? He entertained the idea for a moment, but in the end it just didn't seem likely. She would've had no reason to keep something like that a secret.

On they went, beneath the third, fourth, and fifth bridges. Each time, though people walked along the shore beside them and crossed overhead, not a single gaze flicked in their direction. Theo felt a stirring triumph in his chest. Dolothyia and Demeres had been wrong about the dangers of Kouros. He'd had nothing to fear, and now he was that much closer to saving his parents.

His optimism changed at the last bridge.

Theo could see the Corporis Sea maybe a hundred meters ahead. Cruising at a constant speed, Demeres and Theo floated beneath the last of the bridges, which unlike the others, was deserted. The shadow crossed over Theo and swallowed the boat whole. For a few seconds, the heat of the fires ebbed just a few degrees.

As they neared the other side, Theo's heart sank when he realized they were no longer the only ones in the water. A gondola painted a rich navy blue came slinking out into the center of the canal, blocking their exit from under the bridge. Demeres and Theo's boat came to a halt half in shadow: Demeres in the darkness, Theo in the light.

A broad-shouldered man stood at the front of the gondola. His muscular arms hung at his sides, his feet set slightly apart. Though his facial expression was impassive, his very presence resonated with tension. Light from the plinth fires danced across his slick skin and his dark eyes. Behind him sat another man and a woman, both of whom held oars poised at the ready in the black water. Their faces too were expressionless.

"Welcome to Kouros," the man said. His voice was deep and rumbling. Theo could feel it in his chest. "Are you looking for a place to dock?"

"We are just passing through," Demeres said from behind Theo. "Thank you, but we do not need a welcome."

Theo felt his pulse quicken. He was sweating now. Beads of moisture trickled down his back. The man looked from Theo to Demeres to Theo again. He broke into a wide grin, though the intensity of his gaze did not soften, and his posture did not change.

"Surely you would not come through our canal if you did not wish to stay?"

"This is not our stop," Demeres said. She sounded more commanding than Theo had yet heard her. He wished he could shrink into the shadow covering the back end of the boat. Yet changing seats now seemed unwise, any movement could break the tension keeping the man at a distance.

Demeres continued, "We were only using this canal as a shorter way to—"

"Caelum?" The man's smile widened, if that was possible. Theo thought of the grinning marauders he'd heard tale of as a child, bandits who wandered the woods and begged travelers for help. They appeared friendly, but as soon as the traveler stopped, the marauders attacked, robbing them of their possessions and potentially their life. This man wore the same insincere grin Theo had always pictured on the bandits' faces. It was a grin he might see at night, staring at him through the darkness.

"Yes," Demeres conceded, "Caelum."

"Ah, then the boy does not belong here." The man clasped his hands together, and Theo noticed the way his muscles rippled beneath his skin when he moved. "But... neither does he belong in Caelum. Am I wrong?"

"Don't be ridiculous," Demeres said. "How could you know? You are not a ferryman."

"You're right—I can't know. I was told by someone who does. He saw you coming."

"Who?" Theo asked, afraid.

"The boy is of no business to you," Demeres said. "Let us pass."

"But we are intrigued by your arrival." The man spoke to Theo now, looking him straight in the eye. The stare gripped him like an iron trap. Despite his fear, Theo could not look away and was no longer certain he even wanted to.

"Don't talk to him," Demeres snapped. It was unclear toward whom the command was directed.

"You crossed our borders—I feel that gives us the right," the man said. "And there's someone who wants to meet you, boy."

Demeres gasped involuntarily. "What could Palakostos want with him? Leave us alone. What does the boy possibly have to offer?"

"What an interesting question. If only you knew."

"Let us through and I won't ram your boat."

"You would risk damaging your own?" The smile lingered for only a moment longer, and then the man's eyes darkened and his mouth thinned into a straight line. "The more interesting question is this, ferrywoman: why are you helping the boy? Why are you transporting him through our realm when he doesn't belong here?"

"Please, just let us through."

"No," the man growled. "We won't sacrifice a treat such as he. Palakostos would love to meet him."

Very suddenly, shadows descended upon Theo from the bridge above. He was seized around the middle by a pair of arms, and before he could even react, he was hoisted into the air. Beneath him, the floor of the ferryboat fell away. Demeres screamed and lunged forward to grab him, but it was too late. He was out of reach and beyond her help.

16
Temple Entombed

"Get your fucking hands off me!" Theo snarled, attempting to twist away from his captor. He tumbled to his knees as the arms released him, grunting as he collided with the hard stone ground. Before he could regain his footing, he was seized by two women who had been hiding atop the bridge.

Beneath him, Theo could hear Demeres shouting. Curses flew from her mouth. The man in the gondola responded calmly in his booming voice.

"You may continue on your way, ferrywoman," he said. "The boy is no longer your burden."

"Fight them, Theo! Get away from them and run to the water. I'll find you," she screamed. "I'll wait for you!"

Theo was hauled to his feet and propelled forward.

Ashore, the island became a fiery maze of narrow stone passages between towering buildings. Theo did his best not to fall, though the pace of his captors was unforgiving. He remained upright mostly due to the efforts of the two women who held tight to his arms. Judging by their expressions, this was not an act of mercy but a begrudging necessity. He might have been a sack of flour they hoisted between them for all they cared.

Without warning, they came to a sudden halt. The women released him, and again Theo fell to the unforgiving ground. Pain coursed through his knees as they hit. His palms slapped the stone surface. He lay completely prone, out of breath, still in shock after being snatched from the boat.

As he lay there, a pair of feet clad in muddy brown boots came to rest before him.

Theo rose to his knees and backed away before looking up at the man from the gondola. Up close, Theo could see the man wasn't as old as he would have guessed—maybe ten years his senior but nothing more, perhaps the same age as the ferrywoman. The man looked down at him with a hungry expression, as if Theo were a meal waiting to be consumed.

"Thank you for joining us," he said. "Palakostos will be pleased."

"I didn't have much of a choice," Theo said.

The man seemed to take this as a compliment. He gave a slight bow. "Call me Peitho."

"I don't give a damn what your name is."

"Come now, where are your manners? This is where you introduce yourself." Peitho held out his hand, waiting for an answer. "Hmm?"

Theo looked around at the dozen pairs of expectant eyes trained on him. Each member of the gang of captors stood ready to barricade any attempted escape. Though they acted like servants to this Peitho, Theo could see a lingering hunger in their expressions. Just beyond their obedience lay malice. It wouldn't take much for that unruly nature to come free. Theo's heart sank. Ideas of escape morphed into farfetched hopes. Dolothyia and Demeres had been right after all. Now, not only might he be too late to reach his parents, he likely wouldn't escape Kouros at all.

"Well," Peitho continued, "if we are not observing pleasantries, *Theo*, I suppose we will waste no more time. Up."

At the last word, a boy to Theo's left, who could only have been a few years older than he, seized his arm and dragged him to his feet. Then they were off again.

Without a sun or moon, Theo had trouble keeping directions straight, but maintaining his bearings was the only useful task of which Theo was capable. As far as he could tell, they'd headed away from the canal, though rather than diving straight into the heart of the island, they'd favored his right side.

The band of miscreants jogged through the streets past residents faking their daily routines. Had the circumstances been different, Theo might've found their casual, yet exaggerated poses comical. A woman with long black hair repeatedly filled a massive vase in a fountain. An older man paused halfway up a flight of stairs to examine a spot on the railing. Each onlooker tried their best to observe the procession without blatantly displaying interest—almost as if they weren't supposed to know something was happening.

This thought sat rather oddly with Theo. How could they not know something was afoot? He was being led through the city with a twelve-person escort.

Soon enough, however, the buildings began to thin. Squat houses replaced gangly ones. The road became worn and ill kept. And they left all manner of gawking residents behind. They rounded a rocky outcropping and Theo's heart leapt. They were near the shore, somewhere on another side of the isle, though he hoped not too far from the canal.

Maybe a hundred paces on, the island disappeared into a void of nothing. The black waters of the Corporis Sea met the sands of Kouros. Somewhere in that darkness ahead was where he needed to go.

But they were not headed for the water.

At the end of the stony road stood a lone building. Instead of the plain square brickwork found in the densest parts of the island, this wide temple was constructed of large slabs of white stone—though the fiery plinths bathed the walls in orange. Columns rose on either side of the entryway. Below the tiled roof was carved an ornate, geometric molding, but no other intricacies decorated the exterior.

"The Guardian was very pleased to see you coming," Peitho said as they stopped short of the steps to the entrance. "Usually, we have to escape to the surface to capture adolescents, but you came to us."

Theo frowned, trying to show more of the anger he felt than the fear or anxiety. Inside, his stomach twisted in knots, and he wanted to vomit. Who exactly was Palakostos, and what did they want from him? Something in the way Peitho referred to the Guardian made the being seem more like a deity—an unapproachable god—and less like Dolothyia had appeared—as a person.

Theo made a secret pledge to agree with everything Demeres said if he made it off the island alive. Peitho smiled, and again Theo felt himself shiver. Had Palakostos not been expecting Theo, this man might have tried to devour him.

"Go on then," Peitho said. He nodded toward the temple.

"You aren't going to bring me to the Guardian?" Theo asked, although he wouldn't mind if this was the last he saw of this man and his comrades.

"We will make sure you go in, but you will be guided the rest of the way by someone else," Peitho said. "I do not enter the temple."

These souls—or were they "beings," Theo couldn't tell whether they'd ever been human—did the bidding of Palakostos, but were not allowed to enter his home? Or maybe they were allowed and refused to out of fear. Neither possibility comforted Theo, who looked up at the wall of great stone slabs with apprehension. In his mind, he battled the urge to try and break away now, throw himself down the shore and race to the water. Perhaps they wouldn't swim after him. Perhaps if he at least made it to the sea—

In his peripheral vision, Theo thought he saw something move down by the water, but he didn't dare look and risk giving away his intent. Was it a boat run aground, or anchored just offshore? That could be of use.

"If you don't move on your own, we will force you to go," one of the women said.

Theo's fleeting hope of a plan dissolved as he remembered the dozen intimidating individuals standing around him. He would not make it to the water. Even if he did break away somehow, they would be no more than a step behind. Close enough to reach out and yank him back.

"I'm going," he said. He mounted the first step.

Behind him, the captors fanned out, guarding the bottom of the stairs. Nowhere to go but up. He stopped and turned to face them all. He had one option left in his arsenal. He could try to talk to them. After all, that was how he had persuaded Demeres to help him. Maybe if he appealed to their human memory...

"You don't have to do this," Theo said, hands raised. "I... I'm just a boy. You could let me go. I don't belong here—I should be home with my sister, who's probably distraught because of my disappearance. Please, let me go. I'll go straight back to my home, I promise."

The glowering faces broke into a chorus of malicious laughter.

Peitho smirked. "For bringing you, Palakostos rewards us with more than you could ever afford."

And with that, he reached forward and shoved Theo hard.

Theo stumbled up a few steps, but managed to keep his footing. The short-lived ploy had been worth a try, even if it had proved fruitless. Taking a deep breath, he mounted the remaining steps, his heart throbbing almost painfully in his throat. He realized his right hand had gone to his pocket and was clutching the watch. He brought the other hand to the scarf wound around his neck. The blue fabric was dirtied and wrinkled, but it still carried the same protective feel.

"I'm not finished," he whispered, and passed through the doorway.

The room inside exhibited the same elegant, yet plain architecture as the exterior. A tiled white marble floor stretched out before him, ending at another doorway with a passage that sloped down out of view. Light emanated from a trio of shining orbs arranged on pedestals near the center of the room. Each shone brightly enough that Theo had to shield his eyes with his arm when he faced them.

He heard movement and knew he was not alone.

"Keep coming forward," several serene voices said in unison. Each tone was so pure, they might have been the tolling of bells.

"Palakostos?" Theo asked, wary.

"No," the voices said, again in perfect synchronicity.

Theo considered denying their request, but knew he couldn't go back the way he'd come. Outside, the kidnappers were still waiting for him. He couldn't exit that way. With only one option, Theo edged forth, stepping lightly on the tiles. The bright orbs seemed to ring, a note as high as their gleam was bright. He had to squint as he passed between them, and their brilliance shone through his eyelids.

As soon as he was on the other side, their light dimmed. The effect was immediate, and Theo lowered his arm, confused but grateful. Looking at the orbs from this side of the pedestals, their illumination still filled the room, but the orbs themselves were dull and observable. What strange magic existed in this world.

He turned his attention forward. Six beings stood on either side of the doorway. They were human in form, though Theo was certain they were anything but. As he gaped, searching for words, two of the figures drifted toward him. Walking seemed too crude a term for the way they moved. Their legs alternated sliding forward, but so fluid were their gaits that he couldn't discern where one step ended and the next began.

Neither wore anything more than sheer fabric, which cascaded over their frames as if they were constantly emerging from a pool of water. Theo could see every detail of their figures: their observant eyes watching him, the square or rounded shape of their shoulders, the slimming from torso to waist and back out to hips, the strength in their thighs and calves, and the gentleness of their feet. Though he was afraid, he felt an odd fire spark in his chest, one he hadn't expected nor experienced much before.

Both figures held in their hands a folded article of clothing made of the same silky, translucent material.

"I am Besmin," said the one on the left. Besmin had a feminine body, the most evocative female form Theo had ever seen. Beneath the sheer fabric, her skin glowed, unblemished.

"And I am Erid," the one on the right said. Erid had a masculine body, tall and broad-shouldered with a firm, prominent chest.

Theo had never realized the human body could have so many contours—so many lines of definition. The two before him, Besmin and Erid, were no exception. But *did* they have human bodies? They were far too perfect in form to be anything but an idealist's sculptures, the shapes of deities.

Theo looked quickly back and forth between the two of them, as well as at the four who had stayed back, not wanting his eyes to linger anywhere for too long. His face flushed at their indecency. He'd never seen another naked body besides his own. Yet curiosity fought the instinct to divert his gaze. Erid raised his arms, holding out the cloth to Theo and smiled, nodding. Theo found he couldn't take his eyes away from him.

"It is decided. I will bring you," Erid continued. "Come with me."

Besmin glided away, rejoining the others. Theo watched her go for only a moment before his eyes were drawn again to Erid. The guide was still holding out what Theo assumed to be a garment, though if it was anything nearly as immodest as what Erid wore, he couldn't imagine complying. The thought of this alone was enough to make his face burn hotter. To make matters worse, Theo imagined his own body juxtaposed to Erid's, and his face fell.

"What is it?" he asked, stalling for time. Time that he didn't have.

"I only ask that you wear it over your tunic," Erid said, reading Theo's reluctance. "It is merely a symbolic gesture."

"Yes, but what is it?"

"Gossamer, made by the Great Weaver."

"The Great Weaver?" Theo said. "Sounds impressive when you put it that way. I suppose it's not to get ruined then?"

"This gossamer is incredibly durable."

"Oh. How long will I be in Palakostos's chamber?"

Still smiling in a way that was both mesmerizing and comforting, Erid shrugged.

"Then is there really a reason for me to wear it?" Theo asked.

"Is there reason for you not to?" Erid replied. He emphasized the garment again, and Theo took it.

The fabric was impossibly light. If he hadn't seen Erid hand it to him, he might have thought his hand had passed through a spider's web. It weighed nothing. Wondering how strong it could truly be, Theo tossed one end of it over his shoulder and draped it around himself like a cape.

When he looked up, the guide had started off down the descending passage, his retreating form sliding away. Theo jogged a few hurried steps to catch up, the cloth billowing out behind him.

Strange thoughts floated through his head. He knew he should be trying to find a way out of his situation. He should be scared or anxious about getting closer to Palakostos—and he was—but unrest toward the Guardian had slipped a tier. Instead his palms sweated, his stomach constricted, and his mind raced for another distressing reason. He couldn't help studying the guide who walked beside him and feeling waves of judgment crash over himself. Erid, like the others, epitomized perfection. Theo felt both an urge to embody the separate features of Erid and to reach out and touch them. Theo was not as tall as his guide; he'd not yet had the growth spurt of many other boys his age. The muscles in Theo's arms were not defined as Erid's, nor were the muscles in his back as prominent. He didn't have the square chest, either, and his stomach was thin and undeveloped. The farther they walked, the passage continuing downward as if pulling them into the ground, the more Theo became aware of his youth. When his mind drifted briefly from Erid's form, he compared himself unfavorably to another boy who came to mind, one who cusped manhood: Roman. Perhaps Roman's shoulders were not as broad as Erid's, nor his voice as deep and pure, but he shared more with the guide than Theo did.

The white stone gave way to gray rock. The brick walls were no longer smooth, but jagged and rough-hewn. He could scarcely tell anymore whether the ground was paved or simply stone slab. That Erid should have to step on a path so unfinished seemed almost a crime, but none of the dirt stuck to his feet, nor did it cling to his gossamer robe.

The farther they went, the more enclosed the space felt. The air became stale as well, and damp. Moss grew on the walls and hung down like draperies. Cracks painted themselves with mold. Theo had to lift the blue scarf to cover his nose from the stench.

"Why does Palakostos live out here?"

"He prefers the lack of light and the moisture. He also does not like to be disturbed by the island's residents."

"Isn't he their Guardian?"

"He is Guardian of the island."

"Why does it smell like this?"

Erid didn't answer, but gave Theo a small smile.

"Who is Palakostos?" Theo tried.

"Why, Palakostos is the Guardian of Kouros," Erid replied.

"Yes, I know that," Theo said. "But why does Palakostos want me?"

"For your youth," Erid said without a trace of emotion. "To consume your mind."

Theo's step faltered. His pulse quickened. *To consume my mind?* What did that mean exactly? How could Palakostos want Theo's youth? The Guardian's temple had to be a hundred feet below ground. They had to be—

"Come along," Erid said, coming to a halt as well and holding out a hand. "There is no use trying to escape or fight. We are almost at our destination."

A lump in his throat, Theo began walking again, turning the watch over and over in his pocket. He had to do something. He couldn't just surrender this way, without any struggle. Why hadn't he listened to Demeres? He'd been so stupid.

The passageway ended in a door. It was so plain, so unremarkable, that Theo had trouble believing they'd come to the right place. Erid reached out and placed a hand against the heavy wood, and Theo could hear locks shifting inside. Then it swung open to reveal a long, narrow hall.

At the far end was a set of wooden, double doors. Along the left and right walls were smaller, iron doors matted by rust and grime. They were identical in their repellant appearance. To Theo's dismay, Erid stopped by the first door on the left, and again it opened easily to his touch.

"Come," Erid said.

Theo looked into the darkness through the open door and then glanced up the passageway behind his guide, peering at where the slope disappeared beyond view.

"You will not make it out of the temple," Erid assured him.

Was the guide telling the truth? Theo weighed whether chancing a getaway was worth the risk. But the other deities would be waiting at the mouth of the passage, and beyond would be the band of captors on the steps.

"Palakostos is not this way," Erid said.

"Where does it lead?"

Erid didn't answer. He gazed intently at Theo, who felt as though the circulation of blood inside him had suddenly switched directions. Overcome with a faint dizziness, he blinked up at the guide.

"I don't want to," he said.

"I desire that you do." Erid placed a hand on Theo's shoulder, touching him for the first time. A blossom of confusion unfurled within Theo. He felt fear of Palakostos, fear of the guide, the urge to do as they asked, and a small voice of self-preservation pleading that he run.

In the end, one dominating intent overcame the competing emotions.

Theo jerked forward, dragging his feet into the shadows. The guide touched him still, fingertips lingering on the gossamer cape.

"Inside," Erid breathed. Then Theo was through the doorway.

The instant Erid's touch broke, the fog in his mind dissipated.

The door slammed behind him and locked with resounding finality. Realizing what had happened, Theo spun and threw himself against the solid iron, banging his fists. He shouted, his cries echoing in the room, but he knew already it was of no use. Erid had most likely gone. Theo had walked quietly to his own death.

He stood there pounding on the door until his hands had gone numb, then he sank to the floor, his throat raw from shouting. As the echoes of his yells died, his ears rang. Silence. Complete silence. Enough that even breathing felt too conspicuous. He didn't need sight to know how small the room was. The very walls made their proximity known.

There was nothing on the inside of the door. No handle or latch to speak of. It could only be opened from the outside, which would never happen unless his *guide* had a change of heart. Theo scoffed, thinking how willingly he'd followed along. How he hadn't even shown Erid the resistance he'd demonstrated for Peitho and his crew, and they'd outnumbered him. Theo could say his compliancy had come from his resignation to the inevitable, but another part of him pondered that beauty should be so disarming.

And then Theo fumed, angry at himself for not listening to Demeres or Dolothyia, who had both warned him of the dangers of Kouros. Disobeying Dolothyia was one thing—though she was a *deity*—but disregarding Demeres, who was firmly on his side and risking her neck to save him? Well, he couldn't deny he was to blame for his situation.

Now the minutes ticked past, and his parents slipped away with them.

Theo backed into a corner, his knees to his chest, hugging himself and wishing all the pain would disappear. But there was no one here to comfort him in the impenetrable dark, and though he'd stared in awe at the fantastical world he'd found below the ground, it wasn't until now that he realized how very far away from home he was.

\#

The click of the latch woke him up.

The first thing he noticed when he opened his eyes was that dim light came through a crack in the door. It was open.

Theo crawled forth, quiet and wary. He peered around the side of the iron door and into the hallway, expecting to see who had come for him, but the corridor was empty. Outside his room, a single torch glowed high on the wall, the source of the light. But no shadows cast themselves along the masonry. He was still alone.

Standing, Theo slid out of his cell. He stumbled over to the door he'd come through with Erid, his legs on pins and needles, but of course it remained locked. Each of the other cells had been opened, but he had little use for them as they were all exactly the same as his own: small and square. The pair of doors at the other end of the hall, however, had also been opened.

Theo crept along the corridor, heading for his only exit, sure that if he was being herded this way, it was not for good reason. His heart thudded as he reached the door, ready at any moment to turn and run. He stepped inside.

He found himself in some kind of storage room.

All around him were stacks of wooden crates, each of them unlatched and open on one side. Besides slight differences in their make, nothing about the crates was distinguishable. He could see no labels or inscriptions of any kind. Even their insides were completely empty.

Drawing close to the nearest one, Theo stuck his head inside and looked around. No, there was nothing written there either, though once he'd checked multiple he observed that a few of them had deep gouges on the insides of the walls. The streaks all seemed to come in fives, spaced perfectly apart so that if he put his hands against the marks...

Theo backed away, choking against a yelp that threatened to escape. Each of the boxes was just large enough to fit someone near to his size. A wave of nausea, aided by the rotting stench in the room, hit him, and he wanted to retch. He even bent forward, hands on his knees, and willed himself to take deep breaths through his mouth.

So where had all the captives gone?

Inhaling deeply, Theo shut his eyes and took a moment to clear his senses. He was more determined now than ever to get out—he just had to find a way. The pocket watch felt cool in his hand. Over and over and over again he turned it. Somehow this small, inconsequential act stirred him.

Crouching still, Theo crept through the piles of crates, peering between each for a way out of the room. The task did not take him long.

The far wall held a pair of intimidating wooden doors—much larger than the ones through which he'd entered. The heavy, massive planks were stained by years of submersion in this damp air—black patches of mold and dirt patterned the corners, in all likelihood adding to the foul odor in the room. The doors were held in place by rusty hinges that matched the iron handles set at shoulder height.

Theo was fairly certain this grand entrance would lead to Palakostos, and that was the last place Theo wanted to be. He stepped back, holding his breath, hoping none of the sounds he made were audible on the other side of the thick wooden barrier, where the Guardian might be listening for him. No, perhaps there was another way. He turned to the right instead.

Another door appeared, this one a normal size. A rush of adrenaline flooded Theo. This looked like a promising option. He warded off the pessimistic thoughts that rushed forth. Yes, if it was a broom cupboard it would be of no use, and if it was another passage it would probably be locked. But some locked doors could be broken open, and this was the possibility he hoped for. Yes, just maybe they had unwittingly left him a way out.

Theo seized the knob. He took a deep breath, trying to mitigate the quell of expectations. Whatever was or was not on the other side, he wouldn't give up hope. He had his parents to think of. And Demeres, although he was certain the ferrywoman could handle herself. Exhaling, he turned the knob.

The door opened.

On the other side was a small chamber—no bigger than his bedroom, or what used to be his bedroom—made entirely of stone bricks. Faint purple light emanated from a glowing patch of stones in the wall opposite, but it was too dim for Theo to see much except that the room appeared to be completely empty.

He entered.

But the chamber was a dead end. Not a single door or window to speak of. What a pointless, infuriating room. Theo felt his frustration begin to build. He had been holding back the hopelessness without realizing how quickly it pooled, and now it overflowed. There was nothing left for him to try. Every slim glimmer of hope was inevitably extinguished. He was going to have to face Palakostos.

No sooner had the thought occurred to him than he heard a voice. It was deep—deeper than any voice he had heard before. Deeper even than that of Peitho, the subjugator who'd brought him to the temple. The voice emanated not from a single source, but at once from a great area. An entire wall. Or maybe the ceiling. The room could've been speaking to him. He looked around, but saw nothing in the dim purple light.

"Hello, my boy," the voice said. "Welcome to my temple. I am Palakostos."

17
Palakostos

Theo dared not move.

He heard a faint rustling before a wet slap as something dropped to the damp stones. Theo swallowed, the metallic taste of his own fear coating his tongue. In the purple light, he saw the silhouette of a snake raising its head to look at him.

"Palakostos," he whispered. He couldn't tell whether he felt some measure of relief that the Guardian took the form of a large serpent instead of the monstrous being he'd begun to imagine. He hadn't encountered many real snakes himself, but Roman had crossed paths with several during his travels, and spoke of their great agility and cunning. Some were poisonous enough to kill you with one bite.

At this memory, Theo's fear rebounded. He backed toward the exit, trying not to broadcast his intent, and searched for the door out of the corner of his eye. The serpent remained stationary.

"It is I," Palakostos said. His voice was clear, enunciating each syllable with deep, resonating intonation.

Theo could feel sweat beading on his brow though the room was cold and damp. "I've been told of your greatness," he said, stalling for time. "Many have warned me of your incredible power."

The Guardian let out a low, amused laugh that made Theo's stomach clench. He willed himself not to show his panic, though his efforts were probably in vain. If he could taste his own fear, no doubt the serpent could do the same.

"Of course they did. You have every reason to fear me, boy."

"Then maybe you'll consider showing mercy," Theo said.

"Mercy?" Palakostos said, taunting. "I am unfamiliar with the concept."

"I'm only one, unimportant boy," Theo said, hands clasped before him. "Surely you don't need every child that's brought to you."

When the Guardian replied, Theo could hear a smile in his voice. He couldn't imagine a snake's smile as anything but sinister. "I do not *need* you. I want you. And that is enough for me."

"Please."

"I will show you mercy by being brief."

The serpent darted forth.

Theo spun and fled. He yanked the door shut behind, the loud *bang* reverberating through the storage vestibule. Theo ran his hand over the handle, but there was no lock. The room wouldn't stay closed for long. He sprinted through the piles of crates, back the way he'd come. Perhaps he could hide in his cell.

Theo crashed into the door out of the vestibule, someone had locked it. A brief barrage of pounding fists and pulling ensued, but to no avail. He was trapped. With this exit blocked, all Theo had left were the massive, double doors on the other side of the room. He was just about to turn and run in that direction when he heard the small chamber creak open.

He needed to hide.

Theo ducked behind a pile of stacked crates. His teeth clenched and his heart raced. In the silence he could just make out the sound of the serpent slithering on its belly across the floor. Theo leaned to one side and peered around the corner. His view was restricted, but he could see the snake's tail against the stone.

"You may have been told of me," came the omnipresent voice again, "but you do not understand my great powers."

The sleek, scaly body began to writhe. For a moment, Theo allowed himself to believe they were undulations of pain. Perhaps something had gone wrong when the snake left his dwelling. This frail thread of optimism wasn't truly convincing, but it was all he had left. The truth became apparent moments later. And the longer he watched, the further he felt from hope.

The diameter of Palakostos' narrow, limbless body grew. The tail elongated, twisting past the place where Theo hid. Layers and layers of green-silver scales went from pen tips to coin-sized in seconds, until the Guardian was as thick around as Theo and at least twelve feet long. Theo had to clench his teeth to keep from making any noise as he watched. Suddenly the chamber felt very crowded.

Palakostos laughed. "Run from me now, boy."

Theo could do nothing else.

Taking a deep breath, his eyes trained on the double doors, he sprinted from his hiding spot just as the massive serpent began to slither away. He crossed the room in a few bounds, feeling the focus of yellow eyes on his back. Theo leapt over the snake's body, bounding away from the last rows of crates and up to the great wooden doors.

Grasping the iron handles, he pulled, throwing all his weight into the effort. Despite their tremendous size, the doors swung easily.

Without a second thought, he threw himself through the doorway as soon as the gap was wide enough—

And nearly tumbled to his death.

On the other side was a landing poised at the edge of a great sunken room at least two hundred meters long. At the opposite end, a grand altar stretched from the mosaic floor all the way to the cavernous ceiling above. Theo didn't have much time to observe any details. To either side, symmetric flights of stairs folded back and forth, descending to the ground below. Instinct carried him to the left.

As Theo descended into the massive hall, he felt himself diminish. This chamber was by far larger than any enclosed space he'd ever seen—perhaps larger even than the cavern below the Gateway. The steady sound of falling water echoed through the emptiness, though it was soon masked by the cacophony of his feet slapping against the stone steps.

Heavy slithering was soon to follow.

Theo fled, skipping as many steps at a time as he dared. Above, he could see Palakostos entering the yawning chamber. His scaly body shimmered in the orange light of the fires burning along the walls. Theo hastily scanned the room. He couldn't see a second door anywhere. The chamber was another dead end. He was out of options.

At the top of the stairs, Palakostos had brought his entire body onto the landing. The serpent threw his head back, opening his great maw skyward and baring fangs the length of Theo's forearm. With a tremendous shiver, Palakostos let out a cry of unmistakable glee and malice.

His body grew again.

Once more, the girth of the beast widened until he was as thick around as the metaliberus trees all over Eirini. The tail jutted out, unraveling like a thick spool of thread until it traveled halfway down the flights of stairs. Palakostos' oblong head inflated until he could have fit the boy whole inside his mouth without concern, and the fangs likewise expanded to the size of Theo's legs. Theo nearly tripped as he watched this unfold. In this new, colossal chamber, Palakostos had grown to fill the same portion of space as he had in the previous two rooms.

The hiss that followed filled Theo's head, pounding against his eardrums.

"Please, boy, keep wandering into greater spaces so I may demonstrate my true grandeur."

Theo had nowhere to go. He would never make it up the stairs and past the gigantic serpent. He had no hiding places left. He had been cornered.

Water splashed around his feet. Theo looked down. Puddles had formed on the mosaic floor at the base of the great stone altar. The water was coming from somewhere in the ceiling, he could hear it better now that he was closer. His eyes scanned the many levels of the altar as he approached. He could climb. It wasn't much, but it was somewhere to go.

Footsteps pounding faster with the new direction, Theo sprinted to the base of the structure. Behind him, the beast slithered down the stairs. The ground rumbled as Palakostos moved, sounding like low, distant thunder.

Theo scrambled up the front of the altar, ascending by way of one of the fluted pillars, and hoisted himself onto the first of four platforms. The facets in the designs gave him enough purchase to continue his climb. The floor fell away beneath him. Up and up he clambered, hand over hand and foot over foot. Once or twice, he almost slipped from the mold and moss that clung to the damp surfaces, but each time he managed to hold on. He was almost to the top when the giant snaked slithered to a stop at the base of the altar, staring up at his prey.

"Your resistance is amusing," Palakostos said. "But I am not one to tease a reward."

Theo did not reply, grunting with exertion as he pulled himself toward the pinnacle. Another ten feet and he would be there. The Guardian would have to wait for him to climb down.

"You will learn soon enough that you cannot escape from me," the snake said. Then he wrapped his body around the first column. Horror gripped Theo as the serpent began to wind his way up the structure. He hadn't counted on the Guardian's ability to climb. How was that possible without limbs?

Crying out in frustration, Theo renewed the speed of his ascent, though there was no longer much purpose. Gripping the top ledge, he pulled himself over the roof of the altar, his arms shaking. The climb had weakened him. Sweat drenched his dirt-caked tunic, the scarf about his neck, and the gossamer cloth still draped around his shoulders.

He looked up from where he lay.

Black water streamed down from a crack in the ceiling, gathering at low points on the roof and spilling down the sides of the structure. Black water. That meant he had to be somewhere below the Corporis Sea. Considering the trajectory of his descent with Erid, this shouldn't have surprised Theo. Yet, the sudden realization compounded his sense of isolation, crushing him as if the weight of the sea were sinking onto his shoulders.

Feeling defeated, Theo stood.

THUD.

His head collided with the sloped ceiling. In the dim lighting this far above the torches, he'd misjudged how much room there was to stand. Stars exploded before Theo's eyes, temporarily blinding him. He swayed, vaguely aware of the possibility that he just might topple over the edge before the serpent even reached him. He fought to stay balanced, and while the room spun, he was taken back to the underground passage at Eldra's house.

An idea occurred to him.

Finding stable footing, Theo clenched his hands into fists and waited for the great serpent to crest the top of the altar. He didn't have to wait long. Just as his dizziness ebbed to a dull ache, Palakostos' triangular head rose into view. The eyes were a lusty deep gold, his sharp fangs bared. The serpent swayed, assessing his prey, and Theo stared straight back at him with his chin jutting defiantly. He held his ground, daring the Guardian to take him.

With an angry hiss, Palakostos attacked. His head darted forth. His black-and-red throat opened to greet Theo, anxious to consume him, but the boy moved. Just as the serpent struck, Theo dived under the lunging body, narrowly missing the bottom jaw by centimeters. He slid, twisting to see if his plan had worked. He only had one shot, and it had to be strong enough to count.

With incredible force that shook the entire altar, Palakostos' head struck the cracked ceiling. The Guardian cried out in agony, his shouts reverberating throughout the vast chamber.

A deep rumbling followed, but Theo couldn't stay and watch. The giant snake recoiled from the impact, injured and disoriented. Blood patterned the scales on his head. He fell back and his grip on the column released.

Theo was there to meet him. He leapt from the roof of the altar and collided with the scaly body, clinging as they toppled. The floor of the chamber rushed up to meet them, but the snake absorbed most of the impact from the fall. Theo tumbled away across the floor, rolling to a stop on his back. He stared up at the ceiling, watching the shadowed place above the altar where the cracks widened, and widened, and widened.

Then the ceiling gave way.

Palakostos was still writhing beside him, but he seemed to have realized his temple was crumbling, and this renewed his anguish. Theo ran again. The static of rushing water filled his ears. Already he could feel the spray of the cascading sea on the back of his neck. He could see nothing but the stairs stretching up toward the vestibule.

Somewhere behind him, Palakostos was thrashing against the onslaught of water, hurling curses at Theo. "Insolent boy! I will eviscerate your mortal form. I will rip you from skull to perineum."

He wouldn't stay disoriented for long.

Theo reached the stairs and began his ascent, taking the steps two at a time. If he was correct, the Guardian would be forced to follow him into the storage room, where he would change to a more manageable size. Five flights and only a few more steps to go. Black water had begun to gather on the floor of the chamber, sloshing about like the great waves of an angry tide. The serpent was headed toward him now, more furious than before. Theo could hear the water splashing around him.

Theo threw himself between the wooden doors and slammed them shut. He had to be quick. No room for hesitation. No room for error. He darted to the right, grabbing the first lengthy item he saw—an iron candlestick, perhaps; he didn't take the time to determine what it was—and threaded it through the door handles.

It should buy him an extra second or two.

He ran past the first set of crates, then the next, until he found what he sought: a crate on its side. Theo undid the latch and swung the lid up to look into the narrow, dark space. For a brief instant, the gouge marks on the interior sent a chill down his spine. He couldn't imagine being trapped inside one of these, stolen away from his home above.

Hurriedly, he pulled the gossamer cape over his head, dragging it across his face. So light was the fabric that it resisted his movements, billowed by every disturbance in the air. Theo shoved it into the crate and let the lid swing shut. One end of the cape hung free between the seam, waving at him in slow motion, but he let it be.

THUD.

Palakostos had reached the doors.

Leaping across the aisle, Theo undid the latch on another crate. Teeth clenched, he slid himself inside and carefully closed the lid over his head. The darkness was instant.

CRASH.

The doors gave way. Theo heard wood splintering as they burst apart, debris showering the room. He could also make out the clang of his makeshift lock as it hit the stone, then the gasps of the Guardian as he changed shape, shrinking to a proportional size for his surroundings—his involuntary morphing. He grew after entering a larger space, and shrank before entering a smaller one. Was that why he preferred to hide his temple as far away from the surface as he could? What would happen if the Guardian found himself in open air?

Theo shook the curiosity out of his mind. The serpent was moving again, his form still far too large to fight. Theo mouthed repeatedly to himself that his plan would work. His silent mantra cycled through his thoughts like the blood through his veins. *This will work. This will work.*

Careful not to make a sound, Theo pushed two fingers against the lid, applying more and more pressure until it opened just a crack. He peered through. A portion of the shattered door was visible, swung wide on its obliterated hinges. He could see the next row of crates with the assortment of dull and rusted treasures leaning against them.

The serpent's tail moved below him.

Theo nearly gasped, his body going rigid. The snake had slithered up to his hiding spot, but he wasn't looking at Theo's crate. As he'd hoped, Palakostos had seen the tail of the cloth Erid had given the boy. He imagined a sinister smile plastered on the serpent's face, the tongue darting out and back into the wide slit of a mouth, tasting the air. Tasting Theo's scent.

This will work.

Theo would have to be quick. He would have but a moment.

Palakostos reached out his pointed tail, curling it around the bottom of the crate's lid. As he did so, his body shuddered and shrank in size. Once again, he was no larger than a normal serpent. Theo pushed his fingers a bit harder until the crack had grown to an inch. Then two.

In one swift movement, the serpent flicked up the lid of the crate and darted inside. The lid swung down again behind Palakostos as Theo threw himself from his crate and across the aisle. Heart racing, he flipped the latches shut. The box shook as the Guardian bellowed with rage from inside, but in his diminished form there wasn't much he could do. Theo backed away, breathing heavily, uncertain how long it would take Palakostos to break free.

He turned and flew back toward the cavern.

On the landing beyond the shattered doors, he stopped. Already, the chamber floor was submerged beneath churning black water. The surface couldn't be more than a few meters below him. When he looked across the way to the altar, he saw that the first platform was nearly submerged.

Darting back into the vestibule, Theo got down on his knees and began sliding a large chunk of the broken door across the stone. It was heavy, but large enough for him to sit on, which was what mattered. He grabbed a shard of broken board along the way. When he reached the landing again, Theo knelt with one leg on the door and used the other to push himself out into the room.

His makeshift raft crashed into the black water, sinking for a few terrifying moments before resurfacing. Theo clung to it with all his might until he was sure it would float, then paddled as fast as he could using the other piece of wood he'd grabbed. What he wouldn't have given to have the ferrywoman's powers in that moment. His oar was narrow and didn't provide much propulsion, and by the time he'd made it across the long chamber he was panting and his arms ached, but he had no time to rest.

Theo began his climb.

If he'd found the ascent difficult before, the challenge had increased trifold this time around. Water cascaded over every surface, splashing Theo in the eyes. The smoother sections had become slippery, and several times he had to scramble to regain his hold. Yet, though his progress was slow, he continued to climb until the turbulent influx of water crashed deafeningly in his ears. Finally, he pulled himself over the edge of the altar's roof.

The falling black sea poured into the room, a torrent gushing from the hole. His feet were instantly buried beneath the current as it raced toward the altar's edge. Theo trudged until he was beside the fissure. With difficulty, he grabbed one of the edges of the hole, feeling the terrifying velocity of the water rushing past his fingers. Already he felt submerged, the spray soaking his clothes. He had wondered before what it would be like to dip his head beneath the surface of the Corporis Sea. He would find out much sooner than he'd anticipated.

Bracing himself, Theo filled his lungs with as much air as they could hold.

He closed his eyes, then heaved himself up into the fissure.

The current pushed against him. A relentless jet of thundering force. It squeezed the life from him: stripped him of sight, of breath, and of sound. Theo's boots slid against the rocky sides of the fissure. His hands struggled to maintain their grip. Every muscle in his body tensed as he fought to get himself through the hole.

The pain from rowing flared in his arms and extended into his shoulders, but he began to gain ground. His fingers scraped against the stone. Water grabbed at his hair, trying to pull him back, trying to part his lips and fill his mouth, his lungs. His torso was through now. He got a knee out and onto the exterior surface. Then a foot. He was pushing himself away from the opening—

The current weakened.

Theo let his eyes open. For a moment he was lost.

He could see none of the things he expected to see. Not the temple beneath him, nor the underwater landscape of Kouros beside him. He was instead suspended in a field of stars. Impenetrable blackness surrounded him in every direction, but dotted throughout the blackness pressing in on him were gold-white pinpoints of lights, some close enough that he might reach out and touch them. Captivated by the unexpected vision, Theo remained frozen, hanging in place, unable to believe his eyes.

His lungs began to burn, but as Theo made to swim away, he beheld a new terrifying sight.

Up from the depths beneath him appeared thousands of corpses. They materialized from the darkness, rising, as if suddenly buoyant, toward the surface. Their eyes were closed, their bodies uncorrupted by the water as if they were merely floating in air. Theo kicked toward the surface and his flailing disrupted the astral illusion, shaking the stars from their stillness and plunging him into the blind submersion he had been expecting. His heart throbbed, his head swam, his feet thrashed, his lungs screamed. He didn't know if he was swimming toward the surface or away from it. He wasn't sure how deeply submerged the chamber had been. All this effort to find his parents and he might die after all. If no one should find him, would his soul stay suspended in this underwater starscape for all eternity? He might become like the bodies around him, drifting in the void.

The terrifying thoughts converged on him, swallowing him like the black water. He flailed against them too, the pain culling tears from his eyes that became lost to the sea.

18

The Ferrywoman's Tale

Theo had given up when he was pulled from the water. The darkness fell away, as did the sight of the rising corpses. He slid roughly into the bottom of a boat, where he lay sputtering and gasping for breath. His head throbbed. So did his chest. Theo continued sobbing, his tears mixed with the black waters that soaked him through and dripped from his skin, hair, and clothing.

He'd almost died. Had another second or two passed, Theo was certain his life would've ended in the Corporis Sea. In the moments preceding death, he'd felt nothing but fear. What an ugly way to go.

He couldn't stop himself crying. He didn't even know who had saved him, though only one possibility seemed likely given he wasn't being threatened. Demeres sat beside him, her hand resting on his back. At her touch, Theo looked up into her face. She could've been angry or upset. Instead, she looked worried and saddened by the sight of him.

"I'm sorry," Theo choked. He grasped at her knees, taking handfuls of her dress in his palms. "It's all my fault."

"Theo," she said, "are you alright?"

He scraped his hair back from his forehead. "I'm sorry. I wasn't listening. I wasn't thinking. I'm a shit son."

"Theo."

"I just wanted to get to my parents."

"You must calm down."

"He almost killed me. I was drowning."

"Theo—"

"I—"

"Theo!" Demeres took his head in her hands. She stared directly into his eyes and didn't move until he looked back at her. "Theo, please, calm down."

He sat up suddenly. Panicked again. "We need to go. They're going to come after me."

The ferrywoman lingered, her gaze flicking back and forth as she focused on each of his eyes in turn. She was afraid for him, or at least she had been. He could see worry creasing her forehead, and in the way her lips thinned into a straight line. She'd been afraid, which only deepened Theo's regret. Finally, she moved to the back of the boat and touched a hand to the tiller. They jerked forward.

"Can we go faster?" Theo asked.

"This is as fast as I can go," Demeres replied. Her tone had hushed. "It's alright now, Theo. They can't catch up to us by rowing."

As Kouros shrank behind them, Theo's breath slowed and his heart calmed. He ran a hand through his hair again, squeezing out the black water. It fell in cold splashes down the back of his neck, further soaking his garments. He doubted whether he would dry again completely without warmth. Sitting in his soaked clothes became uncomfortable. He imagined some heat must come from the lantern, and so he moved closer to the bow. Whether it helped him or not, huddling by the light soothed his nerves.

Once more, Theo was exhausted—emotionally drained by everything that had happened on Kouros. He had no idea whether he'd been on the island for a few hours or a few days. He couldn't tell anything about time here because of that damn unchanging sky. The constant state of tension and true fear of death had bled him of energy. What he had left was a strange emptiness. A helplessness. He wanted nothing more in this moment than to curl up at the front of the boat and drift.

"How did you find me?" Theo asked. He stared into the light of the lantern.

"I knew they would take you to Palakostos," Demeres said. "I'd heard rumors that his temple lay on one of the island's shores. It was all I could go off of, so I had to trust it was true. I sailed there, hoping I might see you."

"You were there when we arrived at the temple," Theo said, remembering. "I didn't look because I didn't want to draw their attention."

"Yes. I watched them force you inside, but I couldn't follow."

"That building on the shore—that wasn't really the temple. It was only an entrance hall of some sort."

"He wasn't inside?"

"No," Theo said. "There were guides waiting for me."

"Erid and Besmin."

"And others. You know them?"

"I know of them. Most humans meet them at some point in their life, whether they're aware or not."

Theo was silent, staring into the lantern. He didn't want to tell Demeres how the guides had made him feel. How their presence, while eliciting fear and apprehension, had also been encapsulating. The subtle calm of Erid's hypnotic, sinewy movements was still fresh. Perhaps she knew some of this. If she had met them while alive—whether aware of it or not—maybe she already understood.

"His temple was underwater," Theo continued.

"Was it?" Demeres asked.

Theo nodded. "When I realized that, I managed to trick him into breaking through a weak part of the ceiling. It caved in. I was able to escape."

"Up through the black waters."

Theo nodded again.

"I felt you dying," Demeres said. They briefly locked eyes. Her stare carried a tender expression he didn't quite understand. A concern, a longing, though not for her own sake. "I can tell you are alive because you don't feel the way the other souls do. You have a vibrancy they no longer contain. I could feel you dying, and that's how I knew where to pull you from the sea."

Silence followed, which told him that she knew what he'd seen while submerged. He wondered if she'd seen for herself, or if she'd come into the knowledge when she became a ferrywoman. Then again, she could also have been told by another passenger who'd fallen in. Theo couldn't imagine he was the first.

But when he turned back to face her, the far-off look in her eyes told him that the knowledge came from memory—her own memory—and that it was not a fond recollection. Again he saw the innumerable bodies rising from the depths. Had he remained beneath the surface, Theo imagined the bodies would've continued to rise until they met him; perhaps at the moment he died.

"When I was sick," Theo began, "my father used to stay home with me. He'd sing me songs and play games with me and cook me soups that would warm my insides. He'd hold me until I slept and run hot baths to sweat the fever from my body.

"My mother would bring books home from the library to read to me. They were always fantastical stories—she loved to read about magic and spells and all that. I loved hearing about them. I think that's why I was so keen to have real-life adventures of my own. She should've known I'd got that from her whenever she told me to get my head out of the clouds."

Demeres smiled.

"A couple times as a child," Theo continued, "I got real sick with fever. I could barely eat anything. The doctor told my parents not to stay in the room with me for too long. They should try to minimize contact because I was likely contagious and they couldn't afford to catch what I had.

"But the warning didn't stop them. Though they kept my sister Laila out of harm's way, they continued to care for me in my room. Doing all the things they did before. Not worried about the danger. I think that's what love is."

Theo had brought out the pocket watch and was turning it over in his hands by the lantern light. The dull surface shone yellow. Specks of moisture had breached the face, likely from his dip in the sea. He wished it was still ticking.

"I had a daughter," Demeres said.

Theo looked up at the ferrywoman. "You did?"

She nodded. "The most beautiful little girl you'd ever seen. She had the blackest hair, so dark you'd swear it wasn't there at night, and these round green eyes. And when she smiled—those dimples could've stopped any argument. Her name was Iligenia."

"That's a pretty name."

"It is," Demeres agreed. "She was my baby girl. I loved her with all my heart."

"How old is she now?"

"Not old enough." The last lights of Kouros faded into the darkness, and again Theo was left with the strange sensation that they were floating in a void of nothingness. All of the sky and sea was a black canvas. Theo and Demeres sat alone, the sole travelers in a dreamless sleep. Demeres closed her eyes, though she kept her hand to the tiller. "Iligenia was born frail. I was told I would be lucky to survive the pregnancy, but I continued forth. I wanted to prove the doubters wrong. When my daughter was born, they told me it was a miracle she lived. I was triumphant. I had shown them that I could do it. I could survive childbirth."

Demeres paused, though Theo knew the story wasn't over. He knew what was to come, and it made his heart heavy. Demeres wept. "I had her for five years. The last winter, she caught ill and was gone in five days."

Theo didn't know what to say. He watched Demeres as she struggled against the sorrow that still plagued her. She gripped the wooden pole with a tight hand. A hand that didn't want to let go.

"Nothing made sense after her death, nothing comforted me. So I fled into the woods. I ignored everyone who tried to stop me, warning me about the storm." Demeres' entire torso crumpled as she relived imaginary terrors. "It was so dark and cold. Snow piled up around my feet. I couldn't see anything, though I didn't much care to. I delved deeper and deeper into the trees, trying to leave the body of my deceased Iligenia behind.

"My husband found me. He carried me back to Ipsitfel." She opened her eyes to look at Theo, and he saw how red they were. "That night, I lost not only my darling daughter, but my sister as well, the person with whom I had shared everything since I was born. She went out looking for me and was not found until three days later."

Theo wished he had the words to heal Demeres, to make her feel better, but he found he could say nothing more than "I'm sorry."

She nodded, accepting his condolences though the words affected no real change.

"Death is cruel," she whispered, another tear trembling on the lower lid of her left eye. "Death took so much from me. We held the ceremony for both on the same evening. I couldn't pull the rope, so my husband did it for me. I watched my daughter disappear into the darkness, and then my sister.

"I took my own life that night," Demeres said, and looked away.

Theo's eyes widened.

"Demeres..." he said, but again words evaded him.

"That is why I am a ferrywoman. That is my appointment for what I did."

"So every ferry person... all of you—"

"Are the souls of those who took their own lives."

"Is it your task forever?" Theo asked.

"No." Demeres wiped at her eyes. "That is why the dead pay us for passage. After we have ferried so many souls to their place of rest, we are able to pay off our debt."

"And how far are you from paying off yours?" Theo asked.

Demeres didn't answer right away, avoiding his gaze. Instead she watched the wake of the boat as it fanned out around and behind them. She sighed. "I have already collected enough to pay it."

"You have?"

"Yes, maybe two times over."

"Then why do you stay a ferrywoman?"

"There are two reasons." Demeres shifted in her seat, and for the first time, Theo noticed a wooden box resting on the floor beneath her. "One is that I hope to see my husband once he has passed. I want to tell him that I'm sorry for leaving. In my grief, I hadn't taken the time to realize that he'd also lost a daughter. I could have confided in him, but instead I increased his pain.

"The other is that I'm afraid I will not be assigned to the same island as Iligenia, and if I am, she will have already forgotten me."

"Are family members not on the same island?"

"Most of the time, but not *all* the time. This is what scares me most."

"And you would rather stay a ferrywoman than find out?"

Demeres nodded, then after a few moments, shook her head. Emotion had made her weary too. Theo understood. Hearing the tragedies of her life and her eventual death had torn his heart. He could only imagine how deeply it affected her. They'd both lost family members too firmly etched in their souls for them to heal properly. Death had also seemed an inviting option to him in the days following the fire. Who knew if he'd have found himself in her position had he not chased his parents down the Gateway instead.

"Why are you punished for taking your own life?" Theo asked.

Demeres took a while to answer, long enough that Theo wasn't sure whether she would. Eventually, she replied in a hushed voice, "Many things remain a mystery in Nochlan, even to souls like myself or beings like the Guardians. I have heard talk though, and while some theories are so farfetched I'd never let myself believe them, some might have at least a strand of truth."

"What have you heard?"

"I've been told that Death envies and despises those who take their own lives, for their ability to do so. And that envy has only worsened with time. You see, Death once fell in love with a human, but they couldn't be together. Death cannot die, and humans... well, we're mortal. We live a second life in this world, but eventually we disappear, becoming part of a greater peace—at least, that's what I've heard. Death punishes us, therefore, by making us earn our right t o die."

"That sounds unfair to me," Theo said.

Demeres smiled joylessly. "Death is cruel," she repeated.

Theo scoffed. "Is there really anything to envy in dying?"

Demeres nodded. "Yes, of course. You may not agree with me now, but there is a certain beauty to our mortality, that we have a beginning, middle, and end through which to dimension ourselves. After all, a tale that continues forever could never be as elegant as a well-ended story."

"But that's terrible! Once you die, you're gone forever—at least to those you leave behind. You're just nothing."

"That's not entirely true," Demeres said. "Yes, we grieve for the loved ones we lose, but they don't completely leave us. That's the pain we feel: they become memories, the stories we tell, finished elegies. If they went completely, we wouldn't mind death, but what a waste of life to leave nothing behind. I couldn't weather that pain, though I understand it now. I was afraid and I didn't allow myself to find peace." Her eyes watered now. "I'm still afraid of many things, but I hope to find peace someday."

Theo looked down at the pocket watch still clutched in his hand. It seemed the more he was told, the less he knew. As always there were so many things he wanted to ask, but the breadth of everything she'd just told him weighed heavily on his mind. Again, he thought of how many ferries there were, now with the added notion that each of their owners had taken their own life. He didn't want to dwell on the idea, but it refused to leave him.

"You should rest again," Demeres said.

Theo shook his head. "I don't know that I can." He was no longer tired, and his wet clothes were uncomfortable.

"You should try."

"How much further do we have to go?"

"Long enough for you to rest."

Begrudgingly, Theo nodded, and lowered himself to the floor of the boat. He stared upward, his mind racing—arguments fought every phrase of what Demeres had said about appreciating mortality. He couldn't possibly fall asleep.

Yet as he peered into the black canvas, exhaustion met him again. He found his eyes closed without memory of closing them, while the coherence of his thoughts faltered. Before he slept, he mumbled, "Wake me before we arrive at Caelum?" But he was gone before the answer came.

"We're almost there," Demeres said suddenly.

Theo awoke at the words. Every part of his body tensed, including the hand still clasped around his father's trinket. He hadn't expected them to reach their destination so abruptly, but without reference he couldn't tell how long he'd been asleep.

Theo slid up onto the plank seat and looked around, searching for the foretold mountain of clouds. Instead, all that emerged from the dark was an endless cliffside stretching up and out of sight, as if they had reached the very limit of the underworld. Scraggly arches and outcroppings jutted up from the sea at the foot of the rock face, and their boat weaved between them. The closer they got to the cliffs, the denser the rock formations became.

Theo's eyes turned upward, searching for the top of the cliff. As he watched, a pair of massive orange and white fish soared out of the dark. They swam through the air, bobbing up and down, left and right as they weaved, almost playful. Each was easily twice the length of the boat and at least as wide around as a horse cart. Theo followed them with his eyes, mouth open, until they had passed out of sight.

"Were they..."

"Guardians? I believe so," Demeres said. "I don't know much about Caelum. I've never met the Guardians, but it seems they don't find you threatening."

"They know we're here?"

Demeres pondered. "I don't think they know where exactly, but I would guess they feel you, even as an innocuous addition to the souls they already keep. They don't appear agitated."

"That's a relief," Theo said, preferring this endless cliffside to the fiery profile of Kouros. He shook the image away. "Perhaps that means I won't run into problems here."

"Perhaps..." Demeres repeated, a distant echo. She was no longer looking at Theo. Her gaze had moved beyond him, to a place out in front of the boat. She wasn't afraid, but she was no longer relaxed. Feeling the hairs on the back of his neck stand on end, Theo spun around to see what had silenced his companion. He nearly fell backward off his seat.

Hovering about a foot above the water in front of the boat was a figure draped in a long, flowing brown cloak. No part of the being within could be seen, even with the shadowed opening of the hood facing their direction. As the fabric billowed in its own phantom breeze, however, it outlined features of a skeletal frame—pointed shoulders and a waist too narrow to allow for human organs.

Perhaps they were not being welcomed after all.

19

Matanda and the Weeping Cavern

Theo gripped the sides of the boat with both hands. He would not be taken captive again, not without a fight. This time, he was prepared—though in actuality, any immortal being in Nochlan was likely to be far stronger than a waifish adolescent boy. He wanted to tell Demeres to back the boat away but couldn't do so without breaking the tense silence. Instead, the ferrywoman spoke after a bout of silence.

"Who are you?" she asked.

"I have many names," the figure said. His voice—for Theo would have labeled it a male after hearing it speak—was deep and hoarse. "I have been referred to as Matanda, and you may do the same."

"Matanda," Theo said. Somehow the name felt familiar.

A sensation overcame him—that he'd never said the name when he was very young but had heard and repeated it more as he grew older. This couldn't be true though. He was certain he'd *never* heard or said the name before. It belonged to no villager in Ipsitfel he knew of, nor was it part of any colloquialism. Yet as it came off his tongue, another sentiment struck him—that he shouldn't be as frightened of the specter as he was. "May we pass? We're on our way to Caelum."

"I know that you are," Matanda said. Thus far, the figure had shown no physical indication at all that he interacted with them. His head did not move when he spoke, nor did his arms gesture. He remained perpetually in his slow-moving billow. Theo reassessed his earlier thoughts; the heavy cloak flowed more as if it were underwater, rather than in a breeze. "I cannot let you pass yet."

The familiarity continued to plague Theo, so he asked, "Do I know you?"

"I have been observing you for some time. We have never met face to face, but I watched you as a boy following the crowds to your precious Gateway. I watched you as a young man, scampering through the streets, skirting the responsibilities that disinterested you. I watched you tempt the unknown in the woods."

Images flashed through Theo's mind: shadows lingering behind him, fading into alleyways. He saw darkness peeking through doors left ajar, hovering out of a lamp's reach.

"Are... are you Death?" Theo's heart pounded as he asked the question, uncertain what he wanted the answer to be.

"No," Matanda said, "but Death and I are siblings, in a sense."

"What do you want?" Demeres said.

"It is not what I want, but what you want." Matanda's raspy drawl lingered in the air between them. Neither Demeres nor Theo spoke, unsure of what to say. The words hadn't sounded like an accusation, but they certainly didn't imply good news. This figure had just admitted to being related to Death, siblings even. What exactly did he know about their intent? "I have been watching for some time," Matanda repeated. "I know why this young boy has sacred threshold between the land of the living and that of the dead. I know what you've agreed to help him do, ferrywoman. I have followed you both across the Corporis Sea, from Eirini to Kouros, and now to Caelum. You, Theo, have come to bring your parents back from the underworld."

A flush crept up Theo's face the way it did whenever he had been caught doing something he was not supposed to. He glanced back at Demeres. The ferrywoman was at a loss, petrified with her jaw clenched as if she wished she could say something, but nothing came to her. Somehow, everyone in Nochlan seemed to know who Theo was and what he and the ferrywoman sought to do. That did not bode well for their attempts to skirt Death's attention.

"Are you going to stop us?" Theo asked.

"It is not my duty to patrol the sea, seeking to send unsolicited beings back to their realms. I do not enforce rules; I am merely a guide like your friend here, but of another variety," Matanda said. "I keep all the knowledge of the underworld and parse it out to those who seek it or who have earned it."

"Then why have you come to us?" Demeres asked. "If not to stop us, why do you appear now?"

Behind the hooded figure, Theo watched the giant fish Guardians swim past, spiraling around each other in a suspended ballet of light and color. It pained him to think that their visual beauty should be lost if ever there were no light around to illuminate them.

"I interest myself in few lives of the mortal kind," Matanda said. "I have watched Theo only because I sensed he would do something of great magnitude."

Why is Age watching you?

Mary Alba's austere premonition came back to him all at once. The way her manner had changed without warning. What else had she said? That he would be crushed by the sea—and encounter an endless forest. He'd nearly drowned in the Corporis Sea. Would Eirini count as the endless forest? There'd been a fourth thing too, but the phrase escaped him. Given the way in which she'd delivered the words, Theo had taken them to be a warning, but he'd survived everything she'd predicted thus far. Perhaps her vision had simply been a map of the path he should take to succeed.

"You will fail," Matanda said as if reading his thoughts. He continued to float, wispy brown draperies flowing around him while Theo's heart sank. "You will fail without the knowledge I can give you."

"What kind of knowledge?"

"Careful, Theo," Demeres said. "Nothing is freely given."

"Knowledge of how to reach the souls of Damon and Medina Sahiron, and how to retain them once they've been found," Matanda said. "But yes, your friend is correct. I'm afraid I cannot tell you what you need to know without payment."

"I don't have any money left with me," Theo said. "I used it all to gain passage."

"If coin is all that's required, I can pay."

Surprised, Theo turned to face Demeres. "What?"

She sighed. "I said, I can pay."

"Are you sure?"

"Yes—"

"But your debt?" Theo said. She hadn't taken a moment to consider, hadn't put any thought into how much payment might be required. He climbed over the center seat, kneeling in the boat before his guide. "You don't have to do this."

"I am sure, Theo," Demeres said. She ran a hand through his hair. It was still a bit damp, but only just. "I have plenty, and if it's more than my surplus, well, I'm not ready to pay off my debt yet anyway."

Gratitude filled Theo, and a smile broke over his face.

"This is a kind gesture," Matanda said, "but I do not seek physical currency as payment."

"I was afraid of that," Demeres said. Her face fell, and her hand came to rest on Theo's shoulder.

"Then what do you want?" Theo asked, confused.

At this, the hooded figure finally moved. He lowered his arms to his sides, his clothes falling limp. Then he sank slowly toward the sea until the bottommost tips of his cloak touched the water. "I am not greedy," Matanda said. "I will not ask for much. I will not even ask for all of anything you own. I have three items of knowledge to pass along to you, and for each I will ask of you a trait."

Theo looked again at his companion, but though Demeres briefly locked eyes with him, she said nothing. Likely, she was none the wiser about what the being might ask for, but it didn't hurt to hear his proposition. Theo could always refuse if the cost of knowledge was too high.

"For the first trade, I ask for one-third of all your wonder," Matanda said. "For the second trade, I ask for one-half of your willful ignorance, and for the last trade..." He paused, considering what would be a befitting exchange. "I request a quarter of your curiosity."

Theo was flabbergasted. He had no idea how he was supposed to present the hooded figure with any of these traits, but moreover, this payment implied startling effects. Unlike a monetary exchange, he would be directly altered—permanently. Theo suspected that traits like these did not replenish themselves.

"Wonder, curiosity, and... and..."

"Willful ignorance," Matanda finished for him. "These are what I ask."

"And if I don't agree to give you these?"

"I must allow you to go on your way, to attempt your task without my knowledge, and to fail."

"Can I trade for other traits?" he asked, though he couldn't imagine what else he would offer in return.

"I desire none such as these," Matanda said. "They are very valuable to me. If you were to choose another, I would need to take all of it."

That was definitely out of the question.

"You will not consider gifting me the knowledge without payment?"

"True knowledge is never gained without something paid. Otherwise, it is simply information without understanding."

Theo turned again to Demeres. She had dropped her gaze to the floor of the boat.

"Demeres?" he said, but she shook her head.

"I cannot tell you what to choose," she said. "These are your traits, a cost only you can bear. I have no say."

"Do you trust him?"

"I do. No immortal would lie about their relation to Death."

Theo peered into Matanda's hood again, but it remained a black void. The being didn't wish to persuade him either way. The decision would have to be his own. Should he refuse, then he would have come all this way just to face certain failure. He would never forgive himself if he ignored Matanda and came away emptyhanded. The choice became relatively simple then, even if he was wary about the cost. Portions of his wonder, willful ignorance, and curiosity were not such a steep price to pay for the return of his parents. At least he would retain some of each.

"How do I know that what you wish to tell me is necessary?"

"You cannot," Matanda admitted, "but I have no reason to trick you. Being a sibling to Death means that they have always the final say, and I am always cut short. I have no allegiance, and I gain no pleasure from your failure."

Theo weighed the options again in his mind, but he was running out of time. So much of it had been lost on Kouros, admittedly due to his own recklessness. He needed to decide.

"I'll do it."

Matanda nodded, and rose again a few feet into the air. "You were right not to approach Caelum from the harbor side. Caelum's Guardians are kind but firm, and they stop anyone who tries to enter the island through the main gates. Many who have not earned their stay here try to force their way in because of the island's peace and beauty.

"There is another way, one that I implore you to take advantage of. If you continue along these cliffs, you will come to the Weeping Cavern. Enter while the Guardians cannot see you. A secret passage lies inside, guarded by an echo. Open the door by telling the echo Death says you may enter. This is the first piece of knowledge I give to you."

Theo nodded, mumbling under his breath everything Matanda had just said. He looked to Demeres, who nodded to say that she had heard everything as well.

"When you go through the door," Matanda continued, "you will enter the Valley of Limbo. Walk straight ahead. Do not hesitate, do not doubt, do not turn around. Your walk may be very short, or it may take hours, but if you do any of these things you will be lost endlessly. That is the second piece of knowledge I give to you."

Theo felt his heart flutter. How was he supposed to keep himself from doubting? Wasn't doubt involuntary? If the threshold for doubt was absolute zero, then he couldn't see any way to succeed. If not, how much doubt was considered too much? Before he could ask any of these things, Matanda had moved on to the third item.

"I believe you will be able to find your parents, and you will be able to convince them to come back with you, but once they cross the threshold into the Weeping Cavern, you must keep their faces veiled. If you do not, Death will find them and know what you have done. That is my final piece of knowledge."

With that, the hooded figure went silent.

Each of Matanda's three pieces of knowledge churned sequentially in Theo's mind. He repeated them to himself, making sure he didn't forget anything. Even though the repercussions were daunting, the tasks themselves were straightforward. That constituted some relief. Nothing conjured confusion with more efficiency than complex instruction.

"Thank you," Theo said. His voice shook; he was so close now.

"I wish you well, Theo Sahiron," Matanda said. "I hope what you gain is satisfying."

He turned and began to drift away, his cloak billowing once again as if floating underwater.

"Wait!" Theo called. "You haven't taken your payment."

"When you bring your parents up through the Gateway, your payment will have been made," Matanda said. In the next instant, he vanished into shadow.

⸺•⸺

Demeres and Theo meandered below the cliffs in the direction Matanda had indicated, drifting between the rocky outcroppings. They kept track each time the fish Guardians passed, counting how long it took for them to come back again. Although the count wasn't always the same, they determined a reliable range—plenty of time to pass through a cave opening in the cliffs and out of sight before the Guardians returned. Theo wondered if the two spent their entire time patrolling this way—dancing endlessly—or if they did so only under suspicious circumstances. After all, they were never gone long enough to have circled the entire island, and always returned from the direction in which they'd last disappeared. A sort of pacing in the air. He felt less welcome each time they passed, but reckoned he was mostly at fault, since he was the one breaking into their home.

At last, Demeres spotted a triangular opening in the rock face large enough for their boat to pass through. After pointing it out, she slowed them to a crawl, trying not to be obvious about their intent. She brought the craft around a large, jagged outcropping, tucking the two of them out of sight of the cliffside. Theo kept his eyes trained in the direction from which the gigantic multi-colored fish would return. It should be any minute now. In the next instant, Demeres had dimmed the light until Theo almost couldn't see it, even while sitting closest to the lantern.

He nervously wrung the scarf with his hands. In his mind, Theo repeated Matanda's words. Without following these instructions, he would fail. Though he was grateful to have run into the immortal, he couldn't help but feel that Matanda's warnings meant other difficulties could present themselves once he'd entered the island. Dangers that didn't necessarily mean immediate failure, but ones for which he wouldn't be prepared.

A shimmer of white.

Theo's grip on the boat tightened. It was hard to tell whether the shimmer was real without the lantern. He had to rely on the glow off the sea from the phantom moon. The barest of details emerged from the darkness. Demeres caught his change in behavior and straightened. She was ready to move.

The fish Guardians continued their balletic dance through the air, weaving around each other in perfectly synchronized movements as if they shared a mental connection or were, quite possibly, one being. Down toward the water they dove, coming just close enough to brush the surface with a fin. Then back up along the cliff face they rose, spiraling around each other all the while. Theo had never imagined that creatures so large could embody this level of grace—he'd been taught to fear anything much bigger than a horse—but he was ready to admit his sparse knowledge of the world contained gaping holes. In this underground realm, those holes grew to chasms.

The Guardians passed over the entrance in the cliff wall, showing no change in demeanor or acknowledgment. They swirled and dove and rose until they had disappeared once again into the darkness.

Demeres held the tiller tight and they surged forward. Theo had to brace his feet to keep from toppling over. The ferrywoman expertly navigated through the cluttered water, dodging both large pillars of rock standing firm in their way and small, sharp boulders threatening to tear through the boat's hull by peeking just above the water level.

With a final turn, the boat broke into the narrow strip of un-inhibited sea directly below the cliff. The triangular entrance grew until it was large enough to fit them. No sign of the Guardians, though it was much too soon for them to be back yet.

At the last moment, Demeres pulled on the tiller and the boat slowed. They passed through the mouth of the cave at a comfortable pace, Theo reaching out a hand to brush the rock. He could hear trickling, like falling water. The sound came from all around them in the darkness, and even before Demeres had reignited the lantern, he knew the tight passage had grown.

They were in a cave the size of Eldra Vromía's conservatory. The sounds resolved into visible phenomena: black water seeped through cracks all around the rock walls and ceiling. It ran in rivers down the contours in the stone and fell from above like rain. Theo felt droplets touch the skin of his face and arms. He held out his palms and watched the moisture gather on his hands like many dripping tears.

They had entered the Weeping Cavern.

Theo drank in every angle of the room, lost in the austere beauty. Being enveloped in the cavern had a calming effect. The constant trickle spoke kindly to his heart and mind until they slowed to a pace he hadn't encountered since entering Nochlan.

"Hello," he called.

"*Hello*," came the response.

"There's the echo," Demeres muttered. She stopped the boat when they reached the center of the cavern. From every angle the sounds of dripping or running water greeted them.

"That's right," Theo said. He didn't exactly know why, but he stood. It felt like a more formal way of greeting the sentinel. Perhaps the echo would act kindly toward him if he showed respect. He called out again: "I'm Theo Sahiron."

"*I'm Theo Sahiron.*"

But this felt odd. Theo had never spoken to an echo as if it were a sentient being before—at least, not in a serious manner, not since he was a very young boy. He and Demeres were the only real people in the cavern, weren't they? His hands—which he'd raised to his mouth to shout—lowered.

"Well, go on," Demeres said, tapping his calf with encouragement. "Say the thing."

All the water sounds were getting to his head, distracting him. He needed to think straight.

"Death says I may enter," Theo said.

"*Death says I may enter,*" the echo replied.

But nothing happened. No hidden doors in the rock walls opened, no light came pouring out of an obscured hole. Nothing.

They continued to float on the placid water, and the cavern about them continued to weep, unchanged.

"Death says I may enter," Theo enunciated.

"*Death says I may enter*," the echo enunciated back.

Again, nothing happened. Already, he was failing. They hadn't even made land on the island yet and he couldn't carry out the instructions Matanda had given him. Theo shook his head. What was he missing? Had the door revealed itself and he just couldn't see it in the shadows? He considered asking Demeres to sail them closer to the opposite end of the cavern just in case, but reasoned that the opening would've presented itself in a more conspicuous manner had he been successful. These kinds of things always came with impressive reveals.

"Are you saying it exactly how Matanda told you to?" Demeres asked.

"Yes," said Theo. "He told me the door was guarded by the echo and I had to tell it that Death..."

His voice drifted beneath the trickle of a stream.

"What?" Demeres asked.

How could he be so stupid? The answer was simple.

Theo cleared his throat. "Death says you may enter."

"*Death says you may enter.*"

A low rumble built from within the rock around them. Water rained down with greater persistence as it was shaken from the walls and ceiling. The seismic activity created waves in the enclosed space, and Theo practically fell into his seat to keep from being thrown overboard. Light that was not theirs flooded the cavern from the far corner. A slab of rock detached itself from the rest and slid downward to reveal a passage through the stone. When the slab had sunken far enough to create a step up into the passage, it stopped, and the violent shaking ceased.

"I don't think that door's been used recently," Theo said, smiling a little though his heart hammered inside his chest. Demeres returned a weak laugh, but mostly he could tell she was shaken as well.

"That would be it, then," she said.

Theo nodded. "I suppose so."

"Do you remember the rest of what he told you?"

Theo nodded again but said nothing. He had just remembered that Demeres could not set foot on any island where human souls resided. That meant that she couldn't help him going forth. She'd have to wait here in the cavern until he returned, hopefully with his parents. He would be alone until then.

His guide placed a hand on the tiller and the boat glided over to the open door. The sounds of falling water had reclaimed the cavern once the shaking ceased, but they were not able to calm him as much as they had before. He couldn't forget what was coming next. He couldn't speak, his eyes trained on the lit passage before him. These were the last steps to reaching his parents, and any false move could end all of his efforts.

"You're going to be alright," Demeres said. The boat gently bumped the step. "Never lose sight of what you came to do. You'll find your parents, I know it. And you'll convince them to come back with you. I'll be waiting right here when you return."

Theo saw that Demeres wept. Streams of tears leaked from her eyes even as she hurried to wipe them away. He wished he could make her stop. He hadn't seen many adults cry before, he realized. The sight broke a cardinal rule he'd assumed to be true whether he'd ever voiced it aloud or not: the idea that adulthood was based on emotional pragmatism, that adults had the ability to remain resolute where adolescence may have yielded. The long-held idea began to dissolve in his mind, became silly even. Maybe adults hid their emotions from children to protect them—but that too was silly. Demeres wept with him, and without her help he never would have made it this far.

"Thank you," Theo said. "I—I'll be back."

Demeres nodded. "Now hurry before you run out of time."

Theo wiped his face and stood, forcing himself to breathe deep, slow breaths. His mind hummed, and he repeated Matanda's words over and over to himself as he stepped out of the boat and into the passageway.

It was time to travel the Valley of Limbo.

20

A Mountain Made of Clouds

The passage was short and straight but steep, leading up through the rock and lit by flaming torches. Theo walked with trepidation at first, but by the end he was scrambling, practically crawling against the incline to get out into the open air.

He emerged in a brilliant white-and-peach-colored forest. The bark on the trees was papery and pale, the trunks thin, though they branched wildly outward just above his head. None of them had leaves, only light pink petals that could have been stolen from budding roses. Beneath his feet, the ground was dry but soft, and the same grayish-white as the tree bark, which he might've mistaken for snow were he not standing on it. The sky overhead was light as well, lighter than any sky he'd seen in Nochlan, like an overcast day aboveground.

Theo stopped to appreciate his surroundings. Instinctively, he gripped the front of the scarf around his neck—tarnished and dirty but unmistakably, almost abhorrently blue in this setting—and the watch in his pocket. Reminders of his parents. He was here to find them. He mustn't be distracted.

He also realized then that he was completely alone. Nothing around him moved or gave any signs of life besides the trees. There would be nobody to talk to, nobody to ask directions from should he become lost, or questions were he confused.

He had only to walk straight.

So he went on.

His footfalls kept him company. The eerie beauty of the paper forest held its silence like a breath. Traversing this landscape felt like walking through a painting more than an actual wood. How could any real place be so *unaffected*?

On Kouros, the city had been teeming with souls. They spilled out of every building and every alleyway. They walked along streets and gathered in plazas. On Eirini, there were no people, but the liberi had come to meet him on the shore and Dolothyia had followed soon afterward. This place was completely deserted—it didn't look as if it had ever been touched by hand or foot. Nothing but solid forest. He continued to walk and walk and walk, but nothing changed. He couldn't even tell if he was walking in a straight line anymore or if he had gone in a circle without realizing.

He should—no. He was not supposed to hesitate—or doubt, for that matter—but it might already be too late for that. The trouble was whether the forest knew if he doubted internally, or only if he showed doubt. No hesitation. These were abstract terms. They could only be inferred.

Never mind. He just had to keep walking straight. That was what Matanda had told him. That was all he had to do, and he would find his mother and father.

Trying to distract himself, Theo began to hum. He hummed all the songs he knew: the ones his parents had sung to him when he was young and couldn't sleep; the ones the folk in Ipsitfel often sang at parties, songs about the founders and "Tabitha Rose with the Twinkle Toes" and "Barney's a Fella with One Eye." He laughed thinking about those two, but when he got to "Lower Me, Friends,

Into Death's Arms," he found he couldn't finish it and fell as quiet as the forest. A long time had passed since he'd last sung those songs, but he'd heard them so many times he felt he might never forget them, even in death.

Hopefully, the same was true of his parents. Hopefully they still remembered the songs of Ipsitfel. Hopefully they still remembered their home on Zemeckis Street. The Stick River, which wound partway around the outside of the town until it cut straight through the streets and under Ashmore's Bridge by their home. Hopefully, they remembered him and Laila.

In this way, seconds became minutes and minutes became hours.

Theo stopped walking. He lifted his head to look around. His feet hurt, unused to walking for this long without a break, while the rest of his body ached from uncomfortable travel without much rest or food. He hadn't been hungry, but just as he hadn't felt sleepy, perhaps he didn't recognize his need to eat even if it still existed. The forest remained unchanged, as if mocking him and his efforts. He could walk unceasing for days and wouldn't be surprised to never find anything, even the opposite shore of the island. Somehow, he'd already failed to navigate the valley. Somewhere, he must have gone wrong. He must've shown doubt or hesitation. Matanda had told him the path would vary in length, but the time he'd spent walking *had* to exceed that. This couldn't be correct. Simply couldn't be.

Theo sighed. His shoulders slumped. He sank to the ground and sat cross-legged on the pale gray dirt. He'd run out of songs to sing. His breaths grew slow and long all on their own, like the rhythmic whisper of a breeze. Perhaps he had failed from the start. He had believed in fated success, believed beyond reason that his wish just *had* to come true because he wanted it badly enough. How could he, a boy who'd never done anything spectacular in his life, have possibly thought he would succeed in bringing his parents back from death?

Grief had blinded him. It had exaggerated his bravery, or perhaps goaded his foolishness. He'd tried to change a system that had existed since the beginning of time. He'd sought to outmaneuver a god.

Or perhaps his only crime was wanting to see his parents again.

He was only a boy; he wasn't supposed to lose them yet.

Theo lay on his back, staring up at the gray sky beyond the petaled treetops. He brought the pocket watch out from his trousers and held it up above him, admiring the dull tin surface. His fingers swept the smooth sides, traced the seam, and pinched the hinge. The thin chain dangled onto his chest. He closed his hands around the watch and rested them on his stomach. The watch rose and fell with each breath.

Then he reached up with both hands—leaving the watch on his chest—and unwound the scarf. With his neck exposed, he realized what a difference the scarf had made, the warmth it had afforded him. He spread it across his forearms so that it covered the sky for a moment. The once royal blue was marred with streaks of brown and black, but he could still see the color underneath. He crumpled it in his hand, clutching both the fabric and the pocket watch to his heart.

Theo shut his eyes. "I'm sorry," he said. "I thought I could do it. I wanted to give these back to you."

And he wept.

It was not the same as when he cried on the boat after Demeres pulled him from the Corporis Sea. This time, his tears were hot, and leaked silently from the corners of his eyes. They ran in rivers across his temples. His breath never caught. He never sobbed nor hiccoughed. He simply lay on the ground while the minutes collected, thinking of his parents' faces and trying to remember every single detail he could—and even those little things he may have forgotten. When was the last time his father had sat him down to teach him something? At the time Theo might have resisted; made confident by his youthful independence. He regretted that now. When had he last held his mother's hand and not pulled away when she made to kiss him goodnight? He'd probably accused her of treating him like a child.

Finally, he opened his eyes.

Theo sat up and rolled onto his knees. Delicately, he set the watch aside and unfolded the scarf on the ground, taking care to push out every crease along the edges.

All he wanted was to find his parents.

He took the watch and placed it in the center of the scarf, then brought the corners together to make a pouch. Theo held it before him, his arm outstretched, afraid that if he brought it any closer, he wouldn't be able to follow through with what he was doing. He walked over to the nearest tree and reached up, taking a second to find a branch that fit some undefined criteria in his mind. The perfect branch. When he found one, he tied the pouch to it. The weight of the watch pulled the scarf straight down. The mixture of deep blue, brown, and black hung stark against the white and pale pink of the trees. Inside, he felt his heart twinge. He didn't know if the spell would work—if he'd done everything he was supposed to. There was no room left for doubt, only faith.

He backed a few steps away from the chosen tree, then turned and walked on, heading in a straight line. He wouldn't allow himself to look back, and not doing so required all his will. Instead, he lumbered forth through the woods again. His heart swelled in his throat, and he thought he might break into a run, but restrained himself. Running wouldn't get him there any faster, and he was much too exhausted.

Around him, the forest melded in a blur of whites and peaches. But the spell would work. The spell was his only remaining chance. He had nothing left he could think of.

All he wanted was to find his parents.

The scarf and the watch had been his final payment. Now he had nothing left of theirs to keep. If he didn't find them, they'd be gone forever. He'd have only his memories to rely on. He knew memories faded. He knew they couldn't be trusted to hold true, warped by the years that would come.

A small alabaster carving of a house lay in his path.

Theo bent to pick it up. His hand was just large enough to hold it. The house was rectangular with a pitched roof. A door was painted on one side and a window on another. Other than that, the figurine was white, leaving the rest of its details—the roof shingles, the eaves—to the shape. The house felt incredibly fragile. He set it back down and looked up.

He was staring down a long outdoor marketplace. Buildings lined either side of the street. Though they varied in design, each was made of the same, white wood with pitched teal-tiled roofs that curled up at the eaves. Lanterns, which looked to be made of the peach petals clinging to the trees, hung from ropes strung over the street. People milled about, deep in conversation. Some looked at him as he approached, but most ignored him completely, going about their business as if he weren't there at all. He preferred these to the strangers that made eye contact with him. If people ignored him, he felt less like an intruder.

The curve of the road hid where it led, but Theo could guess what lay at the end. The looming shadow made him pause in the middle of the street to stare.

The town had been built at the foot of an enormous mountain. Unlike the ones he'd seen around his home, this mountain was formed entirely of lavender clouds. In form, it retained the conical shape of a mountain, building toward a peak high in the gray sky, but the surface billowed and churned. He could see spirals of vapor folding in and around each other all along the slopes. He wanted to know what walking on those clouds felt like, but he knew—somehow *knew*—he would never have the chance to experience this.

Theo began walking again, looking around at all the faces as he went. His parents were here somewhere, but would they be out in the open or inside one of the buildings? He wasn't even sure they'd look the same, though he couldn't imagine why their appearance should be any different. The thought also crossed his mind that maybe he should call out to them, but attracting attention seemed like a bad idea. Though the people at the market talked to each other, it was nothing like being in Cirillo Square at midday when everyone conversed so loudly he could barely hear himself think. Conversation in this market remained at a comfortable volume, as if louder noises couldn't exist.

Theo kept walking. Something inside him said he'd know when he was in the right place. He wasn't yet there. Perhaps this was some side effect of having cast the finders spell. After all, he didn't mean to stop in front of one of the unremarkable houses, but he did. There was no front door. Instead, an open archway welcomed him inside.

Furniture decorated the interior, similar to the furniture in his family home before it burned down. Similar sofa, tables, trinkets. Everything similar, but none of it the same. He walked through the entryway, a living room, and a kitchen with a standalone oven tucked into the corner. Already he was at the back of the house—another open doorway—and could see into a small enclosed yard.

There they were.

Theo's knees nearly gave way.

"Father?" he said. "Mother?"

21

Matters of Memory

They looked up at him from beneath a pink-and-white tree. Petals fell over them like light rain. Both wore garments similar in style to what they might have worn back in Ipsitfel, though these were pure white. His mother's dress cascaded from her collarbones to her ankles, the waistline accentuated by a wide sash. The thin, silky sleeves came down from just below her shoulders and fanned outward. Her hair was pulled back into the same tight bun as always, her round face tinted by rose-colored cheeks. Beneath his father's bushy eyebrows and slate-gray eyes, his shirt appeared neatly pressed, and fit as though it had been made especially for him. Likewise, the trousers he wore were a similar silky material. Even his parents looked similar though subtly different. Their faces were fuller, wrinkles scrubbed away save for those that had more to do with expressions than age. They had more color to their cheeks, a deeper hue in their eyes.

And they looked at him surprised, but also strangely unfocused, startled to find a visitor in their midst.

When they said nothing, he tried again. "Mother, Father. It's me, Theo."

Medina Sahiron opened her mouth briefly, drawing in breath. She closed it again. Then opened it once more, exhaling the name. "Theo," she said. "Theo. I know you."

Theo felt a stabbing pain in his heart at her airy tone. She lifted her hand before her as if his image were a blurry memory and she could wipe away the smudges. Her brow furrowed in concentration. She looked angry with herself for not remembering something which was clearly important. But how could she forget to begin with? He was Theo, her one and only son. She had spent the past fifteen years raising him, nurturing him, teaching him, and watching him grow. That couldn't all be lost already.

Damon stood beside her, silent.

"Please," Theo pleaded. "It's me, Theo. I'm here. I've come to take you back with me."

He pointed to the door, looking back and forth between the two of them. His parents stood beneath the tree, errant petals raining down on them sporadically. Their vague expressions lacked recognition. He was but a curiosity.

How he wanted to shake them, to run at them and grip them both by the shoulders, daring them with a locked gaze to remember him. They had cooked him meals, sat at his bedside when he was ill, scolded him when he disobeyed them—which had been far more often than he wanted to admit now. Ice ran through his veins, a cold realization that he might be too late after all. He had come all this way only to find them when his rescue efforts were no longer of any use.

His parents continued to observe him, his mother looking inquisitive and frustrated at her deficient memory, his father immobile and unreadable. They looked like the parents he loved, but would that suffice if only their appearance was the same?

"Please," he pleaded. "I'm your son."

"Theo?" His father's voice became sharp with recognition. His face brightened and his hands flew up.

His mother's memory returned a moment later. She clasped her hands over her mouth. Tears welled in her eyes, and she shook her head in disbelief, while Damon rushed forward.

In one swift movement, Theo's father wrapped his arms around him and lifted him into the air, spinning around. The embrace was firm. In a flash Theo felt like a child again, laughing joyously. The world swung around him, objects devolving into blurs of motion. The impossible had proved possible. His parents were here, together, and he hadn't been too late. He would need to thank Demeres a million times over for her help. Ismena would be in awe that his plan had worked. He would have to keep his mother and father a secret, of course, but maybe he could tell some people. Roman would understand. Yes, he could tell Roman. How would he reintroduce them to Laila?

Laila. How would his sister take their return? He could imagine her surprise when she saw them standing in the light of day. She was always so reserved, but certainly this would be an elation she couldn't mask.

The world stopped spinning and he was set back down again. As the grass met his feet, his mother rushed forward and threw her arms around his neck. Then she kissed him on both cheeks and held his head in her hands.

"Theo, what are you doing here?" she asked. "How did you get here?"

"And what happened to you?" Damon said, looking at Theo's tattered and soiled clothing. The tunic was unrecognizable. Brown covered far more of the cloth than white. Parts of the material had been shredded along one side and his back.

"How did you find us?" his mother asked. Then her eyes widened in fear. "You're not... You didn't... Are you?"

"I'm still alive," Theo said. Both his parents breathed a sigh of relief. "I went through the Gateway—Ismena helped me. She lowered me down a couple days after your Descension ceremony. We went at night, so nobody saw.

"Then I met this ferrywoman. She's been helping me find you. She took me across the sea in her boat. We had to ask which island you'd been sent to, but I had to hurry because you were going to forget what it was like to be above. The Guardian of Eirini, Dolothyia, didn't know how much time I could spare. So I made Demeres take me through the canal at Kouros," Theo had started slow, but the more he talked, the faster his words came. He hadn't realized how much he needed to explain what he'd been through, but telling his parents comforted him. Perhaps it reminded him of running to his mother and father in times of difficulty. They didn't interrupt his rambling, waiting until he'd finished speaking and stood in the yard heaving labored breaths.

Damon grabbed Theo by the shoulders and stooped to look at him. Theo didn't remember the graying stubble on his father's face, though the crow's feet by the corners of his eyes were familiar. The prominent chin and the wide shoulders were still the same, but his irises, though bold in hue, weren't quite the same color. Also, his hair could have been dusted with ash; it was grayer than before. He might have imagined it, but Theo thought Damon already looked different from when he'd first entered the yard.

"Why did you come here?" his father asked.

Theo struggled to find words. "I... I needed you, and you were gone—both of you. I'd left for—for an hour, if that much, to get a scarf for Mom. And you were both taken from me. It isn't fair, because we were supposed to be together for much longer than that. You aren't supposed to die. You're supposed to be with me and Laila. We don't—we don't... What's going to happen to us? I don't know what to do. Now is when I need you most, and maybe it's because you're gone that I need you, but that's the problem, isn't it?" He was rambling again.

Medina had drawn closer while he talked. She stood beside her husband, both of them staring at him with expressions of despair. Helplessness.

"Theo, I'm so sorry," his mother said.

"It's not your fault—"

"The fire—"

"I know." Theo wasn't sure he was ready to hear what she was about to say.

"—spread so quickly. We didn't realize what was happening until it had engulfed the ground floor."

"We were almost out of the house when we realized Laila was still in her room," his father continued.

"I ran back up the stairs to try and find her," Medina said. She was hugging herself, staring ahead, unfocused. "I screamed her name, inhaling smoke. The fire was so hot—I couldn't believe how hot. I remember a loud crack and my body jerked. I lost consciousness. That must have been when I died."

Damon nodded. "A portion of the roof collapsed. I heard the crack too and ran after you, but was hit by falling debris. That fire spread so fast, I never saw anything like it. I think I was hit by a falling beam. I don't know if that's what did it or if the fire killed me afterward."

Theo stared back and forth between the two of them, his insides terribly knotted at hearing the firsthand accounts of their own deaths. If he hadn't been in trouble that day... if he hadn't taken his time going to the market...

"Laila wasn't in the house," he said. "She must've left without you noticing."

"She did?" Medina said.

"Where did she go?" his father asked.

"She went after me," Theo said. "She knew I hadn't learned my lesson. She knew I would do something stupid, so she followed me. She found me at the edge of the woods."

Neither of his parents made a sound. Their expressions may have faltered for the briefest of instances, but they showed no further reaction to his confession.

"Ismena came to tell us what was happening," Theo said. "We saw the smoke as we were running home."

"My poor darlings," Medina muttered.

"Laila doesn't know I came," Theo said. "Otherwise she would've tried to stop me."

"As well she probably should have," Damon said.

"I came to bring you back."

At his admission, tension thinned the air. Again, neither of his parents showed much outward reaction, but a subtle shift in their stances told him that his statement had completely floored them. Petals fell like raindrops while his declaration gathered overhead in a dark, thick cloud.

"What did you say?" his mother asked.

"I said I'm going to take you back with me."

"That's not possible," Damon said.

"It is," Theo said. Admitting now that his plan could work, a sudden light dawned inside him. He'd had help from the Guardians of Nochlan, and while they'd cautioned him against the dangers of his goal, they hadn't dismissed him outright. Here he stood with both his parents, poised to succeed. A smile wound its way onto his lips, a smile he couldn't seem to wipe from his face. "Matanda explained it to me."

"But... *how?*" Damon asked. "We're dead."

"I came with a ferrywoman, my friend, Demeres. She's the one who brought me here. She'll take us back to the Gateway. Then you can come back to Ipsitfel with me."

"Theo—"

"Laila and I need you both. We miss you so much."

"My son," his mother tried to interject, but Theo would have none of it.

"We're not ready to be without you. Laila is smart and responsible, but she can't lead a household."

"Listen—"

"We don't have a home." Theo hadn't meant to raise his voice. Realizing how exasperated he'd become, he willed himself to calm down. "We don't have anywhere to live. Our house is gone, our parents are gone. We must rely on the kindness of our friends and their families, but there's a very real chance that this means Laila and I will be separated for good."

He could only hope his words were having some effect. As he said them, he realized truths even he hadn't yet considered: that he and Laila might never live under the same roof again. He was too old to properly start anew as someone's child, yet too young to live independently. He couldn't keep the pleading from his expression as he waited for his parents' response. Tears leaked from his father's eyes and his mother looked at a loss for words, her worst fears come to be.

As if on cue, Damon and Medina turned to each other. Theo couldn't control his trepidation. They were still his parents, and try as he might, he couldn't make them do anything they didn't want to, especially not this. The decision had to come from them.

"If you say you know the way," Medina said, "we will come back with you."

22

Leaving Caelum

"You will?" Theo almost couldn't believe what he was hearing. He'd expected more resistance, for them to tell him he was being impulsive. To have them agree without much argument was more than he could have hoped for.

His mother nodded, then looked to his father, who nodded as well.

"Thank you!" Theo bounded forward and wrapped both of them in an embrace. For a moment, all he wanted was to breathe them in, to feel how it was to hold them close again. They tensed at first, an odd reaction he barely noticed but for a flicker of doubt, then relaxed into his arms. "Thank you so much."

"We didn't mean to leave you," his mother said. "I just hope we can make things better."

His parents didn't bring anything with them as they followed their son out of the house. Theo sensed that nothing there truly belonged to them anyway. The items were placeholders, existing to provide a sense of familiarity.

They wandered out onto the street of the bustling marketplace. Although nobody paid him any more attention than they had on his arrival, Theo couldn't help his rising anxiety. The feeling was contagious, and he sensed it spreading to his parents. Their heads swiveled this way and that, quickly assessing anyone who looked their way or approached them. None of the marketgoers spoke to them directly though, and they made it to the end of the street without hassle. The small figurine of the house lay on the ground where Theo had left it. He resisted the urge to pick it up again. His curiosities were best held at bay until he felt safe. When they passed the figurine, the noise from the marketplace died away and Theo found he couldn't see it anymore when they rounded the bend in the path.

He and his parents breathed a collective sigh of relief. Even so, Theo kept glancing behind them from the corner of his eye as they continued to walk. If anyone followed, he didn't want to be caught off guard. But no one did. The path behind them remained clear.

Were his mind at ease, Theo might have stopped to wonder how he knew the way back, but the immense relief at having convinced his parents instilled in him a confidence he'd lost. He recognized the differences in the trees, the ones he'd passed and the ones he hadn't. In the distance, the mountain of clouds loomed, and he used that too as a compass to guide the way. He walked without hesitation and his parents followed, always a step behind. Part of him was surprised that neither of them spoke as they walked through the Valley of Limbo. But he had the idea that his parents wouldn't trust themselves with words until they were off the island, and perhaps they didn't want to distract him from retracing the way. Neither did Theo feel the need yet to speak, letting his mind carve the path through the wood. A small part of him even hoped that he might round a bend in the trail and see the spell still hanging from one of the branches, but Dolothyia had explained that the ingredients would be consumed.

After a time, which seemed both longer than and only a fraction of the time it had taken to find the village, Theo spotted the tunnel in the distance. As soon as the entrance came into sight, he wanted to start running, but now was not the time to rush things. Yes, he wanted to get back, but he didn't think his parents were in any state to chase after him. They seemed slower than they had been in the village. Their pace became methodical.

Perhaps dying had its side effects.

Still, they followed him without question as the path dipped downward and the ground curled up around them. The forest retreated from sight until the only signs of it were the tips of branches peeking over the lips of the ground above.

At last, the tunnel opened its maw to swallow them. The moment Theo's foot entered the passageway, the torches sprang to life again. He could hear his parents inhale sharply, anxious that they were soon to leave what was meant to be their final resting place. Three sets of feet clicked on the stone ground, the clatter echoing off the rocks. Up ahead Theo could see the doorway back into the Weeping Cavern. Almost there. All that would be left was to get across the sea. Then he'd sneak them back aboveground without anyone noticing...

Theo stopped, and his parents came to a halt behind him.

"What is it?" his mother asked.

Theo spun on the spot to face them. "I almost forgot," he said. "We have to cover your faces."

"Cover our faces?" his father asked.

"Yes." Theo felt a little guilty for forgetting this detail. He hadn't made his parents fully aware of the circumstances under which they could return to the surface. "That's part of what you have to do for this to work. We have to keep you hidden so that Death doesn't know I've stolen you."

The silence that followed—though only a few seconds long—felt insurmountable.

"How do you know this?" Medina asked.

"I spoke with Death's brother, Matanda. He told me that was one of the conditions."

"We must hide from Death?" Damon asked. Theo nodded. "That's a fearful prospect."

Theo averted his gaze. "It's a small price to pay for me to keep my parents," he said. In the end he sighed, and turned back to his mother and father, who hadn't wiped the worried expressions off their faces. "If it was impossible, none of the Guardians would have helped me."

"I suppose that's true," his father said.

Theo thought for a moment more, then reached down to grab the hem of his tunic. He found a tear, which he pulled at, ripping off a chunk of the cloth. Then he tore that chunk in two to create swathes large enough to cover their faces. It would have to do for now. The dirty cloth he handed them was in stark contrast to their pure white clothes. His parents tied the fabric around their heads so that only their eyes were visible. Matanda hadn't said exactly how much of the face had to be covered, so he hoped this would be enough.

Was this as much as he would ever see of his parents' faces again?

Shaking the thought away, Theo turned and led the way to the door. The light from the passageway filtered out into the dark cavern. Theo listened to the trickle of water seeping down the rock walls, searching the darkness for the lantern light.

"Demeres?" he said in a harsh whisper. Beside him, his mother held the cloth to her face and tried to see what he was looking for. The name echoed. He came down onto the step, leaving the enclosed passageway.

Theo was about to call for the ferrywoman again when her light appeared from around a corner, piercing through the darkness. She sat at the back of the boat, hand on the tiller, guiding the watercraft through the shadows.

The boat came to a stop, bobbing gently before Theo.

"You're alright, then?" she said, looking him up and down.

Theo nodded. He let a smile break over his face. "Demeres, meet my parents."

With a swift gesture of his arm, Theo directed her gaze over to the doorway where his parents stood. The flickering torchlight embellished the dark shadows created by their masks. Their eyes were marred by apprehension. Demeres gasped.

"You... They're... You found them," she said.

"Yes."

"And you brought them back."

"I did."

"I wasn't sure—I guess I knew you would, I just didn't imagine it could happen." Demeres put a hand over her heart, her eyes transfixed.

Theo waved his parents over. "It's alright," he said. "She's the one who brought me here."

Very cautiously, his father left the doorway. Damon held Theo's arm as he stepped down into the boat, and when he brought the other foot forward, a strange unease seemed to overcome him. Damon shook as if unbalanced, clutching tightly at his son. He was out of breath.

"This is Demeres," Theo said. His brows creased in concern.

"Hello," Demeres said.

"Damon Sahiron." Theo's father looked back toward his wife, who lingered in the passageway.

Theo's mother still had a hand to her face, holding the cloth as if afraid it might fall. She kept looking back and forth from Theo to the boat, the wariness in her eyes unwavering.

"Please, Mother," Theo pleaded.

"You're certain this will stop Death from finding us?" she asked. "This will work?"

"Yes," Theo said, though he would be lying if he said he was *absolutely* certain. He couldn't tell whether Death knew what was happening or not. Not until they were above ground again, and even then, who knew? He imagined hooded figures like Matanda flying across the water toward them, ready to seize his father and mother. Or perhaps a large, impenetrable shadow—his own interpretation of Death—would be waiting for them by the shore. He couldn't gauge whether their efforts were succeeding or not, just that his father sat resolutely in the ferry, completely off the island.

"What will happen if we are found out?" Medina asked.

Theo turned to look at the ferrywoman. "There are no islands of punishment, right?"

Demeres struggled to answer. "Well, yes, but that doesn't mean there aren't consequences."

His eyes lingered on her hand which held the tiller. The seat under which she kept the payment she needed to settle her debt with Death. If this was her punishment, what other punishments might exist?

His mother backed away a step. "What if we are never granted peace?"

Again, Theo looked to Demeres for answers. She shook her head, frustrated by the questions and her own uncertainty. "Death is jealous and quick-tempered, but they are not known for being cruel."

"I...don't know what will happen if you are found out," Theo answered truthfully. "I didn't think that far ahead."

Medina Sahiron glanced up the passage, clearly longing to be back in that quiet village at the base of the mountain. For a moment, he thought she might actually decide to go back on her word. He felt the press of time at his back, not just for them this time but for himself. Then she came down onto the step beside Theo and he breathed a sigh of relief. She too held his arm while she entered the boat. Again, the same sort of momentary imbalance passed through her, but afterward she seemed unchanged.

His mother looked to their guide. "I'm Medina Sahiron," she said.

"Demeres." The ferrywoman nodded, but Medina didn't sit down just yet.

"You look... familiar," she said, frowning.

Demeres turned her face away, as if ashamed of being recognized. She cleared her throat. "I was from Ipsitfel when I was alive."

"Were you?" Medina said. Her tone drifted, and her rhetorical question went unanswered as she sank onto her seat.

Theo followed them in, sitting on the narrow bench near the bow where he'd spent most of the journey. This time, he sat backward, facing his parents and Demeres. His heart thundered, and he tried not to blink too much, afraid that in a flash his mother and father might disappear. Between their heads, he witnessed the wary expression on the ferrywoman's face.

Her hand on the tiller, she adjusted her posture, and the boat moved away from the step.

"To home?" Theo asked in a purposefully light voice.

"No," Demeres said. All eyes turned to her. "There is somewhere you should go first."

"But—but we need to get back to our shore," Theo said. "We shouldn't stay here any longer."

Demeres held firm. "No, Theo. You've had your say, but this time you will listen to me."

23

The Weaver's Gift

The boat drifted so slowly that at times Theo had to stare hard into the black surface beneath them to make sure they were still moving. He'd been surprised to hear Demeres mention the Great Weaver.

"Areope, she's called," explained Demeres, and though she knew Theo was anxious to return to his shore, she'd insisted a visit would be best for both his mother and father. Despite his impatience, Theo conceded.

But he'd expected them to arrive at another island. Perhaps a small one, if this Areope lived alone. However, drifting along at their painstakingly slow pace, they still hadn't arrived anywhere notable. Their surroundings remained as impenetrable and black as ever, the sea indistinguishable from the sky.

His worry wasn't helped much by his parents' continued silence. Since they'd boarded the ferry, neither had spoken a single word. Theo wrote this off as their apprehension about being unexpected fugitives. But he wished they'd have at least asked some questions. All in due time. When they reached aboveground, safe from prying ears, he'd explain everything.

The boat came to a stop, though there was no land around them.

"We've arrived," Demeres said.

Theo stammered, trying to find a question to summarize the obvious.

"The Great Weaver, Areope, lives here. It's known as Rimi." The ferrywoman raised a hand to gesture off the port side.

Theo stared into the darkness, straining his eyes. For a moment, there was nothing, then two small flickers of light appeared out of the gloom no less than a hundred meters from where he floated. The longer he stared, the more flickering lights appeared out of the swollen black canvas.

"Can't we get any closer?" Theo asked.

Demeres shook her head. "We can't. The water is too shallow."

This confused Theo, who peered over the side of the boat. But trying to see beneath the water was like trying to see through a stone wall.

"Will you stay with my parents?" he asked.

"I will." Demeres looked to Damon and Medina, who turned to face her. "We'll wait for him here."

"I won't be long," Theo said. He stood, and without a moment's hesitation, stepped over the side of the boat and into the sea. For the second time, the water came to meet him, but instead of swallowing him whole as it had before, his foot sank only a few inches below the surface, enough to cover the tops of his shoes. And though his feet were submerged, Theo felt no moisture touch his skin. Instead, walking across the surface felt like having the wind resist his steps.

He waded away from the boat into the open water, feeling the whole of the underworld opening into an unfathomably vast expanse larger than the night sky. Vulnerability dogged his footsteps, but he tried to hold his pace steady and his head high.

Up ahead, the dots of light grew closer. They became twinkling points of brilliance dancing just below the surface. Clusters formed here and there below him, and he was reminded of the stars in Ipsitfel. Theo tried moving a foot to touch one, but the water curling around his ankle distorted the light as if it were only a reflection. Yet when Theo looked up, the sky was still blank and black.

A monument appeared out of the darkness, shimmering opalescent in the pale glow from the water stars. It rose above the surface of the sea over wide stone steps, a great spiral not unlike that of a snail's shell. Theo's best guess was that it stood at least four meters in diameter: greens, blues, yellows, and an entire assortment of other iridescent colors gleaming back at him.

And then he saw, at the foot of the monument, an altar. It was large enough that he could have lain comfortably on it. The stone was yellow, but that could've just been the tint of the lights. The altar stood at Theo's waist, and when he drew level with it, he gazed down on what lay there.

Four pieces of folded cloth were spread across the tabletop. The first looked satiny, emerald and white. Theo could imagine how smooth the fabric would feel, though he was afraid to touch something so regal given his filthy state. The second cloth was the same translucent gossamer Erid and Besmin had worn on Kouros. Material so thin and see-through seemed of little use, so he passed on. The third cloth was heavy and brown, rough like coarse soil woven into fabric. It might do, but appeared overly heavy and opaque. The last was black lace, thick enough that he could see the intricate patterns fanning across the material, but not so much that he couldn't still see a hint of the stone table beneath. He was reminded suddenly of the statues in Roman's home—they'd been covered by a similar fabric.

"You appreciate my work?" came a hoarse voice out of the darkness. It sounded like a very old woman.

Theo looked around, unable to discern the source of the voice. Before he could formulate an answer, it came again, chuckling.

"Do not worry, I mean you no harm."

"You are Areope?" Theo asked. He would have felt much better if the Great Weaver had shown herself.

"I am," the voice said. "And who might you be, boy?"

"I am Theo," he said.

"Theo," Areope breathed. "What is Theo doing in Rimi?"

"I have admired your work and was hoping to ask for some of your fabric."

The Great Weaver was silent, and Theo hoped he hadn't offended Areope somehow. His eyes continued to wander, though he tried not to be too obvious as he searched for the being. Nobody approached him out of the dark. As he came to face the monument again, he noticed the ends of two hairy black ligaments folding over the top of the spiral. Spider legs were the first thought to enter Theo's mind, but he hoped he was wrong. The clinging appendages were at least as thick as his legs.

"I have only ever had Guardians or gods come to my keep," Areope said. The voice was kind, but Theo was wary. "Your answer leaves many questions. Yet I sense that you are in a hurry." One of the legs—if indeed they were legs—shifted a meter to the side, and Theo's stomach squirmed. "You did not come alone."

"No, I didn't."

"I see," Areope said, and she sounded almost sad.

"Does something trouble you?" Theo asked.

"Life as a Weaver is isolation. I am not visited for my company. I am sought out only for my gifts."

At this, Theo felt a stab of guilt. He wished he could stay to speak to the old spirit—although he had not taken his eyes off the leg since it moved—but urgency to return to the surface tugged at him. He was running out of time after all.

"A life as long as mine leaves many stories to tell," Areope said, "and so I weave my stories into the fabrics. Please, have your pick, young Theo. You may take one of the cloths I've laid out for you."

Theo looked down at the four fabrics, then back up at the monument. The Great Weaver was simply going to gift him one of the pieces? This seemed too easy. After all the trials he had gone through in Nochlan, Theo refused to accept that some other danger wasn't waiting—a rule he wasn't aware of, or an attacker lying in wait. This couldn't be as simple as choosing one fabric.

"You are afraid of me," Areope said. "Sometimes you should not fear the unknown so much as what you know already."

Confused, Theo mulled the Weaver's statement over in his mind before reaching out to lift the fourth cloth—the black lace—from the altar. No attacks came; no traps triggered. He held the fabric in his hands, delicate and light. "Thank you," he said.

"You are welcome," Areope replied. "Goodbye, Theo. I hope my gift serves you well."

Theo nodded, holding the cloth in both his hands as if it were an offering. He turned to leave across the starry plain, but froze, contemplating the many desires within him. Finally, he turned back to the monument and sat down. The placid water obliged, making room for his legs and filling his lap. He felt no dampness; in fact, he likened the experience to sitting in a grassy field. He longed to rush back to the boat and Demeres and his parents, but to show kindness to someone who'd offered him a gift—he had time for this. "Will you tell me a story?"

And so Areope told him of Langit, the man who ruled the sky above. He'd had a charming sister, Buwan, whom he'd loved deeply but had lost to the underworld. His terrible grief came in waves as stark as day and night. When he was happy, the sun shone and the sky was blue, and he'd decorate the world with delicate clouds as charming as the sister who'd passed. When grief came again, he wiped the sky clean and left only the moon as a reminder of his great sorrow.

A dear friend to the man and the sister he'd lost, Areope couldn't stand to see Langit's emptiness. So she taught her children to hang the stars each time grief overcame him. They were not as bright as the moon, for no one could replace Buwan, but they would remind him that he was not alone. The comfort of friends could help him find peace again.

When she had finished speaking, Theo wiped his eyes and thanked her.

"You are very welcome," Areope said. "You must go. You have a great task ahead. Keep hold of that fabric I have given you. Listen to its story."

—◇—

Now that they were headed back, now that the questions of where they were going and how they were going to get there had been resolved, the frantic edge of sailing gave way to an almost peaceful melancholy. Rimi retreated behind them. Theo had wondered if Matanda might appear again, but he never showed himself. Perhaps he kept watch from the shadows.

Theo expected he'd need incredible strength to tear the veil he'd been gifted by Areope; after all, the spirit was known as "the Great Weaver." But the cloth tore down the middle at his touch, as if sensing his needs. He replaced the swatches of fabric he'd torn from his tunic, covering his parents' faces with the black, lacy material instead. In this way, although he still couldn't make out their features, he was able to glimpse more of them than he could behind the thick, soiled cloth. Judging by their postures, the finer material was more comfortable to wear too.

Before Theo knew it, the pinpricks of light from Rimi's aquatic milky way were completely gone, and Theo was left staring in silence at the Corporis Sea. In fact, he couldn't find anything to say at all. Instead, he sank into exhaustion and homesickness. He wanted to be in the streets of Ipsitfel again, to walk across cobblestones and down alleyways tucked into hidden corners. He wanted to see Ismena again and talk to Roman—yes, he wanted to tell Roman everything. This was an adventure even Roman couldn't top.

He wanted to see Laila. He missed his sister.

"What happened after we died?" his mother asked, breaking the silence.

Theo looked up at her.

"Well, we came running back to the house," he said. "Folk had gathered around, waiting. Holding us back because we kept trying to go in after you. Eventually, the fire was put out, but you were found dead. They wouldn't let us see. The Bareens took us to their place. I don't even think Ismena had to ask—her mother just did it. We waited there for news. Waited for hours."

"Alayna is such a wonderful woman," Medina said.

"That's terrible," Damon said. He sounded lost.

"How is your sister doing?" Medina asked.

"She's... She's alright, I suppose," Theo said. "She was holding up better than me, at any rate. Or maybe hiding it better. She was staying with Gwendolyn Shears' family."

"Laila is strong," Damon whispered, "but I don't doubt she was putting on a stronger face for the world."

"She had to be the one to release you both during the Descension," Theo said. "I—I couldn't."

"It's okay, dear," his mother said.

"They handed me the cord, but I couldn't bring myself to pull it."

"That's a hard thing to ask of any grieving person," his father said.

"I wonder how she's dealt with your disappearance," Medina said. "I hope she hasn't taken it too hard."

Theo felt suddenly guilty. He hadn't thought about Laila. He hadn't thought about how anyone might react to his disappearance, let alone his sister. Of *course* his abandoning her only days after their parents' death would've caused her distress. On the other hand, he couldn't risk her trying to stop him if he'd explained his plan. Ismena might have told Laila what was happening after he left. When Laila discovered he was gone, no doubt Ismena would've been one of the first people she contacted. Regardless, what pained him most was that he hadn't considered Laila's reaction in the first place.

Everyone in the boat devolved into silence again. His mother's concern hung in the air, filling Theo's mind like a low, throbbing headache. He wished he had something to distract himself, and thought about letting his fingers dip into the sea, but the image of the bodies rising from the depths stopped him. After a long while, his mother sat up straight again and twisted to face Demeres at the stern.

"I think I remember you," Medina said. Her tone was cloudy, deep, irritated by her inability to remember. "What was your sur-name? Something with an *A*?"

The ferrywoman kept her eyes on the black waters, but eventually cleared her throat. "Ainsworth."

"Yes," Medina said. Recognition dragged its feet, and she had to pull it forward with all her might. "You had a daughter, didn't you? A tiny, lovely thing."

Everything about Demeres tensed. Her facial expression, her steering hand, even her posture went rigid.

"I did," she said, then exhaled deeply. "Iligenia."

"That's a beautiful name."

"Thank you." Theo could tell Demeres hoped the conversation might shift. She didn't make eye contact with any of her passengers. "She died when she was very young."

"That's right," Damon said, hanging his head.

Medina didn't stop looking at Demeres—the ferrywoman's face recalled memories—but she did sigh at the grievous information. "I'm sorry to hear that."

Demeres nodded with a sad smile.

"I remember attending your Descension ceremony," Medina continued.

"What?" Demeres asked, shocked.

"Yes, I remember," Medina turned forward to face Theo, "because it was your first time coming to the Descension."

Theo's mouth fell open. He recalled snippets of that evening, of running through the crowd to get a better glimpse of what was happening. He remembered being lifted up, stopped from dashing out into the cleared pathway. He remembered the sobbing man—who he now realized must have been Demeres' husband—and the pull of the cord. Then the moment the rope went slack, her body falling away.

"I remember too," Theo said, although he didn't recognize Demeres as the woman lowered into the Gateway. In his mind, the subject was faceless. The more important aspects of that evening had been the hushed, somber atmosphere, the people in blue cloaks who carried the stretcher, and the horror he'd felt when the body was released. Nightmares had plagued him for weeks, and the thought of a dangling corpse with bold red hair could still bring a twinge of discomfort to him. He locked eyes with the ferrywoman. She sat with her mouth agape. He clarified. "I didn't know it was you—of course, I was so young at the time—but I can remember being th ere."

"You can?"

"Vaguely," Theo said.

"Life finds humor in strange coincidences," she muttered.

"Indeed, it does," Damon agreed.

"Sometimes, I wish I could take it all back," Demeres said. Theo knew what she meant by those words, and her defeated tone pulled at his heart. His parents, who hadn't heard her story and were perhaps unaware of how she came to be a ferrywoman, looked back at her, confused. Evidently sensing the delicate nature of the subject matter, however, they said no more.

"Only sometimes?" Theo asked.

She nodded. "It's hard to remember how great the pain was after losing two of the people I loved most, but I know life rarely seemed worth living afterward."

"I'm sorry."

"Light," Medina said.

Theo, his father, and Demeres all looked around at Medina. She was pointing straight ahead, the tendons in her hand taut from her outstretched finger. Their gazes followed. For a moment, Theo could see nothing, but then the tiniest pinprick of light flashed out at them. A beacon in the night.

"The lighthouse," Theo said.

They were nearing the Gateway.

24

Dark Ascending

While at first the blinking light seemed to linger forever in the distance, the shore was upon them before Theo knew it. The cone of light orbited steadily, either shining out into the endless night or illuminating the sheer rock face behind the beach. Beneath the lighthouse, Theo caught flashes of the coarse sand and smooth boulders encircling the base of the tower. There were no signs that he'd stood on that shore—none that he could see, anyway. The shallow decline down to the still black waters was smooth and undisturbed.

"We... came through here," Damon said, as if unsure.

"Yes," Medina agreed. "We paid for our passage standing by that rock." She pointed toward a pile of large stones that jutted out over the water.

"I don't remember our guide," Damon said. He narrowed his eyes.

Through the gap between them, Theo watched Demeres. She had become morose, not speaking as they drew closer to the shore. Perhaps she was anxious to be bringing not just a living boy but two deceased souls back to the realm above. Perhaps she feared for them, and whether Theo's parents could adjust to human life again. Or perhaps she feared her own fate should they be discovered by Death.

So long as Theo could convince his parents to wear the veils, she shouldn't have to worry.

The boat drove itself halfway onto the beach, the coarse sand grinding beneath the wooden underbelly. The pale yellow glow of the lantern cast a circle of light around them, while the lighthouse continued to rotate above. Silence fell again, and for a moment nobody reacted, paralyzed by the unbelievability of their circumstances. Theo looked to his parents who stared at the sandy shore as if it might rear up and swallow them. They held hands, their white clothes all but glowing in the dimness. Then, as if deciding together, they stood.

"We've made it," Medina muttered.

Damon could only nod.

"You've made it," Demeres agreed. She still hadn't looked at any of them.

Without another word, Theo's parents stepped out of the boat and onto the sand. Their feet sank. The beach welcomed them in. Their hands released. Just as it had when they'd stepped into the boat, a flash of unbalance overcame them both, though it was brief enough that neither fell.

Theo let them be, knowing that some emotion must be welling up inside them. He instead kept watch of Demeres, wishing she would look at him.

"Thank you," he said.

For a few moments, he didn't know whether she'd heard him, but then she nodded, her eyes glued to the placid black water beside her. Theo leaned forward and moved to take his parents' place on the center seat. This close, Demeres couldn't avoid looking at him any longer.

"You be careful," she said. Though her jaw was set, he could see the sadness in her eyes. Theo felt his own twinge of sorrow. More had happened in the few days he'd known Demeres than in all the days that had come before. She was as responsible for everything they'd accomplished as he, maybe more so. Certainly, he would never look at his own world the same way again. Not now that he knew what lay beneath his feet, beneath the dark circle of the Gateway. If any of his cohort voiced doubts about the Descension traditions, he could not see himself refraining from a vehement defense of the old rites—even if he'd set about breaking all of them.

"I couldn't have succeeded without you," Theo said. "I wouldn't have made it off this shore without your help."

"Another ferryboat would have come along eventually," Demeres said.

"But they might not have helped me. They wouldn't have been you."

"Perhaps that would've been for the best." Demeres's words carried a sudden sharpness, though any edge to her voice melted quickly away. "Please, be careful," she repeated. "Death doesn't like to be deceived."

Theo nodded, his stoic expression meant to show he understood the gravitas of her words. Suddenly, he knew how much he would miss the ferrywoman, and not just because of what she'd given him. He would miss her for her company, the way she took him at his word—not as a child but as an adult. He would miss her for her determination, for always knowing what to do, and for her motherly demeanor.

But he had his own mother back now. And that too was thanks to Demeres.

Theo slid forward again, this time to embrace his friend. She didn't expect the gesture, but after the surprise had worn off, she held him close. He wanted to wish her whatever fate would make her happiest, though he didn't want to say so for fear the wish might not come true.

"This is it, then," Demeres said.

"I suppose so."

"Look after them." Demeres nodded toward Damon and Medina. "They will need you now more than they did before."

"I'll miss you," Theo said.

She put her hand to the back of his head, holding him close. "I'll miss you too, Theo."

Then she let go, and so did he, standing up in the small ferryboat half in the Corporis Sea and half on human ground. Or *was* it human ground? Where exactly did his world end and the other begin? Was there a hard line, or a space where the two blended? Either way, stepping out onto the rock and sand added a weight to his body he hadn't felt since departing from this very spot. He turned and backed away, watching as the ferry retreated into the water and sailed away from the shore, The lantern marked the boat's place in the darkness. He waved, unable to help himself, but already he couldn't tell whether the ferrywoman waved back.

Theo turned, leaving the sea behind him. His parents stood waiting. Their ghostly figures stood sentinel in the revolving light, immobile. Waiting for him to lead them. Their presence was almost eerie, and Theo wished they would talk, if only to remind him who it was beneath the draped cloth.

"This way," he said, walking between them up the shore. The sheer cliff stood resolute, but when the lighthouse illuminated the wall, he could see the opening through which he'd come. Neither his mother nor his father responded, but before he pulled too far ahead, they followed.

Up the beach they went, the sand grumbling underfoot. He led them over the threshold of the carved passage, where the path changed to stone. Inside, the beam of the lighthouse disappeared quickly until they were traveling in a darkness that allowed only a strange, shadowy visibility. Theo remembered being intrigued by his ability to see without illumination when he'd first entered Nochlan. He would've bet that if they turned around now and went back to the shoreline, the lighthouse would no longer be operating.

He pressed on.

They moved through the neatly carved corridor. His hands traced the walls to either side. The feeling brought a sense of security to the shadows. The trio turned this way and that, burrowing deep into the earth. *Impatience* made the trek feel longer than before, but he reminded himself he just had to keep moving.

Faces of the people he missed above motivated him. Laila astonished but delighted. Roman smiling devilishly, eyes twinkling and impressed. Ismena staring in amazement as he emerged from the Gateway with his parents. Her mouth falling open, because she'd given him up for dead.

At last, the walls of the passage opened unto the great cavern beneath Ipsitfel's Gateway. Theo could feel the dark space expanding, an emptiness that dwarfed him. He slowed to a stop at the end of the path and turned back to his parents. They were seconds behind him, their pace almost trance-like.

"Have we... Have we reached it?" Damon asked. His voice drifted with a lax curiosity.

"We have," Theo said, wishing he had a torch or a lantern so they could see more of the gigantic space than the silver glow allowed. If there was more than that dot of light above them from the Gateway—

"I don't remember any of this," Medina said, treading past him into the cavern.

Damon entered as well, and Theo fell into step. He'd forgotten how eerie it had been, traipsing through the dark while trying to avoid the many bodies that littered the ground around him. Though he could not smell their slowly-rotting flesh, the ferric stench of blood coated his nostrils. While he wove around the scattered bodies, Theo listened to his and his parents' muffled footsteps on the damp floor. Their footfalls came like a chorus, despite the myriad of corpses lying about to stifle the noise. They sounded like more than three people walking.

"Stop," Theo hissed. He and his parents came to a halt and the sounds died. Ringing silence filled his ears and nothing else.

"Do you hear something?" his father asked.

Theo shook his head. "No, it must be my imagination. Keep moving."

But as they started walking again, their impossible chorus of footsteps began as well. Theo was sure of it now; they were not alone. Without saying anything, he skipped forward to get in front of his mother, who hadn't seemed to notice anything out of the ordinary.

"Stop again," he said.

All sounds died. Whoever mimicked their march must possess remarkable reflexes to align their stops and starts with such precision. He could barely distinguish any audible delay between his parents' footfalls and that of their visitor—visitors? Theo peered around the next pile of corpses, squinting into the darkness for signs of anyone else. When he didn't find any, he beckoned his parents forward again.

As soon as they started walking, Theo spotted movement across the cavern. The figures were hard to see, but the silvery sheen was light enough for him to pick out their shapes, traipsing across the ground. They stood at the far side of the cavern beyond the great mountain of corpses. Theo watched, transfixed as the obscured beings moved through the shadows. They came straight for him and his parents. He contemplated stopping again, maybe running, trying to find somewhere to hide. But if the approaching figures—and he could see now that there were two of them—had meant to hurt him or his family, they were being very slow and methodical about it. In fact, their stilted movements suggested injury, contorting as if supported by broken bones. Yet, they stepped when his parents stepped, somehow able to match the cadence heel for heel and sole for sole. The hair on the back of Theo's neck stood up.

"Father?" he said, trying to warn his parents. "Mother?"

Whether they didn't understand his fearful tone or chose to ignore it, his parents continued forward in the trance-like state that had gripped them since the boat ride.

The advancing figure on the left changed its gait. With a tremulous crunch, it stood up straighter, snapping ligaments into place like buttons. The way both it and his father walked was like watching a strangely distorted mirror. The same was true for the entity on the right and Theo's mother. As it reoriented a backwards arm, Medina seemed to sense the metamorphosis and stretched out a hand. Her impression reciprocated the gesture, so that when the two came close enough, their hands touched.

Theo understood what was happening.

He gasped. "Your bodies."

They'd been mangled by the fall through the Gateway. Though they'd rehabilitated their contorted limbs, the bloody gashes had yet to mend. Burnt flesh disfigured their features, crusted over like dried, cracked earth. Theo had been so overjoyed to find his parents' souls that he'd forgotten their physical bodies had been horrifically mangled.

Knowing they could not ascend through the Gateway until their forms united, he drifted toward the four. Nobody in Nochlan had explained to him how the transformation would happen. No spells were suggested, nor rituals described. He hoped the transformation would be instinctual, otherwise he would face yet another unforeseen obstacle.

He needn't have worried.

His parents and their impressions stood with palms pressed to-gether, observing their others with a sort of curiosity—sightless, on the part of the physical forms whose eyes had been mostly charred out of existence. The meeting was peaceful, almost beautiful in a macabre fashion. Theo found himself overwhelmed with emotion.

The tranquility broke as the physicals suddenly gripped their souls tightly by the wrists. In their dispassionate states, the soul forms didn't fight. They stood still as the physicals wheezed, backs bending and arching in agony. They were having conniptions! A small part of Theo told him to intervene, but he was so taken aback by the sudden shift in tone that he couldn't move. He could only watch as their mouths opened to their limits and then past their lim-its, jaws cracking like firewood as tendons ripped and skin strained. Physical Damon tugged the arm of his facsimile toward him and shoved the hand into his gaping mouth. He began to consume the soul form, swallowing it inch by inch like a snake consuming its prey—whole.

As Median did the same, Theo backed away in horror. He re-treated until he felt the mountain of corpses at his back, then re-coiled from that as well with a barbarous yelp. Was there nowhere he could go to avoid the barrage of morbidity?

He covered his face with his arms and crouched low to the ground, cowering as he listened to one form of his parents consume the other. Determining that letting his imagination take the reins was worse, however, Theo emerged from his cocoon just in time to see his father shove the last foot into his chasmic maw, blood trickling from the corners of his mouth. His throat was swollen to bursting, but the skin held. And as the seconds ticked past, it shrank back to its normal size.

Somewhere along the way, both Median and Damon had transferred the black veils to their own faces. The fabric hung now as if nothing untoward had happened, masking any remnants of gore. Their black flakes of charred skin fell away, an ashen mockery of the falling peach petals on Caelum.

Not everything about their former corpses healed, however. As they settled post-absorption, he could see ailments manifesting themselves. His father slumped under an injured back and his mother put a hand to her abdomen, wincing. Life reminded them of pain.

"You're alive again," Theo breathed.

His father stretched out his hands, rotating his arms so that he could look at every inch of the ligaments. *Feel* every inch of them. "How?" he said in amazement. Theo couldn't imagine the sensation of regaining your body after dying, but he reasoned the experience bewildered the senses—and been none too pleasant.

"This," his mother sighed, "is very remarkable indeed."

"We have to get up to the surface now," Theo said. "Wait here."

He approached the mountain of corpses. This was the part he'd been trying to ignore. He took several deep breaths, clenching and unclenching his fists while staring at the severe slope before him. At least the darkness hid the brunt of the gory details. If the cavern were lit well, he didn't think he'd have the stomach for the climb. As it was, Theo did his best not to think about what he was doing.

He leaned forward into the mountainside, climbing hand over hand. He grabbed arms, shoulders, legs, and once a head by mistake, which almost caused him to fall over backward. A few times, his mind tricked him into thinking the limbs reacted to his touch and his heart leapt, but as he stared at the body part in question, he never saw further indication that what he'd felt was real. He kept climbing.

At first, the top never seemed to come any closer, but just as he was beginning to think the mountain would never cease, he reached the plateau and was able to stand. Theo looked down the side. He could barely make out the figures of his parents below. Then he looked up at the Gateway above, preparing to call out to Ismena.

Her name died on his tongue.

Dangling some fifteen feet above him was the end of a rope.

The rope had been looped and knotted, same as it had been when he came down through the hole, but the knot in this one looked far stronger. Theo lifted a hand to his mouth.

"Ismena!" he called, thinking that his friend had to be close by. He couldn't imagine anyone else lowering the knotted rope for him. The night sky was just visible through the open Gateway, shrouded by fog.

Louder this time. "Ismena!"

Or maybe his friend had left the rope a while ago. Maybe it'd been hanging here unnoticed since the night he left. How long ago had that been exactly? Demeres insinuated that time aboveground did not move at the same pace as it had in the underworld.

He cupped both hands around his mouth. "ISMENA!"

The name reverberated around the cavern, echoing distantly. Did an echo guard this cavern as well? "Death says you may leave," Theo said, but though the echo once again rang through the darkness, nothing happened.

Theo jumped, trying to grab the looped rope, but he was far too short. The tantalizing proximity of his escape infuriated him, and at once he grunted in frustration. What could he do? Were they going to have to wait here until morning when people came to Cirillo Square? That was a possibility, but one Theo hoped to avoid. He didn't very much like the idea of emerging from the Gateway—which in and of itself was illegal, since he wasn't allowed to go through it alive to begin with—with his parents, who everyone knew to be dead. Then, of course, there was the possibility that even during the crowded day, he still wouldn't be discovered. He might yell his throat hoarse, but when Ipsitfel's citizens burst onto the square, they rarely did so quietly. He was far enough away from the cavern's mouth that he might go unnoticed beneath their brazen v oices.

No. They needed to find another way out on their own.

Theo ran his hands through his hair, trying to massage ideas out of his head. Perhaps they could grab at the rope from down here. Maybe he could find another rope and get it through the loop. Then he could hoist himself up and pull his parents up afterward. All he'd need was a few extra feet, but he doubted any of these cadavers would have one.

Oh, but that dangling loop was so close. If only he were a little taller. If only he could get on his father's back—but his father was hurt enough as it was after rejoining with his physical form. If only the mountain were a bit taller. If only there were another few layers of... bodies.

Theo's hands froze, his hair half pulled back between his fingers. He closed his eyes and let out a soft groan of reluctance. Even as he pleaded with himself not to try exactly what he was about to try, he could think of no other alternative. He had one somewhat reasonable idea—if he had the strength to follow through.

Theo began to descend the mountain. At first, he tried not to touch anything with his hands, but at a certain point avoiding contact with the dead became less important than efficiency—and safety. If he slid down, the trip was much faster.

At the bottom, he grabbed the first prone corpse he came to, a boy maybe a year or two younger than he. Theo couldn't remember attending the boy's Descension ceremony. How long had he been down here? Theo seized fistfuls of the collar around the boy's neck.

"I don't suppose either of you would be able to help," he said aloud. He looked to his parents, but they showed little sign that they understood, still engrossed in the ailments of coming back to life. Something about their behavior wasn't right. He couldn't help wondering if their rapid despondency was imagined, or if they'd been acting stranger as time passed. He brushed the thought away.

Theo didn't wait for them to answer. Urging himself on with deep, steady breaths, he began to drag the body up the mountainside.

The task was by no means easy, but Theo found it not as difficult as he'd imagined. The body seemed to get lighter as he pulled it up the slope. Twice the decrepit coat he clung to snagged on someone else's protruding limb, but he had only to reach down and shimmy it free before continuing. As an added bonus, traveling backward meant the summit arrived faster than expected. Theo dragged the body over the edge and onto the small plateau, pausing only for a short breath before sliding back down.

He dragged up another corpse—a withered old woman—and another and another, until he'd lost count of how many bodies he'd carried. Sweat drenched his brow, the collar of his tunic, and all along his back. Pain wracked his arms and legs. His lower back was stiff from pulling while bent over. Each meter of movement decreased in speed, and his grunts became louder and louder. As he slid his last body up the peak, he let out a scream of exhaustion and collapsed.

He couldn't even lift his head to see how much of a difference in height he'd made.

Bedraggled breaths inflated his lungs. Tears mingled with the beads of sweat rolling down his face until he couldn't tell which was which. Theo sprawled defeated.

Yet as he lay there, he heard continued movement.

Slow, methodical bursts of sound. Dragging, labored breathing, and every once in a while, a small something breaking away to tumble toward the cavern floor. Theo lifted his head and turned over in time to see both of his parents breech the summit, carrying one body each.

Damon and Medina laid their burdens down and stood again, spent every bit as much as he by their one trip up the mountainside. How he longed to reach forward and brush their masks aside just long enough to see their faces in flesh—real flesh. He even lifted a hand to do so, though he knew he couldn't. Instead, he got to his knees.

"Thank you," he said, standing. Both his parents nodded.

He looked up.

He'd centered the localized mound beneath the loop of rope. His efforts were minuscule compared to the mass upon which they stood, but he'd added quite a bit of height when compared to his own stature. After climbing atop the hill he'd made, Theo found he was just able to grab onto the loop if he jumped.

Now all he had to do was get the rest of the way up. Already, his arms shook, threatening to give out again.

"You should rest," his mother said in a muted voice, observing his quaking limbs. "You won't be able to make it."

"I can't rest," Theo said. "We have to—"

"If you don't rest, you might fail," his mother said. And the way she said *fail* carried with it a finality he couldn't ignore. "If you do, this will all have been in vain."

"But..." Theo let go of the rope and landed on top of the pile he'd made. He knew he wanted to keep going, to get them out of the cavern as soon as possible, but his mother was right. If he fell while climbing, there was no telling whether he'd survive this time. Yet, again they were so close, and still the surface remained out of reach. All he wanted was for this nightmare to be over, to be home again with his family.

"Rest, Theo," his father agreed, and put a strong hand on his son's shoulder.

Theo reluctantly sat beside his parents.

Just as he was about to give in to rest, a voice called out from above. It was full of uncertainty, strained further by fear and worry. They only shouted one word, but it was enough to make Theo, his mother, and his father look up in astonishment.

"Theo?" Ismena called into the darkness.

25
The Help of Friends

Theo was back on his feet at once, the throbbing in his arms and back forgotten. He climbed up to the top of the mound until he was as close to his friend as he could be. She stared down, squinting into the darkness as if he were just beyond the realm of visibility. Theo waved his arms at her.

"Ismena, I'm here," he called.

Her eyes widened in disbelief and she jerked away from the opening. "Theo! Is it really you?"

"It is," he said. Relief flooded him. Ismena was here. She was really here. And she knew he was down below. They were saved after all. They wouldn't have to stay another night in this place.

"I—I can't believe it," she said. "I can't believe you're alive."

Theo might've laughed were he less exhausted. "You'll believe it soon enough when you get a better look at me."

"I've been coming here every night since you left, calling your name down through the Gateway," she said, "and I never heard a single thing. It felt like shouting into the void, it did. I couldn't see anything either. I'd just assumed you were... I'd just thought—"

"Thank you, Ismena," Theo said, feeling a rush of gratitude. He could have grabbed her then and pulled her into the tightest embrace, were he close enough. This wonderful girl. This loyal friend.

"But you're here!" she said. "You went through the Gateway and now you're back."

"Almost," he said.

"Oh, right." Ismena laughed. "I've got to get you out of there."

"Us."

"What?"

"Us," he repeated. "You have to get *us* out of here."

Ismena didn't respond. Theo couldn't see her expression, but he imagined her mouth opening in confusion. Theo gestured to his parents to join him on the mound. They obliged, stepping into what little light was provided by the hole above. Ismena leaned down further, as if trying to make sense of the shapes moving around in the darkness below. But nobody'd ever been able to see down into the Gateway before.

"What's going on, Theo?" she asked.

"I found my parents."

Ismena's hand flew up to cover her mouth. That reaction, he could see. The growing silence was not what he might've hoped for, though. Clearly, she'd expected him to come back empty-handed. After all, his parents had died, and people who died never returned. Especially not after they'd gone through the Gateway. To have her refuse to help them now because she couldn't stand the perversion would be the ultimate disappointment.

"What's happened to them?" she asked, her voice thin.

"It's a long story," Theo said, his neck beginning to ache. His body followed suit as the euphoria wore off. "I can tell you once we're above ground, but they have to keep their faces covered."

"But how do you know they're—"

"We wish to thank you in advance, Ismena, for helping us," Theo's mother said suddenly. Her voice was deep and raspy the way it got when she was stressed. She was trying to hide it, hoping to stave off Ismena's wariness and inaction.

Ismena gasped again, and even retreated a little farther from the mouth of the hole. The voice was unmistakable.

"Missus Sahiron," Ismena said. "Pardon me, this is all so much to absorb."

"I understand."

"I just didn't expect—"

"Ismena," Medina said. Though her tone was kind, it was firm enough to quiet the girl. "Please, help us. All we ask is your assistance in getting out of this *pit*."

Ismena didn't answer for almost a full minute. Then, "I do not wish for my family to fall victim to ill will," she said softly.

She was having second thoughts. While hers was a legitimate concern, Theo could not help feeling her timing was quite poor. Why had she returned to the Gateway each night if not to pull him out? If she'd only meant to help if he failed, then she never should have agreed with his plan to begin with.

"But I can't leave you down there, knowing you're alive," Ismena said at last.

"Thank you," Theo exclaimed, sighing with relief.

"Lowering you is one thing, Theo," Ismena said, "but I can't pull you up myself."

"Is there anyone you trust to help?" Theo asked. "Tom, perhaps?"

Ismena considered for another painstakingly long minute before answering.

"I know who to ask," she said. "I'll be back."

Theo wanted to call out to her, wanted to tell her to stay because he was suddenly afraid he might never return from this underground world, but she was gone in an instant and her name died even as it left his lips. He stared up at the hole above him, not wanting to blink. He was so close to returning home, yet another setback presented itself and the chance to resurface was yanked away. But no matter. He would have to be patient. Ismena would return. He just had to wait.

"A brave girl," Damon said.

"A loyal friend." Medina sounded almost like she was scolding her son. "Did she truly agree to help you, Theo, or was it your insistence that brought her to the Gateway?"

"Of course, she—" Theo cut himself off, suddenly doubtful. Truth be told, getting her to Cirillo Square in the dead of night *had* taken a lot of convincing, but Ismena always needed convincing. That was why their friendship worked. If she didn't have him around, she'd never do anything out of fear of failure. And without her—well, without Ismena, Theo would get in a lot more trouble.

"Do not let go of her," Medina said. "Not as long as she'll have you around."

"I don't intend to let go of her," Theo said, still staring at the glimmer of sky through the Gateway. He could just make out a cluster of stars. Real stars, twinkling in the night.

"You should pay special mind to how you treat her," his mother said. "People with hearts like hers are kind, but once they've been pushed past a breaking point, they don't return."

"Are you insinuating I've hurt her?"

"We cannot always avoid hurting the people around us," his father said. He sat again on the mound at his son's feet, breathing heavily. "Especially those we hold most dear. The difference between decent people and all others is that when decent people recognize they're at fault, they make amends as best they can."

"But I—"

"We're not saying you've treated her poorly," his mother said, resting a hand on Theo's shoulder. "We're speaking to all the relationships you have or will have. Death has a way of encouraging you to contemplate the decisions you've made in your life."

Noise came from above at last—people talking in hushed tones. Theo's heart fluttered. His focus turned again to making their escape, though the flicker of conversation with his parents didn't completely leave him. Ismena's head appeared over the edge of the hole.

"You still there?" she asked.

"We are," Theo replied.

"Good, I've brought help."

Then the face of Roman Alba joined her.

"What's this about Theo bein' down there?" he asked, squinting into the darkness.

"There's not much more to it than that," Ismena said. "We've got to get them out."

"Roman!" Theo called.

"Well fuck me sideways!" Roman exclaimed, but he moved to help Ismena without further question. Theo wanted to think of something to say to him, but the situation was far too pressing to delay any longer.

"Can you reach the rope?" Ismena asked.

"We can," Theo replied.

"Alright, one at a time, grab on and we'll hoist you up."

The three stood on the mountain of corpses and looked at each other, silently deciding in what order they should go.

"I should be last," Theo said.

"And why's that?" his mother asked.

"Because everyone knows you two... that you two aren't supposed to be around anymore," he said. "If we get discovered, it's best if you can get into hiding as quick as possible. They know I'm alive—if they see me down here there's a better chance they'll be willing to help me out. If you're the ones down here, well, I don't know that I'd get a chance to come back."

"We should probably make this quick an' all," came Roman's voice, "seeing as this ain't allowed, strictly speaking."

"Right," Medina said. "Let's just get going."

Theo and his father helped her reach the looped rope and she grabbed on, threading both arms through. The two above began reeling her in, the jerky motion causing Medina to swing from side to side a little. She ascended at a sluggish crawl, every minute leaving ample room for something to go wrong. The rope might snap, the knot come undone, or an Ipsitfelian citizen might awaken and step outside for a nighttime stroll. Inch by inch his mother gained altitude, until at long last his friends were helping her over the lip of the Gateway where she disappeared from sight altogether.

After a moment, the looped rope fell through the opening again.

Theo's father grabbed it, nodding at his son, who smiled solemnly. Damon wrapped his arms through the loop as Medina had done, and then he was slowly dragged skyward. Theo was left staring up at his father's progress from below, willing himself to believe what was happening. His heart hammered in his chest and a lump had formed in his throat, but he dared not make any noises or movements until his father had cleared the lip.

Then it was his turn.

The rope came bounding back down toward him, swinging just beyond his reach. His father, who was taller than he, had been able to grab it while standing. Theo and his father had lifted his mother so she could grab hold. But Theo was alone. He crouched slightly, his tired legs begging him to desist, then leapt into the air.

His hands felt the thick, worn rope, and he snatched it, clinging with all the strength he had left. Before Ismena and Roman could start reeling him in, he quickly wrapped his arms through the loop as his parents had: a more secure hold that required less effort.

His ascension began.

Theo's arms ached, though the pain in his back improved as he dangled. Being pulled from the darkness was much like slowly awakening from a dream. The fantastical elements of the prior days fell away, draining from him like moisture squeezed from a wrung cloth. He came back to a world of living, mortal humans. A world with the townsfolk he had grown up around, who gossiped and gawked and sang spontaneously and knew only of the limited things humans on the surface of the world knew. He was going home, and though the time he'd spent in the other world was relatively brief, he felt like he was returning after a lifetime away.

The landscape of bodies disappeared below him, and for the briefest of moments he was suspended in total blackness. Then he was near enough to the lip of the hole to reach out and touch it. Ismena was holding on to the rope; Roman reached forward and grabbed Theo tight under the arms. The older boy pulled him from the void and they toppled onto the cobblestones.

Theo found himself out of breath. On his hands and knees, he looked up to survey Cirillo Square: the courthouse, the bank, crooked Viseyne Tower, all of it looking just as it had when he'd left. He could have kissed the ground. He could have kissed Ismena for her nightly vigilance. He could have kissed Roman for hoisting him out of the Gateway, which he did, mashing their faces together as they lay across the stones.

Roman laughed, then kissed him back with decidedly better aim.

"If you two are finished," Ismena whispered.

She was right. Theo would have to savor his return to Ipsitfel another time. Right now, they had to get his parents out of view.

"Where shall we go?" Roman asked.

Ismena didn't need to think. "To my house. They can hide in the basement. It's not being used as of late."

Nobody objected. She stood, wrapping the rope in a loose coil and sliding it over her shoulder. The others followed as she opened the gate to let them out. Above, the brightness of dawn was just starting to invade the night sky. The usual fog rolled through the streets. Without a doubt, the earliest risers would have risen by now. So, the group snuck as fast as they could through the alleyways and crooked roads until they reached the Bareen residence.

Ismena led them around the side of the building to the hatch leading down into the basement. She held open the door for them while they slipped inside, creeping one by one into yet another place of darkness. But when the others had gone and only he and Ismena remained above ground, Theo paused.

"What are you doing?" Ismena hissed. "Come on."

Theo cleared his throat. "I know, it's just—before we go, I wanted to say thank you."

"What do you..." she trailed off.

"Thank you, and I'm sorry. I know I don't recognize how incredible a friend you are sometimes. It makes me treat you unfairly."

"Theo, we don't have time."

"You're the most loyal friend I've got."

"Yes, yes. I know."

"I shouldn't forget that." Theo lunged forward, wrapping Ismena in a tight embrace. She let out a soft *oof* before hugging him back, some of her tension ebbing. He meant every word, even if he didn't have the skill to say it elegantly. He would've died trying to attempt his journey to the underworld alone.

After a few more seconds, Ismena snorted, releasing her grip. "Alright, alright. Enough of that, we need to get you hidden."

Though Theo hadn't had his fill of the fresh, crisp air yet, he ducked down into the opening. Ismena followed quickly and let the hatch close behind them.

26

Dark Descending

He stood in shadow, but having grown accustomed to it, he was unafraid, unbothered by his sightless eyes. This darkness was composed of the *known*. Since meeting the unknown, he couldn't imagine ever being afraid of the dark again.

A light flared to life, bathing them in an orange glow. The basement was littered with tools for digging and laying stone. In one corner, stacks of spare buckets rose from the floor, while coils of rope lay in another. The last time Theo was in this house, he'd taken one of those ropes without permission.

Theo's mother found a bare wooden chair in the corner and sat down. His father stood over her, hands at his sides and posture perfect. Roman remained by the foot of the stairs, his gaze flicking back and forth between the Sahirons. Ismena stood on the other side of the room, shaking out a match before closing the glass door of a lantern. She slipped the rope off her shoulder and added it to the pile.

Theo backed away from the center of the basement until he hit the brick wall, then sank to the ground.

"So," Roman said. He was looking at Theo now, hints of the sapphire in his eyes flickering like the blue heart of a flame. "So."

As soon as Theo sat down, exhaustion and hunger hit him. Now that he was aboveground again, the functions of his mortal body were regaining control. He'd never felt so tired before.

"So?" Roman said a third time, raising his eyebrows and nodding toward Theo's parents. "What's in the great fuck is this about then, eh?"

"Can I... Can I rest first?" Theo asked. His stomach growled.

"And eat, it sounds like."

"There are peaches in one of those jars," Ismena said, pointing to a set of shelves on the wall by Theo's parents. "You can have a few of those."

Theo was about to get up, but Roman went instead, crouching as he searched for the jar. He pulled it from the shelf and struggled for only a moment to get the lid off before handing it to Theo.

Theo took it gratefully, reaching in and pulling a few slices from the preserving liquid. His friends watched him eat. Ismena's face was solemn, but Roman looked as though he were in the midst of being told the most interesting tale.

"Thanks," Theo mumbled after a large swallow. He needed to pace himself before he choked.

"Well?" Ismena asked.

"Well what?"

"Tell us what happened."

Theo sighed. "Please, can it wait? I'm really ti—"

"No, it can't wait," she said, her voice rising. She made a visible effort to calm herself, bringing her tone back to a harsh whisper. "You fell through the Gateway and disappeared for seven days. I thought you were dead. I went back to look for you every night because I was afraid I'd *killed* you by letting you go. Then you turn up with your parents." She gestured toward Medina and Damon, who remained inexpressive behind their veils. "No, Theo. I need some sort of explanation."

Theo savored the last bites of the peach in his mouth. He closed the lid of the jar, not wanting to deplete the store in one sitting.

His mind buzzed, exhaustion blurring the edges of his thoughts, but Ismena couldn't be denied. She was providing him and his parents refuge, after all. She had the right to answers.

Roman sat on the stairs, resting his chin on his hands. Theo noticed for the first time that he wasn't wearing his usual elaborate garb. He wore pajamas—loose-fitting cotton trousers and a half-buttoned nightshirt. Theo had never seen him dressed so simply. He must've come straight from bed.

"Under the Gateway is a cavern..." Theo began, and his words flooded the dark basement. He told them everything, or at least, as much as he remembered. He told them of the Corporis Sea, of meeting Demeres, who agreed to ferry him across the water, of Eirini, where the liberi lived and Dolothyia kept the Books of Mortal Names. He explained why he needed to hurry, and rationalized his decision to use the canal that passed through Kouros. Ismena gasped when he told them of his fight with Palakostos, while Roman's eyes brightened with admiration. Theo felt his heart swell. He steered clear of mentioning the guide, Erid, however, though he was unsure why. When he reached Matanda beside Caelum's cliffs, he paused.

"Who was he?" Ismena asked.

"He said he was a relative of Death. A sibling."

"Death's sibling?" she said, then fell silent.

"He told me how to get onto the island undetected and how to get my parents back without Death noticing." Theo turned to his parents, who still hadn't spoken since they'd reached the surface. They showed no signs at all that they were listening. The light of the flame danced over their lacy masks.

"He just... told you?" Roman asked.

"No," Theo said. "I had to trade him."

He didn't want to explain exactly what he'd traded, so he pressed on, describing the island where he'd found his parents. ("I had your scarf and your pocket watch," he said to them. "I meant to give them back to you, but when I got lost, I had to use them in a spell.") He talked about convincing his parents to return with him, and about stopping at Rimi on the journey back.

He neglected to tell them about the mountain of corpses below the Gateway.

"... and now we're here," Theo finished, squeezing his hands between his knees. He started to look at his parents again, but found he couldn't, staring instead at the ground by their feet. He wondered how long they'd been in the Bareens' basement already. Outside, the day was probably in full swing. He'd taken at least an hour to tell his story, probably two. But there was one more proclamation to make. "My sister has to know."

Roman and Ismena exchanged a glance.

"That's not going to be a problem, is it?" Theo said.

"No," Ismena said. Her words came out slowly. "We must be careful, though."

"What do you mean?"

"We can't arouse any suspicions getting her here."

"Not to mention we'll have a time of it reintroducing you to the town," Roman said.

"What? Suspicions? Who's suspicious?" Theo asked.

Again, Ismena's tone was deliberate. "Things have gotten... tense since you left. Many of the townsfolk have become rather paranoid."

"Peering from the windows, they are," Roman said. "Hiding like, and spying on everything that goes on in this place."

"Because of my disappearance?" Theo couldn't believe that was true. Sure, Ipsitfel wasn't a large place, and most everybody knew *of* everyone else at the very least, but he was hardly a prominent member of the community. His disappearance shouldn't have caused any uproar. People went missing occasionally and the foggy atmosphere of Ipsitfel didn't change.

"No," Ismena said, "not *because* of your disappearance, but the paranoia became noticeable around the same time."

"Why's everyone getting all fidgety?"

"Because the ceremony's not working," Ismena said.

"What?"

"Well, that's what townsfolk are saying, but I don't know how many people believe it." She clasped her hands together over her crossed legs. "The fact of the matter is, many of the town's wells have dried up—which is why Tom never needs to come down here anymore. Almost instantly, crops are dying after a season where we got plenty of rain. Livestock are catching diseases…"

"I'd heard mention of that before I left, at Eldra's party."

"But like I've said, people have only started to worry in the past week or so."

"They're all misfortunes that never gave us trouble 'fore," Roman said, suddenly very morose. "When the ceremony was working."

"Does everyone believe this?" Theo asked.

"Not everyone," Ismena said. "Some people have voiced the opinion that the ceremony can't be a catch-all, that things would be worse if we weren't doing it right, and that up until now we've just not noticed when we've had occasional bad years."

"Some deny there's any issue at all," Roman said. "They believe it's a batch of mumbo-jumbo that's been thought up by a town of superstitious twats."

"But many *do* believe that what's happening has to do with the ceremony," Ismena continued. "Some may even be taking matters into their own hands."

Theo's eyes wandered to the covered faces of his parents. They could have been statues, given how still they remained. If he couldn't see the steady movements of their breathing, he might not have believed they were alive at all. Thoughts churned in his mind, chasing implications at first before becoming suspicious. What exactly did Ismena mean by *into their own hands*?

"There have been some mysterious deaths," Ismena said.

"Two," Roman said. He counted them off with his fingers. "Matilda Monson and Robin Deckle."

At last, Theo's mother moved. It was an involuntary twitch, but a movement nonetheless. She'd known Robin Deckle from the library.

"Matilda took a tumble from a second-story window and cracked her head on the cobblestones," Roman said, "and Robin sought his own end in his bathtub."

"His ritual took place last night, before I found you," Ismena said.

Theo thought there was an easy way to test whether Robin had ended his own life or not, one that involved returning to Nochlan, but he didn't say so aloud. Too many other thoughts were competing for his attention, none of which were very pleasant. Two suspicious deaths might lead to more; another fall, a sudden illness, maybe even a fire...

"The zealots," Theo muttered. Ismena didn't balk at his use of the term.

"They been growing in number, they have," Roman said. "These days, you can always find one preaching in some alley or another with an audience hanging on his every word."

Aghast at the events transpiring in Ipsitfel, Theo's mouth hung open. Never before had he worried when wandering the city streets. He'd never had much reason to. The idea that Ipsitfel could be a dangerous place had never once occurred to him; the danger was always in the woods outside the walls. How could a population of harmonious citizens have turned on each other so rapidly? Or had these issues always existed beneath the surface, waiting to emerge?

"Don't take much to figure," Roman said, the flame casting shadows over his sharp features. "The dark is descending on our solemn town."

The discussion continued for a short while before Ismena agreed to let Theo and his parents rest. She disappeared briefly before climbing back down the basement stairs with blankets for them. She apologized that they couldn't sleep in the main house, but Theo understood. After he rejoined the population, the Bareens would probably provide him a place to stay. As for Theo's mother and father, he'd have to find another arrangement. Neither Damon nor Medina complained, however, and took the blankets with vague thank yous before Ismena disappeared again.

She left the lantern and the matches with them.

Roman said his goodbyes shortly thereafter. Theo wanted to ask him to stay, but Roman had a nice, comfortable bed waiting for him at home that was far better than the wooden table Theo planned to sleep on. If Theo asked, he most likely would have agreed, leaving Theo feeling guilty for the aches and pains they'd both feel afterward. As it turned out, he didn't need the warmth of the other boy beside him. Theo had only to lay down on the table before he fell into a deep, uninterrupted sleep.

Falling asleep by candlelight and awakening in pitch darkness left Theo confused for at least a handful of heartbeats when he awoke again. He had no way of telling what time it was, nor could he locate the door or his parents. He could hear their soft breathing, but it seemed to emanate from everywhere at once.

Rolling onto his back, Theo groaned against the stiffness in his body. Sleeping on a wooden table was more comfortable than in the belly of a wooden boat, but not by much. What he wouldn't give to have a bed right now, his own bed. But the bed he longed for had burned up in the fire; it would take time before another felt like his own again.

He heard the door of the basement shudder as someone fiddled with the latch.

Theo sat bolt upright, his eyes clawing at the darkness. Where was that lantern?

"Mother, Father," he hissed. He heard his parents stir, which was confirmation enough that they had awakened. Then he slid off the table, hands outstretched. The lantern had last been beside his parents.

With a low creak, the door opened and Theo could see that it was night outside again. Had he slept through an entire day? Tendrils of the persistent fog drifted into the basement, followed by a silhouetted figure who clambered down the stairs uncertainly. They were followed by a second figure, shorter and stouter, before the door closed again and the moon's glow was shut out.

"Theo, where's the light?" Ismena asked.

The tightness in Theo's chest released. But who was the other person?

Ismena found the lantern first. The light flared as the match hissed, and this small flame was enough to make Theo squint while his eyes adjusted. To his left, his parents were sitting up. His mother had fallen asleep slumped in the chair, and his father had lain on the stone ground. Each of them folded their blankets as they rose.

"Who? Who is this?" Laila asked, stepping into the light. Her face was cast in a hopeful doubt marred by heavy wariness. Then she spotted her brother. "Theo! Theo, by the gods, is that you?"

Without waiting for an answer, she ran to him and pulled him into a tight embrace, gasping with disbelief. She said to Ismena, "Where did you find him? How did you? I can't thank you enough, Ismena. Theo, you're back!"

"He was where I'd said he'd gone," Ismena explained.

Laila laughed, possibly on the verge of tears. She released Theo, held him at arm's length, and surveyed the state he was in. "Come now," she said with another laugh. "You don't really mean to tell me... I mean, you were joking, surely..."

But when she looked from the serious Ismena to Theo—who realized he hadn't washed and was still covered from head to foot in dirt, and blood, and who knew what else—the smile on her face vanished. Without warning, she shoved Theo hard in the arm.

"You reckless ass," she said. "You foul, selfish...cretin! How could you? Did you really think that was a good idea?"

"Laila, I'm sorry," Theo said. She laughed again, but this time it was full of malice.

"Oh, you're sorry. You're sorry? That's all you have to say for yourself?" she hissed. "We lost Mother and Father and then only nights later I lose you too. *She*"—Laila gestured to Ismena, who flinched—"comes to me with some boorish story about you going through the Gateway to chase our parents, which is somehow supposed to help me cope. And all you can say is 'sorry.' What the fuck is wrong with you?"

Theo's heart pained him. He had known Laila would be mad, but seeing her angry like this, on the verge of tears though she held them back admirably, was more than he could handle. He shook, wanting her to stop looking at him with so much hurt in her eyes. Instead of answering, he lifted his arm and pointed to his left.

"What?" Laila asked, looking from him to the veiled individuals sitting against the wall. "What am I supposed to—"

"I brought them back," Theo whispered.

Laila looked furiously back and forth between him and their parents before realization began to dawn on her face and an entirely new emotion took over. This time, it was one Theo had not expected. Aghast, Laila mouth fell open, and she backed away a few steps.

"You don't mean to say," she gasped.

"It's them."

"But, Theo..." Laila stopped retreating. Her chest heaved. Finally, she reached out a hand toward her parents.

"You can't remove the coverings," Theo said. "That's the only thing keeping them here."

"But..."

"He's telling the truth, Laila," Medina said finally. Her voice sounded weak and drained.

The outstretched hand went to cover Laila's mouth instead. "Mother?" she managed.

"Yes," Medina said.

"And Father?"

"I am here."

With another gasp, Laila rushed forth and embraced them both. Her long dark hair swung over her shoulders. She could no longer hold back the tears, so she wept as she embraced her parents, trembling all over. All the anger and pain had retreated enough that for the few minutes she spent clutching them, she was nothing more than a young girl glad of her parents' return. Both Damon and Medina placed an arm across her back to comfort her. The small gesture reduced her further into stifled sobs.

When at last she could stand again, Laila came back to Ismena and Theo, wiping her eyes. "How is this possible?" she asked. "Tell me."

So Theo did. Once again, he relayed everything that had happened below the Gateway, recounting the fantastical events with as many details as he could recall. Unlike Roman and Ismena, his sister remained stoic during his retelling, showing only a flicker of emotion during the most harrowing portions. Even when he had finished, she remained silent for a few minutes, watching their parents with a blank stare. Then she closed her eyes and ran her hands through her hair.

"That was an incredibly stupid thing for you to have done," she said. "You put yourself in so much danger and survived only by luck. If you had died…" She sighed, her brow furrowed. "But you didn't. And it is something to have our parents back, even if we can't see their faces. I'm just wondering what kind of life they have ahead of them."

"I hadn't thought that far ahead," Theo admitted.

Laila looked at him. Was that pity in her eyes? "That much, I'd guessed."

"For now, I think it's safe to keep them here," Ismena said. "I can't guarantee that no one in my family will come down into the basement, but it is rare. Usually, I am the one sent to fetch things."

"Thank you," Laila said. "We'll find a way to feed them so we're not stealing food from your family's table."

Ismena nodded at the agreeable terms, happy that she wouldn't have to steal food from their pantry. Theo knew she'd never been comfortable lying; she was probably relieved the task of providing for his parents was lifted.

Laila stayed for a while longer, trying to talk to Damon and Medina, though they weren't quite as responsive as she might have hoped. Theo sat by her side, and Ismena left them to it, saying she'd return when she could.

For lack of better conversation, Laila told her family about what she'd been doing in their absence: how she'd begun work as an apprentice in the courthouse and how she'd spent the week growing used to the ticks of her new coworkers, many of whom were double her age. She did her best to keep her talk light, she and Theo chuckling at the missteps of her first days at the apprenticeship, but Damon and Medina gave little to no response beyond vague encouragement. Their voices were wispy, thin, and tinged with melancholy. Sparks of elation flickered out in their children as Theo and Laila came to realize that not every part of their parents had returned. Being with them was not quite the same.

27
Murder in Ipsitfel

The next evening, Ismena had Theo come upstairs with her. When he entered the living room, Missus Bareen spotted him and nearly dropped the vase she carried. All manner of questions ensued, which Ismena answered exclusively to avoid errors in their story; she'd seen him stumbling out of the woods earlier that day, and he had very little memory of the last ten days except that he'd wandered through the trees aimlessly.

The story wasn't such a stretch of the imagination, given that he was covered in dirt from head to toe. Missus Bareen decried in a scornful tone that it was a miracle he hadn't been killed by something in the woods, but her manner softened when he looked appropriately ashamed. After all, she couldn't be mad at a boy who'd lost his parents and had troubles coping. He would "learn to go on without them in time."

He was allowed to bathe, which Theo was very excited about. The moment he set foot in the bathtub, the water turned a muddy brown and it became apparent that no further good would come from sitting in the muck. Therefore, he ran himself a second bath, in which he scrubbed every inch of his filthy body until his skin glowed raw. Theo lingered until all heat had left the bath, and left only to avoid causing the Bareens to think he'd disappeared again.

Tom brought Theo some of his clothes to wear. Ismena's older brother was larger than Theo, but closer in size than Mister Bareen, in whose clothing Theo would've drowned. As it was, the clothes were baggy and long, but he didn't mind much.

He was also allowed to sleep on the sofa again, which provided a difference in comfort even Theo and his aching body had underestimated. Still, he took longer to fall asleep than he might have, given the gnawing guilt he felt that his parents were below, sleeping among the dank and dust. He vowed to improve their lodgings.

The next day, Theo marched down to Miss Petunia's to ask if he could have his job back. Miss Petunia, glad but wary to see him again, proclaimed that he'd never been formally let go, but she would allow him his old spot if he promised to be more reliable. Theo swore up and down that he would work six days a week without complaint, knowing this time around he had solid motivation to see his promise through.

And so he worked.

With the money he made, he bought better blankets for his parents to sleep on and food for them to eat. Laila helped with this as well, though they had to do so secretly so they wouldn't be noticed smuggling food beneath the Bareen residence. Theo eventually bought himself better-fitting clothing, and he gave some of the leftover money to the Bareens for his food and lodgings.

Roman made a habit of coming by the bakery for breakfast and lunch. Of course, given these were often the busiest times of day for the bakery, Theo couldn't stop working, but anytime there was a lull in customers, they'd chat while Roman ate. On some days, the older boy would ask in code how Theo's parents were doing, to which Theo would respond that they were fine and everything was going well.

These were the only occasions in which Theo lied to Roman.

The fact of the matter was that the situation with his parents was a mixed bag. They barely ate, no matter what food Theo and

Laila brought them, complaining that they had no appetite, and what they did eat they could barely stomach. Their bodies were starting to look emaciated, their collarbones prominent and their necks pinched. Any time Theo did see an arm or a leg emerge from the folds of their clothing, it was bone-thin and sallow. He brought them water from upstairs to bathe in, which helped them stay clean, but the room itself was so dank and dusty that cleanliness didn't improve their circumstances much.

Their disposition did not improve either. Theo and Laila would talk to them, describing their workdays and whatever else they did. Medina and Damon responded with slow nods or faint praise, but little else. Theo worried any day now, Laila would turn to him and tell him he'd done the wrong thing bringing them back. No matter what new challenge arose, he would be willing to argue that it was better they were present than to be gone and needed again.

The problem was they couldn't leave the basement. If they'd had the chance to go out and inhale some fresh air once in a while, stretch their legs on a walk, he was certain their entire demeanor would change. But of course, that was impossible. If anyone should see them and suspect the truth, then their whole secret arrangement would be over.

It didn't help that all around him, Ipsitfel was growing more desperate. People didn't like to discuss the happenings openly, but Theo would hear friends whispering in line while they waited to pay for their scones. Three days after his return, Russell Gottwald drowned himself in the Stick River—although Theo found his suicide dubious, owing to the injury on the back of his head, which went unquestioned except in whispers. While the Descension that followed was as somber as usual, it also carried with it a mounting tension Theo couldn't dispel. Shifting eyes roamed the gathered citizens, though every time Theo tried to look their way, he found everyone staring straight ahead.

He never felt comfortable bringing up the whispers to any of the customers in line—who would halt their conversation the moment it was their turn at the register, as if Theo couldn't hear them prior to that—because eavesdropping was a sure cause for suspicion.

Instead, he relayed his thoughts to Roman.

Two days after Mister Gottwald's Descension, Theo was preparing to lock up the bakery after closing. Miss Petunia was heading out just as Roman came sauntering up, and she sneered at him while he gave a mock curtsey. His faithful patronage as of late had done nothing to improve her favor toward him. Roman had shrugged off her dismissals.

The bell above the doorway rang as he entered.

"Oy," he called, "how's the baker's lad doin' this evening?"

Theo let the lid of the till box fall closed and locked it with a twist of his key.

"Just. About. Finished," he said, shoving the box into its compartment beneath the counter. "All done. No work tonight?"

"Me mum's finishing off with a coupla customers, but she was keen to close up early on account of she's not feeling well." He tapped a rhythm on one of the tables by the window, staring out at the dusk.

"That's too bad," Theo said. "Hopefully it's nothing serious."

"Nah." Roman dismissed his concern with a wave. "Nothing to worry about. Plus, I thought someone like you might want company on his walk home."

"Oh, so you think I need to be walked home?"

"A wee thing like you—"

"I can't take care of myself?"

"You *do* look a bit frail—"

"I took on the underworld and lived, I'll remind you."

Roman laughed, breaking off Theo's string of mock protests. "That you did, Sahiron, but these is dangerous times."

"True," Theo said, "but if you walk home with me, then there's no one to walk you home. That's just not fair."

Roman's tongue poked out of the corner of his mouth as he thought. "I s'pose you're right. Guess I hadn't thought things through."

But when they'd left the building and Theo had locked the front door, they headed off toward the Bareen residence together. The chill in the night air was starting to take hold, and Theo suppressed a shiver. Wind sent billows of fog rolling through the streets, though the lamps fought the darkness admirably.

They rounded the first corner onto Millicent Lane. For the briefest of moments, Theo made eye contact with a haggard man pulling his pea coat over his neck, before the man darted into the nearest building and slammed the door.

Theo shook his head. "I hate that everyone's talking about what's going on without anyone *actually* talking about it. It's either folk in complete denial or zealots telling us all to off ourselves."

"People are just afraid," Roman said. "S'pose they don't know what they should say and who they should trust."

"Yes, but if people were open about it—"

"Cause a fuss, and you're apt to get attention. No one wants that," Roman said. "Imagine the murderer is about and listening in on folk. They'd know when folks was comin' on to them if they was talkin' out loud. They could retaliate."

He said all this without his usual smile. Theo shook his head. "Five suspicious deaths in twelve days—I've decided to count my parents now too. Just because of a few dried up wells and a few sick animals. I just wish there weren't so many secrets."

"Well, we've got secrets of our own. Haven't we?" Roman put his arm around Theo's shoulders. Theo looked up at him, not wanting to press the argument. If he was being honest with himself, Roman was right. They didn't want to draw any attention to themselves either because they *were* hiding secrets. That didn't stop the unease Theo felt at the sight of the abandoned streets of Ipsitfel. It had been this way every evening since he'd returned to work at the bakery. As soon as the sun started to go down and the regular workday ended, the entire town emptied. The lamps were lit, but shutters were drawn, and doors closed. Children were called into their homes for supper and didn't reemerge until the new day.

"Miss Petunia has been upset lately," Theo said.

"Isn't she always?" Roman said. "Rigid bitch has got that look about her."

Theo chuckled, elbowing his friend in the ribs. "More than that, though. The river water doesn't make as good of bread as the wells did. People have been making comments both to me and her, but she can't do much about it. She says that when the light harvest comes after the season, it's only going to get worse."

Roman nodded. "Bert Rye came 'round a day or two ago. Was telling me mum they'd thought about divertin' the river to get to the crop valley. Never had to do that before, but no well water and no rains yet. We'll not have any food come next year."

Before Theo could respond, Roman had grabbed him by the collar and thrown him against the wall of the nearest building. Theo tried to protest, but Roman flattened himself against the wall as well and put a finger to his lips. He looked past Theo at the street intersection a few buildings down.

A man came stumbling into view. The uneven cobblestones caught his foot, and he tumbled, gasping in pain.

Startled by his appearance, Theo made to help, but Roman threw his arm across Theo's chest to stop him, holding him back against the wall. "Don't move," Roman whispered into his ear, making the skin on Theo's neck prickle.

In the next moment, Theo knew why. On the man's heels came a figure in a blue cape. They descended upon the man, who shouted in protest. Theo thought the racket made by the struggle should've been loud enough to draw attention, but the windows above them remained shuttered and the altercation went uninterrupted.

"Don't look," Roman whispered.

Theo shut his eyes, but as he'd learned before, that only made the situation worse. He was focused on the man's sounds now, listening to him whimper. His shoes scraped across the cobblestones. He was trying to back away, but the figure in the blue cape was too close. With a barely audible thud, the man's pleas turned to a gurgle. Then he was silent altogether. Theo opened his eyes as the caped figure fled, a gold medallion around their neck glinting briefly in the lamplight.

Theo's heart raced. He was shaking, glad that Roman held him against the wall; otherwise he might not have been able to stand. Any doubts about the change in Ipsitfel's atmosphere had been erased from his mind. They'd witnessed a murder from less than thirty paces away—out in the open where anyone could have seen. He locked eyes with Roman, who had a look of sorrow and pity on his face.

"Dark times," Roman said.

"That was," Theo stammered trying to find the words. "They just..."

"Paranoia's the law of the land now. Nobody says nothing 'cause they don't want to be next."

"We have to go. We need to hide."

"I'm surprised you don't want to figure out who's done it."

Theo paused, staring through Roman as if he weren't standing right in front of him. "Would you like me to want to figure out who murdered him?"

"No—I didn't mean that. I'm just surprised is all."

"I can't do anything about it," Theo said. "*Paranoia's the law of the land now*. Think of what it'll look like if we just happened to be walking around after dark and witnessed his murder. They might search where I live. See what else I'm hiding. I can't have that."

Roman nodded, holding him by the shoulders with comforting hands. "Did you see their cloak though, Theo? A blue cape. A cape from the Descension. The bearers?"

Theo didn't speak, his breathing heavy and distraught. He didn't try to shake off Roman's hold on his shoulders, but stood still, willing himself to be calm.

"I'd wager that some of the zealots in this town wouldn't bat an eye if every last soul what calls Ipsitfel home was murdered. At least, not before they'd admit it wouldn't help none," Roman said. "We need to be careful."

Theo glanced at the man lying sprawled on the street. He looked back at Roman and nodded, his pulse finally steady. None of this sat right, but he knew that what the older boy said was true. He'd witnessed firsthand how suspicious every wandering eye became whenever he entered a room full of people. The very tension that lined the streets twisted his stomach into knots. And now murder. Unquestionable, conspicuous murder.

"We need to get inside," Theo said.

"Aye." Roman took him by the hand, and they ran the rest of the way to the Bareens'.

After that evening, Theo's anxiety only increased. The next day, the man's murder was discussed in hushed tones by nearly every pair of customers who entered the bakery. His name had been Lionel Burkhart. He'd been a carpenter who had "always minded his own business," but "must've crossed the wrong person somehow." Each time he heard mention of the murder, Theo began to perspire and had to hope the speaker wouldn't notice. If anyone did, they didn't say so within earshot. Perhaps they assumed it was the heat of the ovens getting to him.

Most surprising of all was that this time people generally agreed it was a murder—although they would have been hard pressed to think otherwise, given the state he was in when discovered. Nobody would audibly admit that the string of deaths might all be related. It was almost as if suggesting this connection was admittance of accomplice, which made no sense to Theo.

He, like everybody else, went to Mister Burkhart's Descension in Cirillo Square. Although Theo felt ages older than at his parents' Descension—the last one he'd attended—he still donned the youthful white tunic. The same silence befell the gathering as the proceedings began. When Governor Sutton spoke about what the ceremony was meant to do for the town, he almost seemed to be begging. His short speech resonated through the square, and for the first time Theo noticed that the words carried with them something he couldn't quite place. The tone had changed, and the governor's disposition had as well. Not until the body was being lowered through the Gateway, the Cimmerian Elegy rising like the moon, could Theo place the feeling.

It was feverish anticipation. A tainted sort of hope.

They were all waiting for something, watching that some sign might present itself once the rope was pulled and the body released.

And Theo was part of the crowd.

The realization hit him and the unease that ensued lingered. He still felt it walking back with the Bareens; he felt it as he visited his parents in the basement; he felt it over the next couple days as he worked at Miss Petunia's bakery.

The people weren't just appalled by the collection of murders; they were encouraging them on some level, hoping that the next would solve their problems. And if that one didn't, then perhaps the one after. As long as nobody seemed to care who in the town was committing them, then they could continue unchallenged.

This last thought made Theo the queasiest. He even made himself sick talking to Roman one evening. Of course, Roman had already come to this conclusion. As he was already disillusioned by human nature, the realization hadn't floored him but he did find it disgusting. Perhaps a year in age could make a big difference after all.

Then, one night two weeks after Theo's return, unthinkable tragedy struck. So devastating was the horrific news that it could not go *un*-exclaimed.

Theo hadn't worked that day, so he was at the Bareens' when Ismena's father burst through the front door and told them all to gather in the living room. One by one, he locked the series of newly installed bolts on the doors and drew all manner of curtains over the windows. The family and Theo waited nervously by the sofa while Mister Bareen checked the whole house for lapses in security, muttering incoherently to himself all the while. Finally, he came stomping back into the room, looking fearful and uncertain. He kept pulling at his tie as he relayed the devastating news he'd just heard in Cirillo Square.

"Eldra Vromía has been suffocated in her conservatory."

Ipsitfel's eldest citizen was dead.

28

Eldra Egressed

Theo stood before the mirror, listening as the bells of Viseyne Tower chimed clear across Ipsitfel. He pulled at his tunic and flattened his hair with his hand, trying to gauge whether there was anything else he could do to make himself more presentable. Only this morning he'd noticed black hairs sprouting over his chin, though they were still too short to need shaving. He couldn't feel excited about the prospect of his adulthood, however, as an unshakable foreboding had lingered inside him throughout the entire day. Every interaction had felt dampened, including the ones between him and his friends. Even the fog had appeared more oppressive than usual. The world around him grieved the loss of Eldra.

He left the bathroom, plodding down the stairs to join the Bareen family gathered at the front door. Ismena wore her own white tunic, her hair braided around the back of her head. She made eye contact with Theo as he descended, worry plastered on her face. Obviously, she sensed the same foreboding as he did.

Mister Bareen was the last to join them, and they departed for Cirillo Square, keeping close together. Even on the night of a ritual, the town was fraught with paranoia. Theo kept pace with Ismena, their eyes shifting to stay aware of their surroundings. Theo half expected to see a shadow darting out of sight each time he turned, but he never did. If Matanda was here, the deity had not made himself known.

"I don't know what anyone thinks can come of this," Theo whispered. "It has to end—killing hasn't helped anything so far, and it's not going to."

"I guess they're not convinced," Ismena said.

"What will convince them?"

"Water flowing in the wells again, rain, no diseases in their livestock."

"What happens if *this* never fixes that?"

"They're not willing to take that chance."

"Who will be next? Children? Teachers? My family? You? Me?" Theo shook his head. He wished Ismena could give him answers, but knew there weren't any to begin with. Reason had fled Ipsitfel. Murder was insanity. If murder was going to work, it would've done so by now.

The Shears, along with Laila, came into view. Theo's sister joined him and Ismena, looking every bit as solemn.

"I visited Mom and Dad this morning," she said, head bowed. "I told them about what happened."

"How did they react?" Theo asked.

"Stronger than I expected. They both sort of gasped and Mother even put a hand to her heart."

Theo nodded. An invigorated response like that was eons more than anything else he'd witnessed since they'd come above ground. A bit of him relaxed. He'd been worried their condition would only worsen; this was a hopeful sign to the contrary.

"They didn't want to believe me either," Laila continued. "I had to assure them that the information was reliable. I think I worried them."

"They have every right to be worried," Theo said.

"Just imagine, though," Ismena said. "They've known Eldra to be a steady constant in Ipsitfel for far longer than we have. If nothing else, they expected her to die a peaceful death. Natural causes. She was well-respected, after all."

Laila nodded. "I think we all expected that."

"Her murder is an undeniable sign that Ipsitfel is crumbling," Ismena said.

Somber silence fell between the three of them. They traveled amid the clicking of heels over cobblestones. All around them, the flock of citizens heading toward Cirillo Square densified. People poured in from side streets and alleyways. Adults drew cloaks around themselves, while children subdued by the morose atmosphere scampered along in their white tunics. So many familiar faces: many Theo knew by name and many he only knew by sight. They converged under the gathering night until the path opened unto the square and they were released at the foot of Viseyne Tower.

The square was filling fast. The Bareens settled into the rows of standing citizens with the Shears close by. Theo scanned the crowd quickly, an unwarranted fear gripping his chest, until he saw Roman across the way. Roman caught sight of him as well and gave a reassuring nod. Beside Roman stood his mother, only tall enough that her head reached his shoulder. She seemed to be in a daze, gazing intently up at the wooden pulley that hung above the Gateway. Theo didn't like the worry in the downturned corners of her mouth.

"Listen, Theo," Ismena whispered. He glanced sideways at her. She looked stricken, but also determined to speak. "I don't want to come off accusatory, but I think you should strongly consider what I have to say."

"Well, get it out then." Theo wasn't comfortable with her tone.

"I think you have to send them back. I think your parents being here is what's causing all these problems."

The accusation was a slap to the face. "How can you say that?" he hissed.

Ismena sighed, exasperated. "Maybe you shouldn't have brought your parents back."

"Not you too, Ismena. You don't believe—"

"I think it's hurt both them and the town."

"That's ridiculous. The problems started before—"

"Shh!" Laila hushed them both with an elbow to Theo's side. He was about to protest when she nodded toward the Gateway.

The governor stepped up on the platform beside the great pit. Although he'd spoken at countless other Descensions for countless other citizens, he appeared overcome by the prospect of eulogizing Eldra. He wrung his hands together, partially mutilating his prepared speech in the process. The crowd had already been deathly quiet for quite some time, but still he waited until the exact moment the clock struck the half hour.

"My friends and fellow residents of Ipsitfel," the governor began, his voice lacking some of its usual confidence. "Today we continue to honor the oldest of all traditions here at Ipsitfel: the Descension through the Gateway. By—by returning our sister to the Earth, may trouble never befall her beloved town."

He cleared his throat, trying to look around at all the people gathered in the square while making eye contact with none of them.

"Yet it is with a heavy heart that we recognize the prominent individual and matriarch of our community who Ipsitfel sends off tonight to her final resting place," he said. "Eldra Vromía was synonymous with the name of our town. She carried with her a living history of what it meant to live in and be a part of the Ipsitfel community, from the days of her birth until the final moments preceding her unfortunate death."

A rustle ran through the crowd, though nobody spoke a word. Still fuming, Theo found himself hard pressed to absorb Governor Sutton's words. Instead, he kept stealing angry glances at Ismena.

"Eldra gave herself to charitable work until late in her life, past when many would have found retirement preferable. She was a passionate gardener with a famously green touch, especially when it came to roses. And though she prized her solitude more than most, she was known to be honest and forthcoming.

"As the last member of a long-running, influential family strongly rooted in Ipsitfel's colorful past, she will be missed. As a voice of charity and vitality, she will be missed. As a friend, she will be missed."

The last of the governor's words echoed through the square just as Theo turned his head to see the approaching procession. With no living family to speak of, Eldra's body was preceded by the dozen or so people under her employ at Vromía Manor. They carried candles before them, and the underlighting cast eerie shadows over their faces. Theo felt it made them look emotionless.

Following them came the six bearers with Eldra's body lying on a board between them. Seeing the blue capes flowing around each figure, Theo became anxious. Someone wearing one of those capes had murdered Lionel Burkhart only a few days before. Had a similar fate come of Eldra? Had the last thing she'd seen been flowing blue fabric descending upon her? He eyed the medallions resting on their chests, surprised he'd never been able to make out the roses embossed on them. The image felt almost impudent now.

Then he was able to see the body, and his breath caught. Eldra was lying on the wooden board just as any of the deceased did when their Descension came. She looked peaceful, oddly unreal, and not like the lively woman he'd met at her birthday party mere weeks ago. Her hair had been pulled back into a neat bun beneath her head and her hands were folded over her stomach. She looked small enough to be a child.

Laid out before them was what Ipsitfel had truly become.

All eyes followed her progress as she neared the Gateway. A collective breath held while the procession crossed the threshold into the enclosed space. The bearers set her down and fastened the ropes around her, handing the thin release cord to the nearest of Eldra's attending employees, a woman with dark, fearful eyes. Her hands shook as she held the end. Then the blue-cloaks raised the body until it swung gently over the opening.

A tension more severe than before held the crowd as the body was lowered down toward the Gateway. The song began, deep and mournful and slow.

"Gently you go, breathing the night
The moon and the stars come, guiding by light."

Fog rolled through the square, but it could not obscure the sight of the body hanging limp over the darkness. Shadows reached up to grab at Eldra's ankles and wrists. Theo imagined her waking. Saw her coming to her senses in time to realize what was happening and tell the blue-cloaked figures to stop. This was all a mistake. Her death would not fix their problems. But of course, she didn't stir even as the first of her limbs dipped below the lip of the Gateway. The crowd's attentive fervor was in full force, increasing the weight on her body until she had been swallowed whole by the dark.

"Pity the mountain that howls and grieves
But tend to the bowed willow, mourning its leaves."

Inch by inch, the harness descended until the six bearers had reached the end of their rope. Realizing her time had come, the fearful woman holding the pulley took a deep, quivering breath and then tugged.

The rope recoiled as its passenger fell away.

Theo didn't trust himself to move. He didn't want to be the one to break the spell, the one to release the flood. He could feel the catastrophic energy so ineptly held at bay. Only seconds could remain of that balance.

The governor broke the silence.

"She will find peace now in—"

"It wasn't enough!" someone shouted, and heads began to turn, searching for the source of the voice.

"What are we going to do?" another cried.

"We're being punished for all our wrongdoings!" bellowed a third, and at this, dangerous cracks in the dam began to form.

The governor put out his hands, trying to calm the flurry of shouts that erupted all around him. "Now, now, everyone," he said, doing his best to sound commanding. Not a soul paid him mind. "We mustn't lose ourselves. Reverence, folks. Reverence. We are still in the middle of a Descension."

"Damn the bloody Descension!"

"No! This is why the wells have gone!"

"We're not safe anymore!"

"We have to sacrifice more souls!"

"Everybody stand down."

Theo was jostled, the crowd around him shifting. He stumbled into Ismena, grabbing her arm to keep steady. The noise grew louder, voices rising in confusion and fear. Theo could feel his blood pumping again. They needed to get out of the square. If the hysteria escalated much more, they could be trampled.

"Laila!" he called, beckoning to his sister. "Stay close."

"Head for the streets," Ismena said.

"I said, everybody stand down," the governor cried again, stomping his foot on the platform.

Before Theo, Ismena, or Laila could move, Governor Sutton let out a cry of great agony. He stumbled around on the stage, trying to reach something behind him. When he turned, Theo could see a knife buried to the handle in his back. A dark stain blossomed at the point of penetration. Sutton turned a few more times, grunting in pain, before he sank to his knees and fell from the platform.

Someone screamed, and then the dam broke.

Chaos shattered the night. One moment they'd been standing, huddled together, and the next people were running in every direction. Shouts, screams, and cries pervaded the air. Folk were knocked over as others ran into them. Some were shoving their way through, using elbows and knees to clear their path. The door into the Gateway's enclosure was ripped from its hinges and went soaring through the air, knocking a few citizens unconscious in the process. People were trampled, calling out for help before going silent.

Theo tried to hold on to Ismena and his sister, but as they turned to exit from Cirillo Square, they were torn apart. He managed to grab Laila's arm again, but Ismena was being corralled back into the fray, her eyes wide. Shrill screams escaped her lungs.

"Ismena!" Theo called, but she was gone, lost in the mass of rioting figures. His shocked gaze wandered to the Gateway, where someone clung for their life as they dangled from the pulley. People hopped the fence into the enclosure if they couldn't get around. The body of the governor was hoisted mercilessly into the air and thrown into the black hole.

"Can you make it out?" Theo asked Laila. They were nearly to the edge of the square, though he kept looking back into the chaos, hoping to catch a glimpse of his friend.

"What?" Laila said. "What are you going to do?"

"Ismena," Theo said.

"No." Laila gripped his arm tighter. "Don't leave."

"Laila, I have to." Theo's mind was racing. He didn't have much time. The longer Ismena was in there, the more likely she was to get hurt.

He and Laila were only a few yards away from the edge of the square now. They ducked into a storefront alcove as a mob of townsfolk rushed past, carrying a flailing body over their heads.

"You don't have to," Laila countered. "We can get to Mom and Dad. We can hide there with them."

"That's a good idea," Theo said. "You should do that. When we get to the street, run. Run as fast as you can. Try to make sure nobody's following you."

"Theo." There were tears in her eyes. "Don't do this. I know she's your friend, but you'll die. They've gone mad."

"I have to try," Theo said. "She never abandoned me—I can't abandon her. Please, make sure Mom and Dad are safe. They need you."

He squeezed his sister's hands. She watched him, and he hoped he looked more determined than scared. Although she wanted him safe, he knew this was the right thing to do. The Bareens hadn't seen their daughter disappear; they wouldn't know to look for her. Someone had to go after Ismena. Laila nodded, resigned. "Please, come back," she whispered. "I already lost you once."

"I will," he said. They locked eyes again, then, at the same moment, they both got up and ran in opposite directions. Theo let himself glance back long enough to see his sister clear the edge of the square and sprint off into the dark streets. He hoped nobody was waiting for her along the way.

He faced forward just in time to see a broad back hurtling his way. Theo dived to the side, narrowly avoiding being crumpled as the man fell hard onto the cobblestones. The attackers who'd thrown him leapt forward to continue their assault. While they were distracted, Theo moved around them and kept threading his way toward the center of Cirillo Square. A woman leapt at him from the side, but Theo ducked down and she soared overhead, disappearing to his left. A swinging fist caught Theo's left arm, but he hadn't been the intended target and he backed away from that brawl without pursuit. A woman Theo recognized as Adonia Sykes had climbed one of the lampposts and was now belting "An Ode to Old Viseyne" at the top of her lungs while a gash in her cheek dripped blood onto the townsfolk beneath her.

Then a white explosion of pain erupted behind Theo's eyes as he was hit over the back of his head. He fell forward, sprawling on the ground, blind and confused. Had someone brought a spade to the ceremony? Or perhaps they'd run home to better equip themselves for the melee. Either way, Theo couldn't steady his vision as he tried to crawl out of reach of his attacker. If they did have a metal weapon, he wasn't going to last long.

Hand over hand, he crawled until he realized a scuffle had ensued behind him. Theo tried to look, but he couldn't make his head move the way he wanted it to. His eyes rolled in their sockets.

Suddenly, he was hoisted into the air as a pair of hands grabbed him beneath the arms. Theo tried to wriggle out of their hold, but they wound an arm across his chest, holding him tight to their body. Theo fought more forcefully, unsure if he could even stand straight on his own yet, but aware of how much worse being captured could be.

"Quit your flounderin', Theo. For fucks sake," the attacker wheezed. Theo stopped struggling at once.

"Roman?"

"Who else would it be?" Roman said, aggravated.

"Did you fight off whoever hit me?" Theo asked, looking around for the person with the spade. At the edge of his vision, he could just make out a slumped figure on the ground.

"Aye," Roman said, "he nearly bit me fingers off."

"Thanks."

"Don't thank me yet. Not till we're outta here."

Theo was carried another few steps before he remembered why he'd come back.

"No! Roman, don't!" he shouted. "I need to go back—Ismena's in there."

"What?"

"Ismena's been dragged into the square!"

"Theo," Roman groaned, though he stopped pushing through the crowd. "It's too dangerous."

"That's why Ismena shouldn't be there either."

"But—"

"Please, she needs help!"

Theo twisted around to face Roman, and as he did Cirillo Square came into view. People climbed the fence in and out of the enclosure around the Gateway. One was a girl trying desperately to extricate herself from a hostile group of townsfolk. She beat them back with a shoe, sliding herself over the iron railing. It was Ismena.

"No!" Theo screamed. He gave an almighty tug and broke free of Roman's grip. The older boy cried out in pain and surprise, but Theo had gotten away. He sprinted back into the mayhem, dodging people on all sides. The ground was littered now with fallen bodies, whether dead or knocked unconscious Theo couldn't tell, but he didn't stop to check. His eyes were trained on Ismena.

"Theo!" Roman called after him, but he could barely hear. Everything had risen to a deafening roar.

Ismena had just slid both her legs to the inside of the enclosure when she was hoisted into the air by a throng of hands. Theo could see her mouth opening in a scream, though from this distance he couldn't hear her. She thrashed, trying to break free.

But they didn't let her go. Instead, Theo watched as a hand bearing a loose cobblestone came down upon the top of her skull.

The stone came away painted red and trailing tendrils of viscous crimson liquid. He screamed as her head lolled back. No! She had only blacked out for a moment; he had to get to her before they could strike her again. She was unable to defend herself, knocked unconscious by the bludgeoning. Blood poured from her injury now, but she would be alright.

Yet even as he sprinted, Theo felt his heart sink further. His breath came in difficult gasps. Sweat poured down the sides of his face and his back.

The mob carrying Ismena showed no intention of putting her down. She was lifted higher into the air, held aloft like a sacrifice. As one, they turned toward the Gateway. Their pace was painfully slow and yet fast enough that Theo knew he'd never make it in time.

His mouth opened in silent terror as his friend was hoisted higher still. Then she was pitched forward, thrown from her captors' grasp. Her body sailed through the air, limp and defenseless. Theo willed her to take flight and soar away from this reprobate community. But she didn't. Instead, she plummeted until she disappeared into darkness, swallowed by the Gateway.

Shock ricocheted through Theo's body. Every muscle threatened to seize. His blood ran cold. Agony erupted in his chest as though he were being bludgeoned by the spade again. If he was crying out, it was involuntary. And yet, his own voice screamed in his ear—throat tearing screams that did nothing to ease the terror.

A loud crack resounded through the din, loud enough to eclipse the chaos. Theo cranked his head around, as did everyone else, in time to see the great Viseyne Tower swaying overhead. The obelisk of stone, plaster, and wood tilted precariously over the stretch of buildings behind it before swinging forward.

At once the balance was lost. Another loud crack emanated from its base. The tower toppled. Those within the Gateway enclosure didn't have the time to escape. Their screams rang out as the glowing clock face collided with the crane which hung over the great, black hole. The crane and the platform and part of the fence splintered under the impact. Then, as one, they went careening over the lip and were swallowed by the darkness.

.

29

The Woods

The shockwave came like an earthquake. Theo stumbled sideways as the ground shook, but unlike many of the people around him, he managed to stay on his feet and kept running. Debris flew through the air, pelting him with shards of splintered wood and stone. Dust kicked up, mixing with the fog. All along the length of the fallen tower, the cobblestones cracked under the weight of the collision.

In truth, Theo barely registered the impact, barely registered the screams. His heart had fallen from his chest and was now lying on the ground somewhere behind him. He didn't dare stop or look. He ran until he not only came to the Gateway but was past it, leaping over the rubble and crossing through the insanity that had overcome Cirillo Square. He ran past the courthouse, down the street beyond until the dimmed lights of Vromía Manor approached. But he didn't stop there either. Theo kept barreling onward until he was at the town's edge where the stone wall bordered the north side of Ipsitfel. Following this path, he sprinted until the gates of the town appeared up ahead and he careened through, uninhibited.

Crossing the threshold was like breaking through an invisible barrier. Beyond the limits of town, he could breathe. He tumbled forward onto the ground, his knees meeting the rough soil. He wrapped his arms around himself, willing the pressure he felt to leave his body. What came out was sobs. Tears spilled from his eyes—large, hot droplets that were almost painful to cry.

He couldn't rid his mind of the images playing over and over in random sequence, dull colors dominated by vivid splashes of red. Townsfolk attacking one another, lunging forth with teeth bared and fists clenched. Other people falling, collapsing onto cobblestones, their heads slapping the ground with sickening thuds. Townsfolk falling into the darkness. Screaming. Blood. Running. Blood.

And the image that reoccurred the most: Ismena lifted high into the air and thrown down through the Gateway.

She couldn't survive a fall from so high.

Theo gripped his head in his hands, but try as he might he could not grab the memories and remove them. The harder he tried, the more vivid they became—and likely, the more permanent as well.

Hunched in the fog, he cried. From out here, nothing of the violence perpetrating Ipsitfel was audible. Nothing existed except for silence, and for this he was grateful. He felt, despite what he'd been told all his life, that the world beyond the wall was comforting him. Theo rolled onto his back, staring up into the mist. His arms fell flat in the dirt beside him. He listened to his heart as it went from a heavy, raucous beat to just below the audible. The outside world remained inscrutably gray and dark. He didn't mind the dark.

There was, he reasoned, only one thing left to do. The *only* thing left to do.

After one last, deep breath, Theo sat up. He got to his feet; his face emotionless. He had felt as much as he could. Emotion would return, but for now he was only hollow and dispirited.

Without so much as a backward glance toward the wall, Theo set off for the woods.

The ground sloped downward, pulling him toward the thick mass of trees and undergrowth. So many stories had been told about the dangers, but in the darkness he could barely even see the woods. They were more of an idea than a villain. The trees wanted nothing from him. They couldn't be any worse than the place he'd left behind.

Theo crossed the threshold into the underbrush. Gnarled hands made of branches and twigs reached out to touch him, but he merely stepped around their outstretched fingers. Inside the woods, the world came alive again.

He heard insects calling out in the darkness. Their monotonous song mimicked the ringing in his ears. The trunks of the trees creaked in the breezes that blew through the canopy overhead. Every few minutes a bird took flight or some creature scampered off into the foliage. Theo listened to them go, but did not react. Wolves were said to prowl the area, but if they did, they paid him no mind.

Theo hadn't wandered in too far before he came to a stone bridge that crossed what he assumed was a narrower portion of the Stick River. The thought that someone in the past had built a bridge in these woods bewildered him. It had to have been a very long time ago, for no one these days would dare. He crossed, tracing fingers over the moss-covered railing, and continued onward.

Theo walked without direction, peering through the darkness though he saw very little. Wandering soothed his soul. Once upon a time, he had thought venturing through the forest would feel exhilarating, perilous. Neither of these sentiments gripped him now. He felt only peace. In the dark, he could see no suffering. Through the droning of insects, he could hear no pain. He'd left behind the place where those terrible things happened. That was not here. Not in these pleasant woods.

Up ahead, the ground sloped sharply upward. Mountains. These must've been the same mountains that had always patterned the very edge of distance. They were not so far after all.

He'd reached the mouth of a cave, hewn from the rock by weather or time. The dark opening was easily twice Theo's height and many times his width. Vines clung to the rock faces, growing in a sort of spiraling pattern that might have been beautiful in the light of day.

Theo surveyed the arched entrance before reaching out his hands and stepping inside. He expected the cave to command utter darkness, but as he walked, the light grew.

How very opposite. The world, he thought, makes a point to disprove your expectations.

All around him were thousands and thousands of candles. Each was simple and white, but varied in size. He looked around, amazed as they grew brighter, flames easing out of the black. Some candles were as large as his legs, while others were no bigger than his little finger. They huddled in groups, melting onto one another, in every state of use. Some looked new, while others had burned down to their end. The grotesque shapes formed by the dripping wax unsettled Theo, though the aroma of burning wicks comforted him.

Once their illumination had reached a plateau, he glanced back the way he'd come. The mouth of the cave now appeared to exit into total darkness.

He sensed movement.

A woman in a flowing black dress stepped into the light. She looked young, maybe only a few years older than Laila, though her features refused to stick in Theo's mind. Even as he stared at her, he found he couldn't recall what she looked like. The details slid past like a river's current.

Immediately, a nervous energy overcame Theo as he realized he'd trespassed on her home. She moved with the immutable elegance of nature. She moved like water. She moved like the moon across the cosmos. Theo was helpless to watch, his feet frozen to the spot.

Their eyes met and neither looked away. She stood in the center of the cave of candles.

"You're Death," Theo said.

"That is what many call me," the woman said. She clasped her hands before her in a stance that should've seemed docile. Theo's hands were shaking. He considered asking her, *What is your true name, then?* But he held his tongue. From what he'd learned in Nochlan, powerful beings didn't like to give out their true names. It was sacred knowledge. Even so, she answered him as if she knew what was on his mind. "My true name would take a lifetime to tell, and I would not waste yours to sit here pondering it."

"You're not how I imagined," Theo said.

"Humans have been trying to imagine me for thousands of years. I am never what they think."

"But you're here." He looked around at the surreal landscape of dancing flames.

Death raised her hands outwardly. "I am."

Theo tapped his fists against his sides, struggling to compose himself. His fear was giving way to frustration, to anger. He felt his mind spinning too fast. Thoughts collided. Standing before Death, he realized the warnings his parents and the elders had always given him were true, and a great many things he'd thought but never expected to say were bottlenecking at his tongue.

"Why?" was what he managed first, but that wasn't enough. Death watched him politely as he began pacing the length of the cave. "Why are you making any of this happen? Why is there so much violence and pain and killing? You sit out here in your cave in the woods while... while people I know are slaughtered in the streets and sacrificed to please *your* ancient deal. Lives are upended. People grieved for spouses or parents or—or their own children. You pick and choose who you want to go without considering who is left behind because you don't care. It's all the same to you. You're Death. It's you we're all afraid of. So why? *Why are you taking everyone I love?"*

Theo was out of breath by the time he finished, and his entire body trembled in fear and anger at the woman standing in front of him. Death didn't stop watching him the entire time, though her expression changed from a look of polite interest to one of concern. When he was done, she let him breathe before responding, gathering her thoughts perhaps, or waiting because she knew he wouldn't listen until he'd taken some time to calm down.

"I'm sorry," she said finally. "What you have experienced is difficult—"

"Don't speak as though you know what I'm going through," Theo shouted, his voice breaking. "You and everyone you know is immortal! Why should you care about dying?"

At this, Theo noticed her composed expression slip. He saw sadness in her eyes and in spite of himself, his anger faltered.

"You are wrong, Theo Sahiron," she said, "Immortality has its price, and it does not touch everyone I've known."

Her gaze slipped, becoming focused on something in the past. A face, perhaps. Theo reminded himself not to let his ire ebb. Maybe she knew *some* mortal beings, but that didn't mean she knew what it felt like to love or be loved by one of them.

"Why did you take my parents?" he asked.

Death sighed. "You, like most, mistake my purpose."

"Is that so? Well, I'd think your name pretty much sums up your purpose."

"I do not murder," she said. "People murder—with knives, with their hands, their neglect. It is not my decision who is selected to die at what time and by what means. That is out of my control.

"When the pain gets to be too much, I am summoned. When the soul is tired and ready for a long rest, I come knocking. Or even when the heart is worn but happy and cannot beat another minute, I am there. I let them leave. I guide them to the underworld where their souls are taken to their final resting places." Her gaze fixated on the candles now. Theo wondered then, looking at her eyes, if the pain, exhaustion, and wear she spoke of was neither created nor destroyed by life or death, but rather transferred. Mercy. That was how she explained her role in the grand scheme of things. He opened his mouth to say something, but nothing came to him.

Instead, the woman he'd been taught to call Death continued, "People have to die, Theo. It is part of living. Without death you would grow indifferent to the thought of fresh morning dew or sunshine, ambivalent toward the first words your child speaks, and numb to love's touch."

"You can't love, then?" Theo asked.

"I have loved," Death replied, "and for that, I had to stay away from love for as long as I could."

"Why?" Theo asked, but she didn't say more. "Is that why you hide out here on your own?"

The thousands of candle flames flickered, their light on the walls shimmering. Were it not for the circumstances, Theo might have thought he was dreaming. But this was all too real. Nothing they spoke of felt dreamlike.

"All magic requires payment," Theo whispered to himself. The image of his mother's scarf hanging from a narrow tree limb with his father's pocket watch inside came to Theo's mind. The memory was fiercely sentimental, and though he had succeeded in bringing his parents back from the underworld, the loss of those trinkets somehow still hurt him. He sighed. "That's it then? This is all part of a spell. Payment in return for exclusion from famine and disease."

He might have asked why his town, but then he thought about how close Ipsitfel was to this cave. *Death lives in the woods*, had been repeated so often throughout his life. A mantra of sorts for the townsfolk. He'd taken it as metaphor for the dangers of the forest, but now its meaning evolved into something more. No other town performed the Descension ceremony, but no other town lived in such close proximity to Death. Somewhere in Ipsitfel's lost history, he supposed someone else had encountered her. Had learnt who she was and maybe pled for her protection.

"I know what you did," Death said.

There was no use denying his actions, not if she truly knew of his crimes. But neither did he want to admit to them, as that fear of her still lingered within him. Everyone who'd spoken of her in Nochlan had said she'd be angry if she found out. Standing here now, he felt either he didn't know how to read her emotions very well or she wasn't angry after all. He decided to remain silent, and if she chose to, she would explain.

"I know you went through the Gateway alive," Death said. "I also know that several Guardians took pity on you, as did a certain ferrywoman, and that it was with their help you succeeded. I know you brought the souls of your parents back aboveground."

"How?" was all Theo could say.

"Isora and Uzume, the Guardians of Caelum, saw you traveling in a ferry with two figures whose faces were hidden," Death said. Heat rose up Theo's collar. "I inferred the rest."

"Oh," Theo said. "But you haven't taken them back?"

Death didn't look upset, but her features sang a song of resignation. She raised her open palms toward him. "The soul communicates with the universe through expression. You have kept them veiled. I would have a very difficult time finding them if I looked."

Theo nodded. What Matanda had told him was true then. And she didn't seem to know it was he who had told Theo how to hide his parents. She didn't seem to know which Guardians had come to his aid either, or she didn't feel the need to name them.

"This cannot happen," Death said. She glided forward, her movements seamless and ethereal. Theo might've shrunk away, but he was so enraptured by her grace that he remained where he was, and she took his hand delicately in hers. "Losing someone you love is terrible." Again that flash of sorrow. "Losing more than that is almost insurmountable, but it cannot be helped. This goes beyond the spell on your town. To break that oath between the living and the dead is to defy a magic as old as the universe."

Theo let her words churn repeatedly in his mind. "But what if I'm not ready to let them go? What if I still need them?"

Death shook her head. "You don't need them, Theo. You love them. You cherish them. But you don't need them to stay here with you. You still have your sister, and friends who also love and care for you."

"I *lost* my best friend," Theo said as Ismena's last few moments replayed in his mind. "She was also taken from me."

The woman in the black dress sighed. "You are so young. More has been taken from you than is fair. Truly, I am sorry."

"But there's nothing you can do?" Theo asked, almost spitefully. A lump was forming in his throat, though he tried to force it down with a resurgence of anger.

"Who has died, has died. The old magic applies to every mortal being." Death shook her head again. "But I cannot force you to set the souls of your parents free."

Tears fell from his eyes for the second time that evening. They tasted salty on his lips, and Theo swiped at his nose. Though he thought he understood, at the same time he didn't want to accept that the way things were was how they had to be. It didn't seem fair, even if Death herself might not be the one to blame. In the span of a few weeks, he'd lost his parents, brought them back again, and in the process set off a chain of events that had cost him his best friend. It seemed that despite what he might be willing to do, the old magic would always find balance in the end. Grief was not a problem to be solved; grief was a state that demanded to be felt. His stomach hurt again. Furthermore, he could no longer deny that bringing them back had taxed his parents' souls, draining the health that had colored their faces when he first found them on Caelum.

"Alright," he said begrudgingly. "Alright. I'll do it. I'll send them back."

"You are doing the right thing. It is where they belong. They will be at peace. All the dead must be returned," Death said. "*All* of them."

Theo looked at her, trying to appear confused, but he knew what she meant. Perhaps he had figured it out long ago. After all, he'd overheard the townsfolk discussing their concerns days before his parents had died. He couldn't be the only one to blame. Regardless, the conversations to come were not conversations he looked forward to having. He nodded and made to leave the cave. For all the comfort the woods had provided, he couldn't help thinking his heart felt heavier than it had before entering. Just before he reached the exit, Theo turned. Death was still in sight, though her back was to him now as she bent to examine a cluster of candles. He noticed the black lace that draped her dress, intricate patterns that revealed themselves only in the light.

"Someone told me you'd fallen in love with a human once," Theo said. He didn't expect Death to answer, but after only a few moments of silence, he heard her soft-spoken response.

"Once."

"Will you tell me who it was?"

Death stood and turned to face him. "Can you think of no one whom I avoided for as long as I could?"

Theo nodded. "I thought so." There was no spite in his voice, only compassion. "And you couldn't be with her?"

Death shook her head.

"I'm sorry for you too, then."

The woman in the flowing black dress acknowledge his condolence with a nodded.

Theo reoriented himself and walked through the mouth of the cave. The light of the candles faded almost immediately, and he reemerged in the woods. The dim crescent moon, visible through a gap in the mist, cast a pale glow on the trees and bushes and the ground. To his delight, he saw around the mouth of the cave a semicircle of blossoming rose bushes. Petals spread wide to the night air. In the darkness he could only see hints of their warm colors, but even their varying shades of gray were beautiful. He marveled at their vivacity; he had never seen flowers so open at night. Come to think of it, only once had he seen flowers flourish so brilliantly in Ipsitfel. Once in a great glass conservatory.

He set off toward home.

30

A Time for Bereavement

Not wanting to chance having to explain himself if the gate sentries returned, Theo followed the river around the north end of Ipsitfel until he could make out Eldra's home on the opposite bank. Her dock reached out into the languid current. He would have to swim, and he didn't fancy how cold the water would be, but in some form or another he thought he might appreciate the shock to his system. The water was black. Nothing but darkness.

Theo waded in, his white tunic—dirtied again so quickly—soaking with water. Indeed, the river was cold, but bearable. He took a breath, then began paddling across.

He hadn't much experience swimming. A portion of the Stick River wound its way through the town by his old house, and he and Laila had been allowed to play in it as children, but that stretch of water wasn't large enough for him to become a strong swimmer, just enough to stay afloat. For this reason, he struggled across the flowing water. More than anything, the swim tested his stamina, and by the time he managed to grab the short dock on the other side, he was desperate for breath.

Theo pulled himself out of the water, feeling colder now that he was in the night air. He swept his hair out of his face and wiped the water from his eyes, blinking furiously. Then he trudged along the dock, past the porch at the rear of the manor where he and Roman had sat during Eldra's party, and through the wild grounds of her estate. He could see lights on in the house—he assumed these belonged to the people she'd employed who still lived there—but he avoided them and ran to the gate under the cover of shadow.

Back within the town, Theo opted to use a smaller, less-traveled street, which ran along a row of buildings behind Cirillo Square. Even this close, he couldn't hear any of the commotion from before. The chaos must have dissipated. Was anyone cleaning up the remains? Sifting through the rubble? Law, perhaps, or a sanitation crew. Or maybe it had been left for the night, too much to deal with too soon. He didn't have the stomach to look.

The house he sought appeared from the mist, set back farther from the road than most, which allowed for a twisting, knotty tree to grow in the front yard. Moss overflowed from the gutters, and the wrought-iron gate stood permanently ajar. Theo entered, walking along the path and up the stairs to the front door.

Before he could knock, the door flung open and he had the wind squeezed out of him. It took Theo a moment to realize it was Roman crushing him. The older boy was speaking too, jabbering away in quick, incoherent strings of words. "Can't believe it's—But I never thought, you was just—Then I couldn't find—They was all over the place and you—I thought I'd never see you again..."

He paused to catch his breath and held Theo at arm's length, stooping to look him in the eyes. Roman's sapphire irises were brilliant even in the darkness, and Theo's heart sank, knowing what was to come.

"I thought you was dead, Theo," Roman said. "I thought I'd seen the last of you."

Theo attempted a weak smile. "I'm here."

Roman hesitated, his eyes searching Theo's face for a moment before he slid his hands behind Theo's head and kissed him full on the mouth.

A rush of excitement jolted through Theo. His body tingled with energy from his head to his toes. For a moment, he forgot what he was there to say. He could weather all the tragedy of the recent weeks if only he could stay here in this instant.

Then, all too soon, Roman pulled away.

The world darkened again.

"I like doing that," Roman said with a crooked smile.

"Me too," Theo said, missing the kiss already.

"Come inside," Roman said. He led the way through the front door and into the dim interior of his home. Faint light came from covered lamps in the entry room where all Mary Alba's various wares hung in the darkness. Theo glanced at the door separating the shop from the rest of the house, but tonight it was shut.

"Is Laila alright?" Roman asked. He sat on the counter and Theo stood before him, wanting to keep as close as possible to the boy. Perhaps the proximity might lessen the eventual pain. As he drew near, he spotted the Seer Stone sitting uncovered on a low shelf behind the counter. Memories of Roman's mother spouting premonitions came to mind. Would it be so wrong to touch it again and find out what lay before him now? What would become of his parents? Him and his sister? But despite the brief temptation, he found the spark wasn't as alluring as it had been before. The desire to touch the brilliant red surface was gone.

"I think Laila's fine," Theo replied. "She got away early on. Went back to our parents."

My parents. He would have to face them tonight too.

"That's good."

"Yeah."

"I... I saw what happened to Ismena," Roman muttered. The look in his eyes said he knew the events might be too recent to discuss, but he was ready to comfort Theo if the need arose. In pain, but out of tears for the time being, Theo nodded. "I'm sorry," Roman said. "I know she was your best friend."

He took Theo's hand and gently squeezed.

"I'm sorry too," Theo said.

"That was downright terrible, what all happened in the square. I barely got me mum and me out. Seemed like everyone'd lost their minds, didn't it?" He stared at the back of the front door as if he could see the quiet street beyond. "Terrible. The whole thing. Who knows how many died, none but Death probably—and I'll bet they're happy."

Theo winced.

"You alright?" Roman asked. "Somethin' wrong?"

"Roman," Theo whispered, bracing himself. *Get it out quick.* "We have to let them go."

"What d'you mean?"

"I know," Theo said. "I saw them in the hallway the day I touched the Seer Stone."

"Who—"

"It's your dad, isn't it? And your grandmother."

"But... How did you—"

"I saw them," Theo said. "I didn't know it at the time—I thought they were statues—but I saw them sitting there on the bench in your house."

Roman was quiet, his head hanging, staring at the counter beneath him. Theo couldn't see his face. He hadn't wanted to hurt Roman. In fact, that was the last thing he wanted. If he could, he'd wrap his arms around him, perhaps share another kiss, and let the world remember its own terrible truths. Roman had only ever been supportive, and funny, and earnest with him. Matched his own spark of mischief and disregard for rules. But this was a rule they couldn't break; the cost was too high, and not theirs to pay. If they were the only two to suffer, then maybe the drawbacks would be worth it, but they couldn't continue if it meant others suffered as wel l.

"Me mum let slip one day how you could go about foolin' Death. I haven't a clue how she found out—probably in that stone of hers, I don't doubt," Roman said. "When my father left, it wasn't 'cause of nothing he'd done. Not like everyone says. They like to talk and so often they're wrong about everything. He'd gone to take care of Gran and was only s'pose to have left for a month or so. But Gran was sicker than we thought. When it was clear she wouldn't live long, she decided she wanted to come here to stay with us until *it* happened. You know?

"I left with some folks who're traveling to the city, said I could come along. I was s'posed to meet up with my father and my grandmother to help with the traveling." Roman sighed. Though he wasn't crying, the words were hard to get out. He gripped Theo's hand, perhaps not realizing how tight, but Theo didn't ask him to loosen his hold. "Packed her things an' all. We was underway, had almost made it here, in fact. Only a day's journey out. Then we was attacked. Didn't stand a chance—there was six of them. They stole most of my gran's belongings and bloodied the two of 'em up. I'd been riding my own horse, but it bucked me off as they was coming. I came to just as the bastards ran off.

"Gran and my father were in a bad state. *So*, so much blood. I could see they weren't going to make it. Not the way they was cut up like that—like slaughtered animals. But I'd remembered what mum said, see. I remembered the tricks she'd told. I could stop them from going—all I'd need was a mirror.

"For my gran, it was easy. One of the trinkets left behind was her hand mirror—must've fallen from her bag. For dad, I had to use me knife." As Roman said this, his free hand went to his hip where the knife hung on his belt. "If you die looking in your own eyes, see, the soul gets confused and goes back in. Then I covered their faces so Death couldn't find them. I didn't know if it'd work, but me mum was right."

He looked shamefully at Theo as he said this.

"When you came back and I saw you'd done the same, I thought it weren't so bad. Not if we'd both done it, see."

Theo stared at Roman for a long time. His mind raced through every scenario he could think of, trying to find some way to keep from hurting Roman—some way they could avoid having to give back the loved ones they'd stolen. Another part of him spoke up, interrupting the flow of alternatives. This wasn't something he could get around. This wasn't a request they could ignore, and he could no longer claim ignorance. The sooner he accepted this, the sooner things could get better for all the townspeople. Besides, he'd made a promise to Death. And that wasn't a promise he thought he should break.

"I know a thing or two about the supernatural," Roman said, "unavoidable with me mum. But I'd never put much stock in the superstitions of old zealots."

"I didn't know what to believe either, until I went after my parents."

"When the crops kept right on living and the livestock weren't ill, I thought I'd got away with it."

"It didn't happen all at once," Theo said, "but I did hear people talking about the early signs of crisis at Eldra's birthday."

Roman nodded. "I heard 'em too, but I'd convinced myself it had nothing to do with me."

"What we've done is wrong," Theo said. "We may not have personally killed all those people in Cirillo Square, but the panic caused by the drying wells, the dying crops, and the diseased livestock... that is our fault."

"We didn't force nobody to murder," Roman said. "They was happy to jump to that conclusion on their own."

"People were afraid."

"I didn't make no one—"

"Roman, I didn't say we made anyone kill. Only we hurt—"

"I didn't mean to..."

"I know," Theo whispered.

Leaning forward, he and Roman rested their foreheads together. Theo had never been so intimate with anyone, but despite how much it made him want to protect his friend's feelings, the intimacy empowered him to keep talking. "I didn't mean to cause any pain either, but we have to correct it. We have to stop it from continuing."

Roman was crying now, afraid and mournful. His tears were silent and unobtrusive. If Theo couldn't see them glistening on his face, he might not have known they were there at all.

"I can't keep 'em here?" Roman whispered.

"No."

"What if I still need them? What if I'm not ready to let go?"

"This is the first step," Theo said, not sure if he believed his own words. "The rest will follow."

"Have I got to do it tonight?"

"I think so."

Roman gave his hand one last squeeze. Theo's impulse was to tell him to stay, but the older boy let go.

"Alright," Roman said. "I'll go wake my mum."

He slid off the counter, his lost gaze scanning the darkened shop as if the fabrics and trinkets were foreign to him. "Thanks for being honest with me, Theo," he said. "I'll see you tomorrow."

"Good night," Theo said, and left.

Laila was already waiting in the basement with his parents. She'd set up a handful of lanterns to give the space ample light. Perhaps she'd grown tired of the darkness. Every head was turned his way as he descended the stairs. His sister looked relieved. Many hours had passed since she'd fled the massacre. Like Roman, she'd probably thought him dead. That was twice now she'd had to contemplate his death, and all because of his own brash decisions.

Though her posture was still as proper as ever, he saw relief flood Laila's expression and her eyes began to water.

"Thank goodness, you're back," she said in a hushed tone. "I'd been worried."

"Sorry," Theo muttered. "Did... Did the Bareens return?"

He was afraid to ask, but needed to know.

Laila nodded. "I heard them come home about a half hour after me. Did you find..."

Theo shook his head. Laila clasped a hand over her mouth.

"I watched them throw her down the Gateway."

"Ismena..." Laila breathed, letting her hand fall away again. "That's terrible. She's... Oh, poor Ismena. We'll have to tell them."

"I know." Theo's heart ached for too many people. "Was everything alright here?"

"Mostly." Laila looked around at their parents. "I didn't light the lanterns until a short while ago. I didn't want anyone to see. A couple times, people came running up to the doors, trying to yank them open—I don't know what for, maybe to hide. But I held them closed, Theo. I held them. I didn't let anyone in. It stopped after a spell."

Theo could see she was sad. For whom or for what precisely he couldn't guess, too many possibilities lingered in the air. She could be sad for all of Ipsitfel, or just for herself and the state her life had been reduced to. She held their family together now, Theo realized. For all his exploits, she was the one with a career and a level head. She was the one saving to buy them a home so they wouldn't spend the rest of their lives dependent on other people's kindness—so they wouldn't have to visit their parents in a damp basement.

"We can't keep them here," Theo said. He expected that she might argue, try to contradict him, but she only nodded. The sad look plastered on her face intensified by a degree. She never stopped looking at their parents.

"I've been thinking the same thing," she said.

"They don't belong here. They're not happy," Theo continued. "I've caused so much hurt."

"You didn't know."

"I think I suspected. When I realized a world existed beyond our own, it made me reconsider all the stories we'd been told. I thought they were just folktales. I could've known then that the reasons we did the ceremony were true. I could've seen the signs."

"It's hard to admit you're wrong when it means losing someone dear to you," Laila said. "In any case, we know the truth about human nature now, don't we?"

"What's that?"

"We're eager to kill one another to preserve a status quo."

"That's not true."

"Say it isn't."

"It's not! What about you? Your first concern was to keep our parents safe."

"I'm not everyone else."

"And neither are the people who murdered."

Laila was silent. She didn't appear to agree with him, but neither did she want to continue arguing. Instead, she folded her hands in her lap.

"I've done terrible things to our town," Theo breathed. She didn't rebuke him.

A minute of silence turned into five.

"I suppose we should say goodbye, then," Laila said.

Theo didn't respond. He walked over to the corner of the basement where his parents sat. Laila followed, forever by his side. He knew it would always be this way, no matter what happened to them. She would never abandon him. Damon and Medina stood as their children drew near.

"Mother, Father," Theo began, "I miss you so very, very much." Each word was agony. Trembling, he raised his eyes to the ceiling. If he looked away, maybe goodbye wouldn't be so hard. Medina took his hand. "But you're not happy here," Theo said. "You don't belong here. And as much as I wish I could keep you with me forever, I don't have the right to decide that—not at the cost of others."

"Theo?" Damon asked, but Theo shook his head.

"It's okay, Father," he said. "We'll be alright."

"My beautiful children," Medina said. She reached out her hands to cup both of their faces. Theo was pleased to see that some warmth and color had returned to her skin. Perhaps their souls could sense their imminent return to where they belonged. "We'll stay as long as you need."

His parents didn't know what it had cost to keep them here. Theo didn't want to burden them with the truth before letting them go.

"We'll be alright," he repeated, forcing a smile. "I've got Laila to keep me company."

Laila nodded. "You've taught us all we need to know."

"Perhaps we'll see you again someday," Damon suggested.

"Perhaps," Theo said, still smiling though it pained him. He knew better than to hope this wish would come true. "If not, just know we love you."

"We love you too, dears," Medina said.

"You should sit," Laila said. She ran to grab another chair from the table so that they'd both have a place to rest.

"What's going to happen?" their father asked, sounding worried for the first time. He and Medina complied, though, sitting in the wooden chairs arranged so that they still maintained their small circle—Theo next to his father, next to Laila, next to their mother, next to Theo again.

Laila looked to her brother, but Theo couldn't answer. "I don't know," he said, "but may I ask one thing?"

"Of course you can," Damon said, placing a hand on his son's arm. "Anything."

Theo took another deep breath. "Once you've removed the mask, keep hold of us, please. Don't let go for as long as you can."

Both his mother and father nodded.

"Alright then," Laila said tightly. "When you're ready." She looked to Theo, terrified but resolute.

These would be his last words to them, but what could he say? Paralyzed, his tongue lay frozen in his mouth as he considered all his life that they would miss. All the life they'd never have the chance to live. How could he apologize for everything? How could he summarize a lifetime in any coherent way? He tried to find the right words, but he couldn't speak.

Instead, a familiar melody found its way to him.

"Gently you go, breathing the night

The moon and the stars come, guiding by light

Pity the mountain that howls and grieves

But tend to the bowed willow, mourning its leaves."

By the end of it, Laila had joined in, singing the low, mournful elegy as they wept.

Damon and Medina let go long enough to reach up and pull the cloths from their faces.

Theo saw his mother, round-faced and rosy-cheeked. She smiled at him, a happiness tainted only somewhat by bereavement. He could remember running around her in the kitchen while she laughed, begging him to stop and help her with the meal. He could see the concentration on her face when she sat by the fireplace reading at night while he wondered to what worlds she traveled.

Theo saw his father. His angular face, with its prominent jaw and brow. Worry lines had only just started to crease his forehead, while crow's-feet sprang from the corners of his eyes, a consequence of smiling so often. He surveyed both his children with a mixture of pride and melancholy. Theo thought of playing in the river, splashing his father until he was lifted high and thrown into the water screaming; he thought of the two of them sitting at the kitchen table, his father teaching him to hem his trousers so he could look presentable at school.

Theo and Laila held to their parents' hands in a darkness fought only by candlelight. They held tight until the expressions began to fade from their parents' eyes. Slowly, their mother and father slouched, their heads sinking down as if in prayer. Their hold to their children weakened until it released altogether. The rise and fall of their chests slowed and grew shallow.

Theo and Laila stared across at each other as the life faded from their parents. They didn't dare look away, their faces stained by tears, wondering when, if ever, they would be okay to let go.

31
Life After

The misty morning was cool, though the smell in the air told of a warmer day to come. Perhaps this would be one of those rare days when the sun would break through the fog.

Theo walked along the street, hands shoved in the pockets of his trousers. He was eager to meet Roman, for it was Sunday, and on Sundays neither the bakery nor the clothier was open. They could spend Sundays together, maybe have breakfast in one of the cafés or escape to climb trees at the edge of the woods. Sometimes they just sat together and read, and this too was fine by him.

As he walked up to the gate, Roman came sauntering through the front door wearing a teal vest of crushed velvet. Theo never had to knock; Roman always *knew* when he was coming. The older boy finished clipping a silver watch on his wrist and gave his signature smirk.

"You alright there, Theo?"

"Yeah, I'm fine."

Roman tilted his chin up with a finger and they shared a kiss. It never ceased to make Theo's heart flutter. As their lips parted, Roman draped an arm over his shoulders. "What says you this morn, eh? I could finish off some of Missus Pearson's scones, myself."

"Missus Pearson's it is, then."

The street led them out into Cirillo Square.

In the days following the tragedy, the square had been scrubbed from corner to corner. Every sign that the scarlet massacre had ever happened had been removed, including the construction of a new pulley, platform, and fence surrounding the Gateway. Yet uncertainty lingered during the entire cleanup—during all of which Theo and Roman had both willingly helped. Obviously, they couldn't hold a Descension for anyone who'd been thrown down the hole, but what to do about the couple dozen townsfolk who had met their fate aboveground?

In the end, they'd held one large Descension ceremony for everyone who'd perished in the riot. The living townspeople were instructed to sing not only the Cimmerian Elegy but all the mournful folksongs they could think of while the bodies were lowered one by one to their final resting place.

Once upon a time, he could not have looked upon the Gateway without a vision of the first Descension he'd attended. The image of Demeres dangling over the hole, flaming red hair reaching toward the darkness below before she was released into the void, was etched so firmly in his brain that he'd refused to acknowledge death out of insurmountable terror. Who knew that same woman would somehow lead him to a greater understanding of loss and grief years later.

In the same strange fashion in which the paranoia had manifested itself before the massacre, everybody seemed to agree that nothing would be said about who had committed the killings. No accusatory fingers were pointed and no grudges were held against suspected perpetrators. Perhaps, they figured, there were too many to count. Perhaps it would be difficult to say who had committed what and whether or not the deaths were a result of attacks or defense. Either way, as the weeks passed, fortune returned to Ipsitfel. The wells filled again, rain fell in abundance, and the diseases of the livestock died out. All was forgiven.

At least, outwardly.

Theo still had mixed feelings about the way things unfolded, but as time passed these feelings ebbed. He felt horrible at the paranoia he'd caused, but he was still shocked at how quickly people had resorted to murder. It was an issue he felt they should confront as a community, which, of course, meant it was unlikely to ever happen. The fanatics especially, did not wish to confront their own moral shortcomings, and everyone else was too timid.

Cirillo Square returned to its normal hustle and bustle.

"Viseyne Tower is open," Roman commented. And at this, Theo's face lit up.

During the insanity of the riot, an unknown group of villagers had come to the conclusion that as the tower was as much a part of Ipsitfel as any of the people, knocking it over would help settle the issue—more mob mentality that followed little logic. They'd set about destroying the support columns, which were already precarious to begin with given the tower's historically shoddy reconstruction. Viseyne Tower had been closed off while the damage was properly fixed. Now the tower was open again, the scaffolding around it removed.

Curious, Theo made for it.

"Theo, wait!" Roman called, jogging to catch up with him.

Theo had crossed the square in a few short seconds, dodging between the groups of gawkers beginning to form. He jogged up to the base of the tower and came to a halt beneath the stone archway.

The inside was shaded, though light streamed through the wide windows set high in the wall. Theo saw that while the archway was made of large, smooth river rocks, the other three walls were composed of rectangular slabs of another type of stone. A shadow of himself looked back through the polished surface. Small writing had been inscribed there as well, starting in the topmost left corner and moving down in neat columns. As he drew closer, he realized—

"They're names."

Roman came up behind Theo and placed his hands on his shoulders.

"Hadn't heard nothing about this," he said.

The names covered nearly the entire lefthand wall, with just a few open rows remaining in the bottom corner. Opposite the entrance, an inscribed dedication in larger, golden letters stood out:

Ipsitfel Remembered

And below it was a special section, separated from the rest by a simple border. It included another heading:

Those Who Perished in the Tragedy

Below this was written a list of at least three dozen individuals. Theo scanned the names until his eyes rested on Ismena Bareen. He felt a heavy weight in his heart and reached out to trace her name with his finger.

The morning after the incident, Theo told Mister and Missus Bareen what had happened to their daughter—how he'd seen her thrown through the Gateway during the chaos. The news sent both of them into mournful sobs, and Theo had stood in ashamed silence for a while as they grieved. But it didn't feel right to stop there. He confessed what he'd done and who he'd been hiding in their basement. Ismena's parents were completely shocked and understandably upset. Still, they were more even-tempered than he could hope for. While they didn't place all the blame for Ismena's death directly on his shoulders, they made it clear they didn't want to see him ever again. Theo felt a pang of guilt and loss at this proclamation, but he understood. He had, after all, taken advantage of their hospitality.

Those who'd perished in the tragedy were not the only inscriptions beneath the tower. Beside Theo were the names of other people who had died in Ipsitfel, countless individuals dating back to who knew how long ago. Theo recognized families, realizing for the first time how long some of these lineages had been living here. And near the end, he found the names he was looking for: Medina Sahiron and Damon Sahiron.

"I like this," Roman said, staring at a pair of names himself. He'd reported the deaths of his father and grandmother, and though his grandmother hadn't been living in Ipsitfel when she passed away, she had been included on the wall as well. "It feels thoughtful," he said, "like the lives lost ain't just a bargaining chip to keep our town running."

"I like it too," Theo said. He vowed silently to visit the wall again soon, and often. He wanted to tell Laila, knowing she would appreciate having somewhere to go to remember their parents. Now that he thought about it, he was surprised no one had started a memorial like this before.

"Come on, we should tell our friends and family," Roman said, as if reading Theo's thoughts. He grabbed Theo's hand and pulled him gently toward the archway. Other people were starting to poke their heads in, and they talked among themselves about what they discovered there. The general reaction seemed to be positive.

The clock began to strike the hour.

A man who makes something of himself is always conscious of time.

His father's words—really his grandfather's words—had struck him as odd initially. A disagreeable personal philosophy. The thought of a life spent racing against the unrelenting hands of a ticking clock felt like a poor trade just to say he'd made something of himself. But perhaps, as with so many things he'd come to discover, his first—and even his second—interpretation had been wrong.

All things require time; sleep, work, and loved ones. As much as he wished he'd had more time, it was a frustratingly finite resource.

After all, time is the most subtle, most persistent thief. Being conscious of time did not mean seeking a calculated efficiency, but rather choosing which things deserved the most of his attention. When he made conscious decisions about his time, he made something of himself. He became the person he wished to be.

"Let's find my sister first," Theo said, looking back at the wall, at the names of his parents and his best friend. He also saw Lyra Burkhart, Matilda Monson, Robin Deckle, and Eldra Vromía. Just as he was turning to leave, Theo saw another name, one that at first he didn't recognize. But it made him pause, if only for a moment. The name was Nathaniel Ainsworth, written in the list of people who'd died in the tragedy.

Theo let himself be dragged away by an eager Roman, though his mind floated elsewhere. The ferries of Nochlan were so small. Perhaps only five or six passengers could fit in any one boat. He couldn't be certain how many ferryfolk roamed the Corporis Sea. Still, he hoped there was some small chance that Demeres had come to the shore and seen her husband standing before her at last.

Their meeting couldn't be joyful, of course—after all, it would mean they'd both died—but maybe it would carry with it some hope. She would welcome him onto her boat and have the chance at last to say all the things she'd wished to say. Demeres could forgive herself then, and make her payment.

Her soul could finally know peace.

And in the end, wasn't peace the only thing that mattered?

Please Read!

You've made it to the end of the book!

Thank you so much for reading 'Of Chaos and Eternal Night.' This book has a very special place in my heart and the story has stuck with me in many shapes and forms for multiple decades now. I'm ecstatic to finally be sharing it with readers.

As much as I believe in this book though, its success is greatly reliant on readers like you. For indie authors, reviews and word of mouth are the quintessential ingredient that gets our stories read. Without reviews, our stories cannot be seen above the millions of other stories that are published each year.

Therefore, regardless of what star-rating you feel it deserves, I encourage you to leave a review for 'Of Chaos and Eternal Night' on Amazon, Goodreads, and anywhere else you go looking for book recommendations. Any review is better than no review!

I hope to keep writing for the remainder of my days, and this is one of the most important ways you can help me do that. I'm so grateful to you, the reader, for giving me your time and attention. Without you, storytelling is nothing more than throwing words down a well.

Warm Regards,

RD Pires

Acknowledgements

There are too many people to thank for this book becoming a reality. So, naturally, I will attempt the futile endeavor of naming them all.

First, Alex—who this book is dedicated to—for being supportive in all things but most especially my writing. My worlds would never see the light of day without your delicate input.

Kate, for always being my first and most enthusiastic reader. I will happily hand over every manuscript to you simply for the thrill of your excitement.

Toby deserves a mention, of course. I am wholly reliant on your reactions in the comments if not also your editorial pen.

Everyone who provided the beautiful artwork that brings this story to life; Ricardo Calvo for the incredible cover and Robin for the character portraits. Words are the flesh and blood of a story, but illustrations are the hair and makeup that make it fabulous.

And last but certainly not least, thank you to all the backers on my kickstarter! Without you, this book might never have seen the light of day. Jackie Bronner, Charles W. Younts III, Alexandra & Will Pittman, Melanie Yoshihara, Stephanie, Chloe Grinberg, Samantha Newberry, Daniel Renth, Hereward, Anne-Mette Brandt, Arianne Godoy, Adam McLain, Camille F, Richie G., Charles Rogers, Mike Gilmore, Thomas, AJ Basa, Briannon Schaeffer, JPSS, Ashley Saindon, Tyler Cheek, Evan Tolmie, Robin, Chris Pires, Kate Shively, Toads Hobbertson, Mike Rouse-Deane, Neil K., Jessica Worgo, Oliver Gomez, quail, Kate Darby, Emily Gibney, Ashley Lotti, Mirann Hughes, Noelle Conway, Trip Galey, Malory, Victoria P, Paul Sturm, Bona Books, Tim Kimball, India Barton, Anonymous, Peter, Louis Sykes, Francisco Domenech, and Caleb Barley.

About the author

RD Pires has found there's always a story to tell, and so he spends his time writing them down. A project is always on his mind, even when there aren't enough hours in a day to work on them.

His blend of literary writing with genre fiction is influenced by his favorite authors, including David Mitchell, Brandon Sanderson, Madeline Miller, and Stephen King.

His works include *Design of Darkness*, the first book in the ongoing *The Tides That Reign* series, *A Vast, Untethered Ocean*, the novella *In Death Do Flowers Grow*, and the collection of short fiction *A Sky Littered With Stories*.

He lives in California with his husband and their daughter.